Smoke From Small Fires

A novel

Anne Powers

Smoke From
Small Fires

Pocahontas Press
Blacksburg, Virginia

Smoke From
Small Fires

Copyright © 2014 by Anne Powers

ISBN 0-926487-78-7

Book design by Michael Abraham

Printed in the United States of America

Pocahontas Press
www.pocahontaspress.com

DEDICATION

In loving memory of Rosetta Jones, who never failed to cheer me with her friendship, cornbread and plainspoken wisdom.

ACKNOWLEDGEMENTS

Thanks to these friends and family for their support and valued opinions: Maggie Bouldin, Patrick Powers, Charlene Dreher, Katherine Dreher, The BJs: Barbara Jean Moore and Elizabeth Kirkham, Marjorie Hicks, Aleeta Christian, Paul Scandlyn, Judy Keller, Bill Black, Jim Knox, Gail Neal, Elizabeth Howard, Kathy Cisson, Laura Booth, and the tireless listening ear of Marty Hall who only wanted to ski in Colorado.

Special thanks to Ibby Greer, Editor and Head Cheerleader, without whose encouragement this book would have never proceeded.

Introductory Quote: Robert Van Vranken
Spanish Assistance: Maria Barriga and Fred Pogue
Cover Designer: Eric L. McNew
Cover Illustration: Anne Powers

Final Editor: Jane Abraham
Typesetting: Michael Abraham
Publisher: Pocahontas Press

Smoke From Small Fires

I have dreamed of a painting that would stop the world.
Harried morning commuters would emerge from
their suburban homes,
crumbling donuts in hand - see the sky - pause and
remember…
Finally, all the simple moments of this earth would be
enough;
Morning and evening opening and closing above us –
Yellowing leaves falling among us, hands of ghosts
And the sound, far off,
Of the laughter of women and the clinking of glasses.

Robert Van Vranken
Artist's Statement

2029 *Morning Glory Ridge Assisted Living*

I, Anna Tollett, lay flat and sunk in my bed, waiting to be assimilated into the universe. Earthbound eighty-one years now, I still claim all my wits. They live in a house of brittle bones that could discombobulate at any minute.

Above me I picture an infinite mist, a sacred ether of all that ever was and ever will be, molecules, microwaves, matter, thoughts and dreams, wisps of soul both innocent and wicked. Then again, maybe it's all just smoke - smoke, dense and boiling - born from tiny fires that flame ravenously, dampen, rekindle and extinguish with a puff - thin tendrils rising into the big dark mystery.

I was once a visual artist and spent my productive years making images and objects - personal interpretations. As a youth I presumed to enlighten an unseeing public. "Ah HA! Eureka!" I was sure they would exclaim, "Oh! Now I see! Now that an artist, a Shaman, has ferreted out the essence and made it clear to me..."

Those in the arts can be egotistical that way, convinced that someone gives a care about their clever imaginings, their precious little pictures or original tunes – when all that's wanted is an appreciating investment, a flash of color to match the draperies, some harmonic notes to float in the background during a dinner party for friends.

I realized that possibility early on - that art might be made mainly for oneself, a masturbatory pleasure, a selfish and solitary pursuit. All the same, my motives were honest. I crafted my work with gusto - harboring hope that once in a great while it would move someone to shiver with new insight.

Defined by my art, I continually reinvented myself, sought meaning, connected with my mountain world. But all that was before, back when I had a life, before I became a citizen of the elderly nation.

Now we boomers are bedridden. Rotting in our cots. What sort of old farts did we expect to be anyway? We became more and more sophisticated through the post war decades. Knowledge, technology, efficiency exploded. We became smarter, sharper, faster, better, cooler in every way. Our art forms raged against barriers. How could we possibly become *old* and out-of-it like our predecessors?

Could we have imagined ourselves permanently prone? Immobile? Unable to wipe our own asses, let alone kick someone else's? We, who screamed Elvi-beatle mania at our black and white TVs, body surfed at concerts, looked good, maybe even hot, at sixty? We were rock-n-rollers, beatniks and hippies, Woodstockers, yippies and the occasional aged Goth.

Who knew we, too, would become the smelly, muttering ancients we once refused to visit in the nursing home, even when our parents insisted. Who, in their wildest dreams, could have pictured an assisted living resident named Tiffany (My roommate, 326-B)? Her mind flits from one reality to the next, never lighting in the same place twice - hearing, seeing, things that aren't there.

When *my* mind wanders, it speeds down Blackshale Road in my cousin's souped up car. When I hear things, it's the Grateful Dead. I still dream up artworks in my head that these shaky fingers can no longer render. My inventive thoughts continue to roll on, you see, even though my bones are crumbling and my body has let me down. I'm still creating, *in there*, in my mind.

Yet my skin crackles and tears when I roll over in bed. Like my dried-up meemaw before me, I bear the bedsore and unguent, wear the fragrance of eau-du-pee, and obsess over hard-earned products of the bowel. "Just like little kernels of corn," she used to say, squinching up her nose to focus on the tip of her finger. I am turned outside in, sucking all my remaining resources inward - into a private world where I tell myself the stories I know best.

"Please," I beg myself, "Please, tell it again." So on they go, in the dilapidated theatre of my fading mind, those things I've lived and heard and seen and made into art, over, over, and over again, until I too will evaporate, dragging my visions behind me.

1958 Blackshale

I am named Anna Grace, but along Blackshale Road, I'm often called *that mortuary child*. I live up over the funeral parlor with my pap Frank Tollett, the only undertaker for fifty miles toward either end of a narrow ribbon of whining black tar. My mama died on a hunting trip this year, startled so by a black cloud of stinkbirds that she fell on her own twenty-two rifle. Mama woulda never hurt me so bad, like ground glass rippin' up my guts, but she had no say in it. It was them stinkbirds.

The woman who birthed me, the other mama I never knew I had until this year, had laid me down in a dresser drawer on the stoop of Tollett's Funeral Home with a note that said, "I can't do this." I guess she figgered somebody who had just bought a tiny, shiny white coffin might take me up as a replacement.

I s'pose some 'round here seen me as a troubled soul, bathed in the daily business of death and left behind not once but twicet. The days of my nine years have been punctuated by the tragic endpoints of lives - sometimes question marks, sometimes exclamations, mostly just periods laid down suddenly with a soft tap. Some of them lives was way too short. I reckon my outlook should be colored with a dim tint, but it ain't.

They say Dory Tollett was never so flabbergasted in her life as that hazy August morning when she sallied forth onto the porch to dig furniture sale flyers out of her tin mailbox. I'm told she'd like to have fell over the wood drawer, quick-stepping and sputtering to get her balance. Squatting down to it, she pulled away the pink blanket printed with cartoon bunnies and stained with yellow, soured milk. She yelled at Frank to come look and swore to him I was smiling, trying to sell the idea of myself on her, a wasted effort.

She had borned two baby girls cold as stones and was sent home with every woman part dripping and aching, and a stern warning that any more tries at motherhood would put her right in the ground. She tried anyway, and lived through bringing a baby boy into the world all by her self, but he was up in Heaven before his second birthday. When Frank seen her raising me up out of that drawer to her shoulder, gone all soft, cooing and cuddling, he knew right off what she would want and knew he'd have to make it happen.

Turned out, the County Court Clerk had given his maw a grander send-off than he could ever pay off - even in reasonable monthly installments - and Frank traded in that debt for the quiet shuffling of papers that turned me, officially and permanently, from Baby Girl Doe into Anna Grace Tollett.

I never give much thought as to how I ended up in a funeral home on a stretch of road with a river in front and a railroad track behind, all running as far as I could imagine in both directions. As to how it was that my redheaded daddy and towheaded mama stuck themselves together and made a baby with coal black hair, I been skeered to ask, and they never said. I had fallen into a loving nest and was happy.

· · · · · · · ·

My pap likes to say we "live up over the store." The Tollett Funeral Home has three floors and we rightly do live on top of it all. Back when we were all together in our house on the upper floor, it was like we were in Heaven, floating above the constant stream of sobbin' goodbyes and bloody work that went on in the hellish rooms below. Mama saw to it right from the start that life in our house she called "the residence" would be sweet as pie, out of sight from Pap's sadstained profession. The upstairs apartment is long and narrow, but tall windows cover the whole back wall. She painted and papered all the other walls with whites and yellows so sunbeams could bounce around in there all day.

When the building went up, not long after she married Pap, she studied on them plans night and day, nagging him to put the hearse entrance on the side with no windows and begging for stairwells with two sets of doors so the sickening smell of flowers and the chemicals of his trade could never sneak upstairs. During the day, she'd turn up the "Midday Merry-Go-Round" show on the radio, singing along to a tune at the top of her lungs, and work herself silly, filling the air with scents - vanilla and yeast, furniture polish and fresh-ironed starch.

You see, my mama craved order and my early years were chock full of it. We came and went by the back stairs. I was too young to know about Pap's work anyways so I was not even allowed on the bottom floors. In fact, the door to the long, steep stairway of concrete blocks was locked up tight. On the bright top floor, I sat crosslegged in streams of sunlight making marks, swashing colors, gluing bits of nothings into somethings. I played by myself, creating, in my own little world.

Mama made sure I had chores to earn my weekly 'lowance. I helped her keep everything tidy by lining things up. It was my job to set the canned goods just so, with each kind of fruit or vegetable together and the front of every tin on a straight line. I was also in charge of the bottom edges of all the towels on the rack, making sure they matched up perfect, and ever time I finished a job, she told me to tap my finger on the cabinet ten times, so we could both mark the very moment the job was done... that it was *accomplished*.

Mama had her jobs too, like putting ever last thing in the medicine cabinet according to the ABC's. Alka Seltzer, Bayer Aspirins, Carter's Little Liver Pills, codliver oil, Dr. Miles' Nervine, were always in a nice row all the way on down to the zinc ointment. In fact, everything in our house was carefully arranged according to some plan or another. Organizing in the most precise manner was what my mama did best.

Truth be told, next to me and my daddy, Dory loved no one better than the Fuller Brush Man. Not like a romantic boyfriend, in the way that Mama's former best friend Sudy Pelfree had her a sweetheart besides her husband Faron, but because the Fuller Brush man came right to our door with the most breathtaking choices of household products. That's exactly what my mama claimed, "These are simply breathtaking!" as if she were talking about movie stars or Florida sunsets! He would carry his case over to the divan and spread out boards displaying his wares across the seat. Dory chose carefully and paid him in cash. When he left, she arranged her purchases for Frank to see when he unlocked the door at the top of the stairs and come home for the night.

Sudy Pelfree was Mama's best friend since forever. Mama called her a pied beauty, 'cause her creamy skin was spattered with flecks the color of raisins. Her eyes and hair was the same reddish brown, kissed with bright copper. They had went to grammar school together in Greenville, South Carolina, junior high and high school too. They even took off to Nursing School arm-in-arm on a Trailways Bus. When Mama left school to marry Frank and moved to Blackshale, Sudy's heart was broke. After she come to be a nurse, she directly moved to Blackshale, too, just a ways down the road. But bosom buddies that they were, Mama would have never known about the romantic boyfriend had it not been for the black telephone that come up through the square hole in the linoleum floor.

Tollett Funeral Home had one telephone but it had the longest cord in the world, and all day long my daddy passed it up and down through holes in the floors. Although he made it perfectly clear a hundred times a day that it was a business telephone, and the line should be kept clear for calls to the funeral home in case somebody up and died, it was also the phone for our house and several neighbors. If he forgot and left it upstairs of a mornin', my mama was led into temptation. She simply could not help listening in on the party line. One morning, when she eased the earpiece up and recognized Sudy's voice, she looked like all the blood had drained clean out of her head. She slammed the receiver down, grabbed her new Fuller Brush Magic Silver Polishing Cloth and took to rubbing her silverware raw.

The next mornin' Aunt Sudy was up to the house, and I could tell Mama was not right. When Sudy said, "Let's paint our toenails!" or "Well I swan, when did you get that new Fuller Brush sweeper?" Mama just turned her back on Sudy and flat refused to talk. I knew good and well if she was missing a chance to brag on her new Fuller Brush product, something was truly off kilter. She made choppy, brisk strides from the coffee table to the chiffarobe to the cherrywood mantle clock that humped up in the middle, flapping her featherduster like a mad rooster. Then she swatted her ivory ceramic figurines one by one, taking forever and ignoring Sudy the whole time. After dusting each one, she arranged them evenly spaced in one of her beloved processionals like they was marching off to war.

Finally Sudy got the message and said, "Ok sister, what's got your panties in a knot?"

Mama wheeled around and flew at Sudy straight on with all her rage.

"I heard, Su! I heard you talking to some strange man."

Aunt Sudy was sure surprised and her mouth opened up into a big round O, but she wasn't one to take it layin' down. "Well, that's what you get for listening in on the party line, and I'll tell you one thing Miss Perfect, you don't know the God's truth about everything in the world!"

Mama stuck out her chin and stammered, "Well - well - anyway, it was an accident. I picked up the phone to call in an order to the store and there you were talking like a - a – tart!" and then she looked over at me and shouted, "Anna Grace, go to your room! Now!"

Which, of course, I did. My room was in front of the apartment lookin' out on the highway and the river. Pap had built in a window seat and sitting right there, listening to the high-pitched drone of cars and coal trucks on the asphalt drawing closer and closer and then farther and farther, I was in my favorite place on God's green earth. That afternoon when Mama and Sudy was about to split the friendship quilt, I was not too awful worried. I got out my scrapbook and a stack of snapshots we had taken with the Kodak and sat in my window seat painting globs of white paste on the backs of pictures, tilting them just so on the black paper pages. As for me, I had no girlfriends to fight with. In fact, I had no friends at all and was beginning to suspect that living over the funeral home had somethin' to do with that. So them pictures in my book were just of Mama, Pap, and me, living our everday life as if we were sure we always would be.

• • • • • • • •

Now of an evenin', when the traffic begins to dwindle and the jar flies start chatterin', I listen a while to the wind suck them brown paper shades in and puff 'em out, flipping the crocheted ring pulls 'round and 'round. I spread papers out on my bed and draw lines around the ideas I had and the things I seen that day, knowing I'll sit here making pictures late tonight. Then I open the drawer in my nightstand, take out my turquoise plastic transistor radio and turn the dial back and forth, back and forth, until I zero in on a station coming to me from Cincinnati, Chicago, or some such far off place. It never stays the same for long for soon a crackling static takes over and drowns out the channel. On a good night though, them voices singing about the loss of love sound so clear and close and true. I look out at the river churning under the stars and feel like I'm part of some great mystery, one where Dory Tollett, somewhere, somehow, still lives on.

2029 Morning Glory Ridge

Over in bed 326-B, Tiffany has made an evil smelling mess of cosmic proportions. I heard it explode with one big, bad blow. She will be lounging around in it awhile, too, as I overheard Carlene and Mrs. Stout talking about a baby shower for the single knocked-up caretaker over on the visually handicapped wing. You can bet on your Depends that when there's a party 'goin on, the residents will take a back bed. I am about one line of tumbling "E"s away from being shipped to the visually handicapped wing myself.

Today I am wearing my favorite chapeau, one of many I brought with me to Morning-Glory-fucking-Ridge when the state, in all its wisdom, determined that I was no longer fit to live alone. It is a banded ivory fedora, just one in my massive collection of headgear. I wear something different every day to throw the caretakers off. We wouldn't want these people sliding into complacency.

There is a reason Tiffany exploded. Her bowels are in a tizzy, courtesy of a sour and abusive aide here we call "Gourdhead." He makes a cocktail called the MOMBomb. MOM stands for Milk of Magnesia, which is mixed with piping hot prune juice to create the bomb. Gourdhead's favorite trick is to mix it too stiff, and turn the victim of the day into an erupting butt volcano so Carlene will have to clean it up over and over, all day long.

I'm fairly sure Gourdhead has a thing about butts anyway. His sweet thang, Julio, comes by every other day and they stand behind our door French kissing with lots of tongue, massaging each other's asses. They feel safe in our room because Tiffany is mute, except for an occasional random, totally inappropriate word, and I am pretending to be out of it. They seem to get off on having an audience, even though it is the senior matinee.

Julio is descended from the bean pickers that came to Blackshale back in the 1990's. No one knew if they were legal, but they stayed long enough to sow the blackheaded seeds of Julio and hundreds of others who now work fast food and yard maintenance, their diminutive piece of the American pie. Julio is pissed all the time except for the flaming romance he's found with Gourdhead, which seems to me like one cold comfort.

Hola, Julio you dipshit! I say in my mind while maintaining a vacant look on my face. Carlene and Mrs. Stout mosey back from the baby shower reeking of cigarette smoke and sugary Crisco icing.

"Oh God!" Carlene exclaims, "Get yourself back in here right now!" She is yelling at the rapidly escaping back of Mrs. Stout, who is running away because she gets the gags from pungent wet shit.

Mrs. Stout just keeps on a truckin'. Carlene curses and grabs a stack of aloe wipes and a fresh pad from the utility cart. She rolls Tiffany, dabbing at her inflamed skin. A bedsore, raging scarlet and seeping, is going to need the attention of the wound nazi. That's what the residents call the wound care specialist, who will soon arrive smiling professionally and wheeling her cart of bandages. She will bathe Tiffany's hindquarters in ultraviolet light before she chooses the right high tech material to protect her broken skin. Tiffany leans forward to focus intently on Carlene's sizable facial mole and yells, "Hopscotch!" Her one word exclamation never has a thing to do with the present moment. Every time her word is delivered, she clinches in her arms, shifts her squinting eyes side-to-side, and waits like a grim troll for the world's reaction.

1939 Blackshale Mountain   *A Backstory*

Albine Yother sought out the path between his cabin and the crick, ankles turning on rock and root. The tamped soil was pore, scraped clean, and the hound on his heels ran a nose with hard purpose from scat pile to foxhole. Ahead the path turned downward, damper, and colder. Here a man could feel in his bones the chill of mountain water.

This was no common day, no sir. Albine Yother would this day claim his bride. She had only been spoken for a week ago Friday, when Albine had stood before her paw, hat spinning in hands, speaking of his acre and promise, and trying to quiet his rattling knees. His nerves and courage were not called for, as the girl's father had long wished for the day when someone else would be obliged to feed his only child. He spat a blessing out along with a blob of thick brown spittle and asked reckon how soon a wedding could commence.

The girl herself, Piney by name, had been a harder sale. First seen by Albine three year back, she had been standing up against an electric light pole down in Blackshale on market day, giving away pups. She looked to him to be the specter of an angel and left him without breath. He had no need of one, but he raised up a wiggling, pissing pup, and lingered as long as he could to gaze into Piney's watery eyes. She gave him not one bit of encouragement, no talk except to say the pup was weaned but still shat wherever he damn well pleased. Slipping the pup under his flannel shirt, he pounded the way home with a strange new fullness in his breast. Albine had never felt love before, nor would he have had much use for it, but the heat of the pup and the memory of Piney's face confused into a pulsing warmth that settled near his heart.

It didn't take long for Albine to ask around for the girl's name and know that she came with her paw to town every week to sell one thing or another, egg or chick or hen. What e'er it was, Albine was in need of it. Whatever got hauled home was quickly eaten, as Albine had no wish to care for anything. The hound pup had been an exception seein' he chased off foxes and made good company, requiring only a table scrap and a good belly scratch oncet in a while.

Over the time of two year, Albine suffered with a patience matched only by his new hunger for poultry, gratified by each new gift Piney saw fit to bestow - a sideways look, the raising of a brow, a shy smile.

The first time he come to call, Piney was knee deep in the crick worshin' out her bloodrags. The air smelled of iron and her hands were stained crimson when she looked up and seen him talkin' to her paw. She run off.

He come back though, a week later, and they sat there in the front room, eyes on the floor. Over a time they commenced talkin'.

· · · · · · · ·

Now, a mile downhill, he met the water, and the hound ran in wild splatters upstream and down. When Albine got to the cabin that lay in the lower holler, Piney was waitin', not with bridejoy, but in a mighty pall, as her paw had that very day up and died from the bite of a copperhead snake.

"I ain't goin' nowhar without Maw. I ain't leavin' her hyare on her own." He could tell Piney was firm and set on it the way her arms was crossed, the toenails of her bare feet clawing into the black soil. So Albine packed up the Young's mule and fashioned a rickety sled to drag behind it. On the sled he roped a mattress full of bedbugs, three goosefeather pillers, a tin percolator, two black iron skillets big and small, a three-legged dutch oven and a rockin' chair pegged together by Piney's paw that very week.

On that day when her life was about to change forever, Vina Young had stood at dawn worshin' a mess of creasy greens and ramps. Out the winder she spied him, weaving towards the house in a blind stagger. She watched him grab his throat, fall, twitch, go still. By afternoon, Albine had done come and put him in the ground, that man she'd laid with up in the bed twenty some odd year, and that very day Piney said she had to up and leave everthang but her spit can. Leave her place.

But the call to her heart was powerful strong, the chorus of tiny voices. Piney was yellin' but Vina run out the back door to see her babes in the ground one last time, down the path to the four stones where she took up bawlin' and beating the ground with her fists. Leave her home place. Leave her babies in the ground.

Piney commenced carrying on, so Vina picked herself up out of the dirt wet with tears and headed on back to the house. On her way, she scooped up a hen, squeezing it so hard it shat. One hard chop, clean through neck, muscle, gullet, bone, and deep into the kitchen table she'd never again set. She took and dispensed the blood of the still flapping critter across the threshold and rubbed it over with angelica root as a gad for the house and souls left behind. For each corner of the house, she did the very same.

Her hands traveled slow across the wall, touching each different thing - root charms and the twistings of every kind of vine, the dried up carcasses of field mouse, tadpole and vole, beads of bones, poultices in ragbags, birdfeet and feathers bound in knotted hide strips.

Piney nagged, "Come on Maw, leave them there thangs hangin' hyare. We got to git up the mountain afore dark."

Vina Young played her hands across the objects one more time and sighing out her heavy heart, crossed the front threshold and closed the door painted birdsegg blue. Albine helt the beast next to the porch so Vina could hike up a lag and hunch up behind Piney, and then he led it, heavy with them two heartsick women, and plodded slowly up the mountain.

· · · · · · · ·

Albine added a lean-to onto his cabin, a room for the widder woman who would be grannie to his four children and help run his household the rest of her natural born days. As soon as the travelin' preacher come 'round, Piney and Albine were joined, hand-to-hand and heart-to-heart, and set to work on them four kids and the two babies they lost to scarlet fever. As the youngins grew up, they sat on the front porch swing and looked out over the smoke rising from the iron furnace. The two boys left home to work the mines in West Virginia and the youngest girl got a job at the drug store soda fountain down in Blackshale.

The oldest girl left home in shame after bearin' a stillborn babe out of wedlock, nary seen agin. She had took to bleeding somethin' awful after the shriveled blue fetus slipped out onto the mattress. Piney knowed hit twr'ent right, the red circle growin' out to the edge of the blue stripe ticking, and her girl goin' all white, eyes rollin' back.

She called Albine in and begged him, "Fetch the wagon! We got to git her down to town!"

Albine set his mouth in a hard poker-straight line, shook his head and declared he weren't gonna have folks hearin' a bastard babe come out no house of his'n. "She kin live or die right chere. In God's mighty hands it lays and ain't much hope 'air with her wallerin' like a sow in sin."

He spat on the floor.

Tears streaming down her face, Piney stood by, watchin' and waitin' for her girl's passing. She paced, spitting snuff into a tin can and studying on the stiff blue baby girl thing, no bigger than a newborn piglet. She spied an extra thumb on the right hand.

"Ahaiiiii," Piney jumped back in a mighty swoon. Grannie Young, havin' seen with her own eyes the devil's mark, told Albine, "Bind that thang up and throw it down in the river a fer piece from hyare!" She commenced to bile the bones of a chicken with sassafras and pokeberry root, gathered it all up in poultice sacks tied up with the feathers of a guinny hen, all of which was hangin' over the doors and winders before sunup.

In spite of all and maybe outta pure spite, the girl come to, near emptied of all her juice and barely livin'. Piney told her true that her babe was tetched by the devil and was throwed in the river, for the sake of all their souls. The girl's screams echoed down the holler, bounced off tin roofs and slid 'round the crick stones, 'til the sound withered and scattered softly on the surface of the river where her girl child slept. As soon as her teats dried up, she hobbled down to the Trailways bus bound for anywheres but Blackshale, but Piney and Albine and Grannie Young stayed right where they were for the rest of their days.

2029 Morning Glory Ridge

Memory's a funny thing. It filters and flattens some items from the catalog of your life, takes creative license with the details of others, and blows some up completely out of whack. This afternoon I'm leafing through a scrapbook I made when I was ten. I had scratched my name, Anna Grace Tollett, in big childish marks into the leatherette cover and rubbed black shoe polish down into the letters. The black paper pages are now faded and brittle, the corners of some crumble off as I turn them over one by one. In my memory, Mama and Pap were like movie stars, but here, in black and white, truth is they look so ordinary.

Dory's crowning glory was her naturally blonde hair that tumbled loosely around her face in soft waves. When she stood in the sun, diamonds of light shimmered across her head. Her eyes were on the small side, even squinty, but were translucent and a peculiar blue - cerulean someone professed – a color not often seen in the eyes of a woman. She had an entire repertoire of unique expressions, one of which is right here, under the tip of my wrinkled finger, in this snapshot of her leaning back against the porch rail. One eyebrow is lifted up in a query, as if to say, "You actually think that Kodak will be able to capture me?" I see now she was not really beautiful, but had elegance and a feisty attitude that set her apart. All her slightly imperfect features came together into an unforgettable whole.

Here, two pages over, she is posed in front of the shiny black hearse, encasing me lovingly in her long, thin arms. I am holding my baby doll in exactly the same way. It was never mentioned that my baby doll's rubber skin was brown, just as it never occurred to me that everyone's family pictures were not made in front of a meat wagon.

As for my pap, his features were nothing spectacular either, but he took great care with his grooming, so the gestalt was a fine looking man. He drank a bit, especially after Dory left us, and the more he drank the rougher he appeared, often unshaven. In these pictures though, he had a smoother, more cosmopolitan look than was normally seen in a mountain town like Blackshale. I imagine there were some who called him a "dandy."

When I think of myself as a child, I only recall the list of flaws I fretted over daily, condemnations about my face and body that stacked up in my mind. But here in this snapshot, I am at the carnival down by the river, a pretty raven-haired girl, holding on to the hand of a giant black man for dear life. I'm smiling, probably because of the fluff of pink cotton candy in my other hand.

· · · · · · · ·

Mrs. Stout has come for my bath, the one remaining human touch of caregiving that isn't relegated to technology. She pitty-patters around me in hurried arcs, arranging paraphernalia for a bed bath. Leaning over me, she taps my screen and chooses some relaxing music. If I am nice, she will throw in some of her massage moves, so I give her an appreciative smile and compliment her new hairdo, which in truth makes her face look like a cowpile.

"Hay darlin'," she says. "did you ever get that masterpiece finished the other night?"

"Huh?" I am clueless.

"I was on nights last Tuesday, and every time I came in here your right hand was up toward the ceiling, drawin' in the air. Looked to me like you were really serious about your work. I sure would have liked to see it!" She flips back the covers so she can start sponging around on me.

I spread my legs open wide, and grin up at her over the top of my scrapbook, "Powder it up good, Stout, the preacher's coming!"

"Where have you been hiding?" she laughs, "We haven't used

talcum powder since back in the nineties! Don't you know that stuff causes the female cancer? And, you, you don't fool me Anna Grace Tollett, you have yet to let a preacher visit!"

Then, out of nowhere, I remember the dream clearly. It was one of those marathon activity dreams that seems to go on all night. I had been creating a group portrait of all my loved ones in the Northern Renaissance style. The painting was massive, and my arms were aching as they stretched to reach the outer borders of the canvas. They were all in it, facing the artist in rigid poses, clothed in brocades and satins - Dory, Frank, Corrine, Pearlie, Hum, and my cousin, Perry. My loves. At the bottom right of the picture, was a tiny black dog on a jeweled leash. I lay the scrapbook aside with a sigh, returning my people to their worldly home under my bedside table and give myself gratefully to Mrs. Stout's practiced and tender touch.

1925 Blackshale   *A Backstory*

Nettie McBee was coming up fast on twelve years old, too old really to be playing with dolls. Regardless, she fished her rag doll Hester out from behind the moldy potato bin on the back porch. She was headed down the dirt road to play with her cousin twice removed, Imogene, who was only ten. Her maw, Eliza, had told her she could go play and stay all afternoon long, a rare and joyful treat. Being a farm child, Nettie spent most days knee deep in chores. She skipped down the road dragging the doll by one cloth hand, stirring up dust, jerking Hester limb-to-limb. Imogene saw her comin' a ways off and sat on the porch, nervously chewing a hay straw and picking her nose in anticipation.

Nettie and Imogene scrambled up the ladder to the loft and sat spread legged on the floor with their dolls and a pile of cloth scraps. With pinkin' shears way too heavy for their little fingers, they were cutting out dresses, aprons, and bonnets that they would spend the afternoon sewing by hand.

"Hey! Let's playlike birthin' babies!" Imogene said suddenly.

Nettie lay down on the floor and stuck her doll up between her legs. She commenced to groaning and carrying-on somethin' awful.

"Push!" Imogene yelled, and Nettie took to hollerin'. Both girls had been right outside the bedroom door when babies were born, and they knew well the narrative of birth. After a time, Imogene, playing the midwife, spread Nettie's knees and pulling the doll up in the air by her cloth heels began to whoop her bottom, feigning birth cries through a pursed-up mouth.

"Oh dear blessit God hit's another girl!" She cried out in disgust, "Another mouth for you'uns to feed!" Apparently she had heard those words somewhere before.

Nettie swooned a while longer, and then held her arms out for her baby. "I swanny, I don't kere. I'll love her anyways! Come here my precious darlin' angel!" She stuck Hester up against her bony flat chest and made slurping sounds. Then she raised the doll up and kissed her face, nearly knocked over by the mixed odor of sweaty little girl privates and potato rot.

"Ugh! I declare! This here babe has a powerful stank!" She pushed Hester away.

Imogene took her turn suffering in mock childbirth, and once both raggedy souls were brought into the world and butt slapped into pretend life, the girls began to sew doll clothes, slipping their needles in and out of gingham and calico. After a time, Nettie turned peevish and accused Imogene of being selfish and grabbing up the best scraps.

"You got all them purty calicos, and left me withn' the flour sacks!"

"Well, you kin jes get on home!" pouted Imogene, "And take that smelly youngin' of your'n too!"

Nettie jumped up and slung Hester over her shoulder. She stomped out vowing, "I'll not play with that big selfish crybaby nary agin!" But halfway home the tears started to fall, plopping dark craters in the dust. She had no other friends, and it could get mighty lonely out on a farm.

Self-pity was not cottoned to on the McBee place, so she tiptoed up the steps to sulk in the privacy of her room. When she started down the hall by her ma's closed bedroom door, there was an unfamiliar suite of dire groanings coming from inside. Nettie flung open the door to identify her Ma's distress.

She learned in that horrible instant what it is that men and women do behind closed doors, and noticed right off that the man was not her father. Her mother was naked and wild about the face, legs wrapped around the waist of a man the girl had never laid eyes on. They were at the pinnacle of coupling, carin' of nothin' else, so they failed to notice Nettie and continued the strange thrusting dance. At first, Nettie thought the man was hurting her mama, but when Eliza took to yelling "Don't stop, Oh God! Please, don't stop!" in an unrecognizable voice, Nettie realized she was a willing and hungry participant. The man swung around and sat on the end of the bed, pulling Eliza McBee up over him, until she was sitting right on top of his privates. It looked to Nettie like that huge unspeakable thing, the thing she had heretofore only seen hanging down out of their prize bull's belly, had to be right smack up inside of her ma. As she stared at her mother's back sliding up and down, she knew something was terribly wrong. Still, she could not break the frozen fascination that kept her standing stock still and wide eyed, leastways, not until the loud cracking noise reported from the hall behind her, the one that started the ragged scarlet hole blooming on her mother's back.

When her father shot and instantly killed her mother, Nettie fainted dead away and stayed passed out for an entire day. She woke up mute as a wooden Indian and lay in her bed for a solid month. So she knew nothing of the door-to-door salesman being shot between the eyes and buried out back, two feet from the hole where his severed man thing lay shriveled like a dead field rat. She was not present when her father dragged her mother's body out to the wagon or when he scrubbed down the bedroom with bleach and Oxydol soap. That day, along with many after it, were a merciful blur.

Later on, when she began to talk right again, her father sat her down on the porch swing and spoke his mind in a voice wound clock spring tight.

"Ain't sure how much you recollect 'bout that day you last laid eyes on yore ma. She's gone, and she's gone on account of bein' a sinnin' whore. She got what she had comin'. If some comes 'round directly askin' after her, that's all you say girl, 'She's gone.' "

That was the last thing Nettie's pa said to her for a solid year.

When he took up talking to her again, he had come to be a bad diabetic and claimed he was losing his eyesight. He had no choice than to order Nettie around and accept her help with a great grudge, and she even more begrudgingly gave it.

And some did come asking after Eliza McBee. The county sheriff and two of his boys smoked Lucky Strikes on the porch and casually inquired as to why she no longer seemed to be around.

"Yore neighbors has seen Nettie hangin' the clothes out on the line, and they ain't seen Eliza for a while," they asserted, peering out through rings of smoke across the field to the adjoining farms. Nettie's pa looked them straight in the eye and allowed as to how she had took off in the middle of an afternoon, leaving him to raise the girl. He figgered the traveling life insurance salesman who'd been coming by regular like had given her a ride to somewhars. And the cinderblocks chained around Eliza's bloated ankles kept her from rising up out of the river and ever telling a different tale.

2029 Morning Glory Ridge

The sad sack face regarding me from the mirror is a swollen and gravity-ridden stranger. Dense with ravines carved deep by time, it droops floorward from its skull. But all is not lost, for above this horror mask floats one of my most animated and charming headpieces. Diddlybobs! They are glittered stars that bounce around on springs attached to a plastic headband - a souvenir of the 1982 World's Fair, which was only an hour from Blackshale in Knoxville. They mercifully draw attention up and away from the sagging flesh below. I'm wearing them just to irritate the help.

"Take that crazy fool thing off your head!" Gourdhead complains, "It's making me dizzy and a woman your age looks ridiculous wearing kiddie stuff." He leans over me and expels his rotten breath into my face, "Hey YOU! Do you hear me you old bag? YOU LOOK STUPID!"

His exhalation is a motley mix of unwashed teeth, cigarettes, last night's whisky, and some foul organic something, the possibly Juliesque origins I'd rather not ponder. Gourdhead feels free to visit verbal abuse on me regularly. He thinks I'm mentally not at home and won't tell. I wiggle my head, sending the springy stars akimbo.

An invisible thought bubble floats above my head. *A woman my age can wear anything she damn well pleases, fagboy!* I love it when he gets pissed off and sashays out of the room.

1932 Blackshale

Nettie McBee spent her teenage years fetchin' and nursing, while the other girls at Blackshale High School went on hayrides and met up with their fellers at dances. Bitterness embraced her like a jealous boyfriend. She grew to hate her pa more and more, and even accused him of faking his bad eyesight to keep her a slave in his house. Her words to anyone, if she ever did speak, were hateful and sarcastic.

When her pa insisted that he'd gone plumb blind, his nephew Jim Ed from Dixie Lee Junction picked him up in a wagon and carried him over to Knoxville General Hospital. He spent six months there. After a while, Jim Ed wrote Nettie a penny postcard saying that her pa had married his nurse and that she was ugly as the back end of a mule. When the couple returned home, Nettie was up on the front porch with her hands on her hips, waiting to view the bride. Sure enough, here was the homeliest creature Nettie had ever set eyes on. She laughed indignantly, and spat at her pa, "Oh God! It's true! You really are blind!"

Unattractive as she was, Callie, cross-eyed and wide of jaw, skin plowed with rough, hairy furrows and sprinkled with moles, took over the care and feeding of Nettie's pa with a tenacious devotion. The groping touch of his blind man's hand was the only one this woeful girl had ever known, and she was grateful for it.

Nettie had graduated Blackshale High without accolades, although she'd been fairly good at math. The hard, unemotional realities of mathematics and accounting appealed to her. By her name in the yearbook, where other girls' activities filled the page, was a glaring white space. Drill team, Future Homemakers of America, Cheering Squad, Marching Band, Homecoming Queen, had all been far out of Nettie's reach. Nettie McBee left Blackshale High without ever once being courted.

Now, free to leave home but too sharp of tongue and hard of heart for marriage prospects, Nettie was at loose ends. Her math teacher had spoken well of her to the owner of the drugstore, who had rung up asking around for an accountant. Nettie was offered the job, and in an unusual stroke of good luck for her, the owner mentioned that he and the wife had a tiny upstairs apartment around back that they would be glad to rent her for a small part of her salary.

Nettie walked into the front room where her pa and Callie, her hairy hands buried in a pile of tatting, sat on opposite ends of the davenport in silence. She had intended to march out without a word, carrying her single carpetbag, and never look back. At the last minute, however, she turned to Callie and cautioned, "Whatever you do, ugly stepmother, don't go messin' around with no other man." Her pa sucked in a tortured breath and cocked an ear, waiting to see if more was forthcoming. But it wasn't. Nettie was already out the door and on to her new life.

1940 Blackshale

The accounting job at Blackshale Drugstore suited Nettie McBee perfectly. She was ensconced in a back room in the company of adding machines and couldn't run off customers with her spite. Mr. Elvaney, the drugstore owner, and his wife were easy-going kinds of folk who overlooked what they joked about in private as Nettie's odd turn.

But one day Nettie had to deal with a human being face-to-face when her adding machine got some kind of obstruction up in its cogs and had to be attended to by a serviceman. He was a local, the eldest Tollett son, Boyd Lee, who had lost a leg in the mines and afterward went over to Chattanooga for training to fix office machines. Because of his disability, he felt like a second-class catch and was sure he'd never be able to land a sweetheart. He, too, like the Elvaneys, was willing to overlook Nettie's odd turn. After all, she was a solid built woman and not all that bad looking in the face, even though she was a little on the sour side. So, after a few more trumped-up visits to the adding machine, he set out to see if he could sweeten her up. On his first go, he asked her to step out and have refreshments at the soda fountain right there in the drugstore. She spit out a "no," acting like she thought him a buffoon. But after a few more tries, there sat Nettie McBee spinning back and forth on a stool sipping orangeade through a straw and softening up bit-by-bit.

Boyd Lee worked hard to get through Nettie's shell, and eventually he succeeded. She had a hard time trusting, but little-by-little she put her confidence in this sweet one-legged man. They married at the courthouse in Pineville, settled down on a tiny farm pushed up against the mountain, and a little over a year from then, she was in a childbirth bed groanin' for real. The long, spindly baby was a boy they named Perry James, and he was the apple of her eye.

In this time of her life, Nettie McBee Tollett learned to love and be loved. Her husband had gained religion when he lost his leg, and he took his family to church every Sunday. Nettie came to enjoy the stories of the Bible. She built her life around Boyd Lee and Perry, and let the bitter poison of her past fade away.

2029 Morning Glory Ridge

My reticence act has its ups and downs. It keeps me from having to attend lame social activities, gets me out of volunteer work, and discourages unwanted visitors. On the other hand, I have no friends. I've seen no one here that I would consider friend material anyway, so for now I am holding off on the social life.

Let's talk technology. We all have an eScreen that swings over our bed and gives us access to anything we might need. It's a giant, high-resolution touch screen that swivels to any angle, so we can tilt it over and choose a keyboard of any size. Even the near blind can zoom up a keyboard big enough to type on. We can use it to watch TV or movies, read any book in the world at any size type, make requests regarding our care, keep up with our medical records, or communicate with anyone at Morning Glory Ridge or out in the great big world. We can join a videoconference of all the residents and staff, or we can have a video chat with just one resident and gossip about all the others. We each have Erapods, so our activities on the eScreen are private. I hope. When I signed into this joint, the contract was clear - we are adults, and we retain our rights to privacy and freedom. So I am assuming that if I want to surf porn, no one would be looking over my shoulder electronically. I can tell you porn is the farthest thing from my mind these days, but I do have an active intellectual life that I am keeping carefully hidden from the authorities.

Even with my Macular Degeneration, this screen lets me read and appreciate most media. So I still devour eBooks, watch movies, and email the few people I know who are not in the ground or an urn. The screen has an eSketchbook and tons of art software, but my hands are too shaky for all that now. I can write music and poetry and play games. Entertainment abounds here for those with the energy to partake, but by the time I eat my meals and nap, there goes another day of my rapidly waning life. Oh, and how could I forget, a good bit of my time is spent roaming the roads of Blackshale in my mind.

1946 Blackshale

Picture Blackshale, Tennessee, a coal mining town with a few thousand souls, a river, a railroad track, the twenty-bed hospital, a grammar and high school, a movie show, and in the summer, a roller skating rink under a red and white striped tent. As summer winds down, the tent is folded into a southbound truck, canoes and fishing boats go bottom up on the banks of the river, and the people are drawn indoors to the warmth of their home fires. Over the autumn, as the leaves begin to spin to the ground in faster and faster spirals, thin grey streams rise from those small fires along Blackshale Highway, one-by-one, until even the most overheated granny comments on the chill and bends down to strike a match at her hearth. And on toward winter, the streams flow upward and meet in a grey haze that hangs heavy in the sky. It stays there, thick and unyielding, until May.

The town is tucked right up underneath the coal-rich mountain, so folks feel sheltered. In 1946 life was pleasant and the faces passing from the soda fountain, to the bank, to the local diner, wore contented smiles. This town was more blessed than others, having lost only two boys and those early on in the war. It was a sweet June, folks relieved and grateful to leave behind the bloody ugliness and loss, lifting their faces hopefully toward the sun, going on with their lives. It was a good place to come home to, and when Frank Tollett came home in one piece from France, he expected he'd go down into the coal mines with his pa.

God knows Frank Tollett never set out to be an undertaker. At first, with the afterimages of exploding shrapnel still burned in his brain, the dark mines seemed serene, the safest, deepest trench a man could crawl into. He couldn't wait to go down into the hole. It would be a canned life, living in a company house and working for scrip to spend in the company store at the end of each week, but anything seemed better than the horrors Frank had just escaped.

As the realities of war began to fade, just as he was laying awake nights thinking how he didn't much want to spend his life bent over down in those tunnels breathing fine coal powder and sweating in the heat, an unforeseen opportunity came along. The only mortician within a hundred miles had a fatal heart attack, laying himself out cold over the body he was working on that morning and leaving two counties lacking services for the recently departed.

Frank was approached by a contingency of well-to-do men who asked if he'd ever thought about mortician's school. If he finished the course in good stead, they promised, he could count on a loan from them to build a fine local funeral home. Held up against a backbreaking life in the mines, this seemed like a right good proposition, so Frank packed up his cardboard suitcase and caught the next bus to Nashville. By that afternoon, he was signed up as an official student of the mortuary sciences.

The first day of mortuary school was designed to promptly identify those who were not cut out for the work. Twenty-two young men filed in around a freshly murdered corpse, and the instructor rapidly and unceremoniously plunged a thick steel needle into her abdomen, drawing out a liter of bloody sludge. Two fainted and three quickly retired to the hall to unload their biscuits and gravy. Frank had seen his share of blood in the war, so he was able to swallow back his bile and look the teacher square in the eye. In the following months, he began to learn what it took to be an embalmer, a mortician, a referee of family politics at the worst of times, and the director of dignified closing ceremonies.

Three weeks into his training, Frank was dispatched over to the adjoining School of Nursing to fetch an assortment of glass tubes. There in the supply closet of Room C-105, Frank happened upon the rear view of Dory Larsen, first-year student nurse. He had never seen the seams on a pair of nylons so unerringly vertical or legs so flawless. She was placing tiny vials along a white enamel shelf in a most meticulous way, so that any two were an identical space apart, and all the labels were flush with the front of the shelf. It was as if that simple, everyday act was a precious ritual, and even before he saw her face, it popped into his head that she, too, was precious.

Frank shifted his weight from one foot to the other, garnering his courage. Responding to a timid squeak from one of his penny loafers, Dory turned suddenly and lifted her gaze upward, assessing whether or not the interruption was worthwhile. He stuttered out his need for a dozen each of three mm, five mm and eight mm glass tubes and signed the invoice in a shaky cursive. Only after searching her hand for a wedding ring did Frank turn to leave, and Dory revolved back around to her perfect shelf. But halfway out the door, he wheeled and spoke quietly to her back, "Hey, if it's coming up on your break time, could I buy you a cup of coffee?"

In the diner, Dory slid demurely into a booth. She removed the white bobby pins from her starched white cap and slapped it on the table, setting loose a wave of light blonde hair to fall down over one eye. She fixed the other eye on Frank as he fidgeted with the brown paper sack of tinkling glass tubes that betrayed his nervous hands. She was amused.

Frank had never had a girlfriend before, let alone sex, unless you counted the guilty pleasures of his own right hand when he was alone in the dark. All through school, he had been as bland as wash water, but being a soldier had matured him to a degree, sharpened his edges. And the pure luck of surviving the war had endowed him with a vague happiness that now resembled a sense of humor. While the conversation rambled around hometowns, reasons for coming to school, their classes, and their families,

Dory saw clearly with her unobscured blue eye the gentle and purposeful man she had been hoping for.

Their courtship progressed in the usual way, from holding hands in the picture show to their first tentative kisses on the back stoop of the nurses' dorm, to sessions of groaning and petting and clothed humping on Frank's rooming house bed that left them both wet between the legs and frustrated by Dory's sense of virginal duty. On account of her, Frank Tollett had a powerful and permanently hard lump in his trousers. By the time Frank stood to accept his certificate, he was fit to bursting with need and heavyhearted with the knowledge that he had to go home, two hundred miles from where Dory had to stay for two more years of school.

On the morning he was packed up and set to leave, Dory knocked on the door of his boarding house room crying. "Frank Tollett, there's something you need to know before you go," she confessed in a torrent of tears, "I'd a whole lot rather be an undertaker's wife than a nurse."

• • • • • • • •

So a few days later Frank put on one of the dark suits the school had advised him to buy for directing the business of funerals, and took Dory, along with her best friend Sudy Pelfree to stand up as a witness, over to the courthouse. The Justice of the Peace was on leave for a long overdue hemorrhoid operation. His substitute was an older man, a retiree who had a tic that produced a quickly expelled "hiiiiic" sound, along with a sudden jerking of his neck that seemed to fling his eyeballs clean sideways.

He began: "Repeat after me-hiiiic. I, Frank Elmer Tollett take thee-hiiiic, Dory Jane Larsen, to be-hiiiic my lawfully wedded wife..."

Now Sudy had a sad history of getting an uncontainable giggling fit for hardly any reason at all. Those two girls had been marched out of the Methodist church more than once, when Sudy had lost her composure and made the whole pew shake. On the regrettable Easter Sunday she spewed the blood of Christ all over a brand new white straw hat of the woman kneeling next to her, it was strongly suggested by the pastor that she please become a Baptist or Presbyterian or Episcopalian or anything else except, of course, a Catholic.

On this, Dory's wedding day, there was a degree of natural nervousness that didn't help matters at all. At first Sudy held it in pretty good, looking down at the floor and concentrating hard as nails on how this was a once-in-a-lifetime occasion of the greatest importance in her best friend's life and how she would never hurt the poor afflicted man's feelings for nothing. But the harder she stared at the floor, his expellations and jerking just got worse. Her shoulders began to shake and that brought on severe warning looks from both Frank and Dory. Then the tears came, and her efforts to hold it all in were just too much strain on her weak bladder. What started as a trickle ended up as a sizable yellow puddle over and around Sudy's white patent leather flats. The substitute Justice of the Peace glanced down at the puddle, but never missed a beat or a tic or a hiiic or a jerk. He finished up that wedding ceremony right quick so all would be said and done.

Frank paid him in cash and, also, the singer who had rendered a quavering, off-key version of "I Love You Truly." When he got outside, Dory was giving Sudy the dickens.

"You *peed*! Sweet Jesus! You peed your pants at my wedding!" Sudy just hung her head and dabbed at the back of her dress with Dory's something borrowed and blue hankie.

Frank gave Dory a reassuring pat and Sudy a long studying look that was neither reassuring nor judgmental. Then he declared, "Well, dag nab it, I reckon gigglin' or no gigglin', piss or no piss, we are still rightly married and Mrs. Tollett, I aim to take you up to my room right now!" And he did.

• • • • • • • •

The mourners of Blackshale were sick and tired of driving fifty miles for funeral services, so the vow that had been made to Frank for a new funeral home was quickly kept. In the middle level of the building, the part Frank called "the store," were the chapel, the Victorian style funeral parlor with red velvet settees, the office where people came to make their arrangements, and a showroom where families argued over the prices of coffins. The basement held the embalming room, a morgue, a workshop, a bathroom, and a storage room. On the top floor were their living quarters, a sunny apartment where Dory, with all her heart, loved being Frank Tollett's wife.

Owing to a long run of Asian flu and a deadly mine accident, business had started out at a trot. Frank "Tonk" Tollett soon owned it all on paper, his debts retired. And, as it happened, Frank's widowed pa had been deep in the mine when the timbers came crashing down, so his boys ended up with a substantial amount of cash that had been stuffing the old miner's mattress. What with turning a profit and his unexpected windfall, Frank soon had other irons in the fire. Frank stayed busy. He bought and sold land, brokered timber, that sort of thing. Not to mention the source of his nickname, "Tonk" (as in Honky), Tonk Tollett thought of his hour, or two some days, at the beer joint as serious and necessary business. It was during his drinkin' time that he talked many a softened up mind into a business deal. He never danced with the women, never even talked to them, and if the beer put him in the mood for romance, he headed home. The office closed up at four and by six, Tonk was usually hiking up Dory's skirt, yanking down her step-ins, and backing her up against the kitchen wall while she looked over his shoulder, watching the cornbread fixing to burn in the stove. So vast was his hunger for Dory that most nights, after the cornbread and greens and okry and salt meat, after the washing and drying of dishes, after a radio show or two, even long after the beer had worn off, Tonk sat by Dory on the divan and started to tickle her ribs and kiss her neck. He would take her by both hands and pull her giggling to their room, turn down the soft cotton sheets and lay her down gently in between them, loving her slowly, sweetly with all his being. And even when that was done, he did not roll over into sleeping and snoring like most men would. Looking into her blue eyes, he poured out his dreams, and listened to hers, loving her on and on with his tender words.

All that love made only one small son. Dory bled out the ill-formed beginnings of two baby girls, one right after the other. Eighteen months after their wedding, she was out back in the garden after supper, hoeing, barely able to see the rows of rutabagas and red potatoes over her belly. She felt like she might bust, when low and behold, she did. The flow gushed from between her legs, nourishing the radishes and drowning a few grubworms along the way.

It took her a few seconds to realize what had happened, but almost immediately, the agony set in, putting any question she might have had right to rest. She leaned against the hoe and lowered herself to the ground. Dory knew she was in a peck of trouble. Frank was gone, and she was out of sight of the highway, out of earshot of the nearest neighbor. For a while she yelled anyway until her throat went dry. She kept telling herself to stay calm, that labor usually went on for hours and Frank would be back directly. But within an hour, there was no time between pains, and she knew this was not the usual, that the baby was coming fast and it was going to be all up to her. In a panic, she prayed, "Good Lord in Heaven am I going to have to do this all alone? Help me!"

Sometimes the answer to prayer is "Sure, OK, here you go!" Sometimes it's a flat "Nope, not in my will, so no." Once in a while it's something weird in between. Dory got an in between. Her hand fell into her apron pocket finding pruning shears and the ball of twine she had brought to tie up her tomato vines. Through the endless walls of pain, she grasped for reason, for life, her life, the life of her child. After the earlier miscarriages, she was afraid this was a risky business even in the best conditions. She crawled on her hands and knees to a tree and squatted against it, holding on to a branch for support. With only instinct to go on, she pushed when she felt like she should. Her body was breaking apart, her flesh ripping. She heard her own cries, but they sounded far away. Finally, she felt the baby slithering between her legs, and she slid to the ground too, half conscious. The baby hit the red earth, shocked into breathing and bawling, eyes wide open, slimy body gathering up dirt from the ground. Dory grabbed the pruning shears, used her last bit of strength to cut the cord, wrapping the twine around both ends. She swaddled the baby in her apron, ripped open her shirt, clamped him to her breast, and passed out cold.

She woke up into pandemonium. It was already the pitch dark of night, but lanterns were swinging around her. The baby was screaming, her body was screaming, and Tonk was screaming too, "Oh God! Hurry Cooper! Oh God!" Some sort of vehicle was bumping down the yard, over the rows of the garden, toward the tree. When the vehicle came close, she knew then for sure, she was dead. Cooper Sutton's black hearse was coming to get her. She passed out again.

The hearse (which had only been pressed into use because the town's one ambulance was down at Joe Oody's Garage getting a new transmission) got Dory and her baby to the hospital just fine. And that baby, that miracle baby born in the radish patch was just fine, just fine. But after a few days, Dory got some kind of raging infection working up inside her and a surgeon was brought in from Knoxville who took out every female part she ever had. She took this with a great sadness, as she was still pining for a little girl, and the just fine, just fine baby, the last one she would ever bear, was a big, strapping boy.

Tonk whiled away several days after that at the beer joint, knee-walkin' drunk. He was having a hard time getting over the guilt of staying at that same establishment late the night his son was born in the garden. The longer he waited to face Dory and go beg forgiveness, the harder it got.

But finally, a week after the operation, Dory had to be fetched and brought home. He entered her room with his head bowed and his hat held low in two hands, shuffling in a respectful silence at the foot of her bed.

"You've about made me mad," snorted Dory, "But, I've laid here and thought on it. You couldn't pull yourself away from your precious honky-tonk, and now I'll never have another child because of it. Part of me will never forgive you that, I don't reckon. But you didn't know I was about to plant our baby in the garden, and I know you love me and if you had known you'd a been there. I'm not going to try and make you swear, swear, never to go drinkin' again. I guess that's a losing battle, for sure. But if you ever pull anything like this again that hurts our child or me I'll learn to shoot my twenty-two rifle, and I'll blast your saggy nuts off. Most of the time you are a good man and a good husband, and I do love you. Now, I never want to speak about this again."

Tonk fell across her legs on the bed, weeping like a woman, cupping her chin with a quivering hand, trying to comprehend her forgiveness, the undeserved grace. He held her for a long time, until a nurse brought in the squirming white bundle and placed it in Dory's arms.

"So, what do you want to name your son?" she asked him, her anger put away.

"How about Adam? Seeing's how he began his life with the soil?"

So Dory, Tonk, and Adam came on back to the house. After that, when Tonk went to the beer joint, he only stayed for one hour and was always home by five. Dory let go of her sadness, her feeling of being cheated, and thanked God that she had been able to bring a healthy son into the world, all by herself.

· · · · · · · ·

As soon as she had recovered from the operation enough to stand up without getting dizzy in the head, Dory ran off the woman Tonk had hired to help out. She set up a bassinet, playpen, and high chair in a corner. This worked out for a time while little Adam could be corralled and penned in. But all too soon, he was popping over the sides of the playpen, climbing the cabinets, and slipping out the screen door. On the day he about pulled a child's casket off on his head, Tonk put his foot down.

"Dory," he pleaded, "You can't be everywhere at once. You can't keep a good eye on the boy and help me downstairs and take care of the house. Now we got the money and you need some help. I know you, and I know you don't want some stranger messing with the order of your house, but I am bringin' a nigra woman over here today whether you like it or not!"

The plain fact was, Dory, who was born a perfectionist and had grown up liking things sparkling clean and organized, had become increasingly overwhelmed by the rigors of housekeeping and motherhood. Things had somehow become loosened at the seams and had fallen completely apart.

She simply said, "OK, what time's she coming around?"

Here came Pearlie Bean that afternoon, tall and straight, marching up the sidewalk into the parlor vestibule. Following close behind her was a bent over, brown titanic of a boyman, a bit vacant in the eyes. Each of them carried two scratched up and misshapen suitcases full of used clothes the church had collected up for them. In their wake tottered and swayed a broken down coon dog, a female thick with puppies.

"I means to stay right here," Pearlie resolved softly. "And Hum, Hum he have to be with me, 'cause he ain't right."

Dory's eyes flew open wide, frantic, searching Tonk's face

for explanation. He was fairly surprised himself, not having previously discussed any arrangements regarding the son with Pearlie.

"Ummmm… Miss Pearlie, would you and Hum mind to wait in here and let me and Mrs. Tollett go up to the house and talk over the particulars for a minute? How about a soda pop? Hum, how about a nice RC coke-a-cola?"

Hum mumbled, "Hummmm." He started in picking his nose and pounding on his crotch, and Dory standing with hands on hips, reddened, and looked away quickly. He held the tip of his blunt finger up high in the air, where a booger sparkled in the sunlight streaming through the window. He focused on it, considering it thoughtfully for some time, his eyes no longer vacant at all. To his credit, he didn't eat it, but smeared it over the back pocket of his overalls.

Tonk slipped the bottle into the opener on the side of the red metal cooler in the office and cranked off the top. He handed Hum a Moon Pie from his desk drawer to boot. The whites of Hum's eyes glimmered and his slack mouth drooled.

Dory stomped up the concrete stairs so hard her rolled up nylons melted down around her ankles. Tonk huffed behind her, grabbing at the hem of her skirt. When they got upstairs, he headed straight for the square hole in the floor, and fit the cover down tight. He sure didn't want Dory's venomous words leaking down into the parlor where Pearlie and Hum sat waiting.

"Have… you… lost… your… fool… mind? You expect me to have this… this… halfwit gorilla living in my home? Why, no tellin' what he is apt to do to us in the middle of the night!" Dory began, but Tonk cut in…

"Baby, baby… think about it. Think! If they stay here, we pay her less because of their room and board… and… she's here all the time. Why, she could watch the baby and we could even go out to the picture show some night. And Hum, well, he don't talk much... but I'm sure he's good for help out in the garden, or totin' and carrying. He seems right sweet, well, in a way. Look baby, we got that storeroom downstairs with an outside door. And well, some fool burnt their house down last week... they really got nowhere to go. This is a good thing, honey... just take a deep breath and give it a good thinking over." He rubbed a hand between her shoulder blades, watching her anger subside with each stroke.

She sighed and shifted her weight, "All right Frank Tollett. We try this out for one week. If I am not happy with her here, they go right back across the river, house or no house. Agreed?"

"Whatever you say." Tonk gave her a wink and picked her up, whirling her around the room and practically dragging her down the stairs. Frank and Dory swept into the parlor hand in hand and proceeded to lay out an agreement to Pearlie. They made a fair offer of a weekly salary and went over her working hours and all them things was fine, fine with Pearlie Bean, who truth be known would a just been happy with a roof over her head.

All four of them worked that afternoon clearing out the storeroom in the basement. They swept out piles of dust and rat pills, cleared cobwebs, and washed the whole place down. Tonk went to town and found a couple of used beds, a table and chairs, a kerosene heater, an enamel chamber pot, and Dory made a Tattersall curtain for the room's one small window. They agreed that Pearlie would cook enough for everyone at each meal, and she would take plates for her and Hum down to their room.

· · · · · · · · ·

The next morning, Tonk rolled over and pecked hard on Dory's shoulder.

"Ummmm... smell that!" He sat up in bed all smiles, and then pulled Dory by the hand into the kitchen, her still indecent in her filmy nightdress.

Pearlie was hunkered over the sink, scrubbing the faucet with a toothbrush. On the kitchen table was a checkered tablecloth, a pitcher of peonies, country ham and redeye gravy, fried eggs over easy, grits, and buttermilk biscuits. The percolator bubbled on the top of the stove.

"Oh... well... *Pearlie*," Dory began to protest, "We usually just have ourselves a bowl of Kellogg's Corn Flakes and sweet milk before we go downstairs."

"Dory," Frank chirped, grinning and grabbing her face in both hands, "Dory! Shut up, honey!"

Well, Dory was just plain shamed. Even before Adam came along, her long days helping run the business didn't leave enough time for keeping the house as perfectly as she would have liked, and her cooking wasn't fit to eat - either tasteless or burnt. The upstairs house was covered with a permanent layer of dust and smelled of dirty laundry. Tonk had been worried about the situation for some time now, mainly because he knew it had to be getting on Dory's last nerve, perfectionist that she was.

Pearlie set right in singing about Jesus and scrubbing with vinegar and ammonia. She cranked every sheet and curtain and garment through the wringer of the Maytag washer out on the porch and hung it all out to dry on the clothesline. That baby boy was bathed squeaky clean, and she cooked up two more square meals. After supper, she took everything down off the line, sweet smelling from drying in the sun and laid it all out on the clean kitchen table. She set up the ironing board, plugged in the iron, sprinkled and starched and pounded until the pile disappeared.

Dory, running her hand over the row of crisp cotton garments, folded tablecloths and curtains on hangers, quickly shed her pride and took Pearlie for the gift from Heaven that she was. That night, after singing Adam to sleep, Dory filled her claw foot bathtub with hot water, poured in a whole bottle of sweet milk and crumbled in dried lavender. She soaked in there for an hour, smiling and humming to herself.

2029 Morning Glory Ridge

No one comes to read me Bible verses or spew out their soccer mom pride, share websites and other things that no longer have meaning for me. I took care of that one right up front and early on by pretending to be incommunicado. Over my years here, I have learned to play my cards close to my chest, imprisoning my words, keeping my options open. I notice that residents labeled "bright" or "sharp" are immediately put to work for the common good as free labor. Get this straight! My volunteer days are over. It's my time for introspection, reckoning with any higher powers I might soon be meeting. It's story hour. I opt to lay low and play dumb. I mean it, this time I'm *really* retired. I want to be alone to review my life, muster forgiveness for my tormentors, clean out the cobwebs, rewrite a few scripts in a more favorable light, seek absolution for the screw-ups that I know good and well would never pass the muster of any decent God.

My feigned lack of small talk skills has, for the most part, kept annoying visitors at bay. Today, despite all my well-planned defenses and my most sincere insouciance, a cloying and overly enthusiastic representative of Jesus Christ comes calling, plastic posy in one hand and tracts in the other.

It is not a good day for a visit. A new compression fracture has come from out of nowhere, setting off muscle spasms up and down my spine. I've been shrieking in pain most of the morning until little cups of pills begin to appear. I usually refuse pain meds, but today I've sucked them in gratefully. The spasms have started to relax, and my mind whirls in a fog. I'm fading into a drugged stupor, feeling no pain, and I want to be alone.

My roommate Tiffany has apparently smoked one too many weed or may have even been a crack head or some such and has nothing left to communicate. The fun thing about her is that dependably spurted out, single, completely random word. It's like the Tiffany "word of the day." As the lady from Jesus charges in Tiffany says, "Cockfight!" I have yet to hear her utter a complete sentence, grunt, or fart, so she is really no threat to my quest for peace and quiet.

This local missionary with the plastic flower is another matter entirely. This sort of thing must simply be nipped in the bud before it gets out of hand. She pulls up a chair. She has swept unfazed past my first line of defense, in which I pretend to be incapable of any meaningful two-way conversation.

You can imagine the speech - tiptoeing, pretty with sugar on top generalities - the usual insipid nonsense manufactured for someone not known from Adam's housecat, spoken much too loudly as everyone knows we are *all* hard of hearing. Oh! The drivel! Can you imagine it persisting for forty-five minutes? I am tired, doped into a fog, and patience was never my long suit anyhoo. Oh! How this woman loves to talk about herself! Oh! How she goes on and on about people I don't even know! Why, oh why would I care? The words, the well meant but irritating word bits, begin to pulse and whirl and jiggle under my skin.

Then comes the moment when the mind can only survive an ugly, inescapable situation by converting it, midstream, to humor. Yes! This is so unbearable, it's funny! I feel my laugh lines curve upward against my will, a tremor struggling against the hysterical impulse to laugh in her face. She misinterprets this. She is now inspired to push on for fifteen more minutes, continuing her banal chattering that is obviously bringing me such joy and filling my lonely moments. Bless my heart.

By now, I'm looking pleased as punch. Encouraged by my response, the Jesus lady is leaning in closer when my angelic smile suddenly fractures into a manic grin.

"FUCKIE!" I shriek wild-eyed, spittle flying. "FUCKIE! FUCKIE!

FUCKIE! FUCKIE! FUCKIE!" *Where in the heck did that come from?* I ask myself, confused.

I focus my eyes absently on a spot over her head and drool.

She recoils, jumps back, and flees all in one motion, banging her chair to the floor in a loud wallop.

I hear her whispering to the nursing assistant, "Excuse me, Miss. Does Mizriz Tollett have that Turin Syndrome?"

I query her silently. *Do I look like I'm already in a frigging shroud, idiot?*

A strange noise fills the room. Tiffany is sitting up in her bed, giggling, looking for all the world happy and stoned. "Blue water tower!" she says.

Please don't get me wrong. I love the Lord Jesus with all my failing heart. I just want to be alone with him, sucking in his grace, and skip the small talk with the do-gooders. I'll admit I do feel a little bit bad about this now as I intended to be a *kind* person here in the last lap, but I lost it. I couldn't help myself. I lost control of my own mouth, and it started spewing words I hardly ever use. I'm *possessed*!

Well anyway, as for the F-word, God invented that whole process in the first place so how can the word really be so crude? Just because it *sounds* dirty, like the suction of body juices, it's gotten a bad rap. As far as the God-given act itself, just where would the human race be without it? Yeah. Think about that!

And besides, it got a nice NO VISITORS PLEASE sign taped on the end of my bed. Me, 1. Visitors, 0. *And BTW you fool woman, it's Tourette Syndrome!*

1948 Blackshale

Tonk glanced sideways at Dory once in a while and felt a sad emptiness for the babies they would never have, maybe some little blondheaded, blue-eyed girls who would have looked so much like her. But when he saw her giving the boy a bath, the little feller smacking the soapy bubbles with his chubby hands, her smiles lifted him up. Adam Larsen Tollett was a blissfully cheerful baby, just bursting with energy. He was never still for a minute, even in his sleep. Later on, they would look back sadly and say, "It was like he knew he had to live his life real fast in the few months he would have on earth."

There was no senseless accident for Dory to feel guilty about. There was no headlong fall on the stairs or accidental trip down the well, no choking on an overlooked small toy, no finger stuck in the light socket when Dory turned her head for just a second to change the radio dial.

That baby was toddling along one minute, giggling and clapping his hands together, patty cake, patty cake, and just keeled over dead. Doc Turner down at Blackshale hospital looked over his spectacles and opinioned that Adam had a bad heart from the get-go, one that couldn't even be patched up by a famous surgeon's knife in a big city hospital. No, not even a pilgrimage to Mayo Clinic could have saved Adam Tollett.

Frank, well, you know how men can be, he felt like he had to take it like a man. He never shed the first tear in front of anybody. But Sudy recalled he looked like somethin' had sucked the life out of him. He couldn't work on his own son, so he called up a buddy from Mortician's school and asked him if he would come to Blackshale and prepare Adam's body. Frank vowed to be a strong shoulder for his completely disoriented and heartbroken wife, and he was. He sure was.

He helped her pick out the pale blue casket barely bigger than a breadbox, and lay out the tiny burying clothes. He held her while she shook and wailed, and sat with her as she ran her fingers around the deckle edges of shiny square snapshots, smiling sadly.

Just like him, Dory was always thinking about what other people might need. Frank asserted she was so far off self-centered, she might go spinning off the edge of the world. Even in her paralyzing sorrow, she organized all the things that had to be done, the things that would help everybody navigate the grief, numbly but systematically checking item after item off the list.

One of those things was the comfort of Pearlie and Hum. They were part of her family now. She was not going to bury Adam without Pearlie and Hum standing with her, and she was not going to have them embarrassed by their lack of decent mourning clothes. She got up early the morning before the funeral and went to Knoxville. She walked into Millers and bought Pearlie a church dress and a pair of pumps, matched to the feet tracings she'd made with Pearlie standing on waxed paper. Then she took the escalator downstairs and bought Hum a suit of clothes. He'd refused to take off his boots, so they'd have to do with a polish.

Pearlie had never had on a store-bought dress before. The four cotton dresses she worked in day after day she'd stitched by hand from the same Butterick pattern Number 145, and her aprons, well, nobody but a pure fool would need a pattern to make an apron. On the morning of the funeral she stood in front of the hall mirror and ran her fingers over the dark grey gabardine edged with lace. She knew it was the devil himself that made her fill up with pride and want to smile back at her own reflection, because she had loved that little dead white baby like her own.

The blameless death left Dory without a clear target for her anger; she couldn't even hurl the black wrath at herself. So for a while it flailed around inside of her, ricocheting off the inside surfaces of her skin. Three weeks after Adam's death, after the wake and the burial, the packing away of little blue sun suits and first shoes, the return of flowered china casserole dishes, and the writing of acknowledgments... thank you for your kind expression of sympathy... sincerely... Dory had herself a small, discreet nervous breakdown.

· · · · · · · ·

On the maternity floor at Saint Mary's Hospital, nurse Sudy Pelfree was about to have a breakdown of her own. She had already chewed out three candy stripers and sent another one home red-faced and bawling. It was a full moon that night and four babies had crowned at the same moment. Sudy was running her legs off, from one howling laborer to another. And of course, there were the new mothers who needed help with their engorged, milk-dripping tits. Sudy patiently showed the breast feeders how to grab up a big handful of mammary flesh and stuff it in the baby's mouth. Most of them started out timidly, offering just the tip of their nipple. Well, that was just asking for a sore titty. Thank God there weren't a lot of those though, as most women these days preferred to boil formula in nice glass bottles and let the rubber nipples take the abuse.

Sudy hadn't even made time for a cigarette or a soda pop, and just as she was about to push through the double doors of the break room, she was called to the nurses' station for a *personal phone call*. She knew it wasn't her imagination that those words rang with a terse recrimination over the loudspeaker. Over the long distance line, Frank spilled out worries about Dory. Sudy had already been to Blackshale for the funeral of course, and had stayed a couple of days to help out. But when she heard the timbre of Frank's voice across the wire, she didn't hesitate. "I'll be there tonight." The head nurse wasn't happy, having to switch around the schedule, but Sudy always insisted "first things first and friends above all." The drive was dark, rainy, curvy, but when Sudy drug her wet suitcase in the back door, Dory knew she would be saved.

After a week of Sudy working her magic, things were better. Sudy and Pearlie pampered Dory and gave her quiet time to work through her grief. Sudy carried in trays with flowers and favorite dishes that Pearlie had lovingly prepared. Dory's best friend since forever was the perfect mix of nurse and friend, cheerleader and protector.

Sudy made sure no visitors made the mistake of saying, "Oh now don't you worry honey, you can try again soon!" She made certain they all knew there would be no more having babies for Dory Tollett, and suggested they stick to safe and cheerful topics.

The day before Sudy was due to leave and go back to work, Dory had an appointment with a psychiatrist at the Blackshale Hospital. Sudy drove her, and Dory insisted that she come in with her to see the doctor. Dory bragged on Sudy, telling the doctor about what a good nurse she was and what a great friend she had been, and how she knew just what to do to make a body feel better.

"Really?" the doctor studied Sudy, "You don't say?"

Sudy's ears turned red and she protested, "Just a pal looking out for a pal."

"Are you working somewhere now?"

"Oh yes! I'm on the Maternity Ward at Saint Mary's in Knoxville."

"Well, the reason I asked, we have an opening here and I thought I might talk you into an interview. The pay is a little better than most small hospitals, since there's some administrative work tacked on."

• • • • • • • • •

Sudy ended up taking the job. The money was a lot less, but she would be farther away from women writhing in the pain of childbirth, something she had not enjoyed at all, and closer to her best friend. Sudy moving to Blackshale cheered Dory up so much that in no time she was back on with life. And yet, it was about that very time that things started getting lined up in even more perfect rows.

2029 Morning Glory Ridge

Today Tiffany is speaking in tongues. Having thought she was semi-mute for so long, this has come as a terrible shock to me. She is considerably younger than me, but much, much farther out to lunch. Her life must have been one long drug trip gone bad. Anyway, her babbling is of no real concern. One can only listen to one's own stories for so long, so at other times, I pop in my Erapods. On the control pad, I can click the name of any song by any artist from any generation and... ping... the satellite delivers my musical heart's desire right into my waxy and waning old ears. I can also choose audio books or lectures on a wide range of topics.

Because of my failing eyesight, I was mostly imagining what Tiffany looked like. But after last night, I know. I was awakened in the middle of the night by something wet oozing into my face. Once my eyes pop open and adjust to the dim light, I see Tiffany leaning right over me, drooling a long string of spittle. Her hair is white, long, and frizzled. You'd think her family would cut it, but I overheard them say she hits anyone who comes near her with shears. Her nose is bulbous and red. I had imagined her eyes to be vacant, but no, they go way beyond emptiness toward a google-eyed madness. She jabs at me with her skeletal hand, and before I can remember I wish to be thought totally out of it, I'm hollering, "Hey, Bozo, get the hell off me, you frickin' clown in a witch suit! Go drool on somebody else!" The nurse lurking in the doorway is amused, but I am not. I have broken my vow of silence. I am busted.

· · · · · · · ·

"Grace," the social director clears her throat and begins, "We would love to understand why you haven't been exactly - ahem -

forthcoming with us." After we realized last week that you are, shall we say, *fully with us*, we did a little checking up on you. I perused your library printout. Fully with us, indeed. I am glad you enjoy Sartre and Skinner and a long list of modern authors, but one would assume such an intellectual would have better manners. I'm referring, of course, to the visit with the church volunteer. What was that episode of totally unacceptable language all about? We'll probably never see those nice people again. You certainly know how to squash the volunteer spirit!"

She gave me a lingering *shamey, shamey* look, like I was a bad child being scolded. Then she went on, "You know, I got to thinking that you've been here awhile and I've never heard you talk like that before. So I pulled the orders from that day, and the truth is, there was a reason you went off the deep end. You were given a muscle relaxer on top of Oxycodone, and some older folks get a little batsy with that combination. As they say, your meds were out of whack. Still, I can't help but think there's some underlying anger that bubbled up and set you off!

I smirk. "OK, fine. You want to know? Have at it. I'm pissed. I'm mad as hell. My mind is still twenty. All my life, I was the creative trickster, and now the ultimate trick has been played on me, having to leave my home and studio. This sucks. This place sucks. You, Ms. Huck-a-bee and your act-iv-i-ties suck. And, BTW, what happened to the privacy clause? My reading material is supposed to be private."

Then I feel some degree of remorse. It is not really the social worker's fault that I am swimming, drowning really, in a miserable pool of old age.

1949 Nashville

The prettiest girl at Tennessee Teachers College had it all. Corrine Baker was a lean framed, black-haired beauty with one of those memorable faces – a look that was crystalline and fresh. Her grades had been stellar, and she seemed destined to succeed.

She never acted as though she suspected any of these things about herself and treated everyone who crossed her path with the same sweet demeanor. Therefore, she was voted "Most Popular Senior" and had been elected both Homecoming Queen and Tennessee Student Teacher of the Year, hands down. Her bright future beckoned; her parents, Harold and Bernice, were so proud! She already had a job lined up which would begin the next school year after graduation.

She also had five months' worth of baby girl growing in her belly.

This had come about quite unexpectedly, as expecting often seems to do. Corrine Baker didn't even have a steady boyfriend, and had there been one, she would have never considered premarital sex until the ring was firmly in place on her left hand. Things happen though, when the right girl ends up at the wrong party and drinks too much of the wrong thing. Corrine was not even sure which partygoer had participated in her current situation - one that has reduced many girls of privilege to desperation.

However, Corrine Baker was an enterprising girl, and she had a plan. Two weeks before graduation, Corrine called up her parents with a cockamamie story about a prize job offer. She'd have to stay in Nashville for a few more months. Then she rented a room and waited out the rest of the summer and her confinement in a daze, facedown on a blow-up float in the YWCA pool.

One night at the end of August she called a cab at three a.m., headed for the hospital, and quickly delivered a six-pound two-ounce female with a head full of wild black hair. She lay there in Saint Thomas Hospital the next three days, struggling with the final details of her plan. The one thing she had not counted on was the fierceness of mother's love that had gripped her heart. Then, a choice she could live with miraculously unfolded. She checked out of the hospital with her unnamed baby girl, picked up her things at the Y, and got on a bus.

She felt rotten about taking the drawer from the motel on the road outside Blackshale, so much so that she left a fifty-dollar bill for a brand new chest of drawers on top of the old one. In the middle of the night, she carried it a short way down the road to the first building she came to. Corrine laid out in the wet grass crying her eyes out, nursing the baby and patting her face until dawn, when she laid the drawer down on the porch and ran in a stagger, tearfully, painfully, back down the road.

· · · · · · · ·

"Corry!" Bernice hurried to the kitchen door leading to the garage the minute she heard the garage door groan. "Your dad's over to the post office, he'll be so surprised!" Bernice was not one to discourage with negative observations, but she said to herself, "That girl looks pale."

Corrine went straight back to her bathroom and took the tablets that were drying up her milk. She changed the soaked hospital pad, then set her train case down beside her childhood bed and lay down gingerly on her back. Tears welled up in her eyes and dripped down the sides of her face to the coverlet. She *had* done the right thing, both for her and for the baby. She *had*, and with any luck of circumstance, she could keep an eye out for her from a distance and still go on with her career. Then why did she feel like a piece of her soul had been ripped out and stomped on? She quickly swabbed at tears when she heard her mother coming down the hall. Bernice tapped lightly on the door facing as she slid through it and came right on in. She sat down on the dressing table stool, tracing a run in her nylons with a manicured finger. Bernice took good care of herself.

"So, how was the job?"

"Oh, it was fine," Corrine reported, deftly changing the subject before she could go into any detail and get caught in a lie. "Say, do you still have that hot water bottle? I've got cramps something awful and I'm tryin' to take a headache, too." Bernice went back out and raffled through the hall closet, returning with a fuzzy pink lamb full of hot water. Corrine laid it across her abdomen and wished her mother would go away. Thankfully, she did.

At suppertime, Corrine set the dining room table and arranged late summer flowers for a centerpiece. She put on a Glenn Miller record and lit pale green tapers. Harold Baker folded his newspaper, and then he came and occupied the father chair at the head of the table. He eased into the chair, as his prostate was feeling a bit tender these days. He studied his beautiful daughter and sighed, not believing she would soon be off to her own life. Her childhood had flown by.

The small talk at the table was the usual middle class suburban chatter. Who was going to college where. Who had moved into whose house when they sold it to move to a higher-class neighborhood. Whose elderly parents had passed away. Where their friends were going on cruises or European vacations.

Corrine gave a carefully crafted report on her final days away at college. Her parents repeated their disappointment that she had been firm on not going through the line, depriving them of the glory of her graduation awards. "What a silly waste of time," Corrine had insisted through tears over the phone.

Then Bernice lowered her voice to a confidential tone.

"You'll eventually hear this in town, so I might as well tell you. That Joyce Sutton you graduated with, she has gotten herself in trouble, you know, in the family way. Not that anyone is surprised. She was always boy crazy and… well… I always suspected she was a bit of a tramp. I just feel so sorry for Waylan and Martha! They plan to let her keep the baby and stay home, but God knows they will end up taking care of it and at their age. Joyce had gotten a scholarship to UT Chattanooga, but she won't be able to go to college now. Her life is ruined, just ruined! We've never had a minute's trouble out of you, sweetheart, and we're thankful. You've been every mother's dream!"

Corrine choked on a glob of dry pot roast, forcing an extra heap of wet clots into the hospital pad between her legs. She asked to be excused.

She stayed at home a week, laundering underwear and shopping for professional clothes, visiting old friends, helping her mother clean the detritus of her own childhood out of closets. She carefully avoided her married friends who were expecting or already pushing baby carriages. When she passed her own baby pictures in the hall, she wanted to die on the spot. On her last night home, she was about to drift off into a troubled sleep when Bernice knocked, and again, entered without waiting for permission.

"Are you already asleep? I thought you'd want to know… Joyce Sutton stepped in front of a freight train in Bristol this morning. The town is in shock!"

"Oh my God," Corrine whispered, so quietly that her mother barely heard.

"She was in my English class senior year, and *Anna Karenina* was her favorite novel." Her mother, who probably did not see the connection, nodded weakly.

"Well," Corrine mused, "I guess Waylan and Martha's problem has been solved."

The next morning Corrine packed up her graduation present, a brand new 1949 Ford coupe, hugged her parents goodbye, and headed up Highway 81 to her teaching job and her new future in Blackshale, Tennessee.

2029 Morning Glory Ridge

"Why, exactly, is it called a WidgieWalker?" I ask, trying my best to sound uninterested. As long as I maintain a mask of ennui, I'm better off here.

"Well, I guess it's because of that little noise it makes when you're moving along... widgie, widgie, widgie..." Carlene is referring to the contraption sitting at the end of my bed, a new arrival. Now that my bones have healed again, I am going to be more active, and supposedly this gizmo is the ticket to mobility.

"What does it do anyway?"

"Well darlin', think of it as a souped-up walker. You can push it along using it for support like the old walkers, but it has lots of features that help you get around and stay mobile. And for those with Osteoporosis, that would be you, it has fantastic shock absorption that greatly reduces the stress on your bones. For instance, if you get down the hall and get tired, it has these doo-flotchies that drop down so you can ride. Remember the old Segways? Kind of like those but with a sophisticated gyro system that makes it impossible for you to fall. It does all the balancing for you. And even when you're riding, it is stimulating your legs electronically, which actually strengthens your bones. It also monitors your vitals and calls the nurse if there's a problem."

Carlene doles out all the instruction, watches me take a test spin, and splits. Now that I have been found out and am no longer keeping up the façade of being in my own little world, I decide it's high time to go shopping for some friends.

I start down the hall... widgie, widgie, widgie... and find an activity room with Led Zeppelin blaring out the door. I am happily surprised to find not one, but three women who still have perfectly good minds.

I introduce myself, and so do they, Mary B., Pauline, and

Daphne. They immediately fill me in on all the gossip - which nurses and aides sleep with which doctors, which residents have been famous or infamous, and who has made puddles on the floor of the dining room. Feeling obligated to contribute some juicy tidbit, I share the story of Julio and Gourdhead sucking face behind my door.

"Ugh, Gourdhead is a real sicko." Daphne screws up her face in disgust, then flips over her hand and studies the chipped red polish on her ridged fingernails. "You think we call him Gourdhead because his head is shaved? Think again, girlfriend!"

Pauline looks shocked, and Mary B. appears pleasantly confused.

Daphne continues, "One night last year, everyone who had their screens on really late got a full screen view of a huge, bulb tipped penis, broadcast by someone who had access to the video studio. We all were sure it was Gourdhead, just because he's the sickest SOB around here, but no one could prove it. ICK! It was disgusting! I kept going back night after night to see if he dared to do it again, but he never did," she snorts in disappointment.

I laugh, "Well, I'm glad to hear you were keeping track of the situation!" I stand up and start to widgie out, heading to my room, worn out from all the sudden social life. I turn around at the door and yell, "Hey, poke me on the screen when you're going to be in here again!" They all grin and punch the air with their wrinkly index fingers. I head out again, leaving behind my new friends with the fading strains of "Stairway to Heaven."

When I return to my bed, the screen lights up and blinking reminders tell me it's time for blood pressure and heart medications. A large labeled picture of each pill appears. I look down at the ePillbox running across under the bottom of my screen. A single compartment opens, and I scoop out the pills and pop them in my pie hole.

The screen asks, "Did you take these pills, Anna?" I touch

the pictures of each pill over their supersized captions, and the computer snoozes back off to sleep. The screensaver is a luscious and joyful sunset, probably chosen by the staff with subliminal intentions. The billowing clouds beckon upward, looking a lot like a stairway to Heaven.

1951 Blackshale

The happy times of Nettie Tollett's marriage, along with her good humor, were short lived. When Perry was only ten, his pa grabbed ahold of a rat-gnawed adding machine cord and was electrocuted. When she lost Boyd Lee, it seemed like her foul attitude returned tenfold. With the exception of the small pocket of twisted and controlling love reserved for her boy, she faced the world with black contempt. Nettie doggedly bookmarked narrow slices of scripture and used them as a lens with which to damn the sins of others, especially the mother who had forsaken her. The passages about love and forgiveness, she left unread.

· · · · · · · ·

Sudy Pelfree had an overactive libido and an intense, abiding disgust for masturbation. Not just because her mother had persistently dwelt on the "you'll go blind if you touch yourself talk" but because it made her feel pathetic to half wake in the middle of the night and find that self-satisfaction was all there was. She always hated herself in the morning. Sudy was twenty-seven and something was missing. Contributing to her sense of deficiency was her ringside seat to the happy Tollett family. Sudy loved her best friend completely, and jealousy was not in her vocabulary, but Dory's perfect life presented Sudy with an illustrated diagram of just what the "something missing" was.

Sudy had become a star of sorts at Blackshale hospital, commanding the respect of her peers. Even the doctors relied on her, especially in cases involving mental or emotional troubles. Sudy had an instinctive way with matters of the heart and mind, even though her own heart was empty and barren. She'd just never met any man who was able to fill it up. Until, quite by accident, she met Faron Templeton.

On a Monday that had already been frantic with patients and their piles of paperwork, in through the emergency room doors wheeled Mrs. Robert E. Templeton. Mrs. Templeton presented with heart palpitations, just as she had practically every week since Sudy had taken the job. So again, they would rule out serious heart problems or any other life threatening condition and send her home with a mild tranquilizer. The psych doctor suggested that Sudy try out her skills on the familiar patient they all now fondly called "Mrs. T", and suggested that she also meet with Mrs. Templeton's son, Faron. Perhaps they could work together and get to the bottom of the recurring attacks of anxiety.

Faron whisked into the conference room dressed to the nines, sat down and casually asked, "Do you mind if I smoke?"

Sudy, a cigarette smoker herself, said, "No, go right ahead."

Instead of a cigarette, Faron lit a cherry wood pipe and then leaned back in the slatted wooden conference chair to study her. He saw a gamine face and short hair on a sturdy, petite figure. His thoughts bubbled - under all this boyish packaging was someone intelligent, capable, and sensible.

The conference was short. It didn't take Sudy long to figure out that Mrs. T came to the hospital every time her son was going away for a business or pleasure trip. Apparently she was desperate for his attention, which Sudy could understand. He was a striking man who exuded sophistication. She gave him her honest assessment about his mother's anxiety, and they talked about ways to help her through it. When he rose to leave, he turned back to her smiling.

"Say, are you married?"

Sudy blushed. "No... I'm a career girl, so far."

"Neither am I," he admitted laughing, "much to my dear mother's chagrin. Look, I know we just met, but would you like to have dinner? There's a fascinating club up above Pineville. Are you busy this Saturday night?"

Sudy's dappled face was now red ear-to-ear, and with her boy short hair it was hard to hide the embarrassed anticipation she was feeling. She accepted, and the days until Saturday drug out like a forty-five record played on a too-slow speed.

• • • • • • • • • •

The Piccadilly Supper Club was at the end of a long series of hairpin curves on top of Blackshale Mountain. On the way up, Faron wore a secretive smile and said, "I have a bit of a surprise for you." When they pulled into the gravel parking lot, it seemed like a sour surprise. It was a sordid dump, and Sudy worked hard to mask her disappointment. The sagging, low-slung building was a patchwork of tarpaper, corrugated tin, concrete block, and every other kind of poor white trash building material. She twisted her rhinestone lavaliere around a finger self-consciously, sure it would not be quite right. This was looking like a faded blue jeans and draft beer kind of place.

Faron came around and opened the door for her, watching her face with amusement. They went in what looked like a back door, forced their way though the slobbery greetings of a dog big as a horse, and sidled up to a timeworn leather bar. While Faron ordered beers from the tap, it began - the most intriguing music she'd ever heard. He guided her to the center of the room where eight musicians sat in a circle, knee-to-knee, around a fat honey-colored candle. There was a dulcimer, a cello, two violins, three drums, and a flute. It was an indescribable mix. Lilting classical, dark blues, hints of Appalachia, with a voodoo drumming thrown in. One minute it was lyrical, tender, the next almost sinister with seductive rhythms. Sudy was mesmerized. Food, really good food, was served, but she barely noticed. Animal heads looked down from the dark walls, their glass eyes glistening gems in the candlelight - stag, elk, black bear, wild boar. Trinkets on the walls glimmered, animated by the dancing flame. Faron lit his pipe and sat back, watching her pleasure in the moment.

On their way down the mountain, after midnight, Sudy finally spoke. "What was *that*?"

He laughed, "*That*, my dear, was some of the South's finest musicians in hiding. You would see their names on the program at the Atlanta Symphony, the Asheville Orchestra, and The Grand Old Opry. They come here incognito to make the music they *want to*, which is quite different from what they play professionally. I think they are inspired by the idea of a drumming circle. Did you like it?"

She smiled and nodded her pleasure.

"Splendid!" Faron said with a satisfied gleam in his eyes.

On their second date, he took her to a play in Nashville, the next, a canoe picnic down the river. They went ballroom dancing, and then they tried square dancing. They took in dog shows, ice skated, attended foreign films, and toured art museums. They had dinner with Faron's mother in Pineville, and Sudy used her South Carolina manners and all the right forks. They went to the Blackshale summer carnival and ate cotton candy. They watched variety shows on television. They did not, however, kiss on the lips or fondle or have sex.

· · · · · · · ·

On their twenty-fourth date he took her to Paris, where they were married under the Eiffel Tower. She wore an iridescent white chemise, a crown of petites fleurs pinned into her short hair, and she did not, thankfully, pee at all during the ceremony.

How could a honeymoon in Paris be anything but romantic? Faron introduced every café and flea market, avenue and museum, theatre and mime, every fresh view of the Seine, to her as if they were presents on a platter, unwrapped for her pleasure alone. He always studied her eyes, this lovely new companion on his arm, measuring her delight. In the privacy of their hotel suite, filled with flowers and candles, he was tender, attentive. He washed her hair, massaged her feet, brought her tea. Their first night as man and wife was wrapped in apprehension for Sudy, who had been thrown for a loop by their chaste courtship. She was mad with desire, but confused. When they stood at the foot of their marriage bed, he peeled her chemise delicately, slipped down the straps of her brassiere, tracing the contours of her body with appreciation, as if she were a sculpture in a Paris museum. Her panties fell to the floor. He laid her down, and explored her completely with his hands, then closing his eyes, he laid himself on her and slowly, as a matter of fact, very slowly, over an unusually extended period of time, pressed his not-quite-rigid organ repeatedly into her. Sudy was not a virgin, which seemed not to surprise or trouble him. Suddenly, with a new urgency, Faron rolled her over on her belly, and more enthusiastically began to pump his now quite sturdy member between her buttocks, holding them tight with his hands. He groaned in release, and as he did, slipped his hands around to her front, pleasuring her with his slender fingers.

From that night on, their sexual journey ploughed down the same rut, so to speak. Certain variations came up along the way, handcuffs, spankings, recurring attempts at an alternate entry. Sudy was unsure, confused, and couldn't even talk to Dory about her uncertainty. With the few boyfriends she'd had at nursing school, sex had been about simple groping and need, explosion with no tenderness thrown in. Faron clearly felt affection and concern for her. She was sure he loved her. But something seemed... unusual. She overlooked the difference, and luxuriated in his attentions and companionship. They returned home and set up housekeeping in a bungalow halfway between Pineville and Blackshale Hospital. They decorated their house, shared gourmet cooking, shaped a life, had fun together, and were the best of friends.

Mrs. Robert E. Templeton was thrilled. Sudy was the pert, smart, hopefully fertile wife she had always pictured for Faron. Her habit of taking trips to the hospital ceased. Instead, she daydreamed about precocious, well-behaved grandchildren in expensive, hand-tailored clothes and took up knitting as a hobby. So as not to be too obvious, she was currently making afghans, socks, scarves, and hats, knit one, purl two, but that was only practice for what would follow, hopefully, soon.

2029 Morning Glory Ridge

Today is Thursday, one of my three afternoons a week for vFun. You know, "v" stands for virtual. All the residents at Morning Glory Ridge have an avatar, a little High-Definition 3D character that can do the things you can no longer do in your old, weak, broken-down body. We all go to the sports room and gather around the hugemongous 3D screen. With the weak movements we can still manage and a little eye motion transmission, we use our fake people to whoop each other's fake asses in a wide variety of sports and games.

Those of us who still have half a brain can customize our own avatars. I have to say, mine is *so* Anna Grace. Today she has on polka dot soccer leggings, a yellow tunic, combat boots and a spewing ponytail on top of her head. Of course, every avatar has a whole collection of clothes, and I have customized a set of headgear for mine. I have to say this stuff has come a long way from when it all started back before the turn of the century. Back then, avatars were pixelated cartoons and walked with jerky motions. Now Anna Grace looks so scarily like me, it creeps me out. My goggles transmit my intentions to her, so her actions are instantaneous, intuitive, at one with my wishes - a fit, youthful version of my ramshackle frame.

She slinks into the sports plaza and challenges Candy's avatar to a game of Ping Pong. Candy's reactions are slow, and I quickly skunk her. Yep, Anna Grace is an asskicker all right! On the screen, Candy hangs her head in shame, and Anna Grace struts in victory, admiring her virtual trophy. The win earns me a vPoint. I save those up to buy access to more games and sports. I contemplate the perky young version of me on the screen and wonder if she will live on after I'm gone.

1954 Blackshale

When I was little, for reasons nobody understood, I ate Kleenex. I'd sit in the middle of my canopy bed, tearing the white squares into strips and then stuff them down my throat. When she caught me at it, Mama banned facial tissues of any kind on the premises (a real hardship for Frank down in the funeral home). She hollered at me for days that I could expect to die at any minute from the huge ball of wet paper pulp that was clogging up my insides. Dory was terrified of losing another child and always kept me closely corralled. I was the doom-threatened, nervous child of a dreadfully anxious mother.

During most of Mama's life, I didn't know I'd had and lost a brother. I also had no idea that she lived every day in a constant, grating fear that someone would one day drive right up to the Tollett Funeral Home to reclaim their bureau drawer and its former contents. Looking back, I can see that those things wrangled her nerves up into a knot and drove her obsessive need to keep things in control. Dory Tollett's quest for perfection and order leaked right out of her and into her visions for me. For as far back as I can recall, each and every one of my worldly possessions were right where they should be. I made my bed with hospital corners every morning, just like Mama showed me, and my toys were neatly arranged on my shelves. When I played with something, I put it back. Mama showed me how to turn all the hangers with my dresses facing the same way over the rod, and made sure my shoes sat snugly together in pairs with their toes lined up with the front edge of the shoe rack. At that age, I never went to other kids' houses to play, but if I'd seen a room with clothes and toys scattered winding or heard a mother yell "Pick Up Your Room!" I might have died of shock right there on the spot. According to my mama's vision, our family's world in the upstairs apartment

was a picture from a glossy women's magazine, a genteel study in
orderliness and charm.

. . . .

Across the railroad tracks and up a ways on the mountain lived
a family that was our opposite in every way. Mama and Pap said
no wonder the Murphys was trouble, as they had bred nothing
but nasty boys, one right after the other. Anyways, Pap had his
suspicions that Walter Lee Murphy was a bootlegger and that his
wife was high on something or other all the time. At least, Frank
had surmised, Walter Lee jerked that pit bull up and down the
side of that mountain to protect some sort of secret. My Aunt
Nettie allowed that if a body held that dope fiend Shirley Murphy
up to the light, you could just see the boy babies working inside
her.

The oldest boys, identical twins, was said to be the meanest
kids for miles around. Some swore they were the very seeds of
Satan himself, and had laid in their ma's belly side by side – baby
devils suckin' their pointy thumbs and hatchin' their evil plans.
Them Murphy twins, Jake and Harley, had been nothing but
troublemakers from day one. They weren't just your ordinary
hooligans, they bubbled with hate and stalked the mountain in
search of victims.

They had three younger brothers coming up, ready to follow
in their big brothers' footsteps - one called BoJack who was a year
older than me but had flunked a year of school, Peanut, who was
my age, and then there was Charley who was the baby but still
meaner than a striped snake.

. . . .

In the middle of one sleeting black night in November, the
bell rang on the front door downstairs and Pap grumbled around,
put on his housecoat and slippers and headed down the stairs.
There was Mr. Murphy sobbing out the sad news that his wife,

Shirley, had passed out and passed on during the night. Pap went with Mr. Murphy back to his house, and found she was already stiff as a flagpole.

Shirley Murphy come from a big family out in West Tennessee, a right good one, but had married far, far beneath her raisin'. She met Walter Murphy in Memphis at a blues bar on Beale Street, one of the many drunken, rollicking stops on his way home from the war. When Walter hooked up with Shirley, a decidedly higher-class woman than the trollops he had previously been able to smooze, he reckoned he might stay a while longer in Memphis. Shirley's folks spotted Walter right away for the con man he was, calling him white trailer trash behind her back, but Walter got her so creamy hot in the pants she just couldn't stand it. Before she knew it she was pregnant with twins, disowned, and on an east bound bus with Walter's hairy, tattooed arm slung around her shoulders. They sang "Goodnight Irene" and played penuchle all the way across Tennessee, when Shirley was not back in the toilet puking up her insides. True to the dire predictions of Shirley's mother, the couple set up housekeeping in a rusty rattletrap trailer.

When it finally hit her who she had took up with and what she'd gotten herself into, Shirley's head was in a bad way. When the twins came, she had to take a nerve pill to get through the day, and before long she was moving on to more potent narcotics, for which Walter traded some of his bootlegged product. Not a one of them concrete blocks that trailer set on was the same height. Whenever Shirley was high, which was most of the time, and dropped a baby bottle it rolled the whole length of the trailer before she could pick it up out of the hairy dust and stick it back in a boy's mouth. Shirley Murphy and her whole stinkin' life was way more'n half a bubble off plumb.

"It was funny though," Pap had joked after I was bigger and could hear such things, "The worse off Shirley got, the more Walter got to truly loving her. Couldn't get enough of her, couldn't stop pumping her full of kids."

The month before she died, Shirley had shed off all her clothes while walking down the hill to the Church of Christ preacher's house, and rang the doorbell. When he came to the door, without a trace of shock on his face, he simply stated, "Why, Mrs. Murphy, you don't have any shoes on!" He put a blanket around her and marched her back up the hill to Walter Murphy, who mumbled something about her medication being out of whack and offered the preacher a swig of homebrew, which was, of course, declined.

Mama vowed that wake was something to behold. All them boys was running around the parlor like it was a happy birthday party instead of a funeral. Walter Lee Murphy stood drunk and weeping by the coffin, his big chunky hands turning pale from grabbing the ruffled white satin so hard. He started shaking his head back and forth, blubbering away, "We never got her picture took. She was always in the family way, or sick, and now I ain't got nothing to remember her by 'cept all these damn kids!" Dory gasped and went over to the youngest boy, Charley, and cuddled him up in her lap. His little snoot was covered with the dirt and snot no one had given a thought to wipe off before the wake. He frowned up into her face confused, not knowin' how to be petted and loved on.

Walter Murphy's kin were plumb crazy. Mama swore there was a harshness to them people, crows and jays and starlin's, cawing at each other across the parlor. One of the younger ones jumped up like she had fire ants in her drawers and yelled, "Hey, go get the Kodak!" and their husbands pried Shirley up out of her casket and stood her up with the whole family looking sour, propping her up on the front row, stiff as a board. About the time they were trying to stuff her back in the casket, with the white satin sticking out ever whichaway, my pap Frank marched in and had hisself a conniption fit.

· · · · · · · ·

One of Hum's jobs was to help Pap lift the heavier bodies onto the table. Mr. Adelai Poole was the biggest body Frank had ever worked on. Once Frank and Hum and Frank's friend, Cooper, had hoisted Mr. Poole up on the steel table, he still lapped generously over both edges. Over his enormous carcass, Frank repeated the legend that Mr. Poole had once unzipped his britches in the picture show, seeking relief from the tightness of his waistband. Eugenia Peavine just happened to be sitting next to him, and when he rose and started to squeeze by her, closing up his barn door, he caught her dress up in the zipper by accident. They stood up in the animated shaft of light, struggling to separate themselves, while the whole house chanted "Down in front, fatties!" Frank chuckled as he patted pancake makeup over Mr. Poole's chins.

On this, Mr. Poole's final day above ground, Hum tarried after the lifting to watch the procedure. Frank had been letting Hum hang around for some time now, as good as he was not to chatter.

Frank made the trocar incision, and glanced up to see how Hum was taking it. He seemed ok, involved as he was in a good nose-pickin', but halfway through the embalming process, Hum gave Frank a troubled, questioning look.

Frank began to explain, not wanting Hum upset or confused. "Well Hum, what I'm doing is removing some of the... uh... juice from Mr. Poole and replacing it with embalming fluid. The fluid in this tank here is called formaldehyde, and it will pretty much preserve Mr. Poole here forever! You know, Hum, kinda like your mama's sweet pickles keep in the jar until we are ready to eat 'em up!"

Hum studied the tank seriously and looked impressed. His concept of forever was vague, but he knew it was a long, long time!

Pearlie had named their dog "Choo Choo" since Hum loved trains so much. Choo Choo had arrived with a belly full of babies but they'd all been borned dead. Hum had slumped down on his knees and poked at the lifeless puppies with a stick, not understanding the lack of life. Now she had another litter on the way, and he had a pretty good idea of what was coming. Dory had let him build a doghouse out in the back, but when the saggy, swollen bitch's time came, Choo Choo crawled up in a cardboard box on the back porch to whelp. Mama and Pap let me watch, thinking it would be a good introduction to the facts of life. My breath caught in surprise when the first slimy sack of wiggling pup slipped out of Choo Choo's backside. Out they came, one by one, until two boys and three girls lay on their sides, tugging hungrily at their mother's teats. Hum jumped up and down on the porch with glee, flapping his hands and shaking the whole house down to the foundation.

Hum and me had a peck of fun holding them little fellers, letting them lick our noses that were full of that new puppy smell. I reckon Hum loved them pups even more than he loved trains. One day when they was a few weeks old, I slipped down to pet them by myself. They were gone! I searched all around the nest that Choo Choo had scratched out under the porch and them puppies was nowhere to be found. Dory came out and joined the hunt, Pearlie followed behind, shouting "Lordy how come!" and wiping her hands on her apron. We all ran around the yard, yelling for Choo Choo, who eventually drug in alone, hanging low.

When Pap come home later that morning from runnin' errands, he went downstairs to clean up the workroom. There sat Hum, with his hands on his knees, looking pleased as punch. Frank followed the gaze of Hum's dullard eyes to the embalming tank where the lifeless puppies floated in circles, preserved forever.

Later that day I stood in tears as the story of the pup's fate came floating upstairs through the square hole in the floor. "Hum's ability to reason only goes so far." Frank was explaining to Dory. "He was obsessed with the idea of keeping the puppies forever, but he wasn't able to understand that they would die in the process. I don't think the boy has a mean bone in his body. I could see in his eyes he thought he'd done something wonderful for them!"

Dory listened quietly to Frank, then she asked, "What do we do about Anna Grace?"

"The puppies are buried and gone. With Hum, it's 'out of sight, out of mind'. He will probably forget about them by tomorrow, and he sure won't be telling Anna Grace anything. The kind thing is to let her think they wandered off."

Dory had agreed. But Frank was wrong about Hum forgetting. The next day, he paced frantically up and down the stairs to study the tank emptied of puppies, his hum a mournful wail. For weeks, he sat out on the back porch sadly petting Choo Choo. Ever so often, he'd lift up her tail, intently studying her butt in mute hope.

• • • • • • • • • •

Sudy Templeton came home early from the hospital one afternoon to find Faron embracing the violinist from the Piccadilly Supper Club. The young man's face was pressed flat up against her Frigidaire door, his hips jutted out, and Faron was wrapped around him in some sort of coupling she could only guess at. Sudy tilted her head quizzically and said, "Let me know when you're done with that so I can grab a beer."

She went upstairs, fell facedown on the bed, and let the tears flow. Sudy loved this man and her life with him, but she had always known on some level that something was not quite right. It hurt like hell to face it, the thing that had always been in a dark, secret place in her heart. After a while she heard the door slam, and Faron's heavy tread on the stairs. She rolled over and fired up a cigarette, blowing the smoke out fiercely with her words, "Guess I didn't know you well enough to marry you."

He handed her a cold beer, but there was nothing Faron could say. He got a pillow and blanket from the linen closet and slunk down to the living room, trailing a dark silence behind him.

The next morning, she went downstairs and watched him sleeping on the settee. She finally reached out and woke him up with a prod.

"I would like to propose an arrangement."

He sat up, abashed, and rubbed his eyes.

"There are different kinds of love. I love you and I am fairly sure you love me in some basic, vital way. It's just that we need different things when it comes to the mechanics of sex. I am willing to keep things like they are. We both go our separate ways for satisfaction, discreetly. All I ask is that you don't bring it here, in our house. I think we can still be happy together. What do you think?"

Faron smiled and marveled, "Mrs. Templeton, I think you are one hell of a woman!"

• • • • • • • •

My pap musta had a way with the undertakin' business, 'cause it was going real well. Mama was always taking trips to the department stores in Knoxville and came back loaded down with hat boxes and shopping bags. She also drove all the way to Knoxville to trade at Cas Walker's grocery store at least oncet a month. We'd been one of the first to have a television set and an electric washing machine instead of a wringer washer. When Pap had started out, he was paying off the building and buying equipment and furnishings, so he settled for a beat-up used van for the business. It didn't look like much, but it could bear a casket to the graveyard and make it up the hills without stallin' out. His friend Cooper owned an old hearse, and sometimes they polished it up to use for funerals.

One afternoon the phone at Tollett's rang twice. I was callin' Mama from kindergarten, "Mama, Mama, Mama! Guess what!

I got the chickenpops!" Pearlie started right in making chicken noodle soup while Mama came to fetch me in the van. They fixed up the divan for me with a pile of soft quilts and feather pillows and set a little table aside it for my soup, a co-cola, and a tall stack of funny books. Then they got back to their work around the house, but every time I wanted anything at all, like a popsicle or a drink of well water, they came runnin'. It felt good to be treated like a princess, until the itchin' started. I scratched for a while, all the time Pearlie and Mama hollering like bossy britches, "Don't you dare scratch, missy! You'll get scars!" Then I got sleepy and snoozed off, still scratchin' in my dreams.

On up in the afternoon, a loud blaring noise shook me out of my sweating sleep. Somebody was honkin' loud, over and over again, out in the parking lot. I jumped up, with Mama yelling, "You stay there! You're not supposed to be fanning around!" but I ignored her and ran to my room to see what all the fuss was about. From my window seat, I saw Frank Tollett jump out of the driver's seat of the longest, shiniest, blackest car I'd ever seen. He had gone and bought himself a Cadillac hearse, and it was a beauty! After they'd tucked me back under the covers, Mama and Pearlie went down and ran their hands over every inch of it, grinning and saying, "Now Frank Tollett, who're you expecting to keep this thing polished up?"

· · · · · · · · · · ·

We lived around mountain people who turned their words in that odd way mountain people do. The higher up and farther back on that mountain, the stranger they talked. When I went off to kindergarten I was soon talking just like them. It made my mama, who had come from an educated family in a more refined southern setting over in Greenville, crazy.

"I can not believe that in this year of our Lord, nineteen hundred and fifty four, there are people who still talk like this. My friends from nursing school would never in a million years believe that these people actually *exist*. Half of these hics who slither down off the mountain don't even have running water and electricity, and they are infecting us with their head lice. Their "you-uns" and "ain't nevers" and "young-ins" shouldn't even be allowed in our school! The nigras have their own school for crying out loud, and so should the hillbillies!" Dory was adamant.

Frank frowned at her over his spectacles. "Dory, they are good, kind, hard-working people - the salt of the earth. Don't you think a good education is just exactly what they need and deserve?" It was a mighty bone of contention between her and Pap.

Mama had very few faults, in fact she aimed for perfection every day of her life, but lookin' back I can now see her one peccadillo. She was a bit snooty. One day, not a month into the school year, I was sitting at the kitchen table arranging the mimeographed pictures I had colored. They had the freshest smell! Mama was leaning into the stove, watching her teapot like to never come to a boil. She loved for us to sit down and have a cup of lemon tea and some pretzels when I got home from school, so she could quiz me on how I done that day. When she turned around with our hot teacups, her eyes fell on the dress I was wearing, the one she and Pearlie had made for me special for the start of school. It had a farm scene, with a barn and trees and cows and white puffy clouds in the sky, all lovingly rendered in hand smocking. Now, long curling threads hung from my chest in tangles.

"Anna Grace, you've picked every last stitch out of your dress!"

"I ain't done it!" Well now of course I *had*, because my nervous little fingers needed something to do since I was no longer allowed to eat Kleenex, which I couldn't a done at school no ways. I had never smarted off before, and just that alone would have been enough for a whoopin', but I had talked back in the language of my peers.

"I swear! Your grammar has become the very bane of my existence!" She slammed out the back screen door, cut a hickory and switched my legs to bloody stripes, stingin' me like a pack of waspers.

After suppertime, I was still pouting in my room. Pap came in and swept his hand softly over my rippled forehead. I was fishin' for sympathy. "Pap, I reckon I'm jus' the skate goat whipping girl for the whole hillbilly country talkin' world."

· · · · · · · ·

Later that year, as if called upon to prove my mama's point in the arguin' between her and Pap, Albine Yother from up on the very top of Blackshale mountain appeared on our doorstep in the middle of one snowy Spring night. He told Pap his mother-in-law -- the grandma of their family -- had passed over the river Jordan from a croup, and they had her layin' up in the back of their wagon. In the back of his drowsy mind, Frank pictured the Vina Young of his childhood. It was the same Vina who had been known for the laying on of leeches and such -- water witch, dowser, root worker.

Pap was still half asleep and wasn't clearly getting' the part about the river Jordan. He was sure there was no river by that name around Blackshale. He tightened the belt on his housecoat and looked down at his own goose bumpy ankles and bare feet, his eyes asquint in the yellow front porch light. After showing him into the vestibule, he asked Mr. Yother, "Now, come again? What exactly happened to your grannie?"

Pap put on his boots and plodded out to the wagon, and surenough there was Grannie Young laid out flat, with about six inches of snow on her, topknot to toe. She looked right peaceful to him. However, Piney Young Yother was up in the wagon carryin' on something fierce. She swooned and commenced to weeping and howlin' against the wind that was still swirling snow into the bed of the wagon.

"We done everthang we could fer Maw, we fried up yaller onions in a polchice and plastered 'em on 'er brast to draw out the pizon, but she just clogged right up and died." Then Piney threw herself down on the frozen corpse and took up hollerin', "Don't go, Maw, please don't go and leave me hyare!"

It was high time for Frank to take control. "Get a rug, Dory!" He yelled into the open door. Albine got up under her bony shoulders and Frank grabbed her by the ankles, and one – two – three – harrrrrump, they hefted Grannie onto the rug and slid her frozen body down the stairs into the embalming room. After they got her settled into a drawer, Frank laid a comforting hand on Albine's shoulder and said, "Now, there, Albine, let's go upstairs and plan a nice service for Mrs. Young."

Piney already had them plans in her mind.

"We ain't laying Maw out down hyare in town. Done slid the kitchen table up thar in the front room for the wake. We brung her down hyare 'cause she made us sware to get 'er hair done up for the viewin' and get her fixed up in a storeboughten box.

That there's the onliest cause. Hit ain't fitten to put Maw in no crooked homemade pine box. We brung 'er this frock," she lamented sadly, handing over a near white, hand embroidered muslin dress.

Albine had more practical things on his mind. "Way this snow's comin' down, this here rig ain't goin' back up the hill tonight."

Frank sat down and pulled off his cold, wet boots and soggy socks, studying on the problem at hand. "Well, Albine, Piney... how about this. I'll call Sheriff Raby and see if he can take y'all home in his Jeep. Then, in a day or two when the roads are better, me and Cooper will drive Grannie, all fixed up in her box, back up in the wagon."

"Ain't no road up to the house." Albine focused on his black-edged fingernails. "The gravel stops a mile afore the dirt road goin' to the house and with all this snowmelt, hit'l be a mor'of a gully."

Frank blinked. "If you got down, I guess we can get up, at least in a few days. When were you wantin' to have the wake? Were you lookin' at Sunday?"

"That'll do."

Frank ushered Piney and Albine into the showroom. Dory shuffled in a sleepy daze behind. Piney's eyes fell on a shiny oak model with brass hardware that went for $1,500, her heart set on it. Albine pulled out a rusty tin snuffbox and started counting out ten-dollar bills. Frank quickly saw the bottom of the snuff can comin' up, and spoke up, "Now that one there would cost you a hundred dollars!" He could see Dory's eyes were teary, but he didn't know if they were wet with pride or murderous rage.

"Thar's one more thing," Albine put in. "You'ns have a sineater to come up or do we need to har us one?" Mama and Pap traded looks.

"Well," Dory quipped, "We haven't had a call for one in a while."

· · · · · · · ·

"A SINEATER!" Dory looked at Frank in amazement. "Have you ever... in all your born days? Do these people honestly - in this day and age - think sineaters exist?"

Frank chuckled, thinking back to his wide-eyed grandmaw telling the sineater tales passed down through her family. Her ancestors had lived way back up on the mountain, far from civilization. The sineater was a mountain man, an outcast who crept in secret out of the forest to feed on offerings from families of the dead. In return, it was believed, he consumed the sins of the deceased. It was forbidden to look on his face, and the children were too terrified to even think of him. Legend had it that some boys had hidden to catch him at his work and had drowned that very night. The hill folk believed the sineater had powerful magic.

"Well, I dunno baby, but it sure makes me hungry for some sin..." He fixed his hands on her butt, pummeling, and started backing her toward their bedroom. He hit the button on the six a.m. alarm that was fixin' to go off, and they started the morning off right.

• • • • • • • •

Two days later it had warmed up right smart, and Frank made plans with Cooper to head up to Yothers that afternoon with the remains of Grannie Young. At breakfast, Dory began to cackle, slapping her thighs.

"Here you have a brand spankin' new Cadillac hearse and you're hauling your ass in a buckwagon to a wake!"

I hate to 'low it, but my mama was enjoying the Yothers' time of sorrow more than she should've.

Cooper come through the back door with his boy, Silas, tagging along. Frank didn't look none too happy about that, as he'd shoved some six-packs in behind the buckboard, thinking they might as well take some pleasure in the ride up the mountain. After all, the horses knew the way. As it turned out, Silas was sleepy, and crawled up behind the coffin in the wagon bed and had himself a good snooze in the spring sunshine. Frank popped the top on a Bud and handed one over to Coop. He hadn't driven a team of horses since high school, but it came back to him real fast, and he relaxed his hold on the reins, letting the team feel their way up the road. That Bud didn't last long, so he had another and then, another - and then some more until he 'bout lost count. Cooper was keepin' up with him, too. On the two-lane road Frank came up behind a Chevy pickup truck full of high school boys and feeling his oats, he flipped on the reins to pass it, yelling "Yee, HAW, Hot Diggity Damn!" Out the driver's side of the pickup, a middle finger shot up in the air.

Sudden like, Silas woke straight up, blinking his eyes in surprise. "Frank, he shot chu a bird!" Surprised at Silas' knowledge of local sign language, Tonk and Cooper about rolled out of the wagon laughin'. "Get up here with us, boy!" Cooper yelled and pulled Silas up and over into the seat, givin' him a proud pat on the leg. By the time they got about half way up the mountain road, Frank's hold on them reins was getting mighty loose! When the paved road ended, the gullywashed gravel road required a clear mind at the reins, which Frank no longer had much of.

But, what the hell, he spurred the team on. "Crimony!" Frank hollered over the bucking of the wagon, "Damn! We got a mile o' this to go!" Cooper just laughed, relishing the adventure, which was a hell of a shot more fun than his job in the mine. Another beer each, and that wagon was jumpin' all over the place, leaping in the air and slappin' down hard, and Frank and Cooper weren't caring much about nothing in the world.

Silas turned and looked back down the rutted road, and without too much worry a'tal, asked, "Holy Smokes! Whut happen't to the box?"

Frank looked back over his shoulder and then screeched, "Oh… OH… God, Jesus, Joseph and Mary!" pulling back hard on the reins, strained the rig to a sudden halt.

Grannie Young had sledded clean off the back of the wagon bed. They tied up the team and skittered down through the slippery mud, hopping trenches. There she was, back around the last corner, and it weren't purty. The box had rolled over, flown open and dumped her out in the dirt. The hard polished oak coffin had escaped without a scratch. It had luckily landed on a grassy spot, but Grannie Young looked like she'd slid into home base. Frank slumped down and buried his head in his hands. "Oh God A'mighty help me! I'm ruined!"

Cooper was a glass half full kind of guy. "Naw, naw… Tonk, now look here… her top ain't muddy a'tal, we kin stuff her back in and cover up the mud on her skirt with the satin in the casket." They each picked up one end of that pore stiff body that had 'bout been through more hard times dead than alive and carried her up the hill to the wagon. Then, they went back and hauled the coffin up and laid her in it. They went to work poking satin here and there and before too long you'd a never knowed about her side trip down the road.

"What are we gonna do about *that*?" Frank worried, pointing at her head. Grannie's faithfully promised hairdo had taken a beatin'.

Silas dug down in his overalls grinnin' and pulled out a red plastic comb. It was missing a few teeth, but it did the job. Before nightfall, they finally pulled up into the Yothers' dirtyard, steering the wagon through pecking chickens and barking hounds. Frank carried the last two six-packs of beer in the front door, into the front room where no clock ticked and black muslin hung over the looking glass. Like a priest with a chalice full of the Holy Eucharist, he held them beer cans up in the air reverently. "Let's all drink to Grannie Young before we open her up for the viewin'!" The beer eased their pain and clouded their eyes, and not a single solitary Yother noticed any strange thing about Grannie Young before she went in the ground up behind the house.

2029 Morning Glory Ridge

My bed breathes. It huffs and puffs and responds to every turn of my aching bones. It is designed to prevent bedsores and blood clots, but mostly it keeps me awake, rolls me around and gives me motion sickness. I am lying on it now, concentrating on the flow of its exhalations as a form of meditation, trying to relax. I have a visit from the resident psychologist this morning. Why they find it necessary to prod around in our minds is beyond me.

She is looking at the clippings of my semi-illustrious career in art. The fact that I was an artist automatically makes me fair game for therapy. When she found out about my collection of Victorian funerary photographs, the ones with deceased babies propped up in their coffins, wide eyes staring and surrounded by banks of flowers, she felt inclined to open up my brain and come right on in. I have hidden my sketchbooks for now, because I know if she sees the creepy stuff in there, the kinds of things that all artists are attracted to just on general principle, she'll have me shipped into the looney wing.

The topic for today is my mother. Mothers are always the root of all evil in psych land. Just to give her something to chew on and write down in her paperwork, I tell her all about Dory's obsessive compulsive disorder. Wanting to mess with her a little, I give lots of examples... the lining up, the alphabetizing, the counting. I had learned early on in high school psych class that there was an official name for my mama's behaviors.

"And how do you think that affected you, Anna Grace?" she pries, with a badly manufactured look of concern on her face.

"Uh... I'm the most organized artist you ever met?" I asked, looking equally concerned that I had gotten the answer right. Just to play with her a little more, I count her steps as she leaves the room. "One, two, three... oops, don't stumble... four, five..."

I'm fine, really, I'm fine. I'd be just peachy if I didn't have to inhale disinfectant all the damn time.

1954 Blackshale

Hum spent most of his time down at the river fishing off the bank. He still didn't talk much. In fact, about all he ever did say was "Hummmm", but he had a real flair for filling up a fish stringer. I reckon the high point of his plain life was when Frank would load Hum up in his wooden boat and take him out to cast up under the trees that bowed over the bank of our river. Me and Dory and Pearlie fretted from the dock as they slid out into the stream, Hum's end of the boat sunk deep. Pap had bought Hum his own rod and reel outfit for Christmas, and Hum sat up straight and held his rig proudly. They'd come home at dusk one way or the other, with Hum holding up some big slimy catfish or limpin'with a plug stuck in his own bleeding leg, but either way he'd be grinnin' and dancing the jitterbug.

Pearlie would fry up a mess of catfish, hushpups, and okry, and we all set down to the table diggin' in. Long past was them first days when Pearlie and Hum took their meals down to the room in the basement.

So about every single breakfast, lunch, and supper, the five of us sat around the kitchen table, passing the salt and pepper, black to white, white to black and never thinking that some might find that strange. Over in the next holler, men in white pointy hoods still marched secretly at night, burning crosses, praying in the name of Jesus Christ for an excuse to use their ropes.

With Hum practically being my big brother, I treated him like one. I teased him unmercifully, making up tales just to watch him squirm. One Tuesday in early summer, Frank had come upstairs at noon, and we were all waiting as Pearlie doled out the hot tamales Mama had heated up out of a can. I began carefully peeling the oily orange paper off a mine, licking my fingers and watching poor Hum tryin' to figure out how to get into the thing, eatin' the paper as often as not.

"Mama, guess what I seen?"

"What, Anna Grace, *what* did you *see*?" Correcting my grammar was her new favorite hobby.

"Hum was down to the well with Lucy Lincoln, and I think he's looking to make her his sweetheart! Hoo… Hoo, Hooty… Hoo!" I jumped up from the table and did myself a little happy dance. I boogied like a fool around the kitchen table until I noticed Pearlie stock stiff in her chair and not laughin'. Lucy was coal black, not good enough for her coffee skinned Hum even though he was a man of few words, so Pearlie didn't like my joke much. I was sorry I'd yapped my mouth, 'cause I wouldn't hurt Pearlie for nothin'. Hum's head lolled over on his shoulder, and his fingers splayed out stiff in all directions. He started making his hummmm-ing sound to beat the band, then he bopped me on the head with a greasy flying tamale.

• • • • • • • •

After lunch, Mama says, "Anna Grace, why don't you and Hum walk up Rambler Road to the meadow and pick us some dewberries so Pearlie can make us all a pie for supper!"

She would a never in ten thousand years let me out of her sight alone, but she knew that Hum would tear anybody to shreds with his bare hands if they tried to hurt me. Hum looked alarmed and moaned "hummmm" in a darker way than usual. New things scared him, and he'd never had to fetch dewberries before.

Dory encouraged him. "Oh com'on Hum! You'll be back in a jiffy and just think of that pie!" She rolled her eyes and licked her lips to juice up the sales pitch. "Here's a poke," she prodded, handing him a paper sack to fill up with berries.

He grinned and grabbed his porkpie hat. Then he tucked his trusty Case knife that Dory had given him for Christmas in the front panel of his overalls and gave it a pat.

We headed toward town, and then in a few minutes turned

right onto Rambler Road, a dirt and gravel lane that wound like a copperhead snake up the mountain. Just after the start of that road was the railroad bridge. Hum and me stood there a while hoping a train would come by so we could pitch rocks down in them coal cars.

Hum loved trains more than anything in the world. Of course he never said that, but I just know he did. I could see his eyes light up when he felt the rumbling of an engine shaking the ground, and he walked alongside the tracks all the time just to be close to that power. Today though, it looked like we'd missed the long freight train that usually came through after lunch, so we finally give up and headed on up the hill.

A ways up that road was a split rail fence, which was our sign to bear off again to the right and head out through the woods, the closest way to the thick clusters of dewberries that edged the meadow. The meadow was to the back of our house as the crow flies, but we were going the way that had fewer brambles, less barbed wire, and not as many cricks to cross. A path of trampled pinestraw and leaf rot stretched out ahead. Hum slogged out in front of me, whistling and lettin' farts, slinging a forked stick, ready to fend off snakes.

When we got into the spooky woods, I got a little skeered and I guess Hum did too, 'cause we both started to run, laughing a little to cover up the fact that we were feeling chicken. We come up over a little hill, and all at once Hum froze and let out a tortured sound. Then I crested the hill behind him and stopped short in my tracks, breaking out in gooseflesh. "I'm gonna puke!" I yelled as I backtracked to the road, running hard between quick stops, when I hurled tamale chunks to the ground. Hum was running right behind me, bawling and slinging snot.

At the top of that hill, we'd come up on a straight row of poles, a foot apart and four, maybe five foot high. Stuck up on the top of each pole was a bleeding head, one for most kinds of dogs that lived around Blackshale. There was a beagle, a collie, a coon dog, a german shepherd, a shaggy terrier, a boxer, several hunting dogs and a large number of mutts. Most of their eyes were propped open with twigs, giving them a look that they were plumb shocked to be dead and up on a pole. At the end of the row was a miniature Chihuahua with its little eyes squinched closed and his tiny pink tongue poking out. Its rhinestone collar sparkled in the splattered sunlight streaming through the pines.

We ran panting all the way home, and when we blasted through the back door Mama yelled out, "Give the berries to Pearlie to rinse, they're probably full of bugs! And wash up your hands good, too!"

"Mama, we ain't *got* no dewberries!" I was shivering, the bones of my little body rattling, and Dory was too worried to take up a grammar lesson.

She knelt down and put her hands up to my face, wiping tears with her dishrag. "Aw... sweetie pie, what happened?"

I started heaving in earnest, and when she looked up and saw tears running down Hum's face, too, she demanded, "Tell me! What happened!" By then I took to caterwaulin' good, and was having a hard time putting what I'd seen into words. Hum was not one bit of help.

Mama soaked the dishrag in cool water and began to sponge off my face, saying "There... there," in the soothing way only mamas can. I snubbed, settling down tear-by-tear.

By that time Frank had heard the commotion through the hole in the floor and came upstairs just in time to hear me spill out the story.

"Mam-m-ma... somebody kilt a whole big bunch of dogs and chopped their heads off. They stuck them heads up on red poles up in the woods! Oh Mama, their eyes was still open so they were looking right at us when we came up over the hill!" I kept on sniveling, and about that time I realized I had wet my pink

Tuesday panties good and soggy.

"God Almighty, Dory, there's some crazy people in these woods, and you let that child go in there with Hum as her only defense!" Hum looked hurt, he may have been wordless but he wasn't stupid. Dory had been so proud of herself for letting go of the reins a little and giving me a chance for some freedom. Now she was mad at herself and sat chewing on the inside of her lip.

"We have to call Sheriff Raby!"

But Frank had already put the cover over the hole in the floor and was heading downstairs to the phone.

· · · · · · · ·

"I'll be down there directly," Harlan Raby told Frank before he hung up the receiver and sat staring at the Indian Chief test pattern on his brand spanking new Philco television set. Harlan was *not* on a party line because the county paid extra for private service. Money well spent. Sure couldn't have people eavesdropping on the unsavory kinds of conversations like the sheriff often had. Like today for instance, when he had to make a most unpleasant call to his personal bootlegger, Walter Lee Murphy.

At least now the mystery of all those missing dogs could be put to rest - not that he was about to march up on Nettie Tollett's front porch with the news that her Chihuahua Pedro's head was now impaled on a pole. Not that he would miss the late coon dog Roscoe, who'd damn near taken a chunk out of his ass last month during the bad check arrest of Roscoe's master, Joe Dean Suggs. Not that he gave a flying crap about any dog on four legs for that matter. He would just as soon sling them all up against a tree his own self.

The troublesome thing was the two sets of tracks in the slick red mud around them bloody poles, two pairs of size 13 boots with identical tread patterns, identical except for a cut in the rubber on just one left foot. Why, oh why them damnfool boys still dressed alike was just another mystery to be solved.

• • • • • • • • •

Even though she spent her days working as a housekeeper, Pearlie was an elegant lady. She wore her earbobs all day long, and was never without one of her fancy starched white aprons. She embellished them with embroidery herself, in the evenings, as she sat down in her room listening to her stories on the radio. Mama adored and admired her.

One winter midmorning Mama was working side-by-side with Pearlie, who was polishing the silver flatware and singing spiritual songs in her soft, rasping voice. Mama was right up next to her, arranging her crystal goblets in the cabinet so they were in straight rows and right at one inch apart. Ever so often she'd run her finger around a rim to hear the crystal sing, as if she willed it to harmonize with Pearlie.

All at once Mama got a whiff of something that made her want to gag! It was coming from Pearlie's direction.

She was trying to be tactful. "Pearlie, do you smell anything funny?" It was the *oddest* smell, like nothing Mama had ever had up in her nose before!

Pearlie sniffed the air around her. "No'me." Dory Tollett had become so fanatic about cleanliness that a thing like this could really get under her skin. She arranged another shelf of crystal, this time sherbets. Pearlie walked to the other end of the kitchen and back into the pantry to get more silver polish. The smell disappeared.

Pearlie came back, and so did the odor. Dory moved closer, and it got worse. Finally she couldn't help herself, "Pearlie, I'm still smelling something just awful! Don't you smell it?"

"No'me, I ain't smelling nothin'. Do it smell like dirty butt stank? Cause I done had a good worshin'!"

Dory had to laugh, and she crowed, "Oh Pearlie darlin', you just slay me!" but the smell remained.

That night, as she and Frank lay in bed sharing their days with each other, Dory told him about the smell and her suspicion that it might be coming from Pearlie's general direction. She was flummoxed by the mystery smell.

Frank was amused, laughing. "Well, *did* it smell like dirty butt?"

"No," Dory answered, "that was the funny thing. It wasn't like body odor. I've never smelled anything quite like it before."

"Well my dear Dory, your most brilliant husband has the answer to your mystery! I've run into this down in the workroom a few times now. It's called an asophidity bag... folks wear it around their necks to ward off all kinds of things. Colds, consumption, ghosts..."

The next day Mama spotted a leather thong peeking out from under Pearlie's collar. "Pearlie, what is that you wear around your neck? If you don't mind me asking." For a while Pearlie kept swabbing the breakfast dish she was dipping in and out of the soapy water, but then she pulled her hands out of the sink and dried them on her apron. She fished a little cloth sack out of her bosom.

"Oh, you talkin' 'bout this here? This here keep them haints in the basement from crawling up in the bed with Pearlie!" She chuckled to herself.

· · · · · · · ·

That was not the only time we had a stink. Pearlie had up and took a Trailways bus trip over to Arkansas to see some kin – her auntie, a word she pronounced in a fancified way, not the same as "ant". I reckon she had never been nowhere but here and decided to go off by herself for a spell. *Somewheres else.* Since Mama worked all day down in the store, she decided it was high time I helped out a little. After lunch, she stood me up on her yellow kitchen stool, elbow deep in a sink of dirty dishes and headed back downstairs.

"Be sure to dry them and put them up after you've given them a good washing!"She smiled proudly at her little growin' up girl.

I looked down into the suds and eyed the hardcrusted pans piled up on the drainboard. I'll be the first to admit, if work did not involve making art, I could be downright lackadaisical. After washing a few, I got tired real fast so I climbed down and took to sticking them crusty pans way up in the back of the cabinets.

When Mama came back upstairs that afternoon, she was tickled pink. There was not a dirty dish to be seen. The next week though, there was a new rot smellin' stink, and it wasn't like dirty butt neither. Mama searched and sniffed, and that picayune nose of hers finally led her to the moldy pots and pans. She was on me like a duck on a June bug and switched my bottom good.

. . . .

It wasn't long after the bout of eating Kleenex that I took to drawin' pictures in earnest. My hands were jittery, in need of purpose. Pap had stacks of scratch pads brought to him by coffin salesmen, and I had a box of pencils Aunt Sudy had bought me as a starting school present. I was no child prodigy, but I could doodle for hours. I would draw one picture in the middle of a sheet, and the second it stopped looking right, I'd rip it off the pad and start all over again. Mama fussed at me. "You're wasting paper, Anna Grace!" You'd think she of all people would have understood my quest for perfection.

. . . .

Early one Sunday morning, Frank came in to breakfast, somehow fumbling his tie into a perfect Windsor knot on the run. Through a mouthful of Pearlie's spoon bread, he mumbled, "Where's Hum this morning? I'm of a mind to set him up with the grave digging crew... he could make himself a little spending dough." Pearlie didn't know where he was at, and didn't seem a bit worried about it.

"Oh," I piped up, "I bet he's out gigging frogs or some fool thing. He'll be back directly." I was mighty fond of big, sweet Hum.

Sunday was Pearlie's night off. Mama would have given her more time off but Pearlie counted us her family now, and she was happiest being right there with us. Of course, if she had took a notion to go to the picture show and sit up in the colored balcony, Mama would a tittered, "Oh honey you go right on!"

Most nights off she would take a plate of scrapple and a glass of sweet tea down to her room. Good thing the basement was cool 'cause all Pearlie had for coolin' was a paper fan with a picture of a red headed, white faced, Jesus Christ the Savior on it. If it ever was too hot down there, or if she was feeling traipsy, she'd stroll down to the river to watch the sunset or see the mist come up when the cool air swept down over the warm water.

Since Mama never got around to mastering cooking, Sunday night supper was almost always a bowl of cereal. We each one picked out our favorite from the package of little boxes... Rice Krispies, Corn Flakes, and Corn Pops. Snap, Crackle, Pop! We could cut the box open and pour the milk right in. Mama wouldn't even have to wash a dish, and we could get right down to watching Ed Sullivan or Walt Disney's "When You Wish Upon a Star!"

On this Sunday night, we were still having a second box of cereal when the party line rang twice, and Frank hopped up and got the phone. He stood listening. I saw his whole body sag, and his hand flew to the top of his head. Then he listened a lot more, sagging lower and lower. When he hung up, he unlocked the apartment door and went downstairs.

The next morning Mama looked like she'd been cryin'. She

said Pearlie would be taking a few days off, that Hum was gone. They were all so solemn, something told me to keep my mouth shut and not ask questions. In my childish brain, I thought "gone" just meant "runned off." As far as I knew, Hum was just *somewheres else*. I thought maybe he had chosen to go off for a spell alone, just like Pearlie had. I missed him, but with my child's faith, I fully expected him to pop up on the back porch with a "hummmm" at any minute. So I went on about my child's business, drawing pictures and playing, waiting for that to happen. After Pearlie came back upstairs to work though, she was never the same. She was as loving to me as she ever was, patient and sweet in her soft-spoken way, but she was steeped in dark sadness like a brown stained teabag.

2029 Morning Glory Ridge

I have awakened in a start from a nightmare, heart racing, mouth dry - a fine sheen of perspiration on my papery skin. The blood pressure alert on my screen is going nuts. The bad dream lingers on the edge of my consciousness. Uncle Faron was in it, and Pap. Then I recall the dream really happened, that rainy day when I was six and learned another thing about the different kinds of love.

Mama was gone to Knoxville, off on what she called a "shoppin' spree." I'd come in from school, fixed myself a snack and turned on Howdy Doody, when I remembered the thing that was down in the bottom of my plaid schoolbag.

We'd had a special visitor at school that day, a bible teacher from the "He Be Raised Up on the Cross Church." One of the boys in my class was slumping down in his seat making fun of her and calling it the "Heebie Jeebies for Jesus Church." First we all sang "I'll Be a Sunbeam for Jesus."

Then she stood up in front of the room, lifting a crooked finger and pointing out at each of us, saying, "Don't hide your light under a bushel! Let your light so shine!" And by golly, she had not come empty handed! For each and every student in the class, she'd brought a miniature white bible, and a special treasure she said we could take with us for when we went into the privacy of our closet to pray to the Lord. Everybody got one, a plastic cross, a ghoulish milky white thing.

"If you set it in the sun awhile," she explained, "it will save up the light of the Gospel and glow in the dark." I couldn't wait to get home and see that!

When I got home, I dug it out of my pencil box and lay it over by the windows, checking it ever so often to see if it would suck up the sun. It had been rainin' on and off, but I figured enough patches of sunny sky were passin' over here and there. Directly, I decided just to try and see the light of the Gospel. I opened Mama's perfectly organized closet and sat down cross legged in the floor. Sure enough, the light was shining! I sat there watching it fade little by little, even until I heard "Yoo Hoo, It's Me, My name is Pinky Lee..." coming from the TV set. I was about to get up when I heard voices right by the door. Through the slit of light around the closet door I saw something - something that made me stay glued stiff in the closet, afraid to show myself.

Pap had come upstairs to get a cold drink, and Uncle Faron was with him. He'd stepped right over next to Pap. All of a sudden, he slipped a hand around the back of Pap's neck, and kissed him right smack on the mouth like a girl! I was so shocked I clamped down hard on the glowin' cross, the light of the gospel cutting into my fingers. Confusion was buzzing in my head. In the first place, he was Aunt Sudy's *husband*, and most of all Pap was a *man*! As stunned as I was, Pap looked shocked plumb out of his skin! He jumped back, practically knocking over Mama's knick-knacks, and yelled, "Whoa! Faron! What the hell?"

"Dammit, man, haven't you known? I've been loving you so long now. You have to know! I thought I saw it in your eyes..." Faron looked down at the floor.

Pap was just plain embarrassed, not knowing what to say at all. "Look, I love my wife with all my heart, and even if I didn't, I, uh, I don't do this! Oh Dear God! SUDY! Does Sudy *know* this?" Pap looked like a man who'd been hit flat upside the face with a rug beater.

"As a matter of fact, we have an arrangement. She does her thing, and I do mine. We make great housemates! Look, I'm sorry if I caught you off guard, old man. I'm going now." And with that he flung open the closet door, grabbed his umbrella and shot out the door, leaving Frank gaping openmouthed at the child hunkered on the closet floor, clutching a glowing cross with all her might.

Of course Frank told Dory, and that night me and Mama was having a serious talk.

"But... but, Mama," I interrogated, "Boys kiss girls. Right? Right, Mama? And Pap, he just wants to kiss you, right, Mama? He don't kiss nobody else, does he Mama? Mama? Does Aunt Sudy know Uncle Faron kisses boys in the mouth? Does she let him do that?" I was in a tizzy and chock full of questions.

Mama cleared her throat, and I could nearly see her words all jumbled up inside her brain, struggling to get out in a straight, sensible line. "Sometimes, Anna Grace, there are men who fall in love with men. They can't help it. They are just made that way. And sometimes, women might fall in love with women, too."

"Well... like you love me, Mama!"

"No... no... not the same at all. I love you to heaven and back, like a mama loves her child. Sometimes women find out they love another woman like... well, kind of like... they would love a boyfriend. Romantic like."

"And Aunt Sudy? What about her? Does Aunt Sudy kiss boys or girls? Please tell me Aunt Sudy does not kiss you or I am going to puke my guts."

Mama couldn't help but laugh, and she pulled me to her tight where I could feel her ribs shaking. "No! Sudy has no wish to kiss me, and I am definitely not interested in kissing her or any other woman, for that matter!"

My shoulders went loose in relief, but I leaned away and looked back into Mama's eyes, still hungry for details. So she continued.

"Well, the truth is, I think Sudy loves Faron in a special way. Not like a boyfriend so much, but she loves him enough to still want to live with him. Maybe more like a brother. I know that may be hard for you to understand, honey."

I looked around the floor of my room, mulling over these strange new ideas in my head. Then I grabbed up my two Ginny dolls, Annette and Justine, and pressed their hard plastic mouths together in a grinding kiss, testing the waters.

1955 Blackshale

One day Perry was a kid like me, bigger'n me, but still a kid. All of a sudden he shot up into a beanstalk! I was most fascinated with his hands. His thin arms had stretched, seemed like to below his knees, and at the end of them, long bony fingers twisted willy-nilly. So commanding were the dances of his hands, my eyeballs were almost wore out keeping up with them. Those hands were all over the place when he'd go to say something, and his voice was all over the place too, warbling and squeaking, until finally it settled into a gravely bass. For a while, I grew shy around this strange new deep-voiced Perry, thinking he had gone over into some other land where I couldn't tag along.

2029 Morning Glory Ridge

With my bent, arthritic index finger, I am tracing the curves of my translucent, 3D brain on the touch screen. Then I sweep my finger sideways and send my brain spinning round and round! It's reassuring to see there are no tumors or aneurisms lurking in there, but what about all those packets of knowledge I worked so hard to commit to memory - those tedious bundles of learning that became obsolete? Where are all those archaic software manuals I memorized? Control - this, Command – that, Option-Shift-whatever, an endless list of keystrokes that are now buried deep and useless. Behind which fold of grey matter hides The Gettysburg Address, The Preamble to the Constitution, Thanatopsis, multiplication tables, three years of conversational Spanish, and four years of Latin? What about all those hours I spent learning to develop film and prints before darkrooms ceased to exist? The thought of all that wasted study just makes me tired. I'm going back to sleep.

1956 Blackshale

By the time Mama signed my first grade report card for the last six weeks, I had enough brains to look forward to summer. With the Five Star picture show, our small movie theatre that always smelled like stale popcorn and unwashed feet, the summer skating rink, a river to swim in, and the arrival of the traveling carnival, Blackshale had more summer fun than most small towns. We had one other fine thing, too, that few towns could boast.

Summer started up, and it got dark later and later, 'til there was lots of time after supper for all of us to do the things we wanted to before bedtime. Mama and Pearlie would take a glass of sweet tea to the screened-in porch and clip recipes. I sat at their feet drawing pictures, making a house of cards, or flipping pick-up sticks. Pap almost always went back down after supper to work on his bookkeeping. If he finished early, he'd yell up through the hole, "Dory, Grace, get your sweaters on and let's go watch 'em dump the pot! I'll yell down and ask Pearlie if she wants to go." She didn't - she was always busy doin' something down in her room.

We'd load into the van and drive all the way through Blackshale. A couple miles on out the road, Pap would turn in toward the mountain. We'd bump our way up a service road, past the mines and the tipple barely there in the dimming dark and pull right up to the chain link fence. Behind the fence loomed the tall smokestacks of the iron furnace. Pap explained they'd made pig iron before the depression and somethin' for the war after. They were still makin' some metal thing nowadays 'cause them stacks were still huffin, but I didn't know what it was.

I pestered him, asking, "When, when, how long 'til it happens, Pap?"

He'd always say, "Directly, directly, just sit back and listen to the radio!" Fidgety and checking his watch, he'd finally say, "Near time." All of a sudden the whole sky flamed up deep scarlet, lookin' like the end of the world! Up behind the furnace, giant round vats of molten metal tipped over and ran red hot out into slag piles. "Hot damn, what a show! And free of charge!" Pap would always say the same thing. On the way back through Blackshale, we'd pull up to Sonny's drive-in and get a cone dipped in hot butterscotch. Then we'd get on back home, wishing the summer would never end.

It did turn out to be a right long summer. The rainy June before starting second grade, I slipped headlong off the back porch and broke my arm. It was a compound fracture and I had to be put to sleep for an operation. Feeling sorry for me having to spend most of the summer in a cast, Mama finally agreed to let me get a little dog. He was a curly black miniature something or other I named Mr. Wiggles, a little feller no bigger than a possum. The first time he licked my face, I fell hopelessly in love.

But my pap didn't care much for Mr. Wiggles. The first week we had him, we were all standing out in the front watching cars go by. Mr. Wiggles, too, but instead of standing still like us, which he never ever done much anyways, he was willywaggin' from leg to leg, jumpin' up, beggin' for a pat on the head.

He was so excited, somethin' funny happened to his little pee pee, and Mama blushed and commented he needed to put his lipstick back in his pocket. Then Pap pointed down at him, and making a joke for Mama's benefit, he observed, "If you ask me that dog there is queer!" He took to chuckling and hooting at his own joke, looking out the road over his sunglasses. Well! Mr. Wiggles waddled straight over to my pap and raised his little black leg, spewing pee all over his best undertakin' suit. Frank stood there steamin' and threatening, "I'll take a stick to that dog!" From then on, Mr. Wiggles was on Frank's bad side and had to count on me and Mama and Pearlie for love and care.

Mr. Wiggles went outside just long enough to wee and make turdies, 'cause Mama was afraid he'd get runned over by a car. One morning, she let him out and was watching to make sure he stayed in the back yard, when a skunk ran out of the bushes and bit him smack on the nose. Why she didn't think nothin' of it. Dogs in the country were all the time snapping after some varmint that snapped right back. She just painted his nose bright orange with mercurochrome, and we went on as usual until Pap noticed Mr. Wiggles was not himself and got frothy chops. The next morning, Mama came in my room and sat down on my bed. She was twirling her hair, never a good sign. "Grace, honey, I'm sorry but I have bad news. Mr. Wiggles ran off last night." I was drenched in despair and took to whimpering, but little did I know that things were about to get a lot worse.

The next day up in the afternoon, I got hungry for a snack. Mama and Frank were downstairs with a family planning a funeral. Pearlie was in the bathroom and I expected she'd be tied up in there some time, as I could hear her moaning with the trots. Helpin' myself with a proud grin, I raided the Frigidaire and pawed though the meat drawer for baloney and cheese, which I slapped on white bread. I shuffled around the pickle beets and chow chow and Tabasco and ketchup on the top shelf trying to find the mayonnaise. I loved mayo so much I could eat it by the spoonfuls right out of the jar, but there wasn't none. Then, I spied a big mayo jar way in the back, sticking up out of a brown grocery sack. When I pulled it out and slid it from the sack, I started screaming bloody murder and threw the glass jar on the floor. It broke in a thousand pieces, and Mr. Wiggle's wet, black head went rollin' across the speckled linoleum in a trail of red sludge. Considering my history with headless dogs and how much I had loved Mr. Wiggles, I was a nutcase by the time Mama, Pap, and Pearlie got to me. They picked me up in a hysterical, quaking wad and carried me to my room. I was in bad shape, but once again, I didn't know things were gonna get a lot worse.

While Mama and Pearlie patted, petted, and made over me in my room, Frank was in the kitchen mopping up the floor and digging out another clean glass jar for Mr. Wiggle's head to occupy until Monday, when a health department worker would pick it up for rabies testing. A few days later, the call came. Mr. Wiggles was a bonafide mad dog, and all of us would get twenty-one straight days of rabies shots.

• • • • • • • •

At the health department clinic up in Pineville, the doctor was trying to reason with me through my hysteria, and explain that my tummy had to be rigid and tight for the injection. It was no ordinary skinny needle neither, but a big sharp hollow tube, more like being stabbed in your hard belly with an ice pick.

In the end, Mama and Pap had to hold me down on the steel table. One week later, the rabies shots still a very bad memory, my arm started up hurting again. Fighting the shots had pulled the ends of my broken bone apart, and it had to be reset. As they were rolling me into the operating room for the second time that miserable summer, I looked up into Mama's face that was dripping with tears.

"Mama, why did you tell me a fib about Mr. Wiggles? That he had runned off?"

Dory explained her thinking, that she thought it might be better for me to think of Mr. Wiggles off somewhere, still alive, maybe even being loved by another little girl, than to know for sure that my Pap had no choice than to take him out back and chop off his curly black head.

• • • • • • • •

I was used to spending a good bit of my summers soaking wet - lolling in a shallow bank of the river with Mama and Sudy. Pop. Scritch. Now here on my cast is a girl tied down with ropes, unable to go into the water. Scritch, scratch. A bust of a black dog wearing a halo and the wings of an angel. Dab, dab, dab… A line of dots runs in a spiral, round and round. Chunka, chunka, chunka, the marker shades back and forth, back and forth blackening in the figure of a boogerman. The pen juts against the raised grains and the line takes a detour. I thank God it was my left arm, not my good right drawin' arm. I have covered over every last square inch of the plaster. I hear Mama comin' down the hall. Uh Oh.

• • • • • • • •

It was a miracle of Jesus that I ever made it to the first day of second grade. Mama had been laying outfits on my bed for a week, sticking sweaters up against my face to test their colors with my skin. They were too short, not warm enough, too babyish, not the right red, the sleeves not long enough and then she would start all over with different combinations. When we got up that morning, she was still frantic, but by then, I didn't care no more, all I wanted was to go color with my new box of crayons, that, and read. Having read all about Dick and Jane and Spot in first grade, I was mor'n ready to move on to Friends and Neighbors. Finally, we settled on a plaid dress with a pair of tan corduroy pants underneath, and a red cardigan sweater with a portrait of a Scotty Dog on the front. That worried me somewhat since I'd not been having good luck with dog heads so far. I had brand new Buster Brown tie-up shoes, ones that I could tie myself now that my cast had come off, but I complained that they looked like the ones worn by children who had gone and caught the polio.

Mama walked with me out to the highway, where we waited for the bus. When she saw the big yellow school bus coming up over the hill, she handed me my new book satchel and my Snow White lunchbox and took a ragged breath. She reached out and tapped the door of the bus ten times, which she had done every day since I'd started school, a personal ritual to insure my safety. I knew, as sure as I knew that I already had blisters on both heels from my new shoes, that she would go home and start lining up something in straight rows.

When I got on, there were several other older girls and boys already on the front seats, going over to the junior high school. I heard one whisper, "That there is the funeral home, and she lives there all the time with dead people."

When the bus pulled up to Rambler Road, the Murphy boys got on the bus. I had learned in first grade to keep away from BoJack and Peanut, who were just plain mean. Mama warned there was no tellin' what they would do next and to just stay away from them. BoJack pushed Peanut into the seat across the aisle from me. He elbowed Peanut, and suggested, "Hey! Let's play charades!" He signaled "Two words, first word." Then he leaned over the aisle and pointed straight at me.

Peanut came to life with evil energy and started throwing out guesses, "Girl... her... ugly." All wrong answers.

"Keep tryin!" BoJack aigged him on.

Peanut tried again, "She!"

BoJack grinned and put his finger on his nose and went on to the second word. He shifted his eyes at Peanut and held up both hands, spreading both out wide and open. This had Peanut stumped, "Hands!.. Keep away!... Give Up!"

BoJack smacked him upside his head, "No dummy! Keep tryin'."

I could see the light come on in Peanut's head. "FINGERS!" he yelled, "SHE FINGERS!" BoJack looked so pleased that his half-wit brother had come up with the answer to his sick puzzle. One of the junior high girls gasped and shot a mean look at BoJack, but the older boys were rolling in laughter. Somethin' was funny, but I didn't understand. I knew it wasn't nice.

The older girl got off the bus first, but she glared at BoJack and yelled "Asshole!" I didn't know what that meant neither.

When I got home from school that day, I told Mama what they'd said, and asked her what it meant. She was furious and stalked back and forth like a caged wildcat. When Pap came up, they sent me to my room, but sitting on my window seat I heard them talking. Dory repeated the two words the Murphys had yelled out about me on the bus. Frank giggled, "Well, what does that mean?" Mama got mad all over again.

"Frank Tollett, don't try to tell me you don't know what it means. I know good and well you know what it means to finger a girl!"

Frank grinned. "Yeah, I think I know, and I wouldn't mind doing it right now!" He grabbed at her, but she was not in the mood to be teased or loved up.

"How can you sit there laughing? Your daughter was made fun of in a very dirty way on the school bus. Call the principal right now and take it up with him!"

"Now Dory, that would not do one bit of good. For one thing, the principal is one of Walter Lee Murphy's best bootleg customers, and he's not about to run up the price of his likker by pickin' on those boys. And besides, I'm sure it all went flyin' right over Grace's head. Why, she'd a never given it a thought if you didn't make such a big deal out of it."

Mama gave up, since what Frank said was usually the last word, but she mumbled as she stomped off, "She knows she was being laughed at. She may not know what it means now, but she will... God knows she will."

·　·　·　·　·　·　·　·　·　··

Sudy Templeton's romantic dreams had floundered on the rocks. That's why, when she met Conley Porter, who had a massive double-wide dick and loved nothing better than to hear Sudy yell "Ride Cowbody Ride!" she was willing to settle for raw sex without the complication of love. Conley was a Tennessee cowboy from Nashville, and she saw him occasionally when he was passing through. In fact it was precisely the words: "Do you want to come and ride me this weekend, cowboy?" that Dory had overheard on the party line a few days before Sudy met Conley at the Blackshale Motor Inn for the twenty-seventh time.

Conley was a free spirit, and when his seed escaped the torn condom and tenaciously took root in Sudy's womb, he was perfectly ok with things staying just as they were. He made no move toward fatherhood, but still parked his boots under Sudy's motel bed once in a while. Between her successful career, her satisfying cowboy, her attentive albeit homosexual husband, and the warmth of baby blossoming in her belly, Sudy Templeton's life was complete.

· · · · · · · ·

My second grade teacher was a vision from Heaven. She stood at the chalkboard in a green gabardine dress with a slim straight skirt, her black hair falling on her shoulders in a perfect pageboy. In her high heel pumps, she was near six foot tall. I scuttled into the classroom head down, feeling plain and small, and slid into the wooden desk. I sniffed the air. Somebody smelled. Carved into the desk attached to the bench in front of me were words and names I did not know. There was a groove across the top to hold my pencil. I got it out of my pencil box and dared to lift my eyes to look at the teacher. She smiled right straight at me.

The bell rang, and the teacher picked up a piece of chalk and screeched her name on the board, M I S S   B A K E R. "Good morning!" she beamed, and we all answered in one voice, right back, "Good morning, teacher." We all put our hands over our hearts and said the pledge to the United States of America. Then Miss Baker called the roll out in the order we were sitting. "Penny Holcomb, Charles Young, Jackson Murphy, James Murphy, Haskell Tenpenny, Abby Sue Frytag, Hershel Penley, Floyd Bacon,

Anna Grace Tollett..." Although she had stopped after each name and looked up to smile at each child, sure as shootin' I'd got the most special one.

The next morning we got our new books, and started right in reading from Friends and Neighbors. I was a good reader, but some kids couldn't read at all, like BoJack and Peanut, who Miss Baker had to say the words for them to repeat, "OH... oh... LOOK... look... SEE... see... SALLY... Sally... RUN... Run."

BoJack leaned over to Peanut and whispered loudly, "Oh LOOK, See... Peanut... piss... his... pants." Peanut whirled around and smacked at him but he missed. Miss Baker looked some vexed.

Before that first day was even over, she had moved Jackson "BoJack" Murphy and his brother James "Peanut" Murphy to far opposite sides of the room, making lots of space between them. The order of the roll was changed the next morning. I could tell Miss Baker was gonna be up the crick with them two.

Every mornin', the bus dropped us grammar school kids off on Blackshale road and kept goin' on to the junior high school and the high school. We walked in scattered clumps along Schoolbell Road on up to the school, unless it was sleetin' or somethin' and then the bus would take us all the way to the door. Every day that fall, I skipped along the lumpy brick sidewalk from the bus to school, bubbling with anticipation. The September air was crisp and the leaves whirled in circles at my feet - green, orange, red, and gold. I could smell the smoke from all the chimneys, the small square ones in the houses along the road and the tall round ones of the furnaces up behind the school. I thought about the small fires more though, about the people gathered around their stoves and fireplaces, burning old newspapers and kindlin', hickory logs, lumps of coal. I thought about the people in my town that I loved and the ones I didn't much care for, and I wondered why God had thought to set me down right here in Blackshale, Tennessee when I could a just as well been borned in India with one of them red spots on my forehead.

• • • • • • • •

Someone had whispered that her first name was Corrine. That sounded to me like a bell ringing. She was the greatest teacher ever. She made sure some room mother brought cupcakes with colored icing every Friday, and that we got to go on field trips to a farm or to the bread factory. Even when one of us behaved badly (usually them Murphy boys), she tried to steer us on the right path with a gentle touch. But sometimes (again, Murphy boys), she was pushed to employ a firmer hand.

Out of all our second grade class, BoJack and Peanut were the top troublemakers. I spent my time doing everthing I could to make sure I was the teacher's pet, but I did get myself in trouble one time.

We were supposed to be working on our arithmetic homework, correcting any problem that had a big X in Miss Baker's red pencil. I was already fidgety that day 'cause the principal had give us a big talk on lookin' out for mushroom clouds in the sky, and showed us all how to duck and cover if them Russians blowed up the world. My fingers started that nervous itchin' and I couldn't help myself. I was hunkered down behind Floyd Bailey, a big fat boy who stunk of bad hair grease, drawing pictures.

As of late, I was drawing people with birds on their heads. It started when my parakeet, Blueboy, who was the color of a perfect blue sky and rode all over the house perched on my head, flew into my mirror and broke his neck. On this afternoon in school, I was drawing each student in the class with a different bird on their head. Some had parakeets and parrots, but there was a wren, a peckerwood, a chicken, a barn owl, a redbird, and others I had seen out in the yard. BoJack and Peanut had evil black crows, their wings spread and their beaks eager to peck. For Miss Baker, I was rendering a magnificent Peacock, whose feathers splayed down over her shoulders. Not a one of them birds had a single thing to do with arithmetic.

I was in so deep a concentration that Miss Baker came up behind me and took up my drawing before I knew what was happening. She was nice though, just said in a quiet voice, "Anna Grace, you're supposed to be correcting your sums right now." The fact that I had earned a word of discipline was more than I could take. I teared up, filled up, and flooded over, a wreck of a child. She said kindly, "Oh… darlin', it's ok. I just want you to get your work done so you won't fall behind." But I went home with my chest aching and burning. I had let my wonderful teacher down.

· · · · · · · ·

On the fourteenth of February, I got a big stack of penny Valentines in little white envelopes. Everyone, except for BoJack and Peanut, had brought one for each child in the room. But the Valentine that made me the happiest was from Miss Baker. It had the head of a white puppy with hearts floating up out of his eyes and said, "Be my special Valentine." For the first time in my life, something good and happy had come from the head of a dog. Each pupil come in from recess to find a red cellophane bundle on their desk. As I unwrapped mine, picking through redhots and pastel candy hearts that said "Be Mine", "Kiss Me" and "Oh You!" I was full to bursting with Valentine love.

When spring come, a chunk of Miss Baker's paycheck went for marshmallow bunnies, fuzzy yellow chicks, colored jellybeans. The basket on every desk had a decorated sugar egg with a tiny scene hiding inside. Miss Baker didn't have no kids. She said we was her children.

· · · · · · · ·

On the first school day after Easter vacation, Miss Baker had on a starched white linen dress, white patent leather shoes and her black hair pulled back in a perky ponytail. I was sure my teacher was the most beautiful one in the whole world. That day during spelling class, we were taking turns at the letter table. She set up a low table with wooden letters, so we could practice making words.

BoJack and Peanut managed to get at the table together, and went right to work spelling words that most second graders didn't know. Shit, fuk, pis. When Miss Baker came around to check their work, BoJack could see on her face that he had finally gone too far. He knew he'd be sent to the principal's office, and he was gonna get it.

He bolted out the door of the school and across the field thinking that he would be long gone, safe from his furious teacher. But when he looked over his shoulder, there she come, charging like a bull after him. He dived down under a barbed wire fence and right through a mud puddle, and she was right behind him. She kept going through the cow chips and the muck, finally caught him, pulled him up by his ears and marched him back to the principal's office. BoJack had not known that his teacher Miss Baker was a track star in high school. When I tried to look at her ruined, muddied white dress and bramble scratched ankles, down to the heel broken off her shoe, I was plumb blinded by the admiration in my eyes.

That afternoon I was still daydreaming, looking out the window where Miss Baker had run like a super woman. I wanted to be just like her someday. Out across the concrete block wall, two cur dogs caught my eye. One had climbed up on the other from behind and humped hisself over like a bale of hay. My jaw dropped wide open.

"Miss Baker," I asked in all innocence, "What in the world are them two dogs out yonder doing?"

The back row boys whistled and cackled. Corrine turned red as the top end of a turnip, but she never skipped a beat. "Well, Anna Grace, that is how doggies show love. That's how they hug!"

• • • • • • • •

That night, Pearlie was spread out in the big easy chair lookin'
greens. All of a sudden I felt so filled up with love for her I just
went right over, straddled her big brown leg and started humpin'
away. Pearlie slapped at me all crazy and jumped up hollerin'.
Greens went everwhere.

"Lord Jesus, child, you done lost your mind!"

I lay weepy on the braided rug where I'd been cast off, my
feelings hurt bad, and then I sulked off to my room thinking
Pearlie didn't want no little white child showing her love.

• • • • • • • • •

The day we were weaving colored ribbons around the Maypole
at school, Sudy Templeton gave birth to a six pound girl she
named Marlene May. Mama reported it was a long and difficult
travail, which changed Sudy's opinion that laboring mothers were
nothin' but big old crybabies. Baby Marlene looked nothing at
all like Mr. Templeton, but Mama claimed Faron was right there
passing out cigars with pink bows. Faron's mother came later that
afternoon and brought with her an entire layette, lovingly hand
knit in pink baby wool.

• • • • • • • • • •

Dory and Pearlie sat together at a corner of the kitchen table,
cooling cups of lemon tea. Dory broke a piece of shortbread in half
and shared it, looking over into the sad brown face. After Dory
finished her shortbread, she pulled a basket from the center of
the table and took up her handwork. She worked a needle up and
down, impaling tiny beads onto a shawl she was making. When
she finished the last row, she held out the few dozen leftover
beads to Pearlie.

"Just throw these away hon... not enough of them to save."

Pearlie took the beads and walked over to the trashcan,
flapping open the lid with her foot on the pedal. But those beads,

they slid into the pocket of her apron as she smiled. She sat back down and circled a spoon in her teacup.

"Do you ever think of Hum, Pearlie?" Mama asked warily.

"Yes'm, I sees Hum everwhar I looks." She glanced out the back door. "Hum, he out dere diggin in de dirt fo a fishin' worm right dis minute. Clear as day."

"We're really not so different, are we Pearlie?" She said, Adam toddling across the kitchen floor in her mind's eye.

"No'me, we both done cryin' time. Our boys done in de ground, cept'n when dey walkin' round in our heads."

· · · · · · · · · ·

A half-mile out of town, where Blackshale road came to be called Highway 21, was a grocery where the screen door was always slamming. Farmers stopped in at lunch to sit on barrels, play checkers, listen to the radio, suck down a grape soda, eat baloney and crackers, predict the weather, and gossip.

The groceries were stacked on tall shelves behind a long wooden counter where my Aunt Nettie Tollett stood up at the cash register, taking orders, collecting goods from the shelves, and ringing up totals. Sometimes, she fed cash money into the compartments of the register drawer, closing it with a clink. More often, she wrote up little tickets and slid them angrily under wire clips where a stack of the month's charges for each customer collected, waiting for payday. The customers came in every month on payday and paid their bill, or not. Nettie Tollett, who Mama called a study in parsimony, had never bought nothing on credit and she had a grievous disdain for them that did. Most of her customers was living hand to mouth, as those in Blackshale who were better off, the ones who had housemaids and played tennis and golf at the Pineville Country Club, refused to walk in Aunt Nettie's store. When asked, "Where do you trade?" by one of their friends, they'd likely say, "Well, not with that hateful Nettie Tollett! I'll drive to Pineville or even all the way to Knoxville before I trade with her!"

She called her one worker "the niggerboy." He made twenty-five cents an hour, unloading delivery trucks and stocking the shelves. He couldn't read, so she'd have to place one can of hominy or black-eyed peas on the shelf so he could put the rest up by matching the labels. That made her mad and she ranted about how stupid he was all the rest of the day. She hated anyone of color, but then again she hated everyone, except for her teenage son, Perry. Especially me. All along, I had a real strong feelin' Aunt Nettie didn't care much for me, and I didn't know what I'd done to deserve her hateful stares and the irate cluck of her tongue.

Aunt Nettie and them lived up over the store, too. Their apartment, always smellin' like cooked cabbage, had tall ceilings and all the rooms were lined up along one long, lightless hall with wooden floors that echoed footsteps. There was something scary about the emptiness of that hall with no pictures or windows. Aunt Nettie was Pap's sister-in-law, the widow of his older brother. Once in a while, Dory and Frank would leave me over there when they went somewheres, and I was not real happy to go except for seeing my only cousin Perry, older than me and my champion. Aunt Nettie and Perry were as different as two people could be. Aunt Nettie was bitter as gall, strict, just plain creepy. The only time I ever saw a put-on smile on her face was when she sold somebody a can of snuff or a sack of flour and she felt the cash money rustle in her hand. Perry was jolly ever day of his life. How he got that way with her for a ma I'll never know.

Mama and Frank never much took vacations. They just couldn't get away from the never-ending business of death, but one day Mama put her foot down and threatened to leave Pap if he didn't take her to Nashville. She had her heart set on going to the Grand Ol' Opry and eating fried chicken biscuits at the Loveless Cafe. So Frank got a room at the Music City Motor Court for a whole week of second honeymoon. Thing was, a pinched up bundle of nerves like Mama could never really relax. Pap told me later that Mama had took the vacuum cleaner from home and hauled it up the sidewalk into their room, pleased as punch. He said the first hour when he floated out in the blue concrete swimming pool looking up at the sky and soaking up the late spring sunshine, he could hear the whine of that vacuum cleaner sucking furiously on the floor of unit number 12.

I'd never been nowhere much without Mama and Pap, except school. That week without them broadened my horizons in many ways. Right off, Perry walked me out in the woods and taught me how to smoke rabbit tobacco. When Aunt Nettie was busy with some customers, we prowled around in the store, and he said I could have anything I wanted, so I loaded up on penny candy and pop. Then he took me down the highway in his jalopy to the drag races. I loved riding in Perry's car. I'd get in the back seat and turn myself clean upside down and hang my head off in the floor, so I could wave at the people behind us with my bare feet. At the races Perry bought me greasy, salty peanuts in a little paper bag. I reckon maybe some of them peanuts was spoilt.

By that night, I had worked up a little bellyache. It was just a tiny one, but I commenced whining to Aunt Nettie. Perry was gone on a double date to the drive-in, and I was feeling left behind anyways. She left the room for a while, and then came back in and demanded stiffly, "Come here!" She got me by the wrist and took me into her bedroom. The walls were a shiny, sick and pale green with no pictures, just the kind of creepy room I'd expect her to have. A bare light bulb, swinging from the tall ceiling by its own long frayed cord, burned with a buzz. On the bed there were towels spread out. Next to them was a faded pink rubber bag, and loops of pink rubber tubing with a hard plastic bulby thing on the end. There was an enamel pan with bubbly water. I had a bad feeling.

"What is that?" I asked. I was only a child, but I was trying to think of where that tube might go. No place seemed good.

"Lay up on the bed. I'm going to fix your tummy ache." Her eyes didn't look like fixing and caring auntie eyes. They looked mean, anxious to hurt. I didn't budge, and she narrowed her eyes. "Please... don't be tiresome," she wheezed with a briny breath, and clamped her hand on my shoulder, forcing me toward the bed.

I minded her. I'd been taught to mind. She pulled down my panties, and when she told me to roll on my side and bend up my knees, I did. And when she spread my butt cheeks apart and jammed in the bulb, I didn't say a word, but my tears were falling hot and fast. All at once, I felt a hot cramping rush, filling me up with pain as she held the bag high up in the air. It hurt bad and felt wrong.

"Take it out!" I screamed. She laughed. I had finally seen a smile on Aunt Nettie's face that was all for me. I reached back and pulled it out myself and flung it straight at her. I rolled off the bed and ran out, bubbling a trail of soapy shitwater down the middle of the long, dark hall.

Aunt Nettie yelled confusing, scathing words after me, "You know you're not their real child like your brother was!" At the end of the hallway, I crumpled into a ball and sobbed.

Perry came home at his curfew time, ten o'clock sharp. I was sitting on the sofa with swollen eyes. "Oh God, what happened!" Perry said. "Did she give you an enema?"

"A what?" I queried, not knowin' the word. Apparently enemas were a favorite hobby of Aunt Nettie's, a regular feature of Perry's childhood. He slammed down his car key and stalked down the hall.

"Ma, what did you do?" She was in her bed reading her Bible out loud. "Anna Grace is not your child to do with as you want to!"

"No," I heard her say, "Anna Grace ain't nobody's child, she is just a little bastard born of some shameless whore's sin." Then she returned to her scripture reading, the words of God marching out of her mouth in a forced cadence.

When Pap and Mama came back the next morning, Perry took me right home and sat down with them on the divan. "Uncle Frank, don't ever leave Anna Grace with Ma again. She's got some funny ideas, and you don't want Anna Grace left alone with 'em." He came over to me and hugged me, "I'll come over here to see you from now on, little cousin. Don't you worry!"

When Mama tucked me in that night, I told her what Aunt Nettie had done, and what she'd said. "What did she mean, Mama, about me having a brother and not being your real child? And Mama what is a bastard?" She pulled me up into her breast and I could hear her breath catch, feel her trembling.

"Before you, Pap and I did have a little baby boy. He died from a bad heart when he was still little. But as for you not being our real child, honeypie, you are as real as a child can get!" She looked down into my teary eyes and softly traced under them with a fingertip. "I think maybe Aunt Nettie is jealous that we have such a pretty little girl to love!"

· · · · · · · ·

At the end of each school day, Corrine Baker walked back down School Bell Road to her small white house, carrying with her the afterimages of Anna Grace Tollett's face. That day's smiles, flashes of insight, grimaces of concentration, were carefully filed away in a catalog of poignant memories. She sat down to her supper alone, and tried not to think of her daughter at the other woman's table. The end of the school year loomed ever closer. Her treasured year would soon be over and then the precious glimpses of Anna would be fewer and farther between. Corrine could feel the sad, empty days coming, like a blackening storm.

· · · · · · · ·

I like to think, lookin' back, that I was the luminous center of Mama's world, but that woman had so much energy for putting things right that she spread herself far on out into the Blackshale community. Tollett Funeral Home was seven miles down the road from the clump of small businesses that was Blackshale, the town. On the other side of town, was Blackshale Hospital. To tell the truth, it was more of a clinic with its one part-time doctor and twenty beds. Anything beyond a normal birth or a garden variety end of life was quickly sent on to Knoxville or Nashville.

Because of her half-hearted whack at a nursing degree, Dory was the one folks called when getting to the hospital would take too long, and her reputation for calm under fire turned her into the community fixer for just about every sort of crisis. Most of the time, it was simple ailments - thrushes and chilblains and vapors.

Living right there at the funeral home, she was naturally around when a family needed a helping hand. Once word had got around about Dory birthing her own baby alone, she became a local obstetric legend. Even though her own experience had been an accidental and one-time thing, she was thought of as an expert on birthing around Blackshale. In the country, there were women who still distrusted hospitals and preferred home confinement. She began to get calls in the middle of the night to help out with this or that home birth, and qualifications aside, she was a caring woman who couldn't bear to say "no" to anyone in need. As time passed, she experienced the gamut of birth scenarios and became a skilled midwife. She knew when the situation called for the hospital and she always got them there.

The family business provided Mama with a handy list of warnings for a child growing up. Keep in mind every child within a hundred miles who did or didn't quite end up dead was on her radar since she helped out with small disasters and knew everything else that went on, mostly from listening in on the party line. Every kid that went sticking a shelly bean up his nose, sniffin' the gas tank, or thinkin' they could fly off the barn roof was held out to me as an example of a child gone bad. Dory Tollett was haunted by the dead children of Blackshale. Even though she didn't have much use for the mountain people with their countrified talk and weak looking eyes, she was still torn up bad when Pap had a child on the table downstairs. So when Mr. Murphy showed up on our doorstep again, this time to bury his baby Charley, Mama took it real hard.

Jake and Harley had got aholt of some beer, two six-packs, and were tryin' to shed their little brother for a while so they could go drink it. Jake held Charley face down in a red clay ditch, while Harley weighted him down with big rocks until he couldn't move. They didn't give a rat's ass that Charley, tough and mean as he was for his age, was snivelin'. They took off popping bottle caps, heading up the mountainside to a favorite bluff where they could look out over Blackshale, see who could cuss the worst and talk about which girls from school they'd like to screw. That led them to drop their pants and see who could jerk off the longest stream while moaning those girls' names. After four beers each, they were feeling good. After six, they didn't even notice the black thunderheads rising up behind them. There was just a single bolt of lightning before the sky opened up.

"Oh shitfire! Charley's still down in the ditch!" Harley jumped up and pulled Jake to his feet. They stumbled down the trail, laughing at their own wobbly legs, but halfway down the mountain their laughter died when the rain began to pelt down harder, by then a real gully washer. By the time they got back down to the ditch, water was raging over Charley's head. They fell on their knees scrabbling at the rocks, but it was too late. Jake pressed his weight down on Charley's chest, and water came gushing out, but the little body was lifeless.

Jake scooped Charley up over his shoulder and yelled at Harley, "Run down and start the truck!"

Harley bounded up the steps and through the screen door, ripping the truck keys off their hook. "What's goin'on?" Walter Murphy boomed. Harley kept moving on out the door.

"It's Charley, Pa! He... he... must a fell in the ditch! We gotta get 'im to Dory Tollett!"

Jake, with Charley limp as a dishrag around his neck, got to the truck just as the screen door flung open and his pa's face went rigid. They all crammed in the truck and flew down Rambler Road in a panic, raising dust and slinging gravel.

"What the hell boys? Jake?" Jake looked sideways at Harley, glad there was no time to answer as they slid sideways into the parking lot of Tollett's. Harley ran up on the porch and banged on the bell.

Dory came to the door, wiping her hands on her apron, and when she saw the boy, she yelled, "Put him on the floor." She laid her ear down on his chest for some time and when she rose up, she asked "How long has he been like this?"

"Too damn long!" Walter Murphy spat.

"I'm terribly sorry but you're right, Mr. Murphy, he's gone."

Murphy tensed his jaw, fighting tears. He straightened up tall and after staring out the picture window for a time, started in punching both boys with all his fury. Dory ran to the hall and screamed at Frank down through the hole in the floor. Frank bolted up the stairs and slid in the blood already splattering on the linoleum. Somehow, spinning around on the slick floor, he managed to get in between the three and break them apart. He stood panting for a minute, looking down at Charley and then he spoke gently.

"You fellers, you go on home now. We'll take good care of your boy for you. Come on back in the morning when you've had time to think things over."

The Murphys glared at each other a few seconds longer before they turned and sulked down the steps. The truck clattered out onto Blackshale highway, and backfired all the way to Rambler Road.

Normally, Dory was not welcome in the embalming room when Frank was working, nor did she want to be there. But this time, she followed her husband as he carried the little boy downstairs. He tenderly laid the child on the slab and placed the child-sized head block under his neck. Dory laid her head over on the little body and began to weep violently. Frank gathered her up in his arms, but she could not be consoled. She was remembering her sorrow for the unwanted child at his mother's wake, and she was reliving the loss of her own baby boy.

"I've got to do my work now honey, you go on up and check on Anna Grace."

Dory rose and went up the stairs, counting every step in a broken voice.

At suppertime, Walter Murphy was sitting at the kitchen table not eating. He was holding the only picture he had of Shirley in a tense grip, the one where she was standin' up dead with her family. He was having a serious talk with her when heavy boots clomped up on the porch. It was the sheriff knocking, and it wasn't by any means the first time. Sheriff Raby had mor'n a suspicion about the bootlegging and although he turned his head away from it in return for a case here and there, he still had to make a show of upliftin' the law. He'd been there a few times about the twins, who'd been working their way up the petty criminal ladder. You might say Walter and Sheriff Raby were on a first name basis. Walter stood up and went to the door.

"Come on in, Harlan, set down."

The two slouched down across from each other. Raby lit up a

Camel and offered one across the table.

"Walter, I was mighty sorry to hear about your boy, mighty sorry." Murphy poked a dirty fingernail at a cherry on the torn vinyl tablecloth.

"I was wondering if Harley and Jake would walk out and show me where Charley, uh... well, you know, where it happened and all."

Murphy started up, "Now look here, Harlan, we've been through enough..." but the sheriff cut him off.

"Fact is, Walter, a feller was in this evening with his little girl. She come home tellin' him that she had been up in the woods and had to pee so she gets behind a tree. About the time she gets her drawers pulled up, she hears these boys coming and was skeered, so she kept on hiding. Says she saw two big boys putting great big rocks on a little boy in a ditch. She couldn't lift the rocks, but she told the little feller she'd run and get some help. That was before the storm. By the time she and her paw got back up there, he was gone."

It was nearin' dark when Jake and Harley led their Pa and the Sheriff to the ditch. The sheriff flipped his flashlight over the ground for several yards until the beam came to rest, shaking, on a stack of big rocks.

Back at the Murphy's kitchen table, Walter and the Sheriff opened a bottle of home brew and commenced to talk man-to-man over the cherry tablecloth.

"Look Walter, this here is a serious thing. Manslaughter, might near. Even if they are just fourteen, these boys of yours have been headed bad to worse for a while now. The best thing to do here is to find them a spot at the reform school over in Nashville. They could straighten right up. If you'll let me do that, I think we can just keep this out of the courts. Maybe give 'em a fighting chance.

What do you say?"

Walter took another swig. "I say, how fast can you get 'em outta here? I have a wake to see to."

· · · · · · · ·

The whole back wall of our apartment was made of windows, from the wood floor to the twelve feet tall ceilings; it was a space where you could breath deep. All day a north light bathed the long living room. On the front side of the building next to the road, were the smaller rooms, the kitchen, the bathrooms and bedrooms, and the laundry. Mama's kitchen was still big enough for a massive, heavy wood table that sat on chunky turned wood legs. It was square, eight feet by eight. Our lives revolved around that table. Seemed like there was always somebody peckin' or poundin' at that beaten wood, carrying out one job or another. Sometimes Mama, sometimes Pearlie, sometimes me. The best times were when all of us were working together, listening to the radio. When Mama finished her task, she'd tap the table ten times to mark the end of it. Then she'd smile over at me and say, "I love you special Anna Grace, I love you all the way to Heaven and back again!"

Pearlie would sit on a high stool, chopping vegetables for homemade soup or chow chow, beating her dough roller against a piecrust, or breaking up string beans. Dory and Pearlie loved each other, and enjoyed workin' side by side, but once in a great while they didn't see eye-to-eye. Mama broke her beans exactly an inch-and-a-half long. No longer, no shorter. If by chance, she misjudged and snapped at the wrong place, whoosh, the bean went down in the garbage sack with the strings and the too far-gone shelly beans. This, Pearlie could not bear. She had grown up dirt poor. They ate things Mama wouldn't even be able to look at without barfin', chittlin', possum, squirrel, piggie foot. The thought of wasting a bit of bean, just because it was not the same size as the others in the pan, made Pearlie loco.

One day, they was breaking beans together, which I knew right up front was a recipe for disaster. Sure enough, Pearlie threw a short bean in the pan. Mama fished it out. Pearlie grunted. Then a bit later a too-long one went in. Right out it came. Finally, Mama let out a deep breath and sputtered, "Oh shoot! Just leave this job to me Pearlie. You go out back and wring us a chicken neck."

Pearlie's feelings were hurt, but she was mad, too. She huffed, "You fixin' to waste them fine lookin' beans." She stomped off, and that chicken got his neck wrung good. Mama would have never been mean to Pearlie, or nobody, but she just couldn't help needing everthing to be just right and in a row, done a certain way. When Pearlie went out back, Mama finished breaking the beans into perfect pieces, all the same size, all three hundred twenty-six of them.

· · · · · · · ·

Mama had a twenty-two rifle that had belonged to her granny. She tried over and over to knock pop cans off the back fence, but she had yet to hit one. She wanted to make that can flip up and spin in the air, like Frank could do every time without even tryin'.

That rifle held a fascination for her. She barely remembered a spring afternoon on her granny's front porch - strange chatter coming from around the blue birdhouse nailed to the porch rail, her child's fingers reaching out to explore the hole, and granny's words, forceful, "Dory stop, back up!" Her granny coming up behind, raising the rifle steady into a single blast. She well recalled the birdhouse in pieces, the copperhead snake twitching in a yellow slime of cracked eggs, the authority of the gun in her granny's hands. I recall her tellin' of it ag'in and ag'in. Looking back, there could a been an omen about that rifle floating in mama's voice, if I'd just been paying close enough attention.

Early in their marriage, Dory started nagging Pap to take her quail hunting. He refused, but she just kept on nagging.

"Heavens to Murgatroyd woman! Do you think I want to be around when you're learning to hit the broad side of a barn? I'd end up on my own slab! What business does a woman have traipsing through the field? Why darlin' you'd just get ticks up between those pretty legs of yours!" Frank laughed from clean down in his belly.

Dory dropped it, but she kept on turning the idea over in her mind. She had her heart set on being out in the autumn air with him, feeling the power of her granny's gun in her hands, watching the quail tumble from the sky, and then bringing them home to fry up in her granny's black iron skillet.

· · · · · · · ·

A lot went on through that square hole in the floor of our apartment. They'd yell back and forth through it all day long, pass Pap down a sandwich and an Orange Crush for lunch, drop down or lift up a pet or a visiting small child. Sometimes, it was only a hand that appeared with a summons or the snapping of fingers. Once, on my birthday, Pap yelled, "Lookee there, Anna Grace!" and I turned to see a red balloon floating up through the hole. I squealed with glee 'cause I loved balloons.

Of a spring afternoon, I come running in from the riverbank, thrilled to have found a flesh colored balloon hanging from a stick out over the bank. I yelled up through the hole, "Mama! Look what I found!"

I passed it up, sticky and dripping man goo, through the square in the floor and couldn't understand why she was actin' hysterical. "Anna Grace, go scrub your hands! I mean good! Right now!"

The day after my eighth birthday, Pap yelled up through the hole that I, Anna Grace Tollett, had gotten a letter. He lifted it up into my eager fingers. I'd never got a letter before. The envelope was pale pink and smelled of some single, vaguely familiar flower.

Just in general, I was sick to death of odorous flowers, thinking of them as putrid instead of pleasing, but this smell made me feel happy. I carried the letter over to Mama's roll top desk, fished out her pink plastic Fuller Brush Man letter opener, and sliced carefully under the flap. The letter was penned by hand. On the single sheet were a few words that made not one bit of sense to a eight-year-old girl who had no boyfriends and nothing but ordinary ideas about her birth.

"I hold you in my heart."

2029 Morning Glory Ridge

My screen beeps and comes to life. There is the lovely Daphne, three inches high from waist to frizzy bun, humped over in a little video window.

"Anna Grace! Wanna widgie out to the arbor with us? It's a pretty day!"

I meet them in the lobby. Mary B. walks on her own steam and the rest of us widgie outside, down the sidewalk, and out to the garden area. The arbor is enclosed in dense topiary, with Morning Glory vines growing across the top. We arrange ourselves on the benches and sniff the fresh air in appreciation.

"I brought y'all a little something to cheer you up! You poor *old* people."

Apparently Pauline knows what's coming, "Oooooo! Happy, happy me!"

Daphne pulls out some joints from a red Chinese pouch, passes them around, and hands out matches.

"Oh my," I protest weakly, "I'm not sure my old brain can take this. I've only done it once before."

"Trust me, it can take it!"

"What can they do to us if we get caught?"

"I guess they can kick us out."

"Oh, OK, that would be good! Fantastic!" I light mine. After a short time, the morning glories become so enthralling! They are swirling limpid pools of purple and pink. I'm fixated on a hummingbird burying his beak down deep in a flower. "Oh look at the pretty bird... ooooh, it's like beak sex."

Pauline inhales deeply, "Honey, this is some fine shit! Where did you get it? I mean, it's not like we get over to the high school a lot."

Daphne is already stoned, "Girrrlfriend, this is fine Mexican shit. I got it from Julio! Ok! Now everybody has to tell about their first time, Sex, not weed!"

Normally, I would have opted out of that game right off. But, it's like I'm watching the group from a distance, so it seems oddly harmless.

Mary B. is going first.

"Girls, if you can believe this, it was long after my honeymoon. I kept my pretty little knees together just like my mama told me to until I got married. I was the bride of a banker's son, president of the biggest bank in Knoxville, old money. My mama thought I'd bagged myself a real treasure! We had a huge wedding - showers all over the place. I got every bit of my silver flatware and china, and we went on a month long jaunt of Europe for our wedding trip. The first night, we drove to Memphis and stayed at the Peabody - damn shitting ducks all over the place. But Lord, it was elegant!

"Up in our room it was the whole nine yards, coming out of the bathroom a shy bride with my flimsy negligee on, and we kissed and kissed and played and played, but he couldn't get it up! Ever! He never did! Oh... well... he was kind enough to give me a little finger consolation prize, but dammit I had saved up my o-so-precious cherry in a savings account, and I wanted the big payoff with interest!

"Honestly! I think I was mighty reasonable about it girls. I waited three years for him to get his Mister working, and then I had myself an affair with my harpsichord instructor. Oh dear GOD. He had scruples, about me being married and all. So I had to pine after him for a year. I was so wet I was afraid the seat would be syrupy when I got up from my lesson. Finally one day, I leaned over and placed my hand on his member instead of middle C. He fell apart, since he had been yearning too. We went up like a house afire!

"I had intercourse with that man every which way, grunting and groaning, making more music than that harpsichord ever did.

Once he even lifted me up on the keyboard and my ass pounded out an original tune on the keys while he kept the percussion rhythm coming from the front. Oh girls, what a love song!

"I went back home and told James I wanted a divorce on the grounds of failure to perform marital duties. He nodded, bland-faced and resigned. I don't think he ever wanted to get married anyway. I got the house and all the damn silver and my music teacher, too. Lord knows I deserved it!"

Now it's Pauline's turn. After a ladylike inhalation of the joint for courage, she begins. "Well, compared to that, I guess I was a slut, a pure slut! However, I would like to point out that I lasted three years in the back seat of my boyfriend's car, parked on country roads, in the moonlight, the sweet smelling summer night air, before I gave in. Kissing, tongue kissing and then when his hand was in my blouse feeling up a nipple, I felt the first buds of unstoppable desire. There was a lot of dry humpin' going on in that car. Every date night, a little more, a little farther, a little bit more naughty.

"He slipped his hand into my panties and through my down there hair, fiddling with my, my, you know, my magic place. I learned what an orgasm was. Well, I was headed for trouble then, wasn't I? Now girls, you know it, I was sunk. It wasn't too long before we were in the back seat, taking off our pants, him laying on top of me, rubbing up against me with his damp tighty whities.

"I wanted so badly to be good, but over the next few weeks he pulled down his underwear and mine, and pressed the slimy head of his shaft against me, rubbing, rubbing. Then one night, when I could stand it no longer, I spread my legs wide and pulled him in. He pushed through, the stinging pain overcome by the pleasure. I was his, he was mine, I was a woman, with all the unspeakable pleasures and troubles that brings, for the rest of my life." Everyone was silent, thinking to themselves how that was the story of so many girl's lives.

Daphne takes a long drag and rolls her eyes, "Well, my pets, you'll never believe this one! My most progressive mama took me to a professional! She said she wanted me to learn what it was like to have foreplay and real sexual satisfaction, so when I finally picked out the man I wanted, I would know if he was a 'slam, bam, thank you mam' kind of guy I'd be better off passin' up! So for my 18th birthday she took me to a cathouse and got me a real tomcat. She had made sure he was clean and free from disease, but knowledgeable in the science of sex! Did that man ever take his time with me. He knew I was a virgin getting my sweet eighteen present, so he took it soooo slooow, and got me hotter than an egg frying on an Arizona sidewalk! Later, when I met Rex, my soul mate, I was pleased to find out that he was not a slam bam man, and we had a wonderful married life. I told Rex about the male hooker and he was ok with it. He even laughed at my mama's unorthodox parenting tactics."

All eyes are on me. I blink back at them through the smoke.

I chicken out. "Uh, well, actually, my first time is too hideous to share. I'm sorry! I'm just not ready girls. Maybe another time. Could I pass?" I know I'm babbling, but I can't seem to help myself.

"Geez!" Daphne exclaims, "I got more than I bargained for." We all sit quietly, mired in introspection, and let Mary Jane's song play out. Then we walk and widgie back to our rooms, and fade away into deep, sound naps.

1957 Blackshale

Don't know why, but I hid that letter from Mama. Frank Tollett forgot all about it and never brought it up. From time-to-time I'd pull it out of the secret compartment in the bottom of my jewelry box and feel confused. Something about the smell of that letter made me strangely happy, but I just couldn't think what it was. One day when we were cleaning up my room, I heard the music box playing "Waltz of the Flowers" and out of the corner of my eye saw the ballerina twirling round and round, then Mama was holding the letter out to me.

"Who is this from, honey?" she asked, her voice tense and rising. There was a little tremble in her voice, which made me feel bad for her. I had no good answer neither and that made it even worse.

"Why Ma, tellin' the honest truth," I said, "I don't rightly know. It came one day and I wondered if it was a surprise from you, that maybe you thought I would be tickled to get something of my own from the mailman. Now Mama, don't you worry! I know it ain't from a boy, cause even if one ever liked me as a girlfriend, which they would not, they'd never write on pink paper and talk proper like that. That letter is a mystery to me."

"No, it's not from me," Dory mused thoughtfully. She turned the envelope over in her hand and inspected the postmark. Of course she did not know the name of the woman who wrote those words, but she had a very good idea who she was. And that very good idea scared the liver out of her.

• • • • • • • •

Corrine Baker met John Evan Miller, the new seventh grade Literature teacher, at the first teachers' meeting of the year. She had just returned to Blackshale after a long and difficult summer. Her father had died from prostate cancer gone quickly amok, and Bernice had made it clear that Corry was needed at home all summer to provide emotional support. Losing a father suddenly had been hard; gaining that much of her mother for an entire summer was almost as distressing. Her relief to be back in Blackshale, where Anna Grace was, and where her mother was not, was overwhelming.

It was not her imagination that John Evan made eye contact several times during the meeting, nor was it coincidence that he hit the break room for a coffee refill at the same time she did every day that fall. So she was not particularly surprised when he asked her to the staff Christmas party. John Evan was light on his feet, leading her expertly as they tango'd, rhumba'd, and jitterbugged under strings of colored Christmas lights.

After that awkward night among their inquisitive peers, when she spilled Christmas punch on the crotch of his trousers, and he closed the car door on her dress, they began to see each other regularly. They had sex early on, urgent, breathless, amazingly inventive. She was lonely, she was hurting, and the passionate intimacy soon became a priority for both of them. Compared to the typical Blackshale male, John Evan was well-spoken and well-read. He told her he had grown up an only child on a horse farm in Virginia and had graduated from UVA. He omitted parts though, the repeated stints in a private sanitarium, the drugs he took daily to keep him from descending into grinding depression.

He hid his issues well. John Evan had a country gentleman quality about him that Corrine found intriguing, and he reveled in his identity as an academic. He played bridge and chess and he gardened. For sport, he enjoyed hunting quail. She found him deeply empathetic and sensitive, which suited perfectly her tragic history. That he loved her intensely, almost crazily, in a way she could never return, was not bothersome to her. She was numbed by the loss of her child, in a perpetual state of mourning, and was sure the gratitude-laced affection she felt for John Evan was the most she'd ever be able to muster with anyone. So, she married him.

Before the wedding, Corrine spilled her guts. One night, after a time of intense intimacy, she gave John Evan her secrets. She told him about her daughter, and the plan she had concocted to be near her. More than she loved him, she needed him, she needed someone to know the pain she was living with day after day. He listened carefully, then jumped up in agitation and rushed to the window, twisting his hands in front of him as he peered out into the blackness. He stood motionless for a long time. She waited in misery, not yet party to his reaction and terrified she had lost him because of her secret past.

When he finally turned back to her, he was weeping. "You've been so brave. I don't know how you bear it." She sighed with relief, knowing she wasn't alone any more.

· · · · · · · ·

Mama claimed that life had a way of givin' and takin'. If something really bad happened to you, then something good would come right along to balance it out, and vicey versy. She called it "karma." My life in second grade had been wonderful, but now I was in third grade, and bad karma had sure enough struck. Its name was Eugenia Peavine.

Miss Peavine's butt, as I was forced to view it when she was writing on the chalkboard, stuck out like a shelf. Looking at that butt was better than looking at her face though. When she turned around to lower her mismatched eyes at us, she was so ugly most of us just had to look away. Her face was a collection of unfortunate landmarks: warts, moles big and small, overachieving facial hairs. Her eyes looked off in different directions, and I swear one was bigger than the other. I knew she couldn't help how she looked, so I tried real hard to be kind and give her an encouraging smile.

Like my Aunt Nettie, Miss Peavine hated children, so she just naturally assumed my smile was a mocking one. She stood me up against the blackboard on my tiptoes for a solid hour, straining to keep my nose in a red circle of chalk. "That will teach you to make fun of people!" she grumbled.

. . . .

That year before Christmas, Mama got up her nerve and took me down to Florida to meet my grandmother for the first time.

"Now when we get down there honey, you can call her Meemaw," Mama had instructed as we shot down the narrow highway lined with tall straight pines.

Her ma was holed up in a tin trailer out on a Palatka scrub thicket. I quickly knew why I'd never met my grandma before. Mama's daddy had passed in Greenville, and was soon replaced with a bottle and a cloud of cigarette smoke.

"I'm tickled to finally meet you Meemaw." I ventured cautiously.

She looked down at me and squinted her eyes.

"I ain't your Goddamn Meemaw," She fumed flatly in a spew of whisky breath, and those shocking words were the last I ever heard from her. We had never went to church, but I'd never heard nobody take the Lord's name in vain, not even them devilish Murphys. I did not like that. I decided right then and there I didn't care much for Meemaw neither.

After two days of trying to talk her mother into going to AA, Dory slapped down a hundred dollar bill on the counter and scooted me out the door saying, "Sometimes, Anna Grace, people are just beyond help."

She slipped into a phone booth to call Frank. I could see her through the dirty glass panel, crying and twisting a hank of hair. When she got back in the car, she reached out and stroked my forehead with a shaky hand.

"Hey doodlebug, you've been a good sport and you deserve something nice. You and me are going to the beach, and then I'm taking you someplace really special before we head back home."

• • • • • • • • •

I'd never had my mama to myself, just us two. We laid out there in the white sand and ran up and back chasing the bubbly edge of the ocean. Then we scraped up stinky seashells by the bagfuls. At night, we went to the noisy boardwalk and ate pizza pie and cotton candy and sucked on snow cones under the colored lights. I was coated head to toe with sandy grit, sunburned and bug bit all over - so happy I could bust. And this was even before we went to the special place.

When we left the beach, we headed inland, and I laid down next to Mama in the front seat of the car. She rested her arm across me, and for some reason I started sucking her elbow. She gave me a startled look, and then she smiled, "Are you still my baby?"

I tucked my head under her arm, embarrassed. All of a sudden, I had just needed her so bad it hurt. It was like I somehow knew she would not always be there. Before I drifted off to sleep, I whispered, "Where we going to, Mama?"

I barely heard her say "Weeki Wachi." I didn't have the slightest idea of what that was, and was too worn out to ask.

• • • • • • • • •

I stared up at the expanse of glass and aqua blue water, mesmerized. The mermaids were the most beautiful things I'd ever seen. After that trip, I saw them everywhere, and they haunted my dreams. From my window seat I could swear I spied them in the river, their serpentine tails rolling in the moonlight, hydrophile scales shimmering. If I woke in the middle of the night, I was sure I could hear their siren songs, inhuman harmonies cooing and keening.

• • • • • • • • •

The spring of third grade was gosh awful hot and humid. I couldn't wait to get outside. It was the fifteenth of April, the magic day every year when Mama said I could finally go barefoot, so I sat down on the back porch step and peeled off my socks and shoes, dug big gobs of toe jam out from between each little piggy, and took off down the path on my tender feet. I hopped gingerly, yelling out, "Ouch, ouch, ouch, yee-ouch!"

I had myself a favorite place to hide and play, off on my own, away from the ever present danger of chores. Down behind the house just at the edge of the woods lay a red clay ditch, and only in the early spring could the scrawny trickle of muddy water almost be called a crick. A Saturday had flown by while I shaped tiny bridges and houses, dug out little roads and ponds. Somewhere over in Knoxville or Chattanooga or Nashville, children were building their towns with store bought Tinker toys or Lincoln logs, but not me! Twig, pebble, acorn, buckeye, and curly weed stuck together with a dab of pine resin was all I had to work with, and I made the best of it. By the time the sun was laying down across the top of the mountain, I had myself a whole town. When Mama yelled at me to come shuck the corn for supper, I stood up and brushed off the bits of ground litter stuck to my bottom, listening for a minute to the peepers and polliwogs tuning up, took deep breaths of sweet April air, and then I scampered on up to the house.

The next mornin' I drug the whole family down to see the surprise - my masterpiece of architecture. But before we even got to the ditch, I let out a groan of disappointment. I could see my demolished town flattened and smashed to bits. Someone had stomped it, and I knew who! That squashed town had Peanut and BoJack Murphy written all over it.

· · · · · · · ·

On Monday I come running in from school, slamming the screen door. Pearlie had been frying up pork chops, and the air was thick with meat smoke and grease. She stood at the stove, brownin' okra and spooning the crispy, done ones over on to a newspaper, "Dear Abby" soaking up lard along with the problems of the world. But that afternoon I had my own problems.

"Where's Mama at?" I blubbered.

Pearlie kept working, but she grinned over her shoulder and said in her gravely voice, "She gone over to de beauty shop."

When I'd gone to get off the bus, Peanut had pushed me out the door straight down on my knees where they ground into the rocks. Ribbons of blood ran down into my white anklets from pebbles still stuck in my knees. Pearlie wiped her hands on her apron and fetched a washcloth, some Bactine and the tin can of bandaids. After she patched me up, we sat down on the divan and, she wrapped me up in her arms. My wet face lay on her bare shoulder.

"How come your skin's brown, Pearlie?" I asked her in a teary voice.

"Child, I reckon the good Lord jes made me that way," She said with one of her big horselaughs. Pearlie laughed with her whole body. When she spoke a sentence, she spat every word out with purpose, emphasizing each one equally.

"Well, he sure done a good job!" I planted my lips on Pearlie's arm, studying on how it was not just brown but thick and smooth.

She patted my head until I stopped snubbing. "Now you dry up and come over here and hep me with these here shelly beans!"

· · · · · · · · ·

The first months of her marriage coincided with a difficult year for Corrine. After having Anna Grace in her class the whole year before, not seeing the child every day was hitting Corrine hard. John Evan listened to her tirelessly and held her when she cried, wiping her tears. Her gratitude became confused with the perception of a stronger love for him. Some men would have said "just get over it," but instead he absorbed her suffering, took it into himself, where it meshed with his madness and festered into a wound out of control, deep down where Corrine couldn't see it happening.

2029 Morning Glory Ridge

I am sitting cross-legged on my bed wearing my Frida Kahlo t-shirt and aviator goggles when the floor supervisor brings two new nurses around. Jethro Tull's "Living in the Past" is streaming into my Erapods and I'm playing air flute - bouncing up and down in time. Trudy Gundersen turns to the other new nurse, Florence Hickey, and says, "Some of them never grow up, and that's probably a good thing."

Florence scowls in disagreement. For my own amusement, I give the staff nicknames. I immediately assign "Flotilla" to Florence Hickey. She has that fat lady way of rolling down the hall like a giant warship, plus it sounds somewhat like Godzilla, a perfect match for her personality. Mrs. Gundersen doesn't get a deprecating nickname because she's a nice kind of harmless person, the sort that tells you all about her tomato plants, her gout, and the preciousness of her grandbabies.

Flotilla is the other kind. By afternoon she's tying Tiffany's wrists down at the side of her bed. I'd had experience with cruelty, and I see that appreciative glint of enjoyment in Flotilla's eyes, the vindictive smile on her face, as she pulls the restraints way too tight, cutting off the circulation in Tiffany's hands. Tiffany is panic stricken.

"Hey! What are you doing? What did she do to deserve that?" I demand.

"Mind your own beeswax, you dried-up old busybody!" she huffs.

I shrug and turn back to my eScreen, supersizing the Bingo window. But under it, in a barely visible mini-window, I fire off an eNote to the director asking if Tiffany really needs to be forcefully restrained. An answer never comes.

But that night, I wake up suddenly with a colossus lurking

over me – Flotilla! She smirks, and awakens my eScreen with a touch. My naked Anna Grace avatar is sprawled and crumpled in the Sports Plaza, virtually dead and relieved of her hands and tongue. They lay remote and bloody on the floor. As I look at my onscreen double, the avatar goes "poof" and completely disappears. Flotilla taunts me, her piercing eyes bearing down on mine, "Nobody likes a tattletale!"

At least Tiffany's restraints have been removed.

1958 Blackshale

Sudy had eventually confided in Mama the story of her married life, so they were best chums again, and for me that was good. Sudy's mother-in-law, Mrs. Templeton, had a big concrete swimming pool. In some of my best times of summer, Sudy and Mama sunbathed and cooed at little Marlene bobbing around in her life jacket while I strapped on my white rubber bathing cap and spent the summer dunked in blue chlorine. I barely came up for air.

There were other girls sometimes, friends of the Templetons, and we played mermaid creatures, sirens of the sea. We slapped across the concrete in our flippers, senses dumbed by noseclips, earplugs, and goggles. Underwater, we battled our sworn enemies, the Cyclops pool light and the evil sucking drain monster that lurked at the bottom. Even more alien creatures, boys, splashed and spun on the sparkling surface above in black inner tubes. One of them girls, older and bolder, shot up and jerked down the boys' swim trunks, laughing her head off underwater at the shriveled worms flapping between them kicking legs. In those years before my life changed abruptly, I was a usual kind of kid - mostly.

But I bet you a dollar to a donut I was the only girl in Tennessee, maybe even the whole country, who spent her days over dead people. Mama said down in New Orleans bodies were stacked up all over the place, sometimes ten high. But them girls, being dead, probably don't give much thought about what's under them. See, I am talking about Pap's secret bone yard underneath our house, which came about because of Frank Tollett's hopelessly generous nature. He had a heart of gold, and mor'n once ther'd been grieving families who could not afford his services and a plot. Some of them bodies come from down at the poor farm, and some were just those mindless and nameless who walked the street over in

Blackshale. He'd just quietly pick out a nice simple pine box and pay for it himself, wholesale, planting the deceased down in our basement, the part under our house that was an extra stretch of dirt space after the workrooms were walled in and floored with linoleum. Mama said this foolishness couldn't go on forever, as we were about to run out of room down there, and we were not going to be stacking bodies up ten high in Blackshale, Tennessee!

· · · · · · · ·

Day's work done, Pearlie two-stepped down to the basement, studying each stair and taking care to hold on tight to the rail. In her room, she stayed busy with her hands. The only relief in the dullness of the small space was one tiny square window. Under the top of the crackled wooden frame lay a sliver of sky, and under that the field and pond and meadow, teeming with life and flickering light. With each changing season, the land pulsed with frenetic energy, weedstubble shifting in the wind, the sudden jerking pathlines of birds and insects in the corner of her eye, the sweep of sunlight and cloudshadow.

· · · · · · · ·

There came about an unforeseen benefit of Corinne's alliance with John Evan. At least it seemed that way at the first. He met Frank Tollett, as fate would have it, one Saturday morning at the hardware store, where they were both stocking up early on shells for quail season.

"Quail hunter, are you?" John Evan guessed over Frank's shoulder. They fell into an easy conversation about bobwhite and the occasional pheasant, and Frank told about the one deer he had shot. "I mounted that head myself, but ended up having to give the damn thing away. Those big glassy eyes just kept following me around the room, and I came down with a bad case of guilt. Funny, after all the human bodies I have worked on, I just couldn't take that deer." John Evan laughed, and went on to answer Frank's friendly questions about where he was from, what he did for a living, whether he had a family. Frank enjoyed the chat, as most of the people he talked to all day didn't talk back. They had ended up having a regular powwow. It came up in the conversation that John Evan and his wife played bridge.

"Ah, great! We'll have a game one night then. I'll have Dory call you." Frank was thrilled to discover a new couple for bridge. Corrine was thrilled too. She now had a punched ticket into Anna's world.

· · · · · · · ·

By the time summer was breathing its last, the Friday night bridge party was a weekly thing. Dory was in her element entertaining their new friends, working her perfection on every evening. She spent the afternoons of those Fridays crafting handmade bridge tallies, choosing music for the hi-fi, placing the starched linens on the card table, waxing furniture, and arranging polished silver just so. Frank had scored himself a two-for-one, a new hunting partner and a new third and fourth for bridge. He teased Dory about being "the hostess with the mostest." Everyone was happy - especially Corrine. Corrine was glowing.

Anna Grace skipped about in taffeta serving drinks and desserts. Her beloved former teacher was right there in her house, and she had her all to herself! When it was Corrine's turn to be dummy, she'd go off hand-in-hand with Anna to her room, turning over every little girl trinket in her hungry hands. She leafed through stacks of drawings, learned the names of all nine guppies in the fishbowl, and rubbed the chenille bedspread between her fingers, all the while memorizing the sights and sounds and smells of Anna's life.

· · · · · · · ·

There had been a changing of the guard at Blackshale Grammar School. Miss Peavine had been moved to fourth grade in the hopes that the older students would grind less on her frayed nerves. Miss Peavine always chose a small, wormy child to pick on. This year it was the motherless Pinky Thomas, whose short, bony frame and haystack hair made her look unloved and vulnerable. Pinky tried to remain invisible, but Miss Peavine zero'd in on her with x-ray vision and called her to the chalkboard for a grilling. Pinky, weak in long division, was purposefully given a hard problem. Peavine knew good and well the child couldn't work it and enjoyed watching her squirm.

Pinky gave it her all, but she got lost in the middle of the problem and shuffled backward into a stall. She looked at it with tilted eyes, perplexed.

"Have you been taking your homework problems home at night, Miss Thomas?" Peavine asked in a razor sharp voice.

"I been aimin' to," Pinky peeped. A chorus of titters filled the classroom.

"Well?" Miss Peavine challenged in a sarcastic tone, her voice rising and hardening, "It's certainly not going to work itself!"

Pinky grinned, "Too bad, hit's lookin' like I ain't goin'to neither." The kids beat their desks and rolled their heads with laughter. A few boys hooted.

Oooo, that made Peavine mad as an old wet hen. She reached in her desk for a roll of cellophane tape and turned on Pinky, slamming her against the black board.

"Stay there!" she screamed while she taped a fat "X" across the girl's mouth. Pinky's lips flattened against the tape. "We'll see how much talking back you do now! You, missy smart mouth, are going to stand here the rest of the day, and not move a muscle. You hear me?" Pinky blinked.

On that Friday, the day children naturally had pent up excitement for the approaching weekend of freedom, somebody put a tack in Miss Peavine's chair. She sat down hard, and yelped, leaping straight up in rage. Her traveling eye jerked even farther west.

"Who... did... this?" she growled, scanning the classroom of heads staring down at their desktops. "Pupils! I am going to the faculty lounge. I'll be back in thirty minutes. When I get back, the name of the person who did this better be on my desk or else!" She slammed the door, puffing a cloud of dust motes out into the room of wide-eyed kids.

When she returned, there was no name on her desk except for the faint remnant of "hateful bitch," which had been carved there in the wood all along, unsuccessfully sandpapered down to almost unreadable. "OK, I want everyone lined up out in the hall, heading in the door, ladies first!" She grabbed up her big wooden paddle. It was drilled with holes to enhance the sting. As the children came through the door, Peavine told them to bend over and grab their ankles. She beat their legs and butts and their hands too, if they dared to attempt a block. The whole class was bawling, except for Pinky Thomas, who clamped her lips and gave Peavine a defiant stare. When it was her turn, Miss Peavine pulled down Pinky's pants and beat her until she was breathless. Pinky never cried. The boys in the line behind her pointed and laughed at Pinky's exposed hips and the holes in her faded panties, even though they were next. Pinky never showed Aunt Dimple, her lackluster substitute for a mother, the red circles and stripes on her bony behind.

The next morning, when Eugenia Peavine arrived at her classroom door with key in hand, there was a condom with yellowed glue in the tip, stretched out over her doorknob. The attached label said, "Some love for you, Miss Bovine!" Above that was a terse, loveless note asking her to see the Principal in his office, as some parents had called with concerns.

· · · · · · · ·

During the last Friday night bridge game, the upcoming quail season was mentioned between hands and Dory started in again pestering Frank about learning to shoot. Frank took advantage of his appreciative audience to poke every manner of fun at her. "Oh sure! I can't wait to be around when you're blasting everything in sight, everything except a bird! How many times are we going to have this argument, my sweets?" he asked, softening his words with a coddling look. "Shooting is just not going to be your forte!" He looked across at John Evan and rolled his laughing eyes. Just then, the downstairs doorbell chimed, and Frank jumped up to answer it. Anna drug Corrine into her room to show off a new chemistry set.

While Anna Grace set out racks of test tubes, Erlenmeyer flasks and beakers, Corrine sat on the bed, shuffling through a tall stack of drawings.

"My goodness, Anna Grace, you are getting to be quite the artist. Do you draw every single day?" She was amazed that the drawings were from life or imagination and not copied from comic books like most kids were prone to do.

Dory and John Evan found themselves in the kitchen alone, brewing more coffee and sliding squares of Pearlie's famous strawberry cake on to china dessert plates. "You know, Dory, I'd be happy to take you out sometime and give you some pointers with your twenty-two. Just think how surprised Frank would be when he sees you picking off quail. The season starts in a few weeks, so think about it."

"Why, thank you, John, how kind. And I don't even have to think ... I'd love nothing better than to show Frank a thing or two. Give me a call after season starts." Dory turned back to the coffee pot and counted the drips, which she noticed, with an amused tilt of her head, were in perfect sync with the ticking of the clock.

· · · · · · · ·

The last morning of Dory Tollett's life dawned blue and glorious. The air was crisp, hickory smoke from autumn fireplaces already riding on the breeze and laying up thick grey mists in the hollows. When John Evan knocked on the back door, Dory called to him, "Come in a minute, I'm making us some joe. It still feels a bit chilly out there to me." She packed the silver lined thermos of coffee and the baloney on crackers she'd wrapped in waxed paper into Frank's old army rucksack.

"What a beautiful day!" Dory bubbled with anticipation.

They set out across the back yard, rifles riding over their shoulders. John Evan's pointer, Soldier, was beside himself with drooling excitement, nose twitching, tail sweeping side-to-side as he zigzagged across the yellowing grass. They crossed the shallow creek and then started up a small grade through the woods. A ten-minute walk and they came to the edge of the meadow and worked their way around some brambles. In the clearing, waves of golden grasses, knee high, swept back and forth in the wind.

The crows were raucous and loud in their cawing. Taking a cue from them but not a warning, Dory, too, began to chatter obsessively. Perhaps she felt awkward being alone with another man besides Frank. Maybe she'd had too much coffee or was nervous about handling the gun. For whatever reasons, her words were racing and fluttering like pullets spilling out of the henhouse gate. Even as she charged out across the meadow, Soldier scouting out ahead, John Evan trailing right behind, Dory could not stop jabbering about Anna Grace.

When they reached the stone wall, John spoke to her back, "Let me hold your gun Dory, so you can cross the stile."

Dory turned slightly, and without even looking at him, handed him the rifle. She started up the stile steps, never missing a beat. She rattled on, "After all, John, I'm her mother... you'd think she would..."

He had stepped to the side of the stile, and when she finally looked down at him, his eyes were wildly inhuman. Hers were questioning and shocked when he said, his voice cold... deliberate, "No... Dory... You're not her mother, Corrine is her mother, and I've watched her suffer with that as long as I can." He tilted the gun over, aiming up under her throat and pulled the trigger - just like that.

She fell backward off the stile. John Evan took out his bandanna and wiped off the gun, letting it fall close to Dory. Then he ran, sprinted back across the meadow, through the woods and across the yard until his breath was charging ragged from his lungs. He ran until he fell gasping up on Frank Tollett's back stairs. He bounded into the apartment, down into the workroom screaming at Frank to call an ambulance, that Dory was hurt bad and something, *something* about stinkbirds.

In the meadow, the last swirling wisps of Dory Tollett's spirit danced through her fading consciousness, encircling images of Frank and Anna Grace with the purest love. As her last blood pumped into the ground, she whispered a prayer for Corrine. She reached out, laid her long fingers on the rifle, and tapped... one, two, three, four, on to ten, and her short, perfect life was accomplished.

· · · · · · · ·

Corrine was head over heels into a project. John Evan's 32nd birthday was coming up, and she had been to the Piggly Wiggly, hurridly throwing the makings of a double chocolate cake, along with neopolitan ice cream, into her buggy. Before that, she'd run by the hardware store to pay off her lay-a-way on the new shotgun he'd had his eye on, which she planned to wrap in paper covered with hunting dogs. Just as Mr. Oody started pecking on the cash register, she had laid the bright orange hunters' suspenders down on the counter for good measure. There were already banners spelling happy birthday, multicolored balloons, and birthday candles stowed away on the top shelf of the pantry, awaiting John Evan's big day.

She glanced nervously at the house, then opened the trunk of her Ford and snuck the gun in its suede case through the open garage door. It fit right under the chest freezer where it would stay hidden until the big event. Perfect! She flew back to the car and hoisted up the box of groceries, then leaning back to bear the weight on her hips, she duck walked her way to the porch. That box was heavy, so Corrine set it down on the porch swing while she fished out her key and unlocked the door, leaving it slightly ajar. She propped open the screen door. Once her hands were under the box again, she butted her way in the door backwards and turned around, heading toward the kitchen, but...

John Evan had knocked out the etched glass transom over the wide doorway between the living and dining rooms, and used that heavy beam to bear the weight of his barely swinging body. His tongue, already blue, veered off sideways and shockingly long. From his crotch down, both inside seams of his corduroys were wet and dripped onto the overturned Queen Anne chair. The cat lapped at the yellow puddle, but looked up and regarded Corrine and her grocery box inquisitively, hoping for something tastier, more substantial. He lacked the word for it, but tunafish was the sensation vibrating in his memory.

On the coffee table, under her Pinchbeck Queen Victoria paperweight, a wedding present from the principal and his wife, was John Evan's tear stained note of farewell.

Corry, heart of my heart,

I have no way of knowing if, by the time you are reading this, you'll know of the untimely death of Dory Tollett. It was not a thing planned ahead, but I am the one who took her life. God help her.

My short time with you has been the best of my life. My love for you filled me with joy, and satisfaction, but also, unbearable aching. I have been witness to your emptiness, shaped by the loss of your baby girl. I've seen you suffer from the sidelines, watching another woman raise your child.

As you know, I'd agreed to teach Dory to shoot her twenty-two. She wanted to surprise Frank and be able to go out with him hunting quail. I'm sure he would have loved that. Today we were headed out to the meadow way out behind Tolletts. There's almost always a covey in the long grass out there. It was a perfect fall day, and the dog was working beautifully, but Dory was walking up ahead of me flapping her mouth like some women can't seem to stop doing. In the first place, no female seems to have the sense to shut the hell up when you're trying to sneak up on birds. It was what she was saying though, "Anna Grace this, Grace that, when my baby was little, our precious little girl, she's growing up so fast..."

All of a sudden it was more than I could bear. In that moment, I was overcome with intense hatred for that woman. I hated her for having the joy of your little girl right under your nose. I know she didn't mean you any harm, but she kept on and kept on until it came into my mind that if she were just... gone... that girl would be motherless. Anna Grace would need you again.

About that time we came up to a stone wall with barbed wire over the top, and we had to cross over at the stile. I offered to hold her gun, so she could go up the stone steps and over the wire. She went ahead of me for a second, and I clicked off the safety. I moved up to the side of the stile, like a real gentleman helping her up the steps and pushing down the wire for her so she wouldn't scratch her dainty, oh so motherly ankles, but with *my other hand I tilted the rifle over at just the right angle and pulled the trigger – just like that.*

I ran back to Frank and told him stinkbirds had flown up in her face, and she fell on her gun. I let him think she might still be alive, but I know she died quickly. There was too much blood, too much. I already knew myself to be a murderer. God help me.

So if you're reading this my darling, you know my life, our life together, is now over. When I saw Frank's face, the enormity of what I'd done became real, and I knew there would be no getting over it, even if I were never found out. As much as I love you, I couldn't live with you in a lie. My only hope is that losing me somehow, someday, helps you to know your daughter. God help you.

Heart of my heart,

John

· · · · · · · · ·

"Stinkbirds, Frank! A big black cloud of 'em! They flew right up in her face from behind the stone fence. I'd doubled back behind her to round up Soldier, fool dog got sidetracked, when I heard the rifle go off."

They were barreling through the woods, carrying a rolled stretcher from the hearse. If there was one thing Frank Tollett had, it was experience with death, so even from a ways off, even before he knelt by Dory and pressed his fingers fruitlessly on her lack of pulse, he knew, he knew, she was gone. He stood staring listlessly out across the field, letting the impossible sink under his burning skin. He turned on John Evan, "What the hell were you two doing out here?"

John Evan hung his head, running both his hands through his long brown hair. "She wanted to surprise you, Frank. She was set on learning to shoot birds so she could come out with you. Bringing home a mess of quail was all she could talk about." *And Anna Grace, Anna Grace, Anna Grace…*

"Go back to the house and meet the ambulance. Tell them to drive up Rambler Road. We'll take her out that way." Frank was already numbing up. John Evan turned and started running back to the house.

"No need to hurry." Frank yelled after him. When John Evan disappeared through the woods, Frank stretched himself out the length of Dory's body and combing her hair with shivering fingers, he wept with total abandon, in the violent way of men who have never allowed themselves to cry.

• • • • • • • •

Frank left the hospital, where the coroner from Pineville ruled accidental death, dreading the task of telling Pearlie and me. He could'a crossed Pearlie off his list. She already knew, since John Evan had filled her in when the ambulance and its blaring siren showed up in the parking lot of Tollett's.

She'd already had her first round of weepin' and wailin', hollerin' "Oh Lord Jesus, Oh Lord Jesus! " over and over until she was plum wore out. Then she got aholt of herself, set about doing the things she knew would have to be done. Before Frank even got home with me in tow and in shock, she had put on the good Sunday tablecloth, got out trivets for all the casseroles she knew would be coming through the door, straightened the sitting room, and picked up all those Blackshale newspapers that would feature Dory's picture in the coming week.

She had set the kitchen table with shot glasses and a fifth of Frank's best whiskey. When he walked in, she poured a double for him and then one for herself.

• • • • • • • •

I had glanced up from page sixty-four of my socials studies

book and saw Miss Peavine and the principal, Mr. Mee, peering at me through the glass panel of the classroom door. Well, one of Miss Peavine's eyes was looking at me. The other one was flailing out into space along the line of ABCs that run around the top of the classroom wall. Mr. Mee crooked a finger at Miss Millican, summoning her to a conference in the hall. After a time, the door creaked open and through the crack Miss Millican called somberly, "Anna Grace."

I squiggled out of my seat, scourin' my mind for any recent sins I might have committed on school property. What in the world had I done that would get the principal called in? I couldn't think of a thing. Not a thing. But when I went through the door and saw Pap standing there everything came flooding together into an unbearable truth, the wretchedness of his tear-streaked face, the siren I had heard earlier wailing down Blackshale Road, the pitying looks of the bystanders... my blessed Mama, dead as I knew her to be down deep in my heart, didn't raise no dummy.

Pearlie told me later on she couldn't think straight how to help me havin' to face such a hard shock. She thought on it and thought on it, and finally reckoned it wasn't fair for her and Pap to be dulled down and me not be. So she poured a glass of that whisky for me too, softening it down with sourwood honey, and made me take it in little sips while she held me on her lap, creaking back and forth in the rocking chair until I cried myself to sleep. She laid me down in my bed, praying to her Jesus to bless my pore little heartbroken soul.

Pap called up his friend from mortuary school again. They brought Mama back from the hospital to get her ready, and like all the other families we had seen through their sorrows, we laid Mama out for her wake in the parlor of Tollett's. I looked on numbly, a little girl in a black dress. Because the gunshot had done more damage to her throat than the best cosmetics could ever hide, the casket was kept closed, and I never got to see my mama again. Pap said that was for the best, for me to remember her like she had looked that last fall morning, beautiful and smiling, her hair blowing in the breeze, when she had walked me out to the road and touched the bus to insure my safety, when she'd watched me tromp up into the yellow stairwell with her sweetest smile, when her last words on earth to me had been, "Gimme some sugar."

When the service was over, Pap asked Perry, old man Oody, and Sheriff Raby to help bear her pall down to the basement, where she was put in the ground. Pap wanted her close by.

·········

Whether it was the devil or God that done it, I can't say. But as soon as I felt my mama slip from the world, her obsessions slid right over into me like a troublesome inheritance. My little paws twitched with urges to draw on everthing in sight. When Pap caught me at the walls, he set me to scrubbin' with vinegar and sent me in disgrace to my room. I sat in my window seat scritching doodles no bigger than potato bugs, inventing ciphers to my mama - stand-ins for the painful words I could not speak. Unable to stop, I slipped them into hiding places all over the house where Pearlie discovered them under cushions and over transoms, tiny bits of pain found piece by piece. With every one she cried "My pore sweet girl!"

As lonely and cast adrift as a child could be, I was saved by my imagination. I rendered and scribbled and journaled the way things were and the way I dreamed them to be. In a dog eared composition book, I wrote in a crippled looking cursive, "When the daylight hours fade away Pap takes his bottle to sit in front of the TV set. I come on in my room, lay on my bed and close my eyes. I float in seaweed, tail barely fanning, tears and scales falling to the ocean floor. I peer out through the murky waters, scanning the depths for the sight of her. I know she is there. I know my mama is a mermaid."

• • • • • • • •

After Mama died, my daddy faded on back to washwater. He did his work at the funeral home and put one foot in front of the other. As for me, I wandered motherless at the edges of his vision, a vague reminder of her but without the blood ties required to be a bonafide souvenir. He never pandered to me, and on the other hand, he was never hateful or stern with me much. He just shuffled back into the woodwork and let Pearlie take over the everyday work of raising me up. After years of shooting at quail, he was deaf as a post. That suited him, I reckon. He could wander all alone, undisturbed in that dark place of grieving in his mind.

• • • • • • • •

There was a sliver of radiance in the overwhelming blackness of my mama's loss. I finally got myself a chum. On the day I returned to school after the funeral, a scrawny mite of a girl set her lunch tray down right next to mine and offered a handshake that seemed to be made entirely of wiggling bones.

"Pinky Anne Thomas my ma died when I was four year old," explaining the who and why and when in one nonstop, breathless string of words. "Been called PinkyToe since I was a baby and I can't get shed of it, so you might just as well call me that too." I regarded her hand suspiciously.

"Gee willikers! Wha...you think I got cooties or sumpin'? Jeepers!"

I slid my hand into hers and said in a serious, grownup way, "Pleased to make your acquaintance."

It was as if I'd draped my words in black, so they'd be proper for a girl in mourning. But that night in my bed I felt guilty for the pocket of happy feeling that was tucked inside my pain. I finally had a friend.

PinkyToe had been running wild for some time. Her mama had died and her daddy had run off a few years later. She lived with her neurotic Aunt Dimple, who spent each and every day suspended in a bubble of doom. No one had ever been more misnamed. In my book, dimples came from a perpetual smile, but the young woman who had been born Betty Jo but nicknamed Dimple never, ever smiled. Them dimples musta just got poked by accident into her sour face. She was the sort of person who fully expected to one day hear the drone of an aircraft grow louder and louder until... WHUMP... its tonnage would flatten her against the ground. Her doctor fed her fear with pills that kept her riding a rollercoaster from dull to frantic. On manic afternoons she fingered her viola with menace, clawing the strings until beads of blood danced on the wires. On those days, Pinky fled and stalked the riverbank, skipping stones until dark.

Whether it was a lack of decent parenting, a mental affliction, some gene way off kilter, plain meanness, or just overactive curiosity, they weren't sure. The school counselors couldn't agree on how to explain away Pinky Thomas. They hemmed and hawed a lot about her and attributed her behavior to orphan-ness but never really came up with a solution to the PinkyToe problem. She had an irresistible urge to mess with things just to see what would happen. While there may have been some desire to show off, entertain, or just punctuate the small town boredom, it was mostly about the pure creative fun of seeing what small havocs she could engineer.

After losing Dory, Frank was so rattled, he left me alone to raise myself. I would have done a serious job of it, too, had I not been a natural-born follower and mesmerized by Pinky's bravado. With my new lack of supervision, I was free to go along on her wild ride. I was so busy relishing her invention process and contemplating the reactions that there was never much time to consider how things might end up going badly wrong.

These events usually began with me and PinkyToe whispering head to head in a tree house, saying things like "What if.." or "OK, wouldn't it be hysterical if..." Once in a while, the "if" turned out to be more than we bargained for. It was like rubbing two baby sticks together just to see if we could get a single spark, not really expecting anything to happen, then reducing things to rubble and smoke.

As a result, she spent a good part of her youth grounded. As it happened, the high point of her behavioral creativity coincided with a shift in punishment trends. Up until puberty, Aunt Dimple gave her a weekly whacking with a Ping-Pong paddle. That always calmed her down for a few days. A good snot slinging boo hooin' and all that dangerous energy just melted away. But when Dr. Spock spoke, paddling became frowned on. Aunt Dimple hated to be frowned on by anyone, so she took up the grounding policy (No leaving the house, no telephone, no TV). This left me and PinkyToe with much more time to plan the next prank. A vicious cycle, you can see.

When PinkyToe was grounded, we had to go out on a limb. She lived across the river and up the road from our house, but no further than the length of a football field as the crow flies. In the summer after supper, when it commenced to get dark, we'd drag our lamps to the windows of our rooms and flash away. We neither one knew a lick of real Morse code, but just the flashing meant "the coast is clear", and we could both sneak out. These days Pap was usually at the beer joint, and Pearlie was downstairs in her fixed-up storage room, drowning the sadness she always carried with more than one cold Budweiser.

When Pinky Toe and me first come to be pals, we still played with dolls. Her cousin Gordon had passed down to her a tree house he'd built in the woods. That was where we took our Ginny dolls, along with their trunks full of store bought and homemade clothes, and made up all kinds of pretend lives for them - pretend fashion model show, pretend dance on American Bandstand, pretend spy girls, pretend run away to Florida, pretend boyfriends, pretend in the family way, pretend here comes the bride.

One day, we got called back up to the house by Aunt Dimple for our lunch - sandwiches made with pimento and pickle loaf on white bread with lots and lots of mayo. We just left our Ginny dolls sittin' right where they were. We forgot to remember that the meanest boys in our school lived up on the mountain, and they were ramblin' all over the place all the time. I don't reckon their daddies laid eyes on them from sunup to sundown. One of them, always dirty and smelling really bad, we called Sodboy. He was BoJack and Peanut Murphy's tagalong – not a real pal – just tolerated as somebody to boss around.

That day after we'd finished our P&P loaf sandwiches and guzzled down our cocolas, we headed back to play but heard laughin' coming from up in our tree house. We decided to creep up and spy on 'em so we got under the floor and peered in between the planks. We were so close to them I could smell the body odors they always wore.

There was Peanut holding up my Ginny doll, who I'd named Annette, and PinkyToe's doll, Frannie. We had took them names off American Bandstand, which we loved to watch after school. He had stripped them nekked.

He was actin' a fool with them dolls:
"Sally Sue,
I love you,
Do you love me,
Hell YES, I do!
Do you know what F... U... C... K means, Sodboy? Well, your Ma and Pa do this all the time!"
With that, he creaked open the hard plastic, poker straight legs of those dolls into V-shapes and rammed their crotches

together, crack, crack, crack, crack. On that day, PinkyToe and me had never heard that word before, and our mouths opened wide!

I knew for a fact that Pap and Mama had never done nothin' nasty like that, and I flinched in shock. It was then I stepped on a stick, and things got real quiet up in the tree house.

"Agggggggh…" BoJack and Peanut came flying down the ladder with Sodboy not far behind.

Pinky grabbed up a fistful of rocks and hit them all hard in the face. While they stood there whimpering and rubbing grit out of their eyes, we ran as fast as we could to Aunt Dimple's back porch. Lookin' back, I thought that right there was the start of a peck of trouble with BoJack's gang and the whole bunch of no count Murphys.

• • • • • • • •

After we outgrew dolls later that year, the tree house became the official headquarters for our new club. Of course it was PinkyToe's idea in the first place to have a secret club for the girls at school who had been left behind in this world by their mamas. She had seen pictures about the Mexican "Day of the Dead" in National Geographic magazine, and I'm sure this give her ideas. There was five members, but nobody at school even knew we were pals, let alone bonded forever in a secret and sacred society. We called our club "Las Abandonadas." That was Spanish for "the forsaken," a fact that I had stumbled upon in the World Book Encyclopedia. (Mama had insisted that Frank pay monthly payments to buy the complete set of World Books for me, and they had sure come in handy.)

There was PinkyToe, who was the self-appointed leader, and me, and three new girls we honored with membership in our sad circle. Joannie Dooley's mother had gotten the cancer in 1954 and didn't last no mor'n six months. I counted Joannie lucky, 'cause at least she'd gotten to say goodbye.

Georgia Mason had left her girl Tilla asleep in her bed one

night to go to Frank Tollett's favorite beer joint and wound up twisted around a telephone pole. Tilla was four when it happened, but she was still in a bad way yearning for her mother.

And there was Penny Hammons, with her wounds still fresh. Her ma had just that winter gone out on the back stoop to wring out her rag mop, and slipped up on a patch of black ice, cracking her head wide open on the gray lead pipe rail. None of us thought for a minute we had been intentionally abandoned by our mamas, but we still felt sadly left behind and forsaken.

We made us a book with a black genuine leatherette cover that said "Las Abandonadas" in large red letters. Underneath that it said "Top Secret" in big capitals, and then "Open This and You Will DIE" in smaller letters. We had decorated the borders with "Day of the Dead" art like Pinky had seen in the National Geographic. On the first page were our names. Then, starting on page one, the details of our meetings were described. We spent hours huddled in the floor of one of our rooms, crafting club rituals. Then each of us had a memorial page for our mama, where we pasted a picture and wrote our favorite things about each one.

I wrote:

Dory Tollett was my blessed mama. She strived ever day to be perfect, and she come close. She give me hugs ever day. When I was little, we'd have us tea parties and take sunbaths and work in the kitchen with Pearlie. My mama said my name like it was all one word, spittin' out the "Anna" real loud, and lettin' the "Grace" trail along behind. The madder she was at me, the louder the "Anna" got. She never much whooped me though, even if she had a mind to, she'd look at me funny like and change her mind. She smelled good like the sweet peas in the back yard. She held me up in her lap even when I was too big and whispered in my ear that I was her girl and she loved me this much, all the way to heaven and back.

PinkyToe's page said:

Maw died when I was four year old, so I only recall her face if I get out the picture book. I love the picture of me up in her arms, held tight, and her looking at me like I was sweet as sugarcake. She had her hand on my hair bow, like she took good kere of me. I know she did. I fount a box with little shoes and socks she bought me, and my baby book. She had wrote down ever single thing I ever done and the day, the very day, I done it. I miss her. I would say God bless her sole but I don't believe in no God that took my maw back when I need her so bad here.

Our weekly secret meeting began with the solemn procession to the tree house. We would meet down behind Pinky's house at twilight, dress in black, and take up our poles. Hanging from each girl's pole was a paper lantern with a candle inside, and under that a string of handmade trinkets and a small picture of her dead mother. We walked along the path, quietly singing the dead mama anthem that we had written earlier while sprawled on my bedroom floor.

Vamos a hablar con nuestras madres
Las que honramos
Es el deseo de nuestro corazón
Estar unidas con ustedes

We sang as we walked along in a soft, mystical harmony, "We go to commune with our mothers, the ones we honor. It is the desire of our hearts to be at one with you." We sang this in Spanish although we had no idea what Spanish sounded like. Had a real live Mexican happened by, he woulda probly fell on the ground and split a gut laughing at us gringo girls butcherin' up his language.

When we come to the tree house and hoisted ourselves and our poles up the ladder, we pulled out the secret stash that we'd hidden under a loose board. First, we set up the altar. There was a picture of each dearly departed mama, which we draped with chains of tiny ground flowers we'd find in the woods. Their faces seemed to come alive in the glimmer of a candle we placed in front of each one. On the boards of the tree house walls, we hung small mementos and belongings. We had collected turkey bones from our sad, motherless thanksgiving tables and sewed little bird skulls and crossed wing bones to cloth bags. PinkyToe called these amulets and filled them with herbs that were said to summon spirits. She'd secretly grown them herself at the back of her Aunt Dimple's garden: yew, lavender, and sweet grass. We also lit a match to them dried herbs in little dishes, one for each mama. We never said it to each other, but I reckon we hoped them lines of smoke from our little fires rose up through the cracks in the roof, all the way up to our mamas in Heaven.

Then we got out the Ouiji board, each Abandonada taking a turn. Before sitting down to the board, we would caress our mamas' possessions on the wall, sometimes holding them in our hands and testing them for lingering scent. I could still detect the faintest remains of Dory's "White Shoulders" on her blue hanky, which always made my eyes well up and sting with tears.

The platen was still at first, then it began to tremble under our fingertips. I accused Tilla of moving it, and she blamed me right back. Neither of our fingers seemed to be moving though. I swear it had a life of its own, and began to slide from letter to letter. "We are here," it spelled.

"Yikes!" PinkyToe yelped, "Holy shit!" and jumped up, knocking over a candle. We all scrambled around in the tiny space, stomping out the flames that quickly spread across the dried herbs scattered on the tree house floor.

If Aunt Nettie's Bible is true, I guess God frowned on our childish incantations - our dabbling in the dark arts. But on the other hand, a higher power had to be looking out for us. It's a million wonders we didn't burn down that tree house and set the woods ablaze with all them candles. I've come to believe God feels a sorrow for his children and forgives heartbroken girls who miss their mamas so much.

2029 Morning Glory Ridge

I can't stand it any more. I must draw something, and the only thing I can see is myself. Shaky hands and blurred vision be damned – I am going to draw! I put my eScreen in mirror mode and ask Gundersen to dump all my headgear out on my bed. Egads! It feels so good to push my pen around again. I could not care less what the end product looks like. It's about the pure joy of drawing. The Anna Grace Tollett "old as dirt" self-portrait series is about to be born!

Every time I change headgear, I pick up a new tool. Slipping on my goggles, I cover the page with cream oil pastel and over that I add a layer of black. I reach for a scribe and scratch through the black to reveal the undercolor, the sgraffito outlining my goggle-eyed self. As I draw, I remember the precise moment I became an artist. I was toddling, maybe not even three, but I clearly recall the scribble of red crayon on Mama's butter colored wall and the discovery that the mark of my hand could illicit a screeching reaction. At five, I was already taking high tech art lessons. I had begged Mama to mail order a special clear plastic stick-on sheet, so I could draw on the TV screen during the "Winky-Dink and You" show.

All afternoon, as the stack of self-portraits grows, my artistic life flashes before me. Before my mama died, I happily regarded and recorded any person, place, or thing in my path.

At Dory's death, my art changed course. It became compulsive and laborious, more subjective, far beyond the usual patience and understanding of a child. I was precocious, driven by the thought that my art was a spirit language, speaking to my mama in the sky. Every little doodle was a message bound for the great beyond.

I branched out. One day when I was eleven, I began to carry river rocks from the crick to the center of the meadow, and carefully lay them in an ever-widening curve, until I had fashioned a spiral that filled up the huge clearing. When it was done, I stood smiling in the middle and gazed up into the heavens, sure that Dory could see my heart's desire to spin upward into her arms.

Frank was pissed as hell. He hollered at me for a solid week. Did I, Anna Grace Tollett, not realize that the meadow had to be mowed, and those rocks would tear up the mower? Did I, Anna Grace Tollett, think the universe revolved around me? (Did I, for a minute there, think he got it, that he actually understood I was alone in the epicenter of a painful, confusing world?) After a week of yelling and cussing, it finally occurred to him just to make me return the rocks to the crick, one by one.

1958 Blackshale

Of a Saturday morning I was standing at the sink with Pearlie. She was washing; I was drying and listening to cartoons with one ear. Aunt Sudy was over to the house, sitting at the kitchen table stuffing herself with Pearlie's blueberry buckle and working a jigsaw puzzle of the Grand Canyon. Marlene toddled around the kitchen, babbling, and tapping a stick on the floor.

Sudy had a cup of hot tea, and when she jumped up and screamed "Oh my lands!" I thought for sure she had spilled tea all over her puzzle pieces and blistered her lap, maybe even down in her private place. But she grabbed a dishtowel, ran to me, scooped me up and raced to the bathroom. She sat me down on the toilet and hung her head, crying and laughing at the same time. It was then I noticed blood was gushing down my legs, and I didn't hardly see how that could be very funny.

"Have I caught the lady's cancer?" I asked gravely.

"No honeypie, you have just become a woman!"

She stuffed the dishrag between my legs, told Pearlie what had transpired and that she'd run to the store for the necessaries. In ten minutes she was back with a sanitary belt, pads, and a bottle of Midol. After she had me all fixed up, she gave me a Midol and put me to bed.

I could hear her telling Frank all about it in the kitchen. Pap moaned, "My God, Sudy, she's just a little girl!"

"It happens Frank," Sudy lamented, "She's an early bloomer."

"My luck," Frank grumbled. By lunch I'd soaked and changed four pads and was bitchy with cramps. After a second dose of Midol, I conked out and slept all day. Every month from then on, I was a bloody floodin' waiting to happen. I guess I was just made that way.

• • • • • • • •

PinkyToe spent a lot of time at our table since Pearlie was a much better cook than her Aunt Dimple whose main talent was with a can opener. On the first day of my next monthly, Pinky was over, and our snouts were buried in big bowls of Pearlie's chicken and dumplins. All at once, I felt the deluge between my thighs.

"Pap, kin I be excused?" Frank kept on shoveling in dumplings.

"Pap, please, kin I be excused?" Again, it fell on unhearing ears.

"PAP, I need a Kotex!" I yelled at the top of my lungs.

When he finally heard me, he heard me wrong. I guess he thought I was turning up my nose to Pearlie's dumplins and was asking for something different to eat.

"Anna Grace, gosh dammit, you'll eat whatever Pearlie puts down in front of you and you'll like it!"

PinkyToe spewed Nehi grape across her brand spankin' new white pedalpushers and Mama's old white tablecloth, which tore Pearlie plumb up, even though Pap had been trying to stick up for her all along.

• • • • • • • •

My mama had been firm. I had never, ever been allowed on the first level of the Tollett Funeral Home. Dory's loss had left Frank numb, and all at once I had the run of the place. I guess he figured, after all I'd been through, I might as well know everthing else there was to know about life and death. So there I'd sit perched on a stool, fairly unconcerned, watching the embalming fluid drip out of the machine into old man Jones or Miss Lulu. I could'a just as well been watching my father plant potatoes or sell nails at the hardware store. To me, death was just everyday life.

One day when I was sitting there bored, watching Pap workin' with his needles and make-up, I had an idea. "Pap, kin I have the bathroom walls down here for my very own? Ain't nobody ever in it but us, and I want to decorate it up."

Frank looked up from his suturing and shook his head like it was a crazy thing to hear me say. "Sure, why not?" Pap didn't really care about nothing no more. He didn't even ask what my plan was.

The downstairs bathroom had been a do-it-yourself job finished after the Funeral Home opened. Since Frank expected to be the only one using it, he did a half-assed job. Pap was Dory's opposite when it came to being a perfectionist; he had slopped up a mix of plaster and concrete and slathered it up and down the walls without an ounce of care. As long as the indoor plumbing worked and the toilet didn't run over, that was all that mattered to Frank, so he'd hired a plumber to do the critical parts. The walls were aged, stained, riddled with cracks, a thing of beauty to my artist's eye. My canvases awaited.

I had been inspired by the railroad cars passing behind the house. I scritched and scratched on the rough white walls a graffiti history of the Tollett's Funeral home, keeping a running tally of the causes of death that landed each customer in our care. I was curious what would get the most votes.

Heart attacks won: mark, mark, mark, mark, SLASH! (In the first year there were three groups of these.) The cancer: mark, mark, mark, mark, SLASH! (Two groups plus two marks.) Bust Appendicks: mark, mark. Drowned: mark, mark, mark. Car wreck: ten marks and two slashes. Sometimes I drew pictures next to the name of the decedent. (A new word I had learnt when Pap was taking himself a correspondence course on obituary writing.) The hardest one to draw was of Mrs. Patty Carson, who Pap claimed had married some crazy Shaker Quaker from up past Pineville. She had tried hard to suck up all that religion, but she failed at it. She snuck back home one night and went wild dancing the hoochie coochie up on the table of a local bar - boogied so hard she had an apoplexy. She flipflopped down twitchin' and died right there on that table in a puddle of beer. Yep, that one was real complicated to draw.

There was a hanging noose and three guns. The head in a noose had been my favorite. I'd had secret fun making the eyes bug out and the hair stand on end. I had no idea at the time that the man in the noose, Pap's former friend John Evan, was the one that had kilt my mama. As for Dory, I didn't want her in with the common group of marks for death by gun. Instead I drew a special picture of my mama in her coffin, a sleeping beauty. Rising up out of it, was the flock of evil black stinkbirds, the very flying force of nature I blamed for her death.

That day I had asked my Pap, "Just what is a stinkbird anyways?"

He said, "Oh, no particular kind of bird, just any ordinary bird a hunter ain't lookin' to shoot and eat. Me, I'm wanting a quail or a pheasant for Pearlie to dress up for the table. Anything else is just a useless old stinkbird to me."

2029 Morning Glory Ridge

It's taken me months to undo Flotilla's virtual abuse. Not only did my avatar have to be remade from scratch, but the witch had erased all my digital files and backups - email, computer files I had brought from home, my collection of books and movies, and music. The most devastating loss, though, is my archive of home movies and pictures. They are gone forever.

My first evening at Morning Glory Ridge, I had stretched across the bed feeling low. I blamed my despondent mood on the sound of rain tapping the window. Then I realized the thready, trickling sound was not rain at all, but the bits and bytes of my life uploading from my home laptop into the hundred Terabyte storage volume in my new eScreen. The only remnants of my loved ones then walked and talked in tiny digital movie windows. Before leaving home, I had transferred all the old 8mm silent movies to digital. I watched them over and over, treasuring the smiles. The movies were all I had from my life in Blackshale with Pinky, Perry, Pearlie, my mothers, Frank.

There is no way Flotilla can be fingered for the digital vandalism. She had slipped me a sleeping pill and worked on my open screen with vinyl gloves. It was the perfect digital crime.

I swing the eScreen around on its arm and squint, straining to read the new message from the Activities Director, Miss Huckabee. I remember the ZOOM button that blows the words up really big, and finally fumble onto it. Under a 3D animation of a goofy, floppy-eared white bunny, is formal text.

*You are cordially invited to a formal Tea Party on the Veranda
Tuesday, April 4 at 4:00 p.m.
Easter Bonnets, or other seasonal costume, Required.
Don't be late! Don't be late! It's a very important date!*

1959 Blackshale

By the time Mama had been planted down in the basement a whole year, me and PinkyToe was like Siamese twins. If I was not down at her house, she was up at mine, or we was both at the tree house just us or with the Abandonadas. If we were not together we kept the phone playin' a busy signal.

We adjusted the secret code of flashing lights. When we had first started up flashin', all it meant was "the coast is clear to sneak out." A few months later Aunt Dimple had been cracking down bad on PinkyToe, and Frank was sometimes distracted and cross. We felt the need to add a special "emergency code." If life in Blackshale were to get altogether too unbearable, we had us a plan to run away. Ten short flashes of light, and those ten returned, clearly meant: "Meet at the tree house with bus fare and your bag packed. We're headin' for Florida to live on the beach!" I'd always had that thing about mermaids. I wasn't exactly sure how a girl got to be one, but I was willin' to try. We hoped to find a little island where we could live on coconuts and grilled crabs. I was the only one Pinky felt like she could count on, no matter what, and I felt the same way about her. We were two peas in a motherless pod.

Pinky was so sure a quick getaway was in our future, she had done crafted the letter she planned to leave on Aunt Dimple's bed pillow. She held it out to me with some pride. There was her usual sloping backhand, the letters looking like they were sliding into home plate. I could picture her writing it with her leftie way, twisted askew with her elbow up in the air, lips pinched, grieving out the strings of a cursive designed for right handed people.

So one night, I made my own goodbye letter on an invoice paper the coffin salesman from Nashville had give me, just in case I might need to leave it for Frank and Pearlie sometime. I wouldn't want them thinking I had been kidnapped or murdered when in fact I would just be leavin' mad as hops. On it I wrote, "To the loved ones at home, best wishes, I've gone to be a mermaid."

Then I doodled all over it, and added a few more farewell comments. I slipped it into my desk drawer, in case it should ever be needed.

There was only one time I led Pinky astray. It was a rare thing that she had not already done something that I had, so with great chest swellin' pride I led her out to the woods to smoke rabbit tobacco. Perry had shown me exactly where to find the thin hollow weeds and how to lean up against a tree and light one, looking cool just like James Dean. I could tell Pink was impressed. Of course the next week, she filched two Pall Malls from her Aunt Dimple's pocketbook and brought them to the tree house. My rabbit tobacco seemed childish up next to them Pall Malls, but we both got sick as dogs from inhaling, so our smoking career was short-lived anyways.

Except for the rabbit tobacco, it was always PinkyToe and her creative streak leading me headlong into trouble. She was fascinated with the forbidden basement floor of Tollett Funeral Home. Pap had set up a rule early on, no friends downstairs. When he was away though, she started in begging to go down there and poke around. I gave in, hoping just to give her a peek here or there, but her mind went right to work thinking of ways to turn the prep room into the hall of pranks.

"NO!" I'd had to yell many times, stomping my foot, "This here is Pap's serious work, and we can't be playing down here."

She pouted, "If you wasn't so grim, Anna Grace, we could really have some fun."

The one time I let Pinky have her way downstairs, fate was set in motion. A solitary event reeled into one revelation after another, 'til my life unfolded into an entirely new version of itself. That single event was the memorable last rites of Miss Eugenia Peavine.

It was way past my bedtime. Frank had said so over and over, but ever time he'd said it, he was on the way to grab another cold one. After a while, he didn't care so much as to whether I was up in the bed or not. When the phone rang, the distance to the phone from the divan was no longer a straight line, and he slurred his hullo like cornmeal mush into the receiver.

"Whaaasat? Wha happened?" I heard him say, "Holy Crap!"

On the other end of the line, a nurse at Blackshale hospital was filling him in with gory details. Miss Peavine had suffered a fatal stroke at home and her only family in Chattanooga didn't miss her for several days. It was the heat of summer and Miss Peavine's body was good and stinkin' ripe. Pap was not looking forward to the prep room the next morning.

He woke with a killer headache. Pearlie knew to set toast and black coffee quietly on the table, and I knew enough to keep my mouth shut. After he got a cup of black coffee down, he was a little more talkative.

"Well, Anna Grace, your third grade teacher, Miss Peavine, has passed on. She will be having a closed casket so I'm afraid you won't be able to pay your last respects face-to-face." He looked at me sideways with a hint of a smile. Normally, Frank had the greatest respect for the folks he worked on, but he knew good and well that ugly old Peavine had been hateful to me, and besides he had a migraine and a hangover. Frank finished up his second cup of coffee and trod down the stairs to meet the ambulance bearing Miss Peavine and begin his foul smelling work.

Pinky was spending the night with me that evenin' because her Aunt Dimple had to sit with a friend in the hospital. After we marched up and down the road twirlin' our silver batons in figure eights for a while, we were tuckered out, so we were in my room playing Clue when the phone rang. Pap had gone to bed early, whisky'd up, worn out from his hard, odoriferous day with Miss Peavine. I ran like a bat outta hell for the phone so it wouldn't wake him up.

"Hello? This is May Bivens speaking. I am Eugenia Peavine's sister, the one that called yesterday to make the arrangements. Is Mr. Tollett there?"

"Well, mam, he's already in the bed 'cause he's wore out. This is his daughter Anna Grace. Can I take a message?"

"Maybe you can help me, honey. We've arrived in from Chattanooga for the service, and I brought a gardenia corsage for Eugenia to be buried in. It's her favorite flower, so could you be sure your daddy tucks it on her bosom? I brought it by this afternoon, but no one ever came to the door, so I laid it out on the back stoop. Could you be a dear and get it for me? Maybe take it downstairs to the cooler?"

"Why certainly, Mrs. Bivens, I'd be mor'n happy to," I promised, crossing my eyes and sticking my tongue out at PinkyToe. She gave me the finger.

The corsage box wasn't where Mrs. Bivens claimed she'd left it. We got ourselves a flashlight and finally found the box out under the bushes where it had fallen off the back stoop. I sighed to Pink, "Come'on. If you promise and hope to die that you'll behave, you kin go with me." I knew better than to let Pinky go downstairs, but the truth was I was chicken to go down with Peavine by myself. If there was ever going to be a spiteful ghost, she would be it.

We planted our feet gingerly on each step, not wanting to wake Pap. Pinky, who was never scared of nothin', looked a little spook-eyed. Once we got down there though, she started in. "Let's look at her! You can tell Frank you had to put the flower in. He won't care! You can tell 'im Peavine's sister said to!"

I was kinda wondering myself just how bad she looked. Closed caskets were usually gruesome anyways, and Peavine was butt-ugly to start with. I looked seriously at Pinky, assessing the possibility that she might could stay in control and not go clean off the deep end.

"If we do this, you have to swear never to tell nobody. Swear on your dead mama's grave!" PinkyToe nodded and crossed her heart.

With a loud voice in my head, booming "No, No, No!" I motioned to Pinky to help me lift the lid. We both reeled back from the putrid smell, covering our noses.

"Gag a maggot!" PinkyToe flailed her bony hands in the air, "Great green gobs of greasy grimy gopher guts, mutilated monkey meat… she smells worser than a ton of dogshit!"

"Oh shut UP! You asked for it!" I took the gardenia out of the box and carefully pinned it on Miss Peavine's sunken bosom. Since I was already there anyways, I leaned over and studied her face. All at once it hit me, why she'd been walleyed. "Look Pink! I think she has a glass eye! Before I could stop her, Pinky leaned over and pressed on both sides of the bigger, browner eye, just like squeezing a zit. Plop! Out it popped. Pinky dished out some choice words and dug down in the satin crevices of the casket for the glossy glass orb. She stood back and held it in her hands, rolling it over and over.

"OK! This here is the single most weirdest thing I have ever done in my whole life!" Then she dropped it. It rolled across the black and white linoleum and up under the casket stand.

We scrambled across the floor on our hands and knees but couldn't reach it. I ran and got a broom and poked under the stand, hit the eyeball straight on and sent it shooting across the floor. Pinky was laughing helplessly, legs crossed at the knees to hold her water. "Oh my stars and garters, you're shootin' pool with Miss Peavine's eyeball! Wait 'til I tell the kids at school!"

"Shush your big yappin' mouth! You promised to keep your

trap shut!" I could see I'd made a big mistake.

I carried the dust coated eye to the sink and washed it off, then leaned over Miss Peavine's face and started trying to pry it back in. You'd think that would'a been easy, but one eyelid would be right and then the other one would fold back under. I finally had to just lay it in between her eyelids staring straight ahead, with her pale eyelashes shooting off at odd angles every whichaway. The fact that her other eye was naturally closed made Peavine look like she was winkin'.

"It don't matter," I told Pinky, "Pap said her coffin won't be opened up at all, even for the family. And God thinks you're beautiful no matter what." That was the wrong thing to say.

Pinky's eyebrows shot up. "Oh? Well then, we might as well have some fun!"

"NO! You've done plenty already," I grumbled in my best wet blanket voice.

Pinky gave me her pitiful look. "Please. If you let me do one little thing to purty plain old Miss Peavine up a little, I swear I'll never ask to do nuthin' else. Wait here... I'll be right back!" and she started up the stairs.

"You be quiet and don't wake Frank up!" I yelled after her. I wasn't too worried, as by that hour he was fairly well smashed and dead to the world.

She was back in a flash with the paints I'd been using to paint the guts in my see-through plastic man. I watched in a mixture of horror, fear and artistic admiration as Pinky painted every one of Miss Peavine's fingernails a different color. Green, purple, orange, blue, everything but red or pink. As awful as Peavine had treated her, I half expected Pink to go bonkers and paint her face up like a Zulu warrior. I was ready for the fun to end.

"ENOUGH! Help me get this thing closed."

"Wait! Just one more thing. Please!" Pink begged. "One more thing important for my mental health!" She ran over to Pap's desk on the other side of the filing cabinets and grabbed a tape dispenser.

"Oh… no… no…" I saw it coming, but not in time to stop Pink from taping an "X" across Peavine's crusty lips. Those old bad-mouthin' lips were sealed for all eternity. "Ok, that's it. Let's go!"

We closed the lid and started up the stairs, but PinkyToe yelled back one more time, reveling in her vengeful hatred, "Rest in Peace, you old witch!" PinkyToe had always held onto a grudge like a snappin' terrapin.

· · · · · · · ·

The next evening, the visitation for Eugenia Peavine was better attended than I would'a ever thought. Besides her family from Chattanooga, there were a few former students, who like me, had been told they had to come out of respect. All the teachers from school, and the secretary and the principal were there. The chapel was nearly full, the service about to start when suddenly Miss Peavine's young niece got downright hysterical. Her mother and father lowered their heads and voices, trying to reason with the willful child, but the brat started yelling, "I WANT TO SEE AUNT GENIE! NOW!"

The parents quickly conferred, and rather than to risk an even bigger scene, gave in. Mother on one side, father on the other, they each clamped down on a hand, and led her to the front of the coffin. They asked Frank, who had strongly advised against it in the first place, to remove the floral spray and open the casket. He had no choice than to oblige.

Pinky and I traded frantic glances and held our breath as the lid opened. The sister passed out cold, sliding down the side of the coffin, delicately, into a lump on the floor. The child screamed and screamed and screamed, like an overacting child star in a scary movie. The brother-in-law headed for Pap in a rage, fists tight.

In addition to the misaligned eyeball half stuffed into its socket, her winking expression, the lips flattened under tape, and the multicolor neon fingernails placed daintily at her waist, there was another horror that Pinky and I were not expecting. During its time on the ground outside our back door, the gardenia had attracted an enterprising fly. That fly had laid its eggs deep down in the bloom - eggs that had hatched overnight into an army of squirming white maggots, now churning industriously all over Miss Peavine's throat and bloated face. Eugenia Peavine was wearing a thick mask of grotesque animation to her funeral.

· · · · · · · ·

"Sit down, Anna Grace." My belly ached with dread and I felt the hot shits coming on. When Pap had that look on his face, I knew I was in for it. And there was an empty glass on the table and a nearly empty bottle of Jack Daniels, which was bound to make it worse.

He was pacing. "Our business, our livelihood, is a serious thing. Not only do we depend on it to put food on our table, our customers count on our reputation to treat their loved ones with dignity. It is a sacred trust!"

I interrupted, "But Pap, them maggots was not our fault!"

"Shut up and listen! You have single handedly destroyed our good name with one thoughtless prank! Well, not exactly all by yourself. I know Pinky was in on this too, She is never welcome here again by the way. NE-VER! Do you hear me? Since your mother... oh God... your mother died, you have run wild. Pinky is decidedly nothing but a bad influence. I have tried to keep you goin' right, but she keeps pulling you... off track, down the wrong path. I hate to say it, but I'm glad your mama's not here to see this!" Every sentence was punctuated with a big gulp of Jack.

He finished off the bottle in one great swig, his tongue becoming looser by the minute, his mind spinning in a senseless swirl, his body swaying. "Dory's the one who... who... picked you up out of that bureau drawer and wanted to keep you for her own, she's the one who wanted you to be her little girl... I figured you'd end up... trouble... I... never... wanted... an... adopted... not... my own... flesh and blood..." He passed out cold, drunker than I'd ever seen him.

I ran out, wanting to close up my ears and send those words back where they were before they'd burned like a hot poker into my brains. But then I knew, Aunt Nettie had been right all along. Anna Grace Tollett was the bastard child of a shameless whore.

I stumbled into my room and prayed that PinkyToe would be in her room too. I flashed the lamp ten times. It took a minute but there they came, ten flashes right back. I quickly threw the twenty dollars I had saved up, my panties and trainer bra, my toothbrush, a picture of Mama, a T-shirt and a pair of blue jeans into my train case, and headed out through the damp night to the tree house.

PinkyToe was waiting faithfully. I told her what had happened, that I was the unwanted child of a shameless whore and she was forever banned from my house. We had no choice. My life would be nothing without Pink so we had to go to Florida. We left the tree house and set out on the seven miles along Blackshale road to the bus station, which was not really a bus station but a rusty, bullet-riddled bus stop sign outside the Black Bear 24-Hour Diner. As we traipsed along the right of way, a transfer truck whizzed by in a cloud of diesel fumes. Feeling small, I reached out for Pinky's hand. We stayed that way for a piece, until she broke away and complained, "Oooo, my hand's sweatin'." Four miles on down the road, we bought tickets to Chattanooga, but the bus only ran at seven in the morning.

So there we set, looking skittish one way down the road and then the other. We swung our legs back and forth out over the dark asphalt which smelled like Frank's outboard motor oil, and I couldn't help picturing him at home the next morning walking the floor and wringing his formaldehyde stinkin' hands.

"Pinky, do you believe in the Lord Jesus?" I was hoping he might be looking out for us.

She didn't even have to study on it. "Hellno" Then she looked at me like I was crazy, and began her reverse evangelism. "Do you mean to tell me that you want to count on some dead guy who made mudballs with spit and plastered 'em on people's eyes? Cause that's what he did. Go look! It is right there in the Bible!"

"Well," I countered, "Pearlie says he's looking out after every sparrow, and it sure won't hurt to have him along."

Pinky kind of agreed, "Hit's lookin' like we could use all the help we can get!"

We fell asleep sitting on the covered bench on the side of the diner, in my opinion a sad excuse for a bus station.

• • • • • • • •

"Well, hello there girls!" I jumped and jerked awake and there was Corrine Miller, standing with her hands on her hips. "Are you taking a field trip?" she asked innocently. The diner owner had called Corrine, thinking that she might recognize two unaccompanied school-age girls that were looking more and more like runaways. By then, we'd had a little time to think about the realities of life alone on the road without enough money and much of a plan, so we were each secretly relieved to see Mrs. Miller.

"Hey, oh hi, Mrs. Miller," I started out right enough but somewhere in there I fell apart, and started blubbering. Corrine sat down and put her arms around me and PinkyToe, stroking our heads in the motherly way that we both missed and needed so much. We hung our heads and cried from the sweet touch.

"Girls, did I ever tell you about the time I ran away from home?" My daddy found me two towns away from where we lived. All I'd had all day was a Hershey bar, and my belly was growlin' something fierce! I was never so glad to see anyone in my life. I guess sometimes, the grass just seems greener on the other side!"

She hugged us both again, and we just sat there awhile, watching the cars speed back and forth along Blackshale Road. Then she took us into the diner and bought big fat double cheeseburgers, onion rings, and vanilla malteds all 'round.

Instead of taking us home in the middle of the night, she took us over to her house and put us to bed on a pallet in her front room. Then she went in and called Frank and Aunt Dimple to let them know we were safe, but neither one of them answered the phone.

When we woke up, she made us pancakes and set us up on her sofa watching cartoons a while. Corrine knew we needed some quiet time after our adventure, but she kept going back to the phone in her bedroom, trying to reach Pap and Aunt Dimple and let them know we were ok and on the way. Frank was still out like a light, but she'd finally been able to rouse Aunt Dimple from her sleeping pill haze. Directly she coaxed, "How would it be if I took you girls on home now?" Pinky and me looked at each other, neither one wanting to be the one to back down. We studied on it for a time, then we both nodded our heads. I agreed, "Yep, it is about time for me and Pearlie to watch her stories." Pearlie was always glued to "As the World Turns" of an afternoon.

We left Corrine's house without me ever seeing her kitchen. I might have wondered why my pictures were the only ones proudly displayed on her refrigerator door.

· · · · · · · ·

Corrine dropped Pinky off first. Aunt Dimple was standing in the driveway tappin' her paddle on her thigh. I could see Pinky was going to get a whoopin'. But even with that, I think Pink was glad to be back home, 'cause she grinned when she saw her Aunt Dimple swinging the paddle back and forth.

When Corrine got back in the car, my words spilled over. "You know what, Mrs. Miller? I ran away because my pap told me something that tore me plumb up. He was drunk and talking out of his head, but I know it's true because my Aunt Nettie had told me before and Mama wouldn't admit it. Frank said I was adopted! Adopted! That Mama found me in a bureau drawer on the front porch of Tollett's!"

I started sniffling, "I KNOW my mama was my mama! You just know a thing like that! My mama loved me special, I know for sure she did, to Heaven and back again!" and I dissolved into a flood of tears, anguish honking up from deep in my chest.

Corrine said, "Aw, honey, your mama loved you more than anything in the world. Everybody in town knew that!" She wrapped me up in her arms. She smelled so good, like lily of the valley. I was thinking how soft and sweetly comforting, how good it felt to be held again. That smell! The smell of the letter in the bottom of my jewelry box flashed into my mind and at that exact minute I noticed Corrine was shaking and breathing funny.

Corrine commenced to talking, but she sounded different. "Anna Grace." She faltered, unable to speak. I could tell that tears were backing up thick in her throat, choking off her voice, keeping her from saying the huge, important, hurtful thing she was trying to say. She started over, "Anna Grace, it was me. I am the one who left you in that drawer. I was not married, and I wanted to leave my baby, you, in a place where you'd have a good home. God knows Dory was the best mother I could have ever picked! I didn't abandon you though, I left you in Blackshale because I already had a job here, and I knew I could keep an eye on you, be around you, love you from a distance, see you grow up." She searched my face for anger.

It took me a few minutes to process all the pieces, to work through all the emotions. Then, like a jigsaw puzzle working itself, they all fell together and smacked me in the face with an unimaginable truth.

"Oh my GOD!" I exclaimed, staring straight ahead through a field of smashed bugs on her car windshield, close to bein' in shock, "You… YOU are the shameless whore?" I was having a hard time matching up the perfect teacher I had worshipped so much with the sinner who had left me a nameless orphan on a porch.

Corrine couldn't help it. She laughed out loud. "I made an awful mistake in judgment when I was young. But it resulted in me having you, the most beautiful person I know. Darlin', I can't be sorry about that."

• • • • • • • •

Corrine and Anna Grace came in through the back door, and walked in to see Frank at the kitchen table, hungover and the new day's first beer already in hand. All three were sheepish, embarrassed, feeling at fault.

"Found them down at the bus station Frank. I think Anna Grace was about ready to come on home though." Corrine looked back and forth between them, trying to negotiate a loving connection.

Frank stood up and took Anna Grace in his arms, burying his face in her hair. It was the first time he'd touched her since Dory's death. "Grace, I never, never meant what I said about not wanting you. You're my angel. I just… I just been hurting so bad, baby. I can't seem to feel what I know in my heart. But when I thought you were gone, I was near crazy thinking I'd let you get out where you might get lost, or hurt…" He turned to Corrine, "Thank you, Corry, thank you for bringing her home."

A week later, Corrine was out on the back stoop, asking to come in. Frank had been told the story, of course, and Pearlie too. Pearlie was peckish about the whole thing, greeting Corrine with only a "Hmmmph!" Frank was more understanding. Corry turned to Anna Grace, "Would you like to take a walk?"

They walked back through the yard and sat down next to the well. Anna Grace swung her legs nervously. Then she picked up stones and threw them in, counting the seconds until they hit the water. For a minute, she could see Hum standin' there in puppylove, grinning at Lucy Lincoln.

Then she looked out through the woods and took a deep breath. "I got somethin' to say. You will never, ever take Dory's place. But, even when I had no idea at all about you birthing me, I looked up to you. I reckon Mama would like me having somebody, someone to look out for me, bein's she can't be here no more. I'm not sure what it is we'll be, you and me. You may be like an aunt, I sure hope a better one than I already got, or we might be like sisters, or just friends, I dunno. I'm thinking though, you can love more than one person at a time, more than one kind of mama at a time."

Corrine was so proud of Anna Grace, her maturity and her loyalty. She was also bursting with joy. Now that her secret was out in the open, and Anna didn't seem to hate her, she couldn't help rejoicing in their relationship - whatever form it might take. Whatever tiny bit of the girl's love she could earn, she would accept gratefully. There was one secret remaining though, and it would have to come out. They had to be told that Dory had died by John Evan's hand.

·········

Corrine asked Frank to sit down at the kitchen table with her and Anna Grace. She went into the laundry where Pearlie was sprinkling shirts with starch water and asked her to please join them. Pearlie slapped down the sprinkler bottle and grunted, "Hmmmph!" but she worked her way to the table and sat. Corry pushed down the storm of panic rising in her chest by breathing in and out slowly. When everyone was settled, she unfolded John Evan's letter and smoothed it out on the table.

Looking sadly around the table at each one, she said, "I've kept this to myself until now for obvious reasons. Please believe I had no idea how disturbed John Evan was, or that he had a history of mental illness. I wanted to tell you this myself, before I take the letter to Sheriff Raby. You have all lost Dory, indirectly, because of me. I'll never get over that."

She read the letter. It was painful to hear, and a gamut of emotions passed around the table. Frank and Anna Grace held it in their hands and read it again for themselves, disbelieving at first.

Pearlie cried out, "Mercy, mercy, Lorda mercy!" again and again.

Frank just looked at the floor and mumbled, "Stinkbirds, my ass."

When they handed her back the letter, she rose and concluded, "I'm going now. I'll talk to y'all later after you've had a chance to digest all this."

She headed for the door, but Anna Grace called, "Wait, I want to give you something." She ran to her room and took the pink envelope out of her jewelry box. At the door, she handed it to Corrine, "This is for you. I reckon it's yours."

Back in her house, at her own kitchen table, Corrine looked down at the words she had written years earlier. She didn't know what the return of the letter meant. Was it simply an acknowledgement of her authorship, an angry refusal of her love, or was it a sign of affection and encouragement? She folded her arms on the table and laid down her spinning head, emotionally drained.

· · · · · · · ·

"Do you have 'em?" I asked Corry.

"Them," she corrected. She reached into her pocket and brought out a leather pouch, loosened the strings around the opening and turned it over, spilling the contents into my upturned hands. I walked over to the stile and counted out ten round stones, placed exactly, perfectly spaced across the top. We sat in the grass for a spell, silent. Then I started picturin' the chiggers, working their way up into the warm, sweaty crevices of our bodies.

I stood up and wove my fingers into Corrine's and said, "Let's go." We walked out across the meadow hand in hand, out where the wet grasses slapped at our bare legs, the June bugs buzzed, and Dory's spirit danced in the sky.

· · · · · · · ·

There were two short rings on the party line, meanin' the call was for us up in the house. I skated across the slick wood floor in my socks, hurryin' to pick it up, and shouted my breathless "Hello!" PinkyToe was out of breath too, her words rolling out in a tangle. I smarted off, "Slow down or shut up!"

"Peanut, BoJack Murphy and them! They're up at the tree house gettin' in our stuff! I got a plan! Meet me in our barn in five minutes!" In three minutes I was out the door and across the steel bridge, staring at PinkyToe shoveling steaming horseshit into four buckets that were about bigger'n us.

"Grab a couple!" she yelled, "We're gonna teach them boys a lesson!"

Up in the tree house, Peanut and his friends were making such a racket, they didn't hear us creep up under the ladder. We piled shit ankle high at the base of the ladder, and then we slapped it thick all over the bottom rungs. We backed away a piece, and then Pink yelled with all her might, "Hey Coondicks! Get your puny peckers outta there!"

All five boys fought to be the first out the door and down the ladder, and when BoJack and Peanut won the contest they was sure sorry. Their feet slipped off the stinking sludge on the rungs, and they all landed in a pile, squirming around in the muck tryin' to stand up and run to get at PinkyToe, who was still taunting them. She was slapping her thighs and laughing her fool head off, being a silly, loud, ball-busting girl, having the time of her life beatin' them boys in a brawl.

The very second I was grabbed from behind and felt the cold metal of the handcuff lock down hard on my wrist, I heard one of BoJack's older twin brothers yell out, "BoJack, you boys skedaddle on back up to the house now." All five of them boys our age set out runnin', and scattered like buckshot.

The older twins, who had dropped out of high school that year and already spent a few years in the reform school, had been drinking whisky all afternoon and I could tell they had it in their minds to stay with us awhile.

One of the twins dragged me to the tree house and locked the other handcuff around a support pole. "Hey, hey little girl," he teased with a sick smile, his eyes dancing wild and demonic. He held down my free hand and started trying his best to kiss me on the mouth but I jerked my head back and forth, and took to kicking him in the shins. He looked me up and down and grinned again when he saw I was already growing a bosom, which he started right in mashin' around on with his big sweaty hand.

"Ooooo-eeee, howdy! Look at them big knockers growin' on this little bitty girl!" He shoved his hand down into my shorts but jerked it right back out, stickywet, crimson, smelling of iron. I was flooding again.

"Bloody bitch!" he spat at me, "Fucking hell Jake, she's bloody with the curse. I ain't touchin' this here cooch." Then his head turned slowly back around to me, black eyed, brooding, thoughtful. "It's ok, don't you worry bloody girl, you can still play with us. Jake, bring that'un over here."

The twin called Jake dragged Pinky over next to me and handcuffed her wrists to a cross pole up under the tree house, stretching her arms high up over her head. Harley held her elbows back so she couldn't move and Jake jerked down her green canvas gym shorts. He smiled at me and spat on the ground, looking around, thinking.

Jake got right up in my face with his whisky breath. Then he lowered his voice and whispered in a voice full of gravel and hate, "Pull down her panties."

I looked him right in the eye and laughed. I said, "You are

crazy in the head."

"I SAID, pull down her panties," he demanded in a wavery, slurred voice.

"And I said NO I AIN'T GONNA DO THAT!"

The other twin stepped back and bent down into the shadows. When he come back up, he cocked a shotgun and pointed it at my head.

Jake unlocked the handcuffs. "Now, little girl have you ever played doctor? What'll it be, bloody bitch? Play doctor or both you'uns eat some 'a our bullet candy?"

I slowly raised my eyes to Pink's. For the first time since I'd known her she couldn't talk. Both our throats had gone dry as sawdust, and we couldn't squeak out a scream. I locked eyes with Jake and spoke with a calm boldness nothin' at all like the quaking jello of my insides, "I reckon I'll just have myself some bullet candy."

Harley moved around in front of me and pointed the muzzle of the shotgun up against my heart. I took a deep breath, and my last thought was maybe, maybe, I'd get to see my mama if I died. I could see Harley's knuckles begin to curl toward the trigger, so I closed my eyes and tried to call up Dory's face.

"WAIT!" Pinky shrieked at Harley. Then she looked at me hard and cried, "Anna Grace Tollett, do it. Do what Jake says. Hit ain't worth dyin' over."

I spoke to her softly, "Pinky, it's gonna be ok." I knelt down and pulled down her panties as gentle as I could. Jake shoved his boot in between her feet and kicked her legs farther apart. He ripped off her shirt, baring her chest. I stood up and hung my head, tears falling.

"Look... at... that... slick... runt... pussy," he laughed scornfully. He wheeled around and socked me hard under the chin, "Open your eyes, bitch, I mean for you to LOOK!" I'd bitten my tongue and was spitting blood.

Pinky was behind me a ways as far as being developed. She hadn't got her period yet, her womanhood was still a girlhood - a smooth mound with only a trace of soft fuzz. Her chest was still flat with the soft, barely swollen buds of little girl nipples no bigger than a dime. She was crying, scared, but awful ashamed of her childish body too.

With the ends of his big, rough fingers Jake spread open her private parts, and while his brother held the gun to my head Jake forced me to rub on her down there with my pointer finger. Her tears ran down on my hand. Harley kept the gun on me while Jake gave me orders.

"Rub on her down there real easy, and she'll like it, she will!" He studied our faces intently with his crazy grin, hungry for the results of his sick experiment. "Keep doin' it! Faster!" he demanded.

Then they both got real quiet, fooling around with the fronts of their blue jeans where they were pullin' tight. Jake's voice sounded funny, weak like, "Yes ma'am, you are two little queer girls now!'" At that, both of them were howling hysterically, drunkenly, slapping their legs. Jake handcuffed me to the tree house again, and Harley laid down the gun.

I was sure they were fixin' to take turns with her after that, doing the thing I had heard about that men do. Making love, Aunt Sudy had called it, but this would be nothin' to do with love, no kind whatsoever. Any fool would know that two great big grunting boys forcing themselves on that tiny little girl thing I'd seen would have to be some awful pain and damage.

But they didn't do that. They were startin' to sober up and have second thoughts. Jake took our handcuffs off, and set us up against a tree. Harley give us a drink of water from a canteen – a strange kindness.

But then Jake threatened, "Listen up little girls. If you ever tell a soul about this, breathe a word to anybody, I swear to God we'll come and kill your maws."

That was when I knew PinkyToe had either lost her mind completely or would end up being ok. Sorely shamed on the inside, scratched and bruised on the outside, she began to laugh helplessly, "Ha ha, ha, fooled you kid-abusin' sons of a bitch, our mamas is done dead."

• • • • • • • •

On our way home, we stopped in the woods. Pinky sunk down onto a big rock and gazed out into the woods with wells of tears gleaming in her eyes. Then she looked straight at me in a wounded stare.

"Pink... I'm sorry, but they made me... they'd a killed us!"

"I don't want nobody ever knowin' about this... nobody! I ain't mad at you. I'm the one that called it. I ain't mad."

"But Pink... you could tell Aunt Dimple, she should call the sheriff!"

"Well I could, but I AIN'T!" She was final.

She pulled out her pocketknife and sliced a red line across her right palm, then held her hand out for mine. I laid my left hand in hers, palm up. Next to what we had just been through, that cut didn't hurt not a bit. She pressed our bleeding hands together, and resolved, "We are blood sisters and swear never to tell this thing to a living soul!" I nodded solemnly, sadly, wound up in a tight knot with the aching hurt I felt for her.

• • • • • • • •

Frank Tollett knew Anna Grace had been floundering. In the past few weeks, though, it seemed much worse, like she'd suddenly grown to be an old, bent over woman weighed down with a heavy black cloak. Something was bad wrong, but he was not able to come out and ask. Talking about private things with a girl was just not in a man like Frank. Pearlie provided Grace with food, clean clothes, and love too, but she had no way with the problems of young girls.

Frank knew what Grace needed more than anything was a mother, and as it happened, he knew where there was one right handy. As Anna Grace and Corrine began to forge a relationship, Frank encouraged it in small ways, and after a time he'd say, "Would you like to invite Corrine over for a pizza pie tonight?" They would all sit down to eat together, and afterwards watch a show on TV. Then Corrine would get up and go home, where she spent her hours at loose ends, lonely and disoriented by her widowhood. She could never see herself trusting in the love of another man.

One night Frank followed her out to the car. She got in and then rolled down the window. "Something on your mind, Frank Tollett?"

He put his hands on the edge of the window and leaned in, his eyes bouncing all around that car, everywhere but on her face, "Corry, I have a practical idea I'd like you to think on."

She turned down the radio, and looked up at his ears that were red as sugar beets.

"Would you consider living here so you could be with Anna Grace? Well, thing is… thing is, we'd have to marry on paper to keep it from bein' a big scandal, but right now seems like you need her and she needs you. Later on, after she gets through school, if you're in more of a mind to take on a real husband, well, we can cross that bridge when we come to it." She was a beautiful woman, but he felt no lust in his loins for her. His heart had flown with Dory and the stinkbirds into the big blue sky.

"Well golly, Frank, that's about the most romantic thing anyone's ever said to me!" Corry laughed, but then glanced up, catching Anna Grace out of the corner of her eye. She was looking down on them from her window seat. "How do you think she would feel about it?" Corry asked, suddenly more serious.

"Fine," Frank confirmed, "I think she'd feel just fine."

. . . .

So Frank Tollett and Corrine Baker Miller kinda got married that fall, standing on a carpet of orange and yellow leaves out in the back yard. Pearlie made deviled eggs and pimento cheese sandwiches, and a small coconut wedding cake filled with lemon curd. When time came to kiss the bride, Frank planted a firm but brotherly smooch on the side of her face.

We settled into a routine, Frank and Corry, me and Pearlie. Pearlie and Corrine came around to a mutual respect. We were a family, even though Pap and Corrine weren't much of a couple. I sat in my window seat every night and talked to Dory Tollett up in the starry sky. I hoped she knew that she would always be my mama. Corrine was a wonderful stepmother and friend though, a joy in my life. I never thought much about her being my birthmother. Dory had been that in my mind for so long, she just kinda stuck there. As I began to turn into a woman though, I looked in the mirror and saw a young Corrine, dark eyes, porcelain white skin, shining straight black hair. Dory was nowhere to be found in the reflection.

2029 Morning Glory Ridge

My bunny ears are flopping in time to a widgie, widgie beat as I make my way downstairs to the tea party. It's a beautiful spring day, and the veranda is thick with plastic morning glory vines and the strains of romantic music. I am personally sick of morning glories, but there are much more important things to complain about at eighty-one, like the fact that something rigid and unmovable feels like it's turned sideways in my rectum. In spite of that, I put on my happy face and sweep onto the veranda.

Daphne has saved me a place at their table, a frou frou tableau of layered white laces over a pale blue cloth. I have to admit someone has gone to a lot of trouble, collecting teapots, cups, and saucers of different patterns. The food people have done their homework too, having prepared scones, cucumber sandwiches, and marzipan Easter eggs. One would think that this idyllic setting will make for the perfect day. One would be horribly wrong.

Flotilla, dressed in a vintage 1950's nurse's costume, weaves between tables pouring from a steaming floral teapot. I unfurl a ruffled napkin into my lap and scoot a scone over to my rose covered plate. Munching on it, I regard the cutesy bonnets perched on my friends' heads. They have gone all out in crafting class, decorating their hats with frippery, flowers, birds, and bows. I like my simple bunny ears better than all that crafty ticky tacky, but to each her own.

As a final course, Gunderson, dressed as the Mad Hatter, comes round to each table with a large round tray of pastel frosted cupcakes in pink, yellow, green, and blue. Each one has "Eat Me" piped in white icing.

When the tray reaches the table behind us, Mr. Ho, who speaks excellent English but has one leg in la la land, jumps up and yells, "AH! Ah HA! EAT ME!"

Apparently the cupcakes have triggered a pleasant memory from his younger, sexually active days. He hops over to Daphne and unzips, laying his Spring surprise right out on her plate. She faints dead away, knocking our rickety card table over, sending china teacups to break into slivers on the stone tile, and bits of food fly everywhere.

Enter the house dogs. Roscoe and Ben, a rowdy pair of Great Mountain Pyrenees, who interpret the noise as playtime and run in tails awaggin', sopping up spilled party food in their jowls. Flotilla comes running in after them, hits the butter smeared on the tile, and slides heels first, catching her skirt on a table leg. It pulls up around her waist. I shall never forget the unsightly fat bulging against her vintage garter belt, obese thighs overflowing her white stockings, and her pantieless pom pom exposed for all to see. Mr. Ho is heading for it, with who knows what intent, but Gourdhead and Julio (screeching "SWEET Mother of God!") arrive just in time to hold him back. His pants are around his knees and Daphne wakes up just in time to see Mr. Ho's moon shot from behind. She passes out all over again.

I should have known that Daphne, who had been introduced to sex in a brothel, would not be so shocked by how Mr. Ho is hung. Later, Mrs. Gundersen fed us the gossip that Daphne's fainting had more to do with her diabetes and the marzipan Easter eggs she'd been filching, hiding them under the lace cloth until the coast was clear to pop them in her sugar starved mouth.

"Well good grief! This whole thing has just turned into a big shitshow!" I puff in exasperation. I've had enough and jump on my WidgieWalker, "I'm outta here!"

1960 Blackshale

Most times, I was what Frank called "a purty good kid." Considering everything that I'd been through at such a young age, I was right normal. I went to school and minded my teachers. At home, I did the things kids did when they were eleven and had no brother or sister to their name. Solitaire, pickup sticks, crossword puzzles, stuffing lightning bugs in a jelly jar. I played paper dolls a lot for a while, drawing and coloring my own clothes for them, until Pink got mad at me and cut the white tabs off all them Mermaid paper dolls Dory had give me for Christmas after our Weeki Wachi trip. That soured me on paper dolls. Mostly, I drew and made stuff.

I got in trouble twicet that one year. First, Pinky talked me into charging admission of a quarter to the washroom stall where Becky Burdine was willing to display the miracle of her third tit. It was not as big as the main two, but it sure was a real honest to gosh tit! Our teacher was furious. We listened to her preach on kindness and human dignity while we dusted erasers for a solid month.

The more serious offense was a snot slinging, blood gushing fistfight, when I held a boy down, pounded him into mush, and poked deep black holes in him with my charcoal pencil. At recess, I was minding my own business, propped up against a tree, drawing Pearlie from memory, shading the tones of her skin just right. Around the other side boys were watching girls jumping rope and playing "Red Rover Come Over." I could hear Peanut entertaining Sodboy and some other misguided fools with comments like "Ooooo, I'd love to dip my dick into THAT," "Yeah, she makes me cream in my jeans!" or "Man, how'd ja like to get a stinky pinky offa HER." One tomboy girl got written off, "Forget her, she's queer."

I was about to move to another tree, when one of Peanut's stooges circled back around the trunk and spied my drawing.

"That your dead mama's black nigger? She look stupider than most, and they all right stupid!"

He was showing off for Peanut, but when he turned grinning to win Peanut's reaction, I was up and on him before he had a chance to defend his sorry ass. I straddled him, hammering him with balled up fists, all the hurt and anger from previous events exploding out of me. For good measure, I stuck my pencil in his arms over and over, stabbing deep and hard, until the lead broke off in his tough, hateful white trash skin.

Peanut stood over him brayin', rubbing it in, "You candyass pussy, gettin' yourself whooped by a girl!" As if he weren't hurt enough, Peanut took to kickin' him.

The teacher on duty was there in a flash, dragging a bloody kid in each hand to the principal's office. Frank was called to the school and had to take me home for three days - suspended in shame. When we got home, I told Frank right out what that boy had said.

Frank made an obligatory speech about how fighting was not usually the best answer to problems. But then, trying to hide his smile, he softened, "But in this case, Anna girl, you did right. You did. Taking up for someone you love, well, I reckon sometimes that makes things different."

· · · · · · · ·

Pinky and me sat in my window seat listening to kids holler up and down the river. That scamp PinkyToe was never satisfied to play a simple game of "Hid'n Go Seek." No siree! She was at loose ends and keen to drag me out in the woods for an adventure.

"Let's go see Deadbabe Cove!" she needled.

"No! Corry would skin me alive if I went off that far."

"Common', you're yellow! Yep, I always knew you was chicken-shit yellow!"

That made me mad, so I laced up my Keds and made for the door, Pink laughing in victory behind. After a while, she fretted, "Are you sore?"

"Naw!" I reasoned, "Leastways I don't get bored with you around."

We hiked for an hour upside the mountain through woods all briars and scrub pine, navigating a dense tangle with no clear direction but up or down. About lost, we hit an old trail, and a mile on, we come up on a ramshackle cabin by a crick. Pinky ran ahead, yelling and flapping her hands, "C'mon! Ain't nobody livin' here. This here cabin is as empty as your brain."

She pressed what puny weight she had against the faded blue door and fell headlong into the room, just missing a rot hole in the floor and the copperhead that slithered down into it, shunning the sudden light. I stepped into her silence, and we both froze, staring in wonder at the sun streaked wall ahead.

At first it appeared to be a confusion of overgrown vines, but when we moved closer to the shapes of sunlight cast by the window, it was a thick knit mesh of many a different thing, both dead and alive. "Let's get the hell out of here," Pinky begged, spooked, heading for the back door.

"Not on your peckerhead life!" I replied. I dug down in my jeans pocket and pulled out my notebook and a pen. "Go do something, just look out for snakes."

As Pink went out the back door, I set my pen moving on the paper and drew like my hand was on fire. Working as fast as I could, I outlined every last dust coated thing hanging across that wall. I knew I didn't have long, that Pink would get antsy to move on. There were living vines, slugs and wormy things, but they twisted and squirmed around the skeletons of creatures long dead and strange objects fashioned by some human hand for questionable purposes.

She was gone apiece, longer than I'd counted on, and she came in the back door yelling, "I found it, I found Deadbabe Cove!" She reached up in wonder and touched a stitched figure, a mangle of root and bone and rotted, crusted muslin.

"I sware I do believe some BooHag lived here."

Out back of the cabin a ways, hand hewn sandstone slabs in a row, names eaten by moss and rain and ice, gave witness to a few short lives with the same date of death. "Dory said the influenza kilt all them babies." The tear that splattered a leaf at my feet was for them now nameless babies, but it was for my mama, too. By the time we found our way out, the woods sparkled with lightning bugs, and we ran ahead of the hoots of night birds and the howlings of who knows what.

The next week, my fingers was sore. I had stitched up a copy of every amulet and object from the cabin wall and hung them in the tree house. Those things I could not make, I drew a picture of and tacked to the wall with Frank's staple gun, which I had temporarily stolen from his workshop. With them evil Murphys creepin' around, we could use any kind of magic we could get.

2029 Morning Glory Ridge

Mrs. Gundersen has brought me a gift from the past today - a cardboard storage box full of personal treasures I don't even remember having, that somehow followed me here to this, my last stand. I see in the box Dory's journals, along with snapshots of her alone or with Sudy, cornered with black triangles.

Here are shiny paper albums of travel pictures. I recall her telling of that trip out west. Her Pa had invited Sudy along on a family trip to Memphis, and when they got out there he said "Well, HELL, we are halfway across the country so we just might as well go on to Californie!" And so in the one pair of rolled up blue jeans they had started out with, they wound their way across Oklahoma and Route 66, the grand Canyon and the orange groves of the San Joaquin valley, until they finally stood, jeans stiff and smelling like soured cabbage, on the stars of bronze planted in the Hollywood sidewalk.

Farther down in the box are fading black and white snapshots of other events in Mama's life, and Sudy in most of them too - elementary school and girl scouts, high school and proms, two fresh-faced young women after a capping ceremony in the first year of nursing school, Mama and Pap on their wedding day and Sudy standing there to the side, the edge of a wet spot barely visible on her dress.

Then came me. There were shots of Mama and Aunt Sudy holding me up to the camera, my chubby legs dangling out of a seersucker sun suit. Here are stacks and stacks of us, Mama and Pap, and me growing up inch by inch by inch, until I was nine and the pictures abruptly stopped.

Here's a picture of some little girl holding a smooth wooden stick almost as tall as she is. At first I don't recognize her, but

then I remember the stick. I flip the photo over and read the back
- Marlene May Templeton. After Mama died and Corry slipped
back into my life, Sudy rarely came around. It probably hurt her
too bad to be around Dory's place with no Dory in it. By then
she'd had Marlene, and her days were filled with work and being
a mama. The few times Sudy came around, toting her daughter
on her hip, Marlene always had that stick. From the time she
was knee high to a grasshopper and walking, she took that stick
everywhere she went, tapping, swinging, poking. Most little girls
clung to a blanket or a ragged stuffed animal, and Pap thought
it was mighty strange that Marlene held onto that stick for dear
life.

At the bottom of the picture pile, here's one of Mama all by
herself. I catch my breath and recognize a familiar dull ache in my
chest. She is filling up the square with a proud smile, her granny's
twenty-two flung across her shoulder, blissfully unaware it will
be the instrument of her death.

1961 Blackshale

Time passes so quickly after the loss of a loved one. Corry and Frank had already worked their way past a second anniversary that went unmarked by kiss or cake or gift made of cotton. Under the façade though, in both of them, something unspoken was beginning to stir. It was just natural that two fine looking people in close proximity, who had no natural animosity, would eventually feel a spark of somethin'. If nothing else, they were both getting powerful horny.

Frank struggled with it though, as he still felt the need to keep faith with Dory. Maybe he wasn't accepting that she was really gone. He half-feared, half-hoped her spirit was hanging around looking over his shoulder.

One night, when Anna Grace was away slumber partyin' at PinkyToe's house, Frank came up behind Corrine at the kitchen sink and wrapped himself around her. She was good and ready by then, had in fact been willing it. She turned around, searching his eyes, kissing his lips with an open, hungry mouth. He lifted her up on the cabinet and slid her shorts and panties off. With her legs around his waist pulling him tight and sucking him in, he gave her a loving poundin'. They were loud, out of control, making an awful racket, and only after they fell down on the sofa laughing did they stop to worry that Pearlie might have heard. She did, and as a matter of fact had climbed up the two flights of stairs just to be sure somebody wasn't killin' somebody. Then, she sunk down on the top step and smiled. "Lord, Lord, de gone wear somebody out!" she breathed aloud.

The next day, she and Corry were rolling out sugar cookies at the kitchen table, when Pearlie took to giggling. "Don't kere what nobody say, ain't never hurt nothin' for a man and his lawfully wedded woman to get a little nookie." She shot Corrine a sly grin, and then they both fell to their knees and lay down laughing in convulsions on the floor. Once they'd recovered, they stood back up, brushed off their aprons, washed their hands, and turned back to the cookie dough.

"Tell me about Hum's daddy," Corry said.

"Oh, Lord Jesus, that ain't purty, no'me, ain't purty a'tall. Hum's daddy. Hum's daddy were my daddy."

Corrine gave her a sad look across the flattened dough, reached out her hand, "Oh Pearlie... oh... darlin'!" she empathized dripping with pity, "Did you never get to have a good time with a man you loved?"

"Well... now... Miz Corry, I never went and said nothin' like that!" Pearlie picked up a cookie cutter and began to cut out stars and circles and hearts, smilin' to herself. She was humming a tune full of sugar-sweet, mouthwatering memories of a fine young soldier she'd once loved before he met up with a bullet in the war.

2029 Morning Glory Ridge

Our river was always hungry. Every few years, it gobbled up a boy or girl, an ill-balanced hound dog, and one time a whole band of gypsies. From my rocking chair here on the veranda of Morning Glory Ridge, I can look down and see it meandering through the valley as if it is in no hurry to run from the law, as if it were an innocent with no memory of its murdering past.

The gypsies went into the river one spring way back when Pearlie was a girl. Once in a while they would come through, their painted wagon clattering behind a team of gaunt horseflesh. Blackshale families scrambled to gather in their children, afraid they would be stolen by those filthy, dark-eyed strangers.

A family of eleven was packed in that wagon like sardines, and jangling along behind were three shriveled, exhausted goats that gave out a few drips of milk when they stopped to camp for the night. Back before the steel bridge was built, there was a shaky wooden one. About the time the gypsies started crossing over, a pack of wild dogs got a whiff of the smelly goats and gave chase, spooking the team. The wooden rails were no match for horses in a blind panic, and the whole family was dumped screaming into the raging river. Some said "good riddance, them dirty, child-stealin' gypsies was no good no way" but the girl, Pearlie, had seen them pretty black-eyed children, sad exotic faces peekin' out from behind the curtain, and she mourned them in her heart.

· · · · · · · · ·

For PinkyToe and me, one of the darkest nights of our lives was on that river, a part of our childhood submerged in the black waters. That summer, we were twelve going on thirteen, girls becoming women, antsy to court risk.

Pinky had a cousin visiting that summer, a Yankee boy of

considerable interest to us. Being from "up north" was like having two heads. He was a little older, a lot more sophisticated. He was from Boston, a man of the world. To Pink, he was just an odd cousin. For me, Jon was an alien attraction like nothing I'd seen in Blackshale before. As the weeks went on, he became my first crush.

As the summer waned, we'd worn out the Blackshale summer standbys, had grown tired of the skating rink, the picture show, the usual. We wanted to give Jon a unique southern mountain experience as a parting shot before he went back north to school. As we often did, we made a plan that involved some degree of subterfuge. Frank thought I was at Pinky's; Aunt Dimple assumed Pink was at my house. Jon was going to wait until Aunt Dimple had her little magic pill for the night and then join us. We took Frank's old army pup tent, flashlights, matches, snacks, and our best intentions to camp overnight on the river.

We chose the section of the river where the land sloped up sharply on each side, knowin' it had a silt beach that had filtered down from the hills and offered a flat, soft place to pitch our tent. It was the place where several creeks from the mountain converged into Blackshale River. Pink and I got the tent pitched and a fire built just in time before dark fell.

We sat on the bank, scanning the clear starry sky in awe, listening to the water's rippling song. An hour later, we saw Jon's flashlight swinging back and forth, as he made his way down the wooded slope. We burnt our weenies and marshmallows on the fire, told scary stories, and listened to my radio, 'til the skeeters went crazy on our damp skin. Somewhere in the middle of all that, Jon had leaned over and given me my first real kiss on the lips. We climbed in the tent and zipped our sleeping bags, looking up at the stars through drooping eyes and the netted door flap - what a feeling! Grown up, out on our own. I fell asleep deeply breathing the pine fresh air, drinking in the sounds of the river.

Everything happened so fast, when I replay the memory, I'm never sure which version is exactly right. I woke up when the rain began to pelt down hard, followed by a lightning bolt, but it must' a been raining for a while because the river had already risen up to our tent.

"Get the stuff, we have to get out of here!" Pink yelled over the yowling wind. We all grabbed at the tent, jerking the pegs up out of the sand, ready to scramble up through the woods when lightning illuminated a huge surge of water upstream, coming down on us. Flashflood!

"Run! Climb up!" Pinky yelled at Jon, but he slipped in the mud and fell facedown. The wall of water hit and he was swept away. I saw his arm sticking up out of the wildly churning stream, his hand spread in a desperate plea toward the flashing sky. We two scared girls climbed to higher ground, breathing hard in panic, tearfully trying to decide what to do. We ran to Aunt Dimple's. She wouldn't wake up, but we called the rescue squad on her phone.

They found Jon a mile downstream, thoroughly bruised and beaten and drowned by the angry river. When they came to tell us, Pink and I were huddled together in a shared hysteria. The door opened and a stern-faced Frank came in. Someone had finally gotten Aunt Dimple up, and she observed the scene through a drugged fog.

"What happened?" Pap demanded, "From the beginning." He listened, and in the end, didn't say much in the way of recrimination. Our grand adventure had cost someone's life. He was wise enough to know that we would bear that guilt the rest of our lives, and nothing he could say would make it any worse or better.

Pinky was again subdued by a crisis, and we both grew up a lot that summer. Of course the two of us were grounded until school started back, but we were too beaten down to sneak out. We stayed in or walked alone and did a lot of soul searching in honor of a boy named Jon.

1963 Blackshale

Corrine and I were sitting at a corner of the square kitchen table, a jigsaw puzzle between us, half worked. It was a Florida garden scene, bursting with tropical hues. I spied some pieces of busy, spectacular colors, and when I fit them into the existing contour there appeared... A Peacock! Out of the quiet concentration, Corry began to chuckle to herself.

"Do you remember," she ventured, "the drawing you did of me with a peacock on my head? The one I had to confiscate, because you were supposed to be doing your arithmetic."

The memory of the embarrassment and tears hit me in the chest, feeling just like yesterday. "Sure I do. It was the low point of my educational career!" Even now my voice was breaking with the recollection.

"Well," Corry confessed, "When I took your drawing, you never asked for it back. It went home with me that night and right up on my refrigerator. It was the joy of my life - a real prize. Kinda got me through a hard time when I thought I might never be around you again after you left my class. It stayed right there on my fridge until I moved here!"

I looked across the table at her, and it hit me, really for the first time, how hard those years had been for her. I had been so near, and yet so far. I still missed Mama, but Corry was a blessing in my life. I reached across and held her hands, and then flattened my face onto the table, groaning.

"A peacock on your head, Lord, what was I thinking?"

· · · · · · · · ·

PinkyToe burst through the back door, slamming the screen behind her. Corrine called, "Do come in!" Corry was dubious about PinkyToe's helter-skelter influence on me, but at the same time harbored a soft spot for Pink's orphan status and admired her spunk. Corry always felt protective of small people. PinkyToe was barely taller than an eight-year-old and was still skin and bones.

"Hey A. T.!" Pink was big on initials now. "Let's take a sunbath!"

We slipped on our two-piece suits and checked the list twice - baby oil, sunglasses, transistor radio, cokes, peanuts to dump in the cokes, old chenille bedspread. We headed to the back yard. We laid out for thirty minutes on each side, frying our oil slathered bodies in the late summer sun. Pinky tanned, I burned.

"I'm heading for the porch." Out of the sun, I opened my pack of peanuts and poured them in the coke bottle. The salt fizzled. I rolled the radio dial until I heard the Supremes.

Pinky plunked up the steps, "What's the matter with you? You're sure as hell in a slapdog mood!"

"I dunno, I'm just itchy in my gut. I got a bad case of the whim-whams. Feels like everthing's lookin' to change." I guzzled my salty coke and belched.

"That's called high school," the eavesdropping Corry put in. "You girls are in for a whole new scenario! Just be yourselves and everything will be fine."

Pinky loved to make up her own song lyrics. Off key as a drunken sailor, she sang along with Diana, Mary, and Florence.

"When my nightlight starts shining in his eyes, Makes me realize he's a poltergeist..."

I gave her a fond poke in the ribs and taunted, "You are an idiot, is what you are."

· · · · · · · ·

That evenin', we sat out on the dewy grass bank along Blackshale Road and breathed in the cooling of the air. Ever so often Corrine's long brown weenie dog would mount one of our baby-oiled legs and start humpin' away. PinkyToe kicked him off and airborne. When a car passed by we yelled, "Hay mister, your wheels are rolling." Then we'd run up the bank, slipping and sliding on the wet grass, and hide behind a boxwood in case they came back.

Back on the bank, looking up at Cassiopeia, the moment felt poignant. The simplest things - the rackety cicadas, a yellowish light flickering on in a house across the road, the distant barking of dogs echoing off the river - seemed weirdly profound. We didn't even talk about nothin', just sat slappin' bugs and listenin' to the wonders of the night, until Corry came to the door and yelled out, "Anna Grace, time to get on in here for your bubble bath."

• • • • • • • •

My first day at Blackshale High was a real eye opener. In grammar school, I'd rode the bus to school, done my work, come home, played with Pinky. There was no social life to be had by a girl in Blackshale, except Girl Scouts and Rainbows, which I thought were a stupid waste of time. Who wants to prance around in a uniform or a pastel formal? Now all of a sudden in high school, there was all this stuff. Everybody was joining lame-o groups or playing sports or wearing "in" fashions to shape their i-den-ti-ties. When them cheerleaders got up in front of the pep rally actin' so prissy and silly, I wanted to hurl. It seemed like everybody was tryin' to be just like everybody else and fit in, wearing the same fashions, talkin' the same talk. Then I got to thinking about what Corry had said, "Just be yourself." I decided right then and there, for the rest of my life, I was just gonna be me, Anna Grace Tollett. Everybody could just like it or lump it!

So when the alarm went off the next morning, I threw the shiny Bass Weejuns Corry had bought me into the back of the closet. Instead, I put on Pap's combat boots with a thick pair of polka dot socks over black tights. Over them, I popped on a short ruffly embroidered dress that Aunt Sudy (actually my flamboyant Uncle Faron) had bought me in Mexico. I had hauled my black hair up into a spiky ponytail that spewed up like a fountain through a stack of red rubber bands. Then I hung one of my favorite amulets from the Abandonadas days from my neck, and for good measure penciled on a tiny beauty mark over my lip. Not a single thing on my body was Bobby Brooks - not a thing! I was the only girl at Blackshale High, besides PinkyToe, not wearing a round-collared madras shirtwaist dress. (She wore a t-shirt and jeans or shorts every day of her life.) I walked down the hall to my locker, and I could hear the catty whispers behind my back, but I was happy, enjoying being different, being me! Pinky sidled up to me at lunch. "Ha!" she marveled, "You are way too out-there to be my best friend. Cool though…" She gave me an admiring look and strutted along with me, acting like she thought she was kind'a cool herself.

The next week at pep rally, the whole school was there milling around in the gym before bell. All of a sudden, PinkyToe exclaimed, "Omygosh, look!" pointing at Diana and Becky, the absolute all-time queens of the popular girls. I blinked. They both had on combat boots. I started looking around the crowd, and sure enough there they were, sprinkled through the crowd, polka dot socks, tights, beauty marks. All the stupid cheerleaders with long hair had spiky ponies on top of their dimwitted, rah, rah, rah heads.

"Holy shit!" I laughed. I had tried so hard not to be a look alike and ended up bein' one anyways. "I can't win for losin'!" From that day on at Blackshale High, I was that cool, artsy-fartsy mortuary girl. And that was totally fine with me.

• • • • • • • •

Black ice can be a problem in Tennessee winters, and one rainy night the mercury took a nosedive after suppertime, sending Harley and Jake Murphy sliding clean off the highway at a hair-raising speed. They hit a thick yellow pine head on and were hell raisers no more. They had been on their way to a peepshow in north Knoxville, where Pussie N. Bloom bared all, and then held a private appreciation party after the show for those with the right stash of cash. When Sheriff Raby came up on the bloody scene, he made their whorin' cash his own before getting on the radio and calling in a 10-50. Listening to the radio crackle, he laughed at the ghostly white skull decals on each side of the truck's rear window. "Now right there is a fine piece of prophecy!" he scoffed to himself.

When the sheriff came to the Murphy's door with the bad news, Walter Lee reached for a home filled bottle and resolved, "Them boys never amounted to nothin' but a double dose of trouble no ways." Then he hung his head and wept violently.

Twin ambulances brought Jake and Harley in. They were messed up bad, and Frank didn't have the heart to start in on them that night. He opted to turn in early, and pulled Corry into bed to watch some TV. "Lord," he confided to his second wife, "them Murphys have sure as hell kept me in business."

I called up Pink's Aunt Dimple, who had already heard the news on her police scanner. "Where's Pinky at?" I couldn't wait to tell her, but half figured by now she already knew.

"She said she was comin' over there... she left an hour ago." Aunt Dimple was already starting to slur her words, doped up for the night.

Thinking back to our days of pranks in the prep room, I ran down the stairs to the parlor and around to the next level down, where the door was standing open.

"Pinky!" I called out, my voice echoing off the stainless steel fixtures. "Pin...ky...," again my sing song voice filled the workroom with her name. I saw two open morgue drawers, the twin bodies, but she wasn't there. Then I heard a whimper from the corner. She was folded down to the floor, her hair falling over a face wet with tears.

"You scared the beJesus out of me!" I sat down on the floor next to her. She buried her head in her hands, elbows propped on her shaking knees. "I was afraid you were doin' something dumb," I confessed.

Pinky reached up and touched my hair. "I wanted to. I wanted to take one of them there tools of your pap's and chop off their tally whackers."

"Why didn't you?"

She looked over at the drawers. "I stood there a long time studyin' on them, and after a while they just looked like big dumb wax dolls. I decided it's time to let it go. Anyways, they're double dead and me - I'm still standin'!"

She stood up, and I hugged her tight, then held her out at arm's length and bent down to her eye level. "Pinky Thomas, you're a brave girl." We turned to go, but of course she had to have the last word. She turned back to the drawers and slammed them shut with an angry thud, then raised her fist defiantly. "Up your maggoty dead ASSES, fuckers!"

2029 Morning Glory Ridge

I wake up bed warm in the dusky drowsy dark. Usually, if I get a good nap, I get up cheerful and rarin' to go, even if the only place I have to go is down the hall. Today I am gloomy. I can't seem to stop thinking about death. Dang! I grew up with death so I ought to be used to it. Oh my soul! How I feel the tiresome weight of it, but the alternative still raises troubling questions.

On Blackshale, I had ample schooling in death. After all, I was the "mortuary child." During Frank's off hours, Pinky and I played undertaker in the basement, cutting up lizards we had anesthetized with the medicine Pap used to numb his corns. Once, we chloroformed a hen and incised her chest to watch the beating heart. When we realized she would die as a result of our experiment and we were about to become cold-blooded killers, panic reigned.

Pinky began to moan, "I'm doomed, doomed!"

"I don't 'spect you go to hell for killin' a chicken; elsewise that neck wringin' Pearlie is in some big trouble."

All the same, I ran upstairs and grabbed needle and thread, and frantically began to sew up the rubbery, pimply chickenflesh. I shouted at Pinky to pour Clorox into the wound as I stitched. That hen lived on for several years out back of Tollett's, clucking away, until her number was finally up one night and a coyote got her.

Field mice trickled into Pap's workroom from the meadow and the grasses down by the river. Up against the walls, under the coffins and tucked in the corners, they shriveled up into a curve and died. Thrilled to find them, I soaked their furry bodies with polymer, and wrapped them in shrouds of thin white tape with only their faces peeking out. "The little dead ones," I called them. I lined them up in solemn rows and studied the differences in their final expressions. Most were blankly frozen, but some bared their tiny pointy teeth in anger at death. I pondered, in the larger scheme of things, on how their small demises stacked up to the bankers and teachers and housewives that lay on Pap's steel table. After Dory died and I was allowed downstairs, I had gotten a closeup look at the variations of human mortality.

The mountain taught me lessons too. One fall afternoon, Frank was bringing me back from the dentist in Pineville when we found ourselves behind a beat-up camouflage pickup. Propped up in the back was a magnificent buck, freshly killed. The hunters had tied him down in a sitting position, and as the truck hit the potholes on Blackshale Road, the whole upper torso heavy with a massive rack flopped back and forth violently. A rivulet of blood zigzagged down from the single wound in his chest. His body was still warm and steamed in the cold air. I stared, picturing him alive, a well-crowned king stalking his wood, yet here he sat minutes later, dead as a doornail in the back of a truck.

Then there was the mass murder I witnessed, committed by a freak of nature. Corry had sent me to the road to get the mail. Strong gusts of wind swept the colored leaves, backed up by the cawing soundtrack of October. A flock of blackbirds shot up out of the trees, in a thick and perfect formation. I stood in awe, questioning if these too were stinkbirds. All of a sudden, a zephyr wind came up fast and furious. It raked across the ridge, met cold air and then sucked downward – violently slamming that whole flock of crows down on the blacktop road. Some twitched and flapped pinions against the tar, until one by one they lay still before the cars that began to stop and pull over, the drivers not believing the company of deaths they had stumbled upon. I stood like a statue, in shock and inert, a line from English class playing in my head, "Quoth the Raven, NEVERMORE!" The real mystery is - mouse, buck, raven or me here flat and sunk in my bed - the sudden change of venue. One second you're there, skittering, running, flying, sucking in breath, and the next you're just... gone.

1966 Blackshale

The Abandonada, Tilla, had took up with boys early on. Me and Pink knew she was on a slippery slope the night her panties took to jangling at a slumber party. She groped down in her drawers and pulled out a silver ID bracelet inscribed "Jackie Wayne." She just giggled, not one bit ashamed.

By junior year, she'd already worked through a string of mostly recreational boyfriends, and ever one had whizzed around the bases to home real fast. You'd a thought that girl's moral gyroscope was off tilt, but it was because of her overpowering need for affection. Me and Pink were worried sick about Tilla. She craved a mother's love so bad, and the bruises she wore to school had us suspectin' her daddy hit her. We was sure the touch she got at home wasn't the lovin' kind.

Then she fell in love, seriously, deeply, with Joey Oody, and he deeply, seriously loved her back. Me and Pink were the only ones that knew the secret, but Tilla and Joey were planning to run off to Bryson City, North Carolina, to get married. She wasn't even knocked up neither. They just wanted to knit that special love they had into a life together.

Then a letter came from Uncle Sam, telling Joey his number had been picked for the honor of serving his country. Tilla felt like a grown up woman sending her man off to war, and even up through that last goodbye on the tarmac, she was grinding her pelvis against him in sincere appreciation. She wrote him a four- or five-page letter rank with perfume every single day, first to Ft. Campbell, then to the US Army APO after Joey ended up scooting through muck and blood on his belly in a Vietnam delta.

As bad luck would have it, she had just delivered a sucking up, home baked sour cream pound cake to her future mother-in-law Thelma Oody when the official U.S. Army car pulled up to the curb.

Thelma, a habitual pessimist, started screaming even before the doorbell rang. This time, pessimism was called for. There would be no remains to send home, as Joey had shared exact coordinates with the largest possible napalm experience, but on the bright side, there had been no time for suffering on his part.

Despite the lack of a body, Frank Tollett was still responsible for a military marker, and a dignified memorial service for a young man who had given up his life for his country. Pap planned up a real nice one for Joey.

Pinky and me sat with Tilla before the service, shorin' her up. "Doc Turner give me these pills," she said hopefully. "He said they'd take the edge off and get me through today." She'd already had one, and she popped another one just in case.

Her swollen eyes kinda glazed over, and she stared like a zombie into space, making a low "who whoo whooo" sound like a mourning dove. She kept on keening, even as the preacher took his place up behind the flag draped casket and the organ played "Onward Christian Soldiers." Out of the corner of my eye, I saw another pill go, whoop, whoop, down the hatch. The preacher made a right long talk about Joey giving his life for his country, and smooth as silk, turned that right around into Jesus giving his life on the cross for you and me. Before you knew it, there was an altar call for any sinners in the crowd who might a been scared witless by Joey's youthful departure. "We never know, thank you Jesus, we never know the hour." He mentioned youth in particular, and all the sins of the flesh that the devil plants in their heads and groins. I could'a swore he was looking right straight at us, although his scrutiny was wasted, sworn off on sex as we both were by then, considerin' our run-in with Jake and Harley. The preacher threatened hellfire loudly, harshly through four verses of "Softly and Tenderly Jesus is Calling" but not a solitary soul came weepin' down the aisle. He'd been lookin' at Tilla.

Up towards the end of the service, two men in uniform headed toward Joey's mama with the puffy triangle of folded flag. I could feel Tilla's hips quiver, and heard her breath go jerky. "Uh oh, somethin' ain't right, maybe one pill too many," I thought to myself. All at once, she popped straight up out of the pew like a jack-in-the-box!

Her voice was ragged but defiant, "OK! WE DID IT! And I'm glad! I'm glad we didn't wait! We did it over and over and over, every which a way, in my own daddy's bed, and leastways now I have something to remember him by and I'm not one bit sorry neither!" She spat these words right straight at the preacher, but they traveled like rampant heat lightning over the pews, shocking folk right and left. More than one old lady had to be fanned back to consciousness by her kin.

Tilla's pa, a retired military man himself, grabbed her by the shoulders, shaking her hard. "Buck up!" he berated, "Get ahold of yourself, girl." She slithered down into the wooden bench, a weepy, wobbly mess.

I rode with Pap in the hearse up through the snowy road to the cemetery, looking back at Tilla and her pa in the black car right behind us. I could see his jaw marching up and down in an angry tirade. Tilla sure wasn't getting' no sympathy from him.

Going up that hill, I looked beyond the family cars and on down the long line of vehicles, their little black funeral flags aflutter. In the other lane, all the cars goin' the other way had pulled off to the side of the road, their drivers showin' respect. A few men had even gotten out of their cars, some waving American flags in sad, slow arcs.

Occasionally, some asshole redneck would fly by the procession, either too ignorant of the custom or too full of themselves to honor the dead soldier. The surviving military fellers took care of that though, with their middle fingers flying at full staff out the rolled down windows of their cars.

1988 Morning Glory Ridge

Nettie Tollett exists in silence, but that doesn't mean she lacks thought or memory. On this rainy afternoon at Morning Glory Ridge, while the other residents are playing bingo, or watching finches shit in the aviary, a bad time from her childhood comes callin' and she can't seem to keep it at bay.

After her mother went to be in the river, Nettie not only patched up the friendship with her cousin twice removed Imogene, she clung to her in desperation. With no affection from her father, and no other relatives to speak of, Nettie found in Imogene her only human lifeline.

The girls were of an age that they could run free, scampering across the farms, or up into the woods a ways, and some days were gone off dawn to dusk. A rugged ravine, carved deep and craggy by mountain flash water, was their favorite place to explore. On a sunny September afternoon, they had packed a picnic of peanut butter sandwiches and root beers, and toted trowels to dig in the mud for fossils.

After they gobbled down their picnic and sat a bit longer pickin' their teeth with weeds and sharing what they knew about boys, which really amounted to nothing, they set out to prospect for the bones of dinosaurs.

Nettie headed downhill, while her cousin climbed up the gorge apiece. Imogene began to chip away at chert buried in the red earth near the top of the ravine. She barely had time to identify the dry chattering before a timber rattler, only two feet long but as thick as a man's arm, came across the grass and struck her right in the jugular vein. She let out a blood-curdling cry, the wound spurting scarlet, and Nettie came running. Nettie heard the snake rattling off into the grass, and took off as fast as she could to get Imogene's Pa.

Blackshale hospital was too far, the girl too scrawny, and the venom too well placed. Imogene never stood a chance.

The next day, the whole extended family, Nettie included, sat in the front room, waiting for the crippled embalmer to come. Two boy cousins, who were only once removed, sat in the back of the room giggling and saying that the twin punctures on Imogene's neck were clearly not snakebite, but the bite of a mountain holler vampire. They also allowed that Nettie, dark and strange and silent and hateful as she was, was undoubtedly the vampire.

The embalmer came in the front door and hobbled over to the body, laid out under a sheet on planks propped up on carpenter's horses.

He pulled up the sheet and observed, "Lord God, this pore child never even got started." He reached down into his black bag and pulled out a giant hypodermic syringe.

"Any you'uns got a bucket?"

Imogene's Pa sidled out on the back porch and dumped moldy beets out of one and brought it in. Without thinking to evacuate the family, not even the young children present, the embalmer went about his work plunging the syringe right into Imogene and sucking out her body fluids. He grinned at an uncle he recognized and made conversation to pass the time while the girl's blood emptied. "How's your mama and them? Where they at?"

"They down at the house. Mama falls out with the vapors at a dyin'."

Nettie stared at the clear cylinder as it filled with crimson slime, then she turned white, eyes big as moons, but she tightened her lips into a determined grim line. She bucked up and swore she'd never have a friend agin, as losin' one was entirely too painful. That night she lay on her bed chokin' back tears, as tears were still not allowed on the McBee farm.

1967 Blackshale

It was spring, the season of new life, and Tilla was nauseous and dizzy and pregnant. She told her father that she wanted to keep her baby, all she had left of Joey, but he gave her $3,000 and ordered, "Fix it any way you want to, just don't ever come home unless it is fixed." She bought an airline ticket to New York, not knowing how, exactly, "it" would be fixed. A friend had rooted out the number of an illegal abortion clinic, which she kept in her pocket, struggling for a decision. On a Sunday afternoon, she boarded a plane and when it landed at LaGuardia, she was alone and planless as a body could be.

In the city and still not showing, she got a job as a telephone operator, buying a few more weeks to think. And think, and think. She sat at the black console saying "number please", jerking plugs in and out, out and in, and thinking and thinking and thinking. There were no good fixes.

She made an appointment at the clinic - the one where they sucked your baby out of you while you prayed to God not to hear it gaspin' for breath. Up on the table in a paper dress (please young lady, there you go, it will all be over soon) but she ripped it off and ran out naked trailing reasons, "I can't do this! It's all that's left of Joey. This is wrong!" Fleeing, leaving the Indian doctor standing there with the scary tool in his hand and his black eyes wide, throwing on clothes, and stumbling into the street.

One day walking home from work, after saying "number please" at least five hundred times, she saw a notice stapled on top of many other staples and bits of torn paper on a telephone pole that said, "Pregnant? Call Murray Hill 5-9555." She did, desperately fishing for options.

It sounded good. All expenses paid at the House of Grace, a Catholic home for unwed mothers on East 72nd street. She could take her time making a choice: find a way to keep her baby or place it with a loving couple and go home as if nothing had ever happened. For a few days she harbored hope of making a life with her child, but reality quickly settled in. Later that week, she took a city bus to the child services agency that handled the adoption, and signed the preliminary papers.

The next month, broke, swollen, and too tired to work, she checked into the home. Most of the residents were Yankee girls - smart talkers, ruffians. One was an Olympic running star, anxious to get rid of her problem and back on track to her fame. During the day, they worked chores, went to doctors' appointments, had counseling sessions with "Mother," the hateful nun in charge. At night, after another round of chores, they sat in the dayroom playing cards, pretending they were regular girls and women living normal lives. When Tilla climbed the stairs and fell into her bed, she lay awake dreaming of the day Joey's child would grow up and find her.

Under her wimple, Mother had one solid opinion. All the girls were plainly sluts - deserving of the agony of childbirth they would soon go through and any other indignities Mother could dole out along the way. If the silverware was not set precisely or beds had sloppy hospital corners, Mother loved to slap face. Mother had no love of Christ in her heart, only reproach. The only happy moment Tilla had at the House of Grace was when Fonda (no last names please) from West Islip stood up at the dinner table and called Mother "a barren bitch" and "an offense to the forgiveness of Jesus Christ" to her face. Although some of the other girls had nicknamed her "Fonda Peters" behind her back, Tilla had a great respect for the girl who had stood up to that hate-filled nun.

At three in the morning two weeks before her due date, Tilla woke up cramping hard. Just her friggin' luck, as she would miss her special "due date dessert." She had been looking forward to her strawberry shortcake with real whipped cream! Mother wordlessly sent her off in a cab alone. At the hospital, she was given an enema with rough hands and strapped down on a bed in a broom closet. After her bowels emptied, Tilla had one horrible contraction that lasted for hours and never stopped. No one came to the closet until after she passed out.

Tilla woke up trapped. She was tied down, wrists and ankles strapped tightly to table and stirrups, a huge bright circle of light in her eyes, crying, feeling like a big baby but unable to control her gut reaction to the pain.

"Please lady, give me somethin', please!" she cried.

"Too late," insisted a faceless nurse voice.

After another hour someone said, "You can push now."

A last screaming groan, from far off, sounds like the voice of some other poor soul. And in her arms, coated in cheesy white goo, a bloody baby girl, six pounds, two ounces, is rooting at her chest. Her baby, her Joey baby, her love.

The nurse clamps down on Tilla's breast and shoves it into the baby's mouth. The baby suckles and calms against her mother. Tilla presses her lips against the downy head, and her tears flow. There has to be another way. She can get a job and keep this baby. She can tell her daddy to go straight to hell. She can.

A nurse yells and grabs the baby, jerking her from Tilla's breast. A mistake has been made. Tilla is wheeled to her room and sleeps.

"Please, can I see my baby?"

"No, it's not for the best."

"Please, I want to have her baptized. Please, please, I'm beggin' you."

A hour later, the nurse wheels Tilla to another broom closet. The hospital chaplain shuffles in, carrying the baby in a pink blanket. He kicks a wide push broom out of the way, stifles a curse, fakes a smile and crosses himself. He hands the baby to Tilla, who baptizes her with tears before the chaplain sprinkles water from a small bottle onto the newborn head. Out of a worn missal, he reads some hurried rite – precious last words she will struggle later to remember.

The day after, a social worker comes to visit, sitting like a vulture on the edge of her chair. "So you love her, do you? Listen up girlie, if you really do love her, you will do the right thing for her. You will give her a real family with two parents, people who have jobs, who are established. You are too young to be a good mother. Do the right thing for your baby, girl." Sobbing and heartsick, Tilla signs the papers.

The next day, she leaves her room with her baby in her arms and hands her to the social worker who shrinks smaller and smaller down the long hall, blurred through tears. Never again. Never. Never is such a long, long time. No, Tilla has to hold on to the dream, hold on tight, or she will go mad.

A year later, things had happened that Tilla never knew. A crooked social worker from the agency sold her baby for a large amount of money to a French Diplomat. The records were amended to show the baby died in the hospital nursery. Tilla's child was lost forever, an ocean away.

· · · · · · · ·

As the years of our childhood passed, Sodboy fell out of favor with BoJack and Peanut's gang. He just didn't have what it took. He wasn't mean hearted enough, he was just… dirty. Really, rotten smelly dirty. I doubted if the tarpaper shack where them sad sack people lived even had running water. With prom coming up, it was the perfect time for the Murphy boys to sucker Sodboy. As a prank, BoJack and Peanut put him up to asking Becky Houser - the most popular girl in school. She was too kind to refuse. They couldn't wait to see him squirm at the prom, a laughing stock exposed and embarrassed in his grimy clothes, the brunt of their cruel joke.

We had our own prom issues. Pink was between a rock and a hard place. She was not wanting to be alone with any boy after what happened with Jake and Harley, but she didn't want to be left out neither. The whole school would be there!

I said to her, "There's no school rule that says you have to go with a date. We're going stag!" Nobody did that. All the girls knocked themselves out with schemes to get some guy, any guy, even a secret second cousin, to take them to the prom. Not to go with a boy and corsage on your arm was a disgrace. I could'a cared less, and I talked Pinky into it. "I'd rather go by myself any day, than go with some pimpleface freak who will just want to grope me up!"

The day before the prom, I came out front at school after the final bell, and there was Pap. For a second, my heart flew up in my throat. I just knew something had happened to Corry. Weird though, he was talking to Sodboy, who went around and got in Pap's car. I quickly looked around to see if anyone was takin' this in. I was half curious, half mortified, and you can bet the minute I got home, I headed straight for Corrine to see what was up.

"Oh, darlin', Frank has taken that poor boy under his wing. They've gone off shopping." When Frank came back with Sodboy, he took him right downstairs to the bathroom with the dead history of Blackshale on the walls. Sodboy was quite impressed with it. In fact, he sadly and proudly pointed out his grandpaw's black lung. "My grandpaw kilt himself bent over down in that mine, his whole life, fillin' himself up with that black dust!" Sodboy mourned.

Frank cleared his throat and came right to the point, but in a kind way. "Well, then, let's see here Haskell," using Sodboy's rarely heard given name, "If a fella is taking a girl to the prom, he'll need to wash up a bit!" He tore open the plastic around the packages of clean underwear and socks. Frank stepped out, closed the door and sat in a chair by the door tapping his feet, waiting for the shower water to start running. After ten minutes, there was still no sound of a spray.

"Haskell, son, is everything ok in there?" He tapped on the door, and it swung open. Sodboy was standing there in his dingy underwear, looking confused.

Then Frank realized, that boy had no idea how a shower worked. Humiliated and head down, Haskell explained that he'd had been excused from PE because of a bad heart, and the only baths he'd had at home had been with crick water in a tin washtub.

"Hit takes a while to heat up that much crick water over the fire, so I don't get much worshin' in the winter."

Frank sympathized, trying to put the boy at ease, "I reckon not."

After his first shower, Haskell came out in his too new blue jeans and plaid shirt. Frank took him as far up the mountain as he could in his car and let him out. Haskell held on tight to the plastic bag holding his new suit, and the box of shoes. He gave Frank a timid wave goodbye. "Much obliged, Mr. Tollett."

· · · · · · · ·

On Saturday morning of the Prom, I had just finished washin' my hair in beer and plastering a strawberry mint mask on my face when the back doorbell of the apartment rang. When I went to get it there was my cousin Perry, looking out over the porch railing with an absent look. When I opened the door and pulled him inside, Perry bent down and wrapped me in one of his big bear hugs and then made a beeline for the bathroom. He came back out grinning. Perry had reached his full height and was bone thin. He looked like a human skyscraper to me. On anybody else, those long fingers would have looked scraggly, but he moved his hands gracefully, with elegance and expression. He'd taken up the fiddle and those fingers served him well - he was fast and furious on that thing. Now they parked on his hips, spreading in time with the monkey grin on his face and the tilt of his head.

"You had me worried there for a minute, Anna Grace. When you hugged me I felt a tickle in my pickle, but I just had to go to the bathroom. That was all!"

I smacked him upside his head, and offered him a cold drink. We took our soda pops out on the back porch and Perry started tellin' me what all he'd been up to. Perry was the brother I never had, a scrawny redneck boy eight years older than me, and I loved him to death. He loved to fish and hunt and canoe. He'd like to have worn that river out. Pearlie came out, wiping her hands on her checkedy apron, and asked could she make us an ice cream sundae.

Perry and I watched her hobble back into the kitchen, slowed down by a little limp these days. There were grey patches working their way into her Brillo pad hair. My gaze followed her with love. Perry saw that and smiled.

I told him, "Hum just disappeared one day. I always thought he'd come back, but he never did. Pearlie's never been the same after that. It always seemed like there was more to it than met the eye, and Pap acted funny when I asked him about it, like there was somethin' he didn't want me to know."

Perry got real quiet and got that look of someone mulling around a big decision in his head. Then he confessed, "I know, Anna Grace. I know what happened to your Hum. Do you want me to tell you, even if it's really God-awful?"

I swallowed back a little gulp and whispered, "Yeah Perry, I reckon I do."

"Back before Ma and Pa bought the store out on the highway, we lived in the dirt hills up against the mountain on a piss poor farm. Saturday was tight shoe day. We all shined up the shoes we never wore much at home and went downtown to see what we could see, and to be seen too. You knew the girls up on the mountain and the girls down at school who would never speak to you. But downtown on Saturday, well, you just might see girls from the other towns - new faces - and they would have slept in pin curls the night before and slipped on some Tangee lipstick the minute they left their mama's sight. You see that was big excitement for a young teenage boy who'd just spent a week of days hauling hay and a week of nights scratching like crazy.

"I stopped in the hardware store and picked up a half-dozen boxes of ten penny nails, a mousetrap, and some Oxydol for Ma. About then the sky took on the color of a stonebruise and started rumbling to beat the band. When it opened up, it dumped everything wet it had up and down the street. First I went in the diner and had steak and biscuits and gravy, and then I ducked into the five and dime and looked at comic books for a time.

"When the rain let up I thought I'd walk on down the street and have a look at our brand new hospital I'd heard about. When I get to the bottom of the hill, about to cross the street, I see a commotion under the red lights over the side door, you know, where they brought in them people that was in a real bad way. A big clump of people was shiftin' around in rings, working like bees. When I got down there, I pushed my way through right fast but came back out a whole lot faster, spewing my greasy breakfast on the sidewalk. My head was still spinning as I struggled to believe what I'd seen.

"They said this colored feller had been walking on the slick wet tracks. He slipped and fell in front of the train - chopped both his legs clean off. It took him a while to die though, cause the pressure mashed the ends of his stumps almost flat. There he lay, and I figgered it was some hobo nobody knew, but when I got closer I saw it was your Hum. His eyes were already glazing, his life bleeding slowly out of both stumps. You see, he'd been turned away at the door because our new hospital was only for whites, since nigras had to go over to their own doctor's office in Pineville.

"There was one doctor who came out to see what was going on, but by the time he got out there, all he could do was shake his head back and forth, that round silver thing strapped around his head sending shafts of light dancing across Hum's brown face and the bloody sidewalk. That Doc lit up a cigarette and stood there blowing smoke rings at the sky, still shaking his head in disbelief. After a bit, he yelled out to a feller to call the nigger hearse and get somebody to clean up that bloody mess for God's sake.

"You could still see them stains on the sidewalk for a long time after that. And that, honeybunch, that's what your pap didn't want you to know."

· · · · · · · ·

After Perry left, I took it up with Pap. He gave up the truth, and he also told me Hum was the only colored person to ever be worked on at Tollett's. They'd brought him, and his legs in a separate bag, in through the back secretly and buried him in the basement. Pearlie visited him down there every night, no longer afraid of haints, at home with them since she now knew one so well. After that talk with Pap, I took the steps down to the downstairs bathroom slowly, one at a time. I opened the door and took up my drawing tools. I engraved my sorrow into the wall:

Runned over by train. One mark. One mark that made me so, so sad.

· · · · · · · ·

I learned something important on prom night. Before, I was of the opinion that all popular girls were silly, self-absorbed airheads. I found out that night that it was possible for people to be well-liked just because they were plain nice. Becky Houser smiled up at Haskell all night, and the only smell of his body was the English Leather my pap had bought for him.

· · · · · · · ·

I drew my way through high school. We had no art class. It was just in me to draw everyone and everything, filing up page after page and book after book with the squigglings of my pen and the strokes of my floppy brush. By the time senior year started, I began to piece together all kinds of stuff, making strange things that people would look at and say, "I wonder what that there means!" I knew when they cocked their head and waited a second before saying anything, I'd given them something to think on - a whole new way of looking at the most everday thing, and that, I reckon, is what artists are in the world for.

2029 Morning Glory Ridge

On my eScreen is the New International Bible in extra large type, the digital pages flipped to the twenty-third Psalm. Yay! Though I walk through the valley of the shadow of death!

Although I sneak and read it once in a while, I'm still not sure how I feel about it. That Old Testament throws me. A supposedly loving God telling the Israelites to go out and smite everybody with their swords – what's that all about? Even back when we had a Bible teacher in grammar school, I was skeptical about all the different interpretations. I recall my child's brain pondering, how the heck do we know who's got it right?

Yet, there came a time when I urgently felt the call of the Spirit. I was around twelve and severely unchurched. Mama had grown up a Methodist and Pap a nothing. The only churches in Blackshale were of no use to me. One was a holy roller Pentecostal reputed to illegally handle snakes and drink the strychnine, and the other was the colored church.

Eventually, I knew it was to this one room frame building that Pearlie sometimes disappeared on Sunday evenings. She never spoke of it to me, just quietly went and came back peaceful and smilin'. Looking back now, I realize that Pearlie Bean was my minister and spiritual mentor. I had grown up hearing her soft praises in song, her constant string of conversation with the good Lord, and had been touched daily by the beauty of her simple faith and kindness. Unwittingly, Pearlie Bean had led me right smack to God.

Fit to be tied with this newfound spiritual awakening, I lay awake night after sweating night begging God to lead me to some group of white believers who eschewed poisonous reptiles. He didn't answer.

One Sunday evening in Indian summer, I followed Pearlie Bean. To my surprise, she didn't walk towards her church building, but down to the river where her Reverend was dipping soul after soul down into the waters of forgiveness. I spied on their salvation from a briar patch, jealous of their joy, atremble with anxiety and excitement, until I was seized by necessity. I stepped brazenly out of the briars into the twilight, and one of the sisters dressed in white saw me and yelled, "GOOD GOD ALMIGHTY!"

I felt the need to make some speech explaining myself, so I coughed up words remembered from grammar school bible class. I spoke forcefully. "I am pore in spirit, and need to be baptized into Jesus Christ. Will you baptize me, Reverend?"

The Reverend looked stricken. He sloshed up out of the water in his black rubber boots, and was met on the bank by a group of wideyed churchmen I took to be the leaders of the congregation. They murmured and grunted together in a huddle. I couldn't hear their deliberation, but a few stomped feet in anger before the Reverend quit the circle and faced me. He looked everywhere but right at me, saying, "Naw, missy, naw we ain't got no bidness baptizin' no white girl."

I stared down at the ground, trying to control my blooming tears. When I looked up a swarm of churchwomen had rapidly encroached on the knot of church fathers, tightening around them, shaking their pointer fingers in the air, beating them down with their adamant voices.

"Whatch you talkin' bout?" Pearlie Bean spat at the Reverend, "This here white girl, she a child of God! Same as you and me! This here white girl needin' a baptizing! You not telling me we shuck her off to no snake church. Hmmmmph!" And while she fell to her creaky knees and waved her hands to the sky, fervently praying for the Reverend his own self, each sister took ahold of her own better half, and gave him what for. After the church fathers reconvened a few minutes later, the Reverend held out his hand and led me on down into the river.

Night was already coming on and the water was cold. My breath caught from the shock of it, but the sisters in their white dresses began to sing some deepswaying harmony and I fell calmly back into the stream, on those brown arms and my newfound faith. I came up saved and shiverin' and blue.

We walked home that night together hand in hand, Pearlie binding me to the ground like a tether. I could have floated clean away, so pure and buoyant was my new soul. I never did attend the colored church, not wanting to cause them trouble, but I took up my own conversations with God, singing my own soft songs, and I figure by the grace of Jesus and my river baptizin', I'll be seeing him before too long.

1967 Blackshale

When the weather was warm enough we were allowed to camp out in the tree house. Pap and Corry reckoned there was safety in numbers and, besides, it was close enough to the back of Aunt Dimple's house that one of us could run for help if anything went wrong. On a crisp Friday night in September, the football team was playing out of town, and it was not too cold to sleep out. I remember loving how the air smelled that night. You could barely detect the warm, burnt smell of the smoke from the furnace when the air started turning cool. Pinky and I never went on dates, and Tilla, well Tilla was still in mourning for Joey and her baby, so we felt sorry for her and asked her to spend the night in the tree house too.

We were too old now for dolls, real or paper, pretend worlds, secret clubs. The Abandonadas had disbanded when Joannie and Georgia moved away, both to the hometowns of new stepmothers. We had left the evidence of the Abandonadas on the walls of the tree house though - the mementos of our mamas still hung there. Through the years other things were added until the walls were completely covered, dense with the art and artifacts of girlhood. From time to time, we'd make a new amulet or talisman from something we'd found or bits of our lives - turkey feet, pinches of soils and sands, feathers of a deceased parakeet bound in ribbons, trinkets, locks of our hair. Even Pearlie had contributed an asophidity bag and a plastic mermaid charm she'd fished from a box of Cracker Jacks up in the colored balcony of the picture show. The glowing plastic Cross of Christ claimed a prominent position.

All these things were suspended over a scribbled web of words, a diary written on our walls. Whenever anyone crossed one of us at school, we commemorated the conflict: "Pinky kicked

Marsha Painter's ASS" or "Polly Sutton can EAT ME RAW!" We still believed that if we had enough hoodoo in our tree house, we could keep the mean boys away.

We stayed up all night that Friday. All of us were already worn out from a busy week at school, and the tree house was too small, the floor too hard for sleeping. We spent half the night jabbering and ended up tangled in an arguing, bawling, gaggle of exhausted girls. When I got home Saturday morning, I was dog tired and just wanted to sleep all day. I stood brushing my teeth, thinking about how good it would feel to flop into the softness of my bed.

O crap! I realized I must have left my transistor radio up in the tree house. That morning Frank and Perry had gone off bright and early with their guns and dogs, yearning for the quail season that was still a ways out. You would have thought that Mama dying on a quail hunt would have turned Pap off of it, but I guess it was a hard habit to break. Corrine was at the grocery and Pearlie was down in her room. I took off and headed back across the bridge. Pinky and them were not home, and then I remembered her saying that they were going over to Pineville that morning to get her a new skateboard. I just kept on going to the tree house, not giving it a second thought. I'd been all over them woods by myself many a time.

I scrambled up the ladder, then froze, studying the floorboards in confusion. I had been used to seeing plenty of strange things there: altar, candles, and other relics of our childhood ceremonies. But now there was something new that looked equally ritualistic, something unfamiliar that wasn't ours. At each of the four corners, wide straps of leather with buckles were nailed to the floor. In the middle, two boards were nailed down and up out of those short, sharp nails pointed to the ceiling. The spikes them Indian swamis walk on flashed through my mind. "What the...?"

There wasn't even time to finish the question. The Murphy boys come up the ladder fast as blazes. BoJack swung hard, knocking the breath out of me. I fell backwards on the floor into points of searing pain where the nails pierced my back and butt. Peanut jumped on me, straddling my middle, and held me down while his brother buckled each wrist and ankle into a leather strap. My, my, my! Look what has fallen into our girltrap. Then he pulled out a hunting knife, sliced my clothes and pulled every stitch of fabric out from under me. I was buck naked under their hateful, glaring eyes. I glared right back, refusing to look weak and embarrassed, not wanting to give them the satisfaction. My boldness came at a price.

Peanut pulled out a small box, the kind a fishing plug came in. I could see its contents through the dull, scratched plastic. It was a stack of single edged razor blades. BoJack held me down and Peanut started at my collarbone, and pressing with all his weight, drew a line of blood straight down into the folds between my legs. He cut just deep enough, not wantin'to kill me right off or make me lose so much blood that I'd die before they got through with me. Then he raised up a bottle of his daddy's home brew and dribbled it down the length of my wound, an extra stinging torture. I passed out from the shock of the pain.

When I came to, BoJack was leaning over me. "Hey Tollett! You ain't much fun conked out. We wanna party! We brung the hooch, you brung the poontang!"

I spit in his face.

"Awww, now… come'on, girlie, you remember that day on the bus in second grade? …Dumb kid, you didn't even know what it meant to get fingered. I'm bettin' you still don't. Allow me to demonstrate!" He shot Peanut a companionable, fun-loving brother grin. He thrust a middle finger into me and jiggled it around, then he raised it up and gave it a lick.

"Ummm, yummmy, yummmm yum. Pussy Popsicle!"

I tried to spit in his face again, but he was too far away. He cut off a piece of my shirt and tied it into a gag. Then BoJack was on me, sliding on my blood, forcing his way inside. After the first searing pain, I survived by going into a kind of trance. Over his shoulder I could see Dory's blue wedding hanky on the wall, used by someone else before she was a bride. All through the rhythmic, painful surging against my busted up cherry, the stinging rub of BoJack's body on the raging fresh gash, and nails tearing against the moving flesh of my backside, I was thinking how strange it was that now here I was too, used up and forever very, very blue.

Then it was Peanut's turn. He flopped around on me a little while and made a big show of grunting and yelling, "YEAH! Yeah! Oh YEAH!" but all I felt was a limp and slippery little mouse flop up against my bruised front. BoJack was about to start in mocking him when Peanut yelled, "Take that damn gag off, they ain't nobody out here and I need to hear her screamin'. Hell, that's half the fun." BoJack yanked off the gag.

I did get a few screams out before Peanut stiffened up and started in on me, and then I had no wind to force out. I knew Aunt Dimple was gone, and there was no one to hear them anyway. In my mind a question formed, one I recalled hearing at school, "If a tree falls in the forest when there is no one there to hear it, does it make a noise anyway?"

It didn't take Peanut long to finish. He stood up, weasly mister still dripping and shrinking. "Now you've had a real man Tollett! Probly the last one you're gonna get!" His brother headed toward me, a blur in the background.

BoJack bent over me with a bucket and a wide paintbrush, smirking.

"Hey Tollett! Didja know I'm an artist too? "He began to paint on me, stroking up and down each violently shaking limb, covering the canvas of my naked and bloody body with manure. Not yet satisfied, he slopped brushfuls in my hair and across my face. I squinched my eyes and mouth against the stench.

He was just finishing up his masterpiece of revenge when I

heard the barks of Pap's hunting dogs. Frank Tollett had heard enough to know the worst. "Come on down boys if you want to live one minute longer!" Frank and Perry trained their shotguns on both boys as they descended the ladder.

Frank was crying, a raw, wretched sound that hurt me almost as bad as all the other. He yelled at the Murphys in between sobs, "The hardest thing I have ever done is to refrain from blowing your useless piggie brains out. If Perry here weren't witness to this whole thing, I swear to God I would."

Perry held the gun on both boys while Frank scrambled up in the tree house, his worst fears realized. By then I was covered in shit, and lay in a large puddle of blood on the verge of shock. He averted his eyes but ripped off his hunting jacket and laid it over me, then scooted around on his knees to unbuckle the straps. He sat me up, encircled me in his arms, and together we wept.

Pap carried me, dripping blood and horseshit. Perry marched BoJack and Peanut across the bridge and down the road to Tollett's where Pap called the sheriff. Then Corrine and Pap took me to the hospital to be examined and treated for the razor cut. They kept me in the hospital for two days, pumping blood into me to replace all that I'd lost. From my collarbone all the way down my body was a perfectly straight column of stitches. At least Peanut had been neat about it and made me a straight scar – a mark I would wear the rest of my life.

The morning we headed for home, Corrine helped me into the back seat and then held my head in her lap, stroking my hair and crying her eyes out. I was groggy from sedatives, but my brain was still straining to make sense of it all. "Pap, I thought you was taking the dogs out on the mountain that day."

"We were, but I kept hearing Dory's voice in my head saying, 'Don't go off too far Frank, go somewhere close to home, so you won't be so far from Anna.' So me and Perry decided to just go over the river."

"Thank God for that." Corry whimpered, her voice still weak. "No tellin' what would have happened if you hadn't gotten there when you did... no tellin'..." She burst into a fresh hysteria.

Frank shot Corry a look, willing her to hush. "You're gonna be okay, Anna Grace. Those boys will wish they were never born. They'll get their just comeuppance!" But Frank and Corry both fell quiet, deep in thought about the terror I'd been through and how close they'd come to losing me.

For several miles down Blackshale Road, the silence in the car roared. Then the trembling voice of a wounded child trickled up through a drugged fog.

"Will y'all still love me?"

· · · · · · · ·

Because of them slicing me up and intending to leave me for dead, BoJack and Peanut were charged with attempted murder. They were sentenced as adults to life in the state penitentiary. The Doc testified that even though the cut was not an immediate mortal wound, it was deep enough that I would have bled to death if Frank had not come along.

PinkyToe reported gleefully that men who mess with kids are hated so bad by other jailbirds that they get messed with themselves. Pink liked to grin demonically and yell "gored in the bunghole," using a twisting fist to demonstrate. Maybe that should make me happy, but it don't.

I have a memory from second grade that somehow muffles my hatred. It was a momentary glimpse, the look of Peanut's face gone soft when he saw that Easter basket from Corrine on his desk. He picked up the yellow chick and rubbed the soft fuzz over a sweet, innocent smile I'd never before seen cross his face. A split second later, BoJack grabbed the chick and stomped it on the floor, grinding it with his dirty boot, the very same thing he had done to Peanut's plastic Cross of Christ. Sometimes I just sit in my window seat and think about them little kids we were and how we all got to where we are now. Inside them boys was somethin' tattered and vulnerable, livin' next to an evil rage, and the evil part got fed. I reckon them Murphys never had a chance in the world.

2029 Morning Glory Ridge

I've been here four years now, since 2025. At seventy-five, I had still been hiking - pacing off the pain of my losses - solitude and fresh air my therapy of choice. I would put one foot in front of the other, oblivious to the unnamed creatures slithering away from the trailside. Here and there lurked the threat of a stumble - the slippery, round rock hiding under wet leaves, laying for me. The turning of an ankle five miles into a frozen dusk was its evil plot. I'd usually recover, flailing in midair, thinking only briefly of the "what ifs." Most of the time, I'd given up worry as a bad habit. After losing all my loved ones I was fearless. Something, someday, sooner or later, was going to get me. "Take a number," I gloated as I courted risk and hiked alone, "Get in line, and wait."

One winter afternoon, a little round stone finally brought me down. I could hear my hipbone crack as I came down hard across a bigger rock. That night it was tryin' to snow. It sure was cold enough, but there was no juice in the air. Three smartass boys on their way back from a pot party in the woods got to be heroes and saved me from freezing to death. I recovered from that break, but over the next few years there was another, and then a third, and finally a bone scan bearing really bad news.

"We believe," the sanctimonious home health caseworker had said, "that it would be in your best interests to consider assisted living. Your bones are so fragile, and you've already had a few falls."

I watched her mouth as she pontificated on. It looked to me like an anus.

"Normally," the anus mouth continued, "The state agrees that staying in one's home is the preferred option, but because of your remote location and lack of family..."

I protested, "It's not my fault my family all died and left me an orphan!" I could have fought on indefinitely, arguing that between home health and the alarm around my neck, I could stay on at home. But, the truth was, I knew the gig was up. My bones were working against me, and the days when I could stand in the studio and work all day on large pieces were over. I was tired - tired of keeping up my house, tired of cooking my own meals, tired of being alone. In assisted living, I would still be able to make art, just on a smaller scale. I signed her papers, because I was ready to be cared for, ready to slow down. I even looked forward to being with other people who were in the same sinking ship as me. But I still hated the sight of that sanctimonious bitch and her prissy butthole mouth.

It's one thing to say you're ready to leave your home and another to actually do it. For one thing, there's so much stuff, and each piece of "stuff" requires a decision as to whether you can live without it or not. Was I really ready to part with my Dremel Tool and all eighty-nine attachments, my huge collection of vintage mannequin heads and hands, or fifty-plus strings of antique Christmas lights. I didn't think so. At that point, I was moving into a fairly spacious private apartment in Morning Glory Ridge Estates. The title somehow gave the impression that it would still actually be my home. So in theory, I could take any possession with me, but I could see them questioning the necessity of certain items. "Why, Ms. Tollett, does a woman your age need one hundred sixty-one vintage mannequin hands? Really?"

After many days of soul searching and mind changing, I had chosen the survivors that would be picked up by the movers. An estate dealer, a paid vulture who would pick, pick, pick through the remains of my life after I was settled at Morning Glory Ridge Estates, would handle the rest.

The day before the movers came, I was a wreck. There's

something unnerving about moving to the final locale of your life. I sat on my deck and cried. I sat in my studio and cried. I squatted on my toilet with the nervous runs and cried. Now that all my loved ones were in the ground or missing in action, I was down to mourning for my studio and my material possessions. They were all I had left, and I was feeling really sorry for myself. So I opened up a bottle of scotch and had myself a real humdinger of a pity party.

• • • • • • • •

My first glorious morning at Morning Glory Ridge was spent filling out stacks of papers, turning over a huge chunk of my assets to the state, surrendering what was left of my dignity, and facing death.

One of the papers was labeled REGARDING YOUR PASSING. There were headings for NATURAL and ASSISTED, under which there were many checkboxes, allowing you to customize your final moments down to the gory detail. I checked NATURAL. There had already been one too many assisted deaths in my family.

The entire afternoon was devoted to a complete physical and an in-depth psychological evaluation. A stubby doctor whistled in to where I sat humped over in a crackling disposable gown.

"Well now, we're going to have to get that thing off and get a good look at your birthday suit! You never know when we might find a nasty little skin cancer hiding out, waiting to cause trouble!" His eyes fell on the scar that bisected my body.

"Oh, MY!" I could see his wheels turning as he tried to think what surgery would have involved an incision that long. "Well dear, how did we get this?"

"WE didn't get it, I did. It happened when I was eighteen. I had a disturbing encounter with a razor blade."

"I see." He returned to my history, and speculated, "So, I see you are an artist. So nice when one can make a living from their vivid imagination!" Then he tapped in his opinion that I had possibly been a cutter and would benefit from therapy.

. . . .

After suffering through all that moving and paperwork and prodding four years ago, the "Estate" stage didn't last long. Two more broken bones and two years later, I got demoted and had to move again. Now I'm in a single bed in one room with nursing care and a nutcase for a roommate. Apparently this train I'm on only goes in one direction – down the hill.

That said, nowadays it's common to live to way past a hundred, but people like me can get to the point where they're really sick and tired of life. Morning Glory Ridge alone has twenty-five residents over one hundred and five. This is not one of my goals. I pray daily for a nice quick halt of heartbeat.

In case my prayers are not answered, they have a special wing for the centenarians, with unique equipment for care of the extra special afflictions of ultra-old age. Mrs. Gundersen told me that there is a woman over on that wing who is one hundred fifteen years old and can still walk some with a stick and hold up her end of a conversation. That poor lucky girl.

. . . .

Today, I've pulled out a stack of sketchbooks from my college years. There are sheets and sheets of nude self-portraits. The figures are jangled, tortured, some splayed out in an X, the black hair on head and crotch is tangled and spiked. Every one has a red line from clitoris to clavicle, a bloody testament traveling up from my sex. I drew my salvation, that's how I worked it out. Maybe it's time I talked about it.

I beeped Daphne. "Can we all go out to the arbor? Do you have any refreshments? I'm ready to talk and I'm going to need some refreshments." She knew just what I had in mind. We met in the lobby and headed for the arbor. Once we were seated and weed was lit all round, I didn't dillydally.

"I decided to take my turn telling about my first time."

The other three traded sideways glances, raised eyebrows, and pursed lips.

"I was attacked. Two malevolent boys strapped me down spread-eagled on a tree house floor with leather shackles, sliced me in half like an avocado with a razor blade and then using their wankers as weapons, brutally pummeled me in my private place. I opened up my flowered house coat a little to show the top of the scar. They all cried out in unison. I never thought I'd have any interest in sex, ever again. But later I had a partner who showed me tenderness and pleasure. So yeah, you old nosy voyeur vultures, I did get to enjoy it!" I took a few more deep drags on the joint, just to get me through the telling of it.

· · · · · · · ·

Normally my reminiscing daydreams live in Blackshale. This week, because of the stack of sketchbooks on the bedside desk, my ramblings are going to college. When the letter came offering an art scholarship to Mount Highland, a small liberal arts college in northern Virginia, I was torn. College had been only vaguely in my plan. I definitely wanted to pursue art on some higher level, but leaving Frank and Corrine felt like ripping some necessary organ out of me.

When they drove off and left me sitting on the veranda of the dorm squalling, I was abandoned once again, with a painful beast running ragged in my chest. It was a college for women, and most of the "women" were from wealthy families up north. Culture shock set in. I was smart enough to drop my mountain lingo like a hot potato. PinkyToe would not have recognized my voice, nor would she have even liked the person I'd become in the blink of an eye. I was a lost wanderer fakin' it in a whole new world, all for the love of art.

In some ways though, my college art classes had little to do with the artist I became. They were about design fundamentals and techniques and history of art, the same foundation that every single art major in the world stands upon when they have figured out just what vison it is they want to show the world. So there at Mount Highland I learned how to draw more confidently, mix colors, use design principles, break rules and construct a canvas that wouldn't fall apart before the grading period was over. As to what I would say with all that, that would come from a lifelong dance with living. And college was part of that dance.

· · · · · · · ·

College had rules: In your room at seven p.m., lights out at ten, no food or boys in the dorm, no shorts or pants on campus unless covered by a completely buttoned up raincoat, no visits home 'til Thanksgiving. Forty girls stood in a long line every night for a short turn at the one pay phone. You were allowed one date per week, on Friday or Saturday night, and you had to be in by 10 p.m. Mount Highland ran a tight ship with its long list of rules, but there was one thing we could do. We could chain smoke cigarettes layin' in our beds. My ashtray stayed full.

The housemother sported steel blue curls over her stern, wizened face. Her smile was knowing and skeptical. She'd seen it all – embryonic humans in the toilet bowl, girls lovin' each other up in the bed, beauty queens sneaking out of their professors' sports cars at the back door. She'd thwarted test cheaters and runaways and girls likker'd up on the dorm roof. She would not be fooled. Her name was Lucille Malone Stone, but we would come to call her Crone Stone.

Aching with homesickness, I haunted the small brass mailboxes stacked to the ceiling in the Student Lounge. Corrine got me through, sending something every day for that first awful quarter of separation. If not a long, hand written, newsy letter thick with pink pages, there would at least be a picture postcard signed "Love, Corry and Frank." At least once a week, a note would tell me to check at the post office window for a package that smelled sweetly of sugar and vanilla and chocolate - brownies or chocolate chip cookies.

The first week was called Slave Week. Freshmen wearing felt beanies were marched by force all night in a freezing rain, in the name of indoctrination. If any upperclassman wanted any little thing, a freshman slave was to provide it, without whining. If a freshman failed to suck it up, their social future at Mount Highland was bleak.

For a few, it wasn't all in fun. When they thought they could get away with it, they pushed and tripped, hit or kicked, taunted with epithets. The worst, a foreign student named Babette, chose the art majors for her special torments, doling out demands to exhausted slaves. As the week wore on, she zero'd in on me. She knocked me down during a rainy night march and once I floundered in the mud, kicked me over and over with her pointy toe boots, cursing me in French. My suitemates circled and saved me. Babette spat on me and backed away laughing. The next week in the dorm, the former slaves on my floor inspected my bruises, grumbling and making revenge plans I nixed.

I guess abusive environments make for strange bedfellows, because my dearest friends in the world, besides PinkyToe, were the half dozen girls who slogged through Slave Week together in nineteen sixty-six. Even though they were sophisticated damnyankees and I was a hick, we were suddenly soul mates. I missed PinkyToe though. She would have kicked Babette's ass to France and back.

I open the sketchbook and turn through a section of shaded portraits - my roommate, Elise, Sunny, and B.K. from across the hall, suitemates Lacey and Sondra, and Crazy Daisy from the second floor. We were partners in crime, co-conspirators, shoulders to cry on for broken hearts or homesick blues. We lived on the top floors of Highland Hall, a small brick dorm that housed forty girls. We were all art majors, but most of us minored in creating havoc.

There was some studying that wild freshman year, most girls' first without parental supervision, but we spent a lot of our time inventing trouble. The weekend after Slave Week, we were full of pent up energy and spite, our mistreatment at the hands of the upperclassmen grinding on our nerves. We weren't bad girls, but meanness was boiling up in us that Friday night. We weren't quite to the point of sneaking out yet, so we had to work within our confinement. At precisely ten-thirty every evening, the night watchman rounded the back corner of Highland Hall. That Friday night we opened our windows and dumped buckets of icewater on his head, withdrawing quickly. A trail of water pointed up to our window, and Crone Stone was immediately at our door with green reprimand slips. Three of those in the course of your college career earned you a bus ticket home.

We laid low for a few weeks, but then the tension built up again. By this time, we had birthed a collective disdain for Crone Stone. She had a fussy apartment on the first floor filled with Victorian furniture and a plethora of silly china curios. She was what Corry would call a fixey lady, but after hours, her blue hair was in pin curls and her substantial makeup removed. Her stout body had gratefully escaped a girdle and waddled freely in a gaudy floral housecoat. We loved to lure her out of her cave for any reason, so we could make fun of her.

Highland Hall had cold, hard stairwells made of polished concrete and steel. They produced resounding echos of the finest quality. Late at night, we gathered at the top and in one chorus, snorted as loud as we could. The sound, like a herd of wild boars, multiplied as it descended, until it fell on Crone Stone's ears. She had already begun to dream of long gone gentleman friends when the clamor came down, but she was out in a flash craning her neck up through three stories of open space, straining for a glimpse of the perpetrator. We were all in our rooms, noses in books, when she came around sniffing for a rat.

"Warnings all 'round girls," she shouted up and down the hallway. "Next time, the whole lot gets reprimands until one of you lassies talks. And Anna Grace Tollett, I heard your big hillbilly mouth loud and clear, so you get a reprimand of your very own right now!" She stomped back in her apartment and slammed the door.

By my first trip back home I had flunked English and French. Frank sat me down and read the riot act. I started studying and brought my grades up, but I was still minoring in creation of havoc. I could have been sent home so many times. We courted felonies, took risks. When we cranked a butane lighter up on high and ignited farts, no one seemed to notice the yard long flame was only an inch from the curtains. When we poured a puddle of turpentine on the linoleum floor of our room, set a match to it and roasted marshmallows, we never stopped to think the old dorm could burn to the ground with lives lost. The nights we left pillows under our covers in our stead for bed check, while we drank too many cocktails and did the watusi in local dives with scary strangers, could have landed us in shallow graves. We didn't think about the dangers, we did stupid things, we were fearless and careless - we were young.

· · · · · · · ·

A Spring Saturday night found some of us in our favorite bar, spending our date night on an all girl drinking party. We were stuffed around a table, smashed. We weren't the only ones. In a booth across from us, eyes bleary and barely able to sit up, was Babette. She was smoking something in a long cigarette holder. Two songs later, something by the Animals and "Louie, Louie," she staggered to the ladies room.

Later, Daisy had to pee and drug me into the john. Washing our hands, we heard a groan from one of the stalls. The door swung open and out swooned Babette soaked in vomit, hanging on the door. Walking was out of the question.

"Oh crap," I whined to Daisy, "Get on the other side of her and let's get her back to the booth." When we drug her out in the hall, Daisy glanced to her right and spied a door with an open padlock hanging in the hasp.

Crazy Daisy had no filters. She was half insane and would do anything. She never forgot an offense and never missed an opportunity for revenge. When her head pivoted slowly around and her eyes met mine, I could see the wheels turning. We dumped the comatose Babette in the floor of the storeroom in a puddle of her own puke and slammed down the padlock.

Back at the table, we got more and more plastered to the wall. We were in stitches, pumping our payback for all it was worth. Some of the girls thought we'd gone too far.

Daisy laughed, "I'll get the manager to let her out before we leave. A little scare will be good for her. *Fuckied-vous, Mademoiselle*?"

We rolled and hooted in laughter. Then we got even drunker... and drunker... and drunker. Closing time came, and the cab, and we blundered to our beds in a haze, passed out and slept until Sunday afternoon.

· · · · · · · ·

"I thought you were going to get her let out!" I was screeching blame at Daisy through my killer headache. We tried calling the bar, which was of course closed. We took a cab to the bar, but no owner's name was on the door. Only a sign that said "Closed on Sundays and Mondays." We went back to the dorm and tried to think. We talked Sunny into calling Babette's room to ask about a class assignment. "She's not here," they reported, "Must be away for the weekend." We called back Monday morning. No answer.

By Monday afternoon panic set in. "What if she died of dehydration? What if she choked on her own puke?" I was throwing bad case scenarios at Daisy faster than she could think.

"Not my fault." She asserted. "Her puke is not my fault. Her puke is her responsibility."

"We have no choice. We have to go to the police and get her let out."

Reluctantly, Daisy nodded. We got our jackets and opened the door to go face the music.

There stood Babette.

She had showered and seemed fairly fresh - in control of the situation. "Sit down girls, and let's have a little chat."

"Luckily the bar manager came in Monday afternoon to pick up something, or I could have died you know. So, I imagine you think I'm going to the dean. Right? Wrong. If I do that you'll get kicked out of school, and I know you don't want that, do you? No, *alors*, I prefer cash. I'll need one thousand dollars in cash in a week. In one hundred dollar bills, *S'il vous plait!*" And she stood up and breezed out the door.

We decided it was worth a thousand dollars not to get kicked out of school. Daisy sold her Yamaha twelve-string for five hundred to a girl on the second floor. I had nothing to sell. I ended up calling Frank and spilling out the whole sordid story. He agreed to loan me the five hundred with the promise that if the bitch asked for any more we would stop the extortion then and there. I promised to pay him back when I got a job and begged him not to tell Corry. A lesson was learned.

• • • • • • • •

After that first year, I decided to go to summer school for a head start on graduation, if I managed not to get kicked out first. Pinky had gone to Nashville, so Blackshale held little interest for me. I'd still have time at the end of summer school to visit Frank and Corry.

Three weeks into the term, I came in from class to find my summer roommate locked in the bathroom, not answering. I called Crone Stone, who came running with her key. Roomie was in our bathtub, reclined in two inches of clotting and blackening blood, eyes transfixed on the coat hangar in her hand. The ambulance came, she lived, no longer with child, but she left school. I luxuriated in my private room for the summer, but a fetus impaled on a coat hanger haunted my dreams.

. . . .

Second year, I grew up, focused on my art classes and channeled my creativity into more productive pursuits. Everybody goes a little wild their first year away from home, all that freedom for the taking. In some ways, I was a classic good girl. Because of my history, I never dated. There were no troubles with boys, no pregnancy scares, no broken-hearted suicide threats, no danger of my name and number being scrawled on the walls of the washroom stall. And for some reason, when I went out one night with a group of Mount Highland art students and they passed around the weed, I sneered, "Nope. I'm not gonna do that. I'll never do that!"

So that night, I left them all stoned and selling their leftovers to freshmen. I called it an early night and hailed a cab. When the bust came down and several of my artbuds were charged down at the police station, I was back at the dorm in my bed. They were all sent packing the next day, home to Roanoke, upstate New York, Boston, New Haven, home to pissed-off parents and jobs at local burger joints. I probably should never have said never, because here comes Daphne now, wanting to widgie out to the arbor... and anyway, we finally realized it's legal now.

. . . .

Here in my hands is my New York sketchbook, the summer between junior and senior year recorded in pen, ink, sepia wash. I took as many classes as I could afford at the Art Students League, drawing nudes, standing in a forest of oil-soaked easels on ancient floors. I can smell the old wood now.

The models were spectacular: a four hundred pound Japanese

woman, a dried-up little man all wrinkles and bones and elongated string of a penis, the tiny Asian girl with perky tits who ran from the stand when she started her period, scattering droplets of blood across the old wooden floors. Glib notes from my instructors were scribbled across my drawings.

My out-of-class work captured a Manhattan experience - the random paths I'd chosen up and down, across and over the grid of the borough, tourist stops seen through my irreverent eyes, a love of the city so different from my mountain home. I drew whatever caught my eye - mannequins in windows, frogs and fish in market barrels, layers of tape and staples on a kiosk pole, the sleeping homeless figure, museum artifacts, the profile of a boy who thought he could save me, change me, with his gentle love.

I liked him, the boy from Figure Illustration class, simply because he seemed so lost himself. At first we stood together at lunch, snarfing down Sabrett hot dogs. He and I began to explore streets together, sometimes going deep into the island, shoring each other's courage up through the riskier jaunts. We cataloged neighborhoods: Little Italy, Hells Kitchen, Chinatown, and Roosevelt Island where legless, partial people paddled around on wheeled pallets. I doled out my trust to him, bit by bit, but when he kissed me and tried to move on, I cried, "No, I can't, I'm sorry, I just can't." He cried too, as his hand pressed down on his needy crotch. I quickly escaped back to my senior year.

· · · · · · · ·

Like many senior years, mine seemed redundant and passed quickly. Seniors have too many things on their do-list, and little time for foolishness. Already looking ahead to the working world, the week before finals, I was tense, prickly, unsettled.

A tall, red-eyed figure slunk across the hall and flopped down on my bed with the grace of an ox. "Do you have a ciggie for B.K.?" I threw a pack of Winstons at her, bonking her on the head, dislodging several jumbo hair rollers.

"We deserve a last blast." she moaned. I couldn't have agreed more, so the girls from the top floor of Mount Highlands planned to sneak along the stone campus wall one last time for a party night out. We hit our bar, and I put down more Tom Collins than I could count, then we walked slowly and crookedly to the river singing Stones songs. We sat on the concrete retaining wall, swinging our legs, shaping our futures, dreading the big change and our weepy goodbyes. The sky was already tinting peach when we drug our sorry asses up the hill to Mount Highland.

All the others assumed Stone was snoring in her bed so they took off their shoes and boldly tiptoed up the stairs right past her apartment door. I was a chicken shit and chose the back door. As I started up the back stair, and turned the corner, I ran splat on into Crone Stone. "Anna Grace," she gloated, "There were pillows sleeping in your bed. And, if my records are correct, you are one reprimand away from being expelled."

I groaned in disbelief! I was going to get kicked out of school right before graduation. Frank and Corry would have my head on a platter!

"Come into my apartment for a conference please." She turned on her heel and slapped her house shoes through her door with me, heart sinking, trailing behind.

"Sit down," she pointed to a red velvet Victorian chair and disappeared into her kitchen. My eyes fell on trinket after trinket. That woman did love her curios. I felt an unexpected stab of pity for her lonely life in the company of knick knacks, tortured by smartass girls.

When she returned, she was holding two flutes of champagne. "Let's drink to your success. I'm going to let your little graduation trip slide. Frankly, you've surprised me, Anna Grace. Your professors rave, and while you've had your fun, sometimes at my expense, I think your raw talent and relentless work ethic will make Mount Highland proud someday." I laughed in surprise and she joined in, raising her glass to mine, Crone Stone gave me her most house motherly smile.

1976 Blackshale

Perry married late in life. Aunt Nettie was still kickin', but she had closed up the store when the Piggly Wiggly moved into Blackshale. She just sat her witch self around the house alone, drawing her social security check, watching soap operas and reading the word of God in vain. Perry had gone off to college at Georgia Tech and had become a heck of an engineer. He went to work tinkering with the workings of steam plants. I understood his need to be out of Blackshale, but I missed him. When he came in, he spent more time with me and Pap than with Nettie.

He'd dated several women, a few seriously. I think he always stopped short of commitment, not wanting to inflict his mother on someone he loved, but then again maybe he'd just never found the right one. When he was thirty-five, word came through the Blackshale grapevine that he had found her.

She was also an engineer, but a UT grad, which made for great football rivalry. He told me later that she loved to yell "Go Vols" when they were making love, just to get his goat. She was a gourmet cook and a low handicap golfer like Perry. She was beautiful, slender, delicate, doe eyed, and black. "Black as the ace of spades," the redneck grapevine had reported.

Perry took her to see his mother Nettie only one time. When they knocked on the door, Nettie thought Perry was bringing a maid or a nurse's aide for an interview, until he said, "I want you to meet Bonnie, my wife." Nettie's undiagnosed high blood pressure spiked to a new record high systolic, and she fell to the floor, forever paralyzed from the waist down, forever speechless, and forever after unable to move her bowels without the help of an enema.

After it was determined that she had survived the stroke, he visited her just once in the Morning Glory Ridge rehabilitation wing, long enough to leave an ornately framed picture of himself with his lovely bride on top of her dresser, where she could be sure to see it every day.

Bonnie and Perry had some great years, and they enjoyed life to the fullest. They built a house on a hill up across the river, all glass across the front. They chased each other through the house naked, daring the fishermen to look up and see them in action. He loved to tell about their rollicking sexploits and their multitudinous collection of sex toys. More information than I wanted, but I was glad that Perry was finally out from under Aunt Nettie's evil thumb and had found someone who filled him with happiness.

As for me, it didn't help that Jake and Harley died in that fiery car crash out on Blackshale Road or that BoJack and Peanut were rotting in prison on a life sentence. Thank God my damage had some limits. I was still able to give and receive love, but as far as sex was concerned I was numb. Since the day I was strapped down in the tree house, I'd mustered no interest in sex of any kind.

1992 Morning Glory Ridge

At the moment her colon burst, flooding a bloody delta out over the landscape of her off-white George Washington bedspread, Aunt Nettie had been seething at the picture of Perry and Bonnie, chanting "niggerbitch, niggerbitch, niggerbitch!" hatefully, silently to herself. The cancer (which, like her hypertension, was also undiagnosed) had left her with paper thin intestinal walls. A male nurse, after raiding the pain med cabinet on his own behalf, punched the enema nozzle in at the wrong angle. Whoops! Aunt Nettie grabbed and scraped greedily for her King James Bible, seeking spiritual succor and sustenance for her last breaths, but it was out of reach.

1993 Blackshale

Most kids finally grow up, as do most towns. Blackshale had only matured to the point of having one Jewish and one Catholic family, a Family Dollar Store, and a half-assed Community Center. I'd become an adult, but I was the only forty-three-year-old I knew still living at home. After college, a stint as a graphic designer in Nashville whiled away some years, but I was utterly unsuited for corporate life. Every time I left my desk to take a whiz, the unbillable minutes of urination had to be carefully logged. I felt like a lab rat on a treadmill and was miserable to the core.

In nineteen eighty-seven, Corrine was diagnosed with MS. Pearlie still lived in the basement, but "old Arthur" was in her joints takin' his toll. She had cut back on her hours but caring for Corry and the house was too much. Pap offered me a deal: "Move home, help look out for Corrine, and I'll build you a rent-free studio apartment in the woods out back." That worked for me, I was hungry to make art no one else would sign off on.

Most women my age had monthly sex with balding husbands. They had grown children, many of who were already moving back home after stalled lives. At this point I was rather nunnish. My happiness was my haven, a beautiful open studio space filled with the trappings of my work. Frank had gone all out. It was a two-story structure, the top level was the studio and a small sitting room. Downstairs was my bedroom, bathroom, and a kitchenette. There was one big window looking out toward Pap and Corrine's, a window I had insisted on so I could still monitor the comings and goings on Blackshale Road. My old room at Tollett's and my window seat, now belonged to Pearlie so she wouldn't have to climb the stairs any more.

On the backside of my sitting room, a wall of windows looked out over the creek and the woods and on out to the meadow. Pap had cleared out the undergrowth. I could see all the way down the stone wall snaking through the meadow to the stile, a sad landmark from my childhood. In spite of its history, my view was still beautiful, heaven on a rocky black earth.

· · · · · · · ·

On a moonlit New Year's Eve, I nest alone in my beanbag chair, sucking down a bottle of Chianti. I'm dressed up like a movie queen, practicing my line, "I vant to be alone." I've turned off all the lights so as to best appreciate snippets of illumination arranged in the room. From the ceiling hang strings of lights with clear amber bulbs. The coffee table is covered with candles in a hundred shades of white, off-white, ivory, oyster, cream and eggshell, and as many different heights and diameters. All the flames dance, bringing to life my mama's collection of white figurines on her walnut buffet, which I had painted with sultry green enamel. Floating happily in my buzz, the ting of my movie star fingernails on the wineglass makes me giggle.

At midnight, I glance out the window toward the meadow. A glint from one of the candles on the glass lines up with the stile on the stone wall. In my left brain, I know good and well that's what it is, I do, but my drunken right brain jumps right in and begins to consider other possibilities. I catalog them out loud in a warped voice: "Ok, a lightening bug whooshed through a time machine to the wrong season, or... a bundle of fairy dust, or... the flashlight of an approaching ax murderer. Maybe it's a leprechaun's lantern... foxfire... the reflection of a car light from over on Rambler Road... a will-o-the-wisp... or possibly, please God, maybe," I blather to myself with a teary smile, "a bit of Dory's luminous soul."

"Happy New Year, dahling!" I say to Dory in my best Garbo. Yeah, I'm smashed all right. I wander back to the family picture gallery covering the hall walls from ceiling to floor. There's

Marlene decked out in a pink tutu and proudly holding her stick, seven year old me in a fetching set of corrugated cardboard wings I had made myself, Pap with his brand new hearse. Aunt Nettie is not represented. I look at my people, maudlin. The loneliness, how it hurts. There is Dory in an Easter dress and peep toe pumps, her lips painted deep magenta beyond the borders of her mouth, Marilyn style. Over the cream underskirt, multicolored dots floated on translucent silk. The dress was designed to show off a décolletage, but Dory lacked cleavage and the spots lay flat against the bony plane of her chest.

Here's Frank with his Model 64 Winchester, standing tall and proud next to a twelve-point buck - the only one he'd scored in all his years of hunting. The buck hangs upside down from a tree, draining, waiting to be field dressed. Pap stuffed the head himself, and hung it over a row of filing cabinets in the basement. As a child I had been fascinated with that head and crown of horns, still existing, yet no longer existing - presiding over the files on dead humans.

My eyes slide up to Frank's picture and his eyes seem to be looking straight at the drink in my hand. "Don't be looking at ME Pap!" I smart talk my dead daddy, "You liked a good buzz, and a whole lot more, didn't you? You know the truth now, over there on the other side, that as you age and see that deathbed looming up in your face, it helps to escape, to soften that harsh reality, even if just for a few hours." I study his face, trying to remember his voice, and cry, "I want my Pap!"

There's a snapshot of Corrine and Frank in later years, settled and solid. When Corrine came into his life, Frank had stayed sober. As for me, I'm totally drunk at the moment and the childish voice in my head whines, "I want my mommies, both of them!"

I walk tipsily back into the studio, looking out over my work. I have a show coming up in Nashville at an important gallery. I love making the work, but I hate the exhibition thing, the marketing, and the expectations of others. It is like standing buck naked in front of a crowd of people while they cast critical eyes on your flaws, be they scars, moles, bunions, toenail fungus, stretch marks, or the heartbreak of psoriasis. I have spread out all the pieces from the last three years on work tables and along the walls. I come to the figurative pieces first.

The figures shimmer to and fro on the picture plane, mutating, animating. Contours disappear and reappear, forcing constant reconsideration of the subject. My style had always been non-committal, favoring techniques that are forgiving - processes that don't require immediate perfection. I think of myself as lacking courage - chicken, yellow. There's an upside though. I draw and paint over, scrub out, scumble, scrape down and redo. In the end, the finished pieces reveal layers of pentimento that invite questions.

In one, Frank stands over a draped corpse on a steel work table, needle in hand. And there is Pearlie out on the chicken path in pursuit of a giant iridescent rooster, her body pulled sideways toward the heavy ax.

Larger than life self-portraits stand side-by-side, one as a mermaid, of course. In another, a young Anna Grace is seeking to cast blame on herself, clothed in a burlap sack dress, a zipper bisecting the front from top to bottom. There are somber versions, dark angels with black wings, poised on tiptoe - considering flight into a stormy sky.

The meadow out back is my only landscape - ever. I've recreated it almost every day, habitually, obsessively, exploring it in different moods of weather or casts of light, its picture plane forever bisected by contrails of the spirit I seek though my art making. I study a large series of those landscapes now, moving along the wall where they are lined up, Norman Greenbalm singing the soundtrack in my head.

There are stacks and stacks of drawings, their surfaces covered with corybantic markings, murky clouds of tone, calligraphic lines, tiny symbols borrowed from my mental catalog of doodles. Many have economical color palettes - ochre with undertones of cobalt - and deep layers of translucent beeswax. I've shunned Chiaroscuro - preferring ghostly, smoky masses spiked with line and sparkling details. Most feature a single, simple object: amulet, stile, talisman, embalming tank with floating puppies.

My favorite pieces are art objects - assemblages - oblique wrappings, found objects reduced to anonymous states with layers of paint. Many are small wooden boxes, shrines and altars, totems, handmade books. Almost everything combines objects in assemblage, inviting the viewer to form connections, meanings between my marks and the tiny bits of ephemera I love to collect and collage. Humble aggregates, snipped bits of nothingness, get glued in place with tweezers and a yearning for community.

On across the room, hundreds of pairs of Dory eyes gaze up at me from the floor where they have fallen out of their folder. They float helter skelter at my feet. I lift up my gaze to quell tears and turn up my glass to dull the pain. *Mama.*

Only one thing nags at me in the rare minutes when I'm not totally absorbed in my work. I am lonely. When it comes to human love, I am an atheist, a vegan, unheld. I have no hug, no touch. My skin is a barbwire border to the rest of the world.

· · · · · · · ·

Pinky moved to Nashville, a little after I did, to become a photographer's assistant. She'd gone to Watkin's Institute and picked up skills. When I moved back to Blackshale, her Aunt Dimple had died of an overdose, and the farm was sold, so Pink stayed planted in middle Tennessee.

I went back to Nashville once in a while. We hit the country music bars and partied hardy, rolled in the floor with laughter, toasted ourselves and ignored the sleazy men circling us like sharks. Sometimes, we just sat in her apartment on Murfreesboro

Road, floated in her aqua pool and reminisced about our Blackshale kidhoods - about the happy-go-lucky, innocent times. The hideously scarring, depraved ones, we never mentioned.

2029 Morning Glory Ridge

Tiffany is speaking sentences today, a rare, but still unwelcome turn of events. She is propped up in her exercise chair by the window, shrieking in her outside voice about a man walking down the middle of the river. She's thinking it's Jesus. She sounds a lot like amplified breaking glass, so I need to get out. I touch the spot on my screen that says eCall and then tap the photo of my new friend, Candy. Up she pops, toothless and grinning.

"Are you free to go to the Activity Room with me? I have to get the hell out of here before Tiffany bursts my eardrums. Put in your teeth and wheel on by. We'll go down and get up a game of bridge."

We wheel our WidgieWalkers on down to the elevator. When we get off, the activity room is just around the corner on the right.

"Allow me to introduce myself," a melodramatic voice floats out into the hall. When we come through the door, a profusion of fuschia feathers fills up what's left of our vision. She is standing on the table, tap dancing.

"Taloola La Rue, as you may suspect, was my stage name, but I got so attached to it I decided to take it to my gravestone!" she says with flourish, throwing a purple boa around her neck. She proceeds to list the Broadway theatres she has graced, "the Fantasia! the Imperial! the Royal!"

You know I was in "Those Town Girls" with Fred Astaire in forty-five. He was such a stunner, that one! She bats her fake eyelashes, and extends a fish netted leg and pointed toe. The tale grows outrageously by leaps and bounds, until I can take no more.

"Bull hockey! This is a big stinking pile of it. Let's go, Candy." I huff, and we wheel out of the performance with our wrinkled old noses held high.

I go right back to bed, but after a second thought touch the eScreen. There are many more up-to-date search tools, but I like good old-fashioned Google. I'm just comfortable with it. I start typing in the search box... T A L O O L A L A... and poof! Up she comes, Taloola La Rue, star of stage and screen. The old broad has a Filmography. On Google.

"Crap! Crapola! Now I'll have to apologize." I slide off the bed, fire up my WidgieWalker, and shuffle penitently down to Taloola's room.

1998 Blackshale

After burying so many folks, Pap died quickly of a massive coronary. He left the world in very much the same way his son Adam had gone abruptly years before. He'd often vowed that sudden cardiac death was the way to go. Corrine saw him fall in the back yard where he was preparing the soil for a spring garden and reached his side in time to say goodbye to the man she had come to love. I heard her through the open window of my studio, yelling at me to call 911. I quickly made the call and ran down, in time to see a glimmer of recognition and feel the squeeze of his hand before his chest stopped rising, before his eyes focused on mysteries far beyond. Corry wrapped me in her arms, but I was inconsolable.

The last funeral conducted by Frank Tollett had been for Albine Yother, the widower from out on the mountain. After looking it up in his rusted metal filing cabinet, Frank confirmed that he had buried Albine's mother-in-law back in the early years of his business. Albine met his horrible demise from a slow eating cancer. His middle-aged daughter, who was the manager down at the drugstore, came to see Frank imploring him to go up the mountain and talk to her Paw about his service, so he could put his mind at rest. She said, "Paw's mind's 'bout gone, but he tol' me, he bagged me, 'I like that feller Tollett, you go get 'em fer me.'"

Frank drove as far as he could, then struggled on foot the rest of the way up the hill. The road was worse than it had been those many years back. He got mighty out of breath doing it, too. He noticed the house was going to fall down in a pile of rotten wood and copperheads on top of Albine Yother if the man didn't get on with dying soon. Frank knocked on the door and a ghostly trickle of voice, weak and breathless, bid him inside.

"Howdy," Frank said quietly, still lacking in breath himself.

The home nurse had propped the bedhead up on wooden crates, as a boon for failing lungs. On the mattress Albine lay flat as a flapjack, except when he bent up to hawk blood-streaked sputum into a kidney-shaped pan. His voice came with much effort, in a thready and high-pitched whine. He was full of tubes.

"Ain't nothin' much left up hyare. I says to my girl Alamandra, 'If'n I was you I'd scritch a match to the house and that barn up yeunder, then call up the Blackshale Fire truck so's the whole mountain don't go up.' She ain't got no use fer it, her girl got kilt cookin' meth up hyare in a trailer. Blew sky high. Now Alamandra's raisin' up a grandboy – Josiah, but he won't have no need fer this scruffy plot neither. Tollett! This pore scrap ain't good for much, but hit's all yor'es in trade for my wake and buryin'. You kin sell it fer a little, I reckon. Hyare's the deed I done signed. Yore an honorable man and I know you'll let me live out what little I got left right'chere. After I'm done, hit's yores.

I done tol' my girl Alamandra, 'I like that feller', and I kin tell you why that is now that Piney's dead and gone."

He chuckled, bringing on a spate of whistling, hacking coughs. That spell of carrying on lasted for a while, but Frank sat patient and quiet, waiting for it to pass so he could hear why it was he was liked. As an undertaker, he did not hear that too often.

"May be I'm wrong, but I'm purty dam well shore you dumped Piney's maw out the back of my wagon that day before her buryin', and sent her sorry naggin' ass shootin' down the gully. That old hoodoo crone was straight from the devil, made my married life a livin' hell and I reckon she went right back to 'im! But Lordy Lord, if you didn't give her a fitten send off!" he cackled. "Haaaaa... yep, you dumped that hateful hag right out in the dirt, ain't that right?" he reminisced happily, his weakening voice trailing off. Frank's color deepened, and he studied the mud on his shoes.

"So how did you know, uh, about the, uh, accident with Mrs.

Young?"

Albine looked a bit guilty. "Well, Viny had brought a little money in a poke from the old house, and we couldn't find it nowhars. I figgered she'd try to take it with her. So that night before the buryin', I pulled back the satin and poked around under there, but all I found was a lot of red mud caked up her arse and on her fat old scratched up ankles. Hit was that, and all them scrape marks going out the back of my wagon."

Frank laughed. "Be sure your sins will find you out. Just out of curiosity, why did we not have the honor of burying Mrs. Yother when she passed?"

"Oh, Piney, she had no use for you. She took a powerful offense when you broke out the brew at her maw's wake."

"But, but... she was suckin' it up, in fact, she was damn near drunk, or else she would have noticed Mrs. Young's hairdo had been... uh... readjusted."

Albine nodded, "Yep, well, she drunk it all right, but she was still sore you brung it, didn't like it not one little bit. Piney Young Yother had her some principles!"

 Frank and Albine worked out the details of a simple service, and agreed on a spot of ground, there on top of the mountain, for his burying. Frank commented on a mason jar of home brew on Albine's bed table. "That's sure good for what ails a feller!"

Albine smiled the patient smile of a dying man. "Take it on home, we got lots more of them there down in the cellar. Been thar three year, and I won't be hyare to drank it up! Yep, the cold hard ground is callin'and I'll be in there directly!"

Frank shook Albine's emaciated hand, took the deed and the mason jar with embarrassed thanks, and slid through the mud back down the gully. He sipped from the jar all the way down the hill.

The next day, Frank ran the deed by the courthouse and recorded it, thinking it hardly worth the trouble. A week later,

Albine passed, and Frank kept his end of the bargain. A week after he buried Albine Yother, Frank himself was in the ground and Corrine Baker Miller Tollett was a widow for the second time in her life. The day Frank died, Corrine finished up the other half of that Mason jar she found parked on the kitchen counter.

· · · · · · · ·

They say death comes in threes and sure enough there was another funeral that same week. Perry's beloved Bonnie was lost to him all too soon. He was out buying seed at the co-op, and came home to find her recently deceased but still warm, lying in the kitchen floor next to a shattered pitcher, a squeezed lemon, and a puddle of sweet tea. An autopsy showed she had died, with little warning, of a burst aorta. A blessing he wasn't, but I reckon if Perry had been standing next to her, he would have heard a loud pop.

He was heartbroken. He lay in their bed soaking up her scent, refusing to change the sheets for three months. After he finally hauled his ass out of bed, he began to spend a lot of time at my studio. He started getting all over my last nerve, so I gave him a job doing my dirty work, thinking it would be good for him. I was making wall pieces and boxes and sculptural towers that had to be built anyway, and Perry loved to saw and hammer and glue. We spent several months side-by-side, our wounded heads buried in projecting.

One afternoon, I had a pot roast in the oven, and he sniffed the air with frank appreciation. I said, "Perry boy, you might as well stay and eat. I have plenty." We snarfed down the roast and potatoes and carrots and a pineapple upsidedown cake I had dug up out of Dory's old recipe file. After dinner we opened a bottle of Maker's Mark, and sat on the sofa watching a movie. The liquid level on that bottle kept going down, down, down, and then there was an unexpected sexy scene of lovemaking in the movie. Perry looked into my eyes and some new feeling tweaked between my legs. I felt a heaviness low in my belly and then an itch I'd never felt before. Perry leaned over and kissed me, and it felt so sweetly forbidden. Then he got in my blouse and tickled around on my nipples, and by then I was a goner. His hand went down my pants and sideways under the elastic of my panties, working over, over slowly like a rambling spider, and I was for the first time willing, desiring to let someone touch me. He gently stroked me, and I watched myself from up in the air like I was someone else, as I pulled him on top of me, into me, and I wanted it. I wanted it all. We lay on the sofa a long time after that, laughing and crying, all our pains and sorrows and abuses melting into a single sweet moment of well-deserved love and joy. Soaked in alcohol and a blurry contentment, my mind was singing out, "Hallelujah!"

· · · · · · · ·

I woke up the next morning sober and cursing. "Jesus H. Christ! I have done the nasty with my own first cousin! Oh good Lord! Adopted or not, the Blackshale biddies would still call that incest!"

Perry wasn't all that concerned. He shrugged his shoulders and giggled with the sweet memory of it all. "Well, me myself, I thought it was pretty swell!"

"Oh… now…" I argued, "this is just plain wrong. You will have to keep on your side of the river from now on." I was crying. I was losing my best male friend, my only male relative, my working partner, and my self-respect in one fell swoop. And he did, he stayed over there across the river a long, long time, but I would be lying if I said I didn't miss him like crazy.

· · · · · · · ·

A month after Perry and I had gone way beyond being kissing cousins, I missed my period for the first time in my life. I was terrified, and there was no one I could confide in. Another month passed and still no period. I was out on the far edge of childbearing years, and the odds of spewing an ill-fated child out of my womb were huge. Two and a half months into my terror, I called Sudy in tears. She got me over to the hospital and did a pregnancy test.

She called laughing hysterically. "Honey, you've gone through the pause!"

I found it weird but comforting that the same person who had pronounced me a woman was now telling me my woman troubles were over forever. I had not named the potential father, but she finally weasled it out of me. Again she laughed. "Well, then, sweetpea, you might as well just go at it for the sake of pure fun, there won't be any babies coming out of you now."

2001 Nashville

On the tenth of September, I met Pinky at Gate 12 of the Nashville Airport. We were going to New York City for a week of gallery hopping. Over the years, she had transitioned from photographer's assistant to successful commercial photographer, then on into a fine art photographer who had a lot to say with her lens. We were looking forward to turning SoHo upside down.

"Hey girl!" I threw myself around her in a full body hug. "Are you excited?"

"I can't wait! Did you know there's a Sally Mann retrospective at the MOMA?" Smugly, I handed her my gallery guide with the show already circled in red. Robert Van Vranken, my favorite painter, was also circled. I was stoked!

She gave me the classic PinkyToe "imp has a secret" look. "Well, I have a fantastic late birthday surprise! You have to wait though. I'll show you on the plane. Hey, here's the johns... do you need to drain your lizard or drop the kids at the pool before we head for the gate? I went before I left home."

I nodded, and wheeled my suitcase through the restroom door and into a stall. I sat down and spread out, thrilled that my oat bran muffin had decided to work just in time. Nothing worse than needing to go bad with two attendants and a drink cart between you and the facilities!

When I stood up and turned to flush, I couldn't believe what I was seeing. I blinked and bent down closer to inspect.

"Look at that!" I said to myself. There in the toilet the product of my bowel had fallen into a precisely crafted circle with a leaning slash, the universal symbol for "don't go there." Ever the artist, I pulled my camera out of my bag and took a picture, and then I marched back out to the American Eagle desk and cancelled the flight. I hated flying anyway, and was superstitious enough that there was no way I was getting on that plane.

"You... did... what?" Pink was livid, understandably. I had paid for the plane tickets on my credit card, and I hadn't even asked her opinion, or if she wanted to go alone. I couldn't explain it, but the poop had spoken. We drove back to her apartment in our separate cars, and by the time we got there she'd had time to get really pissed.

"What the fuck were you thinking? I've been saving up for this trip a solid year, but oh, no! It's always about you and your morbid visual sensitivity. Okay, okie-fuckin-dokie, let me get this straight, your shit told you not to go? Your shit drew a symbol, a diagram in the friggin' crapper telling you not to get on that plane? YOU! You and your prophesying POOP!"

I presented my defense, "Look... here, I took a picture of it... you can see how perfect..."

"You can take your picture of your shit and cram it right back up in your sorry ass where it came from!" She stormed into her bedroom and threw her bags on the bed, snorting and drawing long breaths. I could hear her throwing clothes and shoes, unpacking with a boiling anger.

I hung my head. Then I slithered to the door of her room and tried to sound somehow reasonable, "I know it sounds crazy, but the fact is I simply could not get on that plane. I think I would have died of a heart attack. And if I couldn't get on, I sure couldn't watch you get on either!"

She came back out with a pillow and blanket. "You can sleep on my sofa tonight and eat my stale donuts in the morning, but after that I never want to see you again. I mean it!" I knew she didn't really mean it. We had been through much, much worse together. I turned over my left hand and traced the blood sister scar on my palm.

The next morning at early-thirty, true to her word, she plopped down a plate of stale donuts on the coffee table in front of the sofa where I was still wrapped in a blanket and guilt. I grabbed a donut, but it was so dry it fell apart in my hand and crumbs rained down in my lap.

In an effort to ignore my presence, she flipped on the news. In horror we watched it live. The acrid blue sky, the silver planes, the tumbling of bodies and concrete and structural steel, thickly dusted ghost people running through the streets in terror. We staggered to the bathroom to vomit. For hours, we didn't speak. Pinky made coffee with shaking hands. After a while, she scuttled to her bedroom and pulled an envelope out of her purse.

When she came back, she said, "As hard as it is to believe, there's more. This was your birthday surprise. I guess now I should say I'm sorry." She handed me the envelope. Inside was a reservation confirmation for two on expensive paper.

Breakfast
Windows on the World
September 11, 2001, 8:30 am

2029 Morning Glory Ridge

On a sunny Friday I widgie on down to visit my new friend Taloola. En route to her room, I pass a cast of characters in the common area. There's a clump of imaginary mommies rocking their rubber baby dolls, the long retired music teacher beating time on her knee, and a man who refuses to keep his clothes on. There are also the chronic itch scratchers, skin pickers, eye blinkers, knuckle crackers, foot swingers, and same song singers.

I ask Taloola if she cares to go down to the Activity Room with me and get up a hand of bridge. She does, since her agent only calls on Tuesdays.

That woman is a stickler for hygiene and beauty. First thing, she pulls up her dress, stretches out the waistband of her panties and sprays Febreeze down in there. She makes me sit and watch while she slathers on eye makeup with a trembling hand. She ends up looking scary but I'm not about to be the one to tell her. She whirls her boa around her neck and off we go.

When we arrive, no other bridge players are about. For that matter, there's no one at all to appreciate Taloola's makeup job and nice fresh smell. We pet the dogs a while, letting them slobber on our wrinkled fingers, then we get ice cream and sit out on the veranda.

"So Taloola, tell me a good theatre story." My eyes fall on a greasy spot in the tile I can't look at without laughing. I still see Flotilla flailing there.

"Dahling! I could tell you thousands of stories! Just thousands! But if I had to choose just one, oh, fiddlesticks, let me think. I guess the funniest one happened on opening night of 'Big Top Circus.' There were all kinds of live animals and circus parades through the audience. It was quite the festive atmosphere! Well, dahling! You may, or may not know that the theme song for that musical was 'Love Under the Big Top', a perfectly charming song that was woven throughout. I was suspended from a trapeze just as the main performance of the song got into full swing, forgive the pun. Just then, two of the capuchin monkeys escaped from their trainer, centered themselves perfectly over the proscenium arch, which was appropriately draped like a striped circus tent, and did the dirty with great gusto, screeching and rutting. Every time the audience went wild with laughter, the horny little beasts stopped and peered out with that questioning look they have. Then they'd go right back at it. It was a hoot. The trainer came out totally red faced, and reclaimed his charges. In the next performance, needless to say, the monkey population had been reduced to a single neutered male."

I laugh heartily. "I can imagine you've had quite the life!" I raise my fluted glass ice cream dish and tap it against hers in a toast, "Here's to the fabulous Taloola La Rue!"

She reminisces on for a bit, talking about the stage life, the uncertainty, the travel, the thrill of the applauding crowd, the pure joy of being under lights. Before we rise to go back for our naps, she looks from side-to-side and whispers confidentially.

"You know, I don't say this to just anyone dear, but if you'd like an autograph, I'd be happy to sign one just for you."

I dig in my WidgiePack for a pen and paper. She scribbles wildly all over the page, and even though it is totally unreadable, I'm sure it says, "The fabulous Taloola La Rue."

"Actually, there's something else I'd like. Could I draw you?"

She agrees, of course, thrilled to be in the spotlight once again. I pull out another page, and working quickly, capture her panache, her curling boa, the flamboyant young actress still in there behind an old woman's overly made-up eyes.

• • • • • • • •

This tall stack of sketchbooks represents the hardest time of my life. Not because bad things happened during those years, but it was then that the numbness receded, and I began to feel the weight of the past. This was the time of my life when I finally confronted the demon of memory - and used my art to beat it down into submission. The books are oversized, carved, doodled, taped, stapled, embellished. and torched. Black from cover to cover, these are the visual chronicles of my dark journey.

After graduation, I headed for Nashville. I had a job as a designer waiting there. PinkyToe was already ensconced in a tiny apartment. She was studying to be a photographer's assistant, and had a co-op job with a professional photographer. "Yee Ha! Take me down to the Grand 'Ole Opry!" she liked to say. Pinky still talked countrified, and when I was with her I backslid a little myself. In those early days, we were country bumpkins in Music City.

As the sixties became the strange seventies, Pinky and I pursued second careers as professional barflies. Neither of us had any interest in picking up dates. We just loved the drinking, the funky disco beat and the people watching. The sleazy men with their polyester suits and sideburns were checking out girls with goofy fashions, poufy hair, and sexy legs in platform shoes. There were the usual games - eye contact, cigarette smoke blown just so, pick-up lines, the invitation to a courtship dance, she gets her coat, he smiles victoriously, they split for his pad. Pink and I were only smug spectators.

A few years later we sat at clubs with friends from work, listening to the Ramones, The Avengers, The Clash, Blondie. We were aimless thirty-somethings, with no hankering for the marriage and family track most of our friends were on. Work was a grind, not the creative adventure I'd hoped for, more a repetitive production line for the ideas of others. Hints of depression began to take root. We drank too much and slept too little, which didn't help.

When Punk turned Goth, we went underground to cave-like clubs throbbing with deafening rhythms. Like everyone else, we wore black and spiked metal from head to toe. Oddly enough, I felt younger again, the edginess and disconnection of that world suited my isolation. Everyone danced alone to Sisters of Mercy, eyes closed, pulsing together in one organic mass. Hard drugs were everywhere in the convulsing crowd, but we passed, sucking up instead jello shooters until three in the morning. Those were the days.

Pink and I got tattoos, a single word in twenty-four point black Gothic text, Abandonada, incised in the skin across our hearts. The artist had winced when he had to work across my scar with his letters. I went back to the same tattoo parlor a second time, bent on encircling my ribcage with a line of tiny symbols, but I chickened out at the last minute when the tattoo artist himself warned, "That there's gonna hurt like a sonofabitch!" Instead I got my bellybutton pierced – which was soon infected, landing me in the emergency room. I already had scarification front and back, so no further markings on my body were needed to prove my bravery.

It must have been the specter of forty on the horizon. The hint of depression grew into a gnawing black beast in my gut. My former mermaid psyche was now a gnarled seamonster, rolling in a sun-deprived deep. I was too glum to party, too independent to seek counseling, too glib to let my feelings show, even to Pinky. She was still all about fun. I turned to the only therapy I knew - my art.

It finally hit me that the thing I had been doing at work, with the title "Artist-Designer" on my door, had nothing at all to do with my flailing creative self. I had to find her again.

I converted my second bedroom into a studio, and used all the previous clubbing time for art making. I copied the therapists on TV, asking myself, Tell me about it; how did that feel? I used pages in my books to write it all out. I was brutally honest with myself. Starting with the myth of my childhood, I filled page after page with a quivering, clinched hand. As much as I loved Dory and Frank, it was a myth. It was a happy myth, but a myth all the same. As much as I adored Corrine, there were still feelings about being left on a porch like a Fed Ex package. Aunt Nettie's cruelties loomed large. Then came Jake and Harley forcing me to be the abuser. That one was the hardest. Finally, being buckled down, the slice of the razor, the prick of nails, the loss of my virginity to thugs. In my mind, I danced in a circle around a fire I feared to touch – forgiveness. I dug out and wrote down every memory, every emotion I could find hiding down deep in the abyss with that raging black monster.

When I was done, I began to draw, and draw, and draw non-stop. My anger spawned rough, raw marks and unfettered strokes. My sadness gave birth to a sensitive beauty. The books were filled – memory-by-memory, word-by-word, mark-by-mark – until I felt healing rise up to slay the beast.

2008 Blackshale

Pearlie and I had done our best for Corrine, but her condition was deteriorating rapidly and she needed constant, backbreaking care. Corry and I had inherited enough from Pap's business to place her in an excellent facility in Knoxville, one that specialized in the needs of advanced MS. She saw the toll her care was taking on me and was determined to go. I argued with her week after week, wanting to keep her at home. One night, she tried to get up alone, not wanting to wake me, and fell, shattering her hip and two bones in her right arm. Now she would have no choice but to go into the facility for therapy. Once there, she was content.

As soon as she was settled, I visited, bearing a bouquet of gardenias and framed pictures of Frank and me. She introduced me to all her caretakers and chattered on a while about the rigors of physical therapy. She laughed, "That PT bitch is going to get hers. When I get back on my feet, I'm going to whoop her fat ass and show her what pain is!"

"Well," I laughed at her bluster, "You'll be home before you know it, and all this hard work will be behind you!"

Her face clouded. "Sweetheart, sit. I have something to tell you. I've sold the building. I have no where to go home to." Frank had left her the building, me my studio and the six acres behind it, and split his money between us. It was her right to do what she wanted with the building, but I was a little miffed that she'd done it all without discussion. I knew she was doing it for me though, out of love, to give me back my life.

"Bobby Oody made me a good offer on the front property, and the great part is, he has no plans for the building. He just bought the land for investment, so things will stay pretty much as they are."

"No, not the same!" I pouted, "You won't be there." I was being left behind all over again.

"You can come and see me here any time you want. We'll both be better off."

I knew she was right. She reached out and held up my chin with her hand, now quaking with tremors. Her face was puffy from the steroids, but her love for me was etched, purely, painfully, all over it.

There was only one problem - one huge problem. Pearlie had lived most of her life at Tollett's. I couldn't kick her out on the street, and there wasn't room for her with me. While I was musing over the possibilities, I let Pearlie believe that Corry would be coming home, and kept the sale of the building under my hat. It was a wretched month. I lay awake most of the nights and in what few hours I slept, Pearlie's sweet face and voice haunted my dismal dreams.

There's an old saying, "God moves in mysterious ways." One afternoon, I had gone over to check on Pearlie and pick up a few things for Corry. Pearlie came to the door, looking like the cat that had swallowed a whole cage full of flapping canaries. She had always pushed her words out strong but today they were busting out like steam out of a pressure cooker.

"Oh Lordy! Fixin' to call you. Fixin' to. Oh, Lordy Me." She was pacing the floor and clawing at her chest with her long, arthritic fingers. "Ain't no easy way... Might as well be spittin' it out... Oh, Lordy, Grace... well, fact is... been here near all my life, you a baby girl, Miss Dory, Miss Corry, Mr. Frank... Oh Lord, hep me Jesus to tell it." Pearlie was in a state. She looked like she was about to shoot up clean out of her drawers. "Fact is, I has to quit now, Anna Grace. Oh my sweet babygirl! Mr. Samuel Washington from Pineville, he done got down on his knees and slid a great big rock on my finger! I'm tellin' it, he done axed me to be his bride! I hates to leave you alone, I hates it, but if I got any happy time comin' for my own self, I'm sayin' the time done come!"

I know I stood with my mouth hanging open for a full minute.

"Oh, Pearlie! What will I do without you?" I hugged her, full of mixed emotions. I was so thrilled for her and happy the problem was solved, but life without Pearlie seemed unthinkable.

"There's just one thing now... you don't have yourself a hope chest!"

I took her to Belk's that week and bought her a huge Lane Sweetheart Chest, and we spent the afternoon filling it with crisp new linens, fluffy towels, a set of china and stainless steel flatware. What fun it was, shopping for Pearlie as a bride! As a special treat, I threw in a blender. She'd learned to love a good Margarita, but referred to it as "her special lemonade" so as not to offend the folks down at the church.

When we got back to the house, Pearlie sank down in her rocking chair with one of her special lemonades, tuckered out. She lifted her wrinkled brown hand in the air, pointing over to her bureau. "Anna Grace, child, would you open up that top drawer and hand me that little red box?"

She opened the box and handed me its contents. It was Hum's Case knife. It was a beauty, the pearl handle tracker. "This here is for you, to 'member Hum and me."

I closed my eyes and rubbed my fingers over the handle. I could swear it vibrated with a satisfied "hummmm."

A few days later, Mr. Samuel Washington came in the back door and shook my hand with a firm grip.

"I am so glad to meet you, but that said, you better be good to this woman or you'll answer to me!" I gave him the stink eye, followed by a friendly smile.

He assured me there was no doubt about him treating her fine.

Then all at once he started grunting, "Oooooo, ummm, ummmm, ummm. Your breath is so fresh and minty, like a young person!" I laughed. He seemed genuine and sweet, and I felt like Pearlie was going to be in good hands.

As I watched Pearlie and Sam chug off in his old Pontiac with her hope chest and her few other possessions dragging behind in a U-Haul, I was an Abandonada once again. One of the last remaining props of my life had been pulled out from under me.

········

I went back home and hired some men with a truck to cart off the familiar possessions of my loved ones, Dory, Corrine and Frank. The keepers were moved up to my place, especially the vast, timeworn square of kitchen table where the women of Tollett's had worked side by side, preparing food, cutting out dress patterns, crafting the small details of family life. It would become the centerpiece of my studio, where I'd now work on alone, making art instead of fried apple pies or penuche fudge. All the rest of the housewares were taken to a junk dealer. The loose ends were tied up.

Six weeks into my new alone time, there was a timid knock at the door. Perry was standing there, looking at the floor, seriously down at the mouth. There was not a hint of a smile to be seen on his usually mirthful face.

"I know, I know I'm on the wrong damn side of the river, but I'm in shit deep need of a best friend and like it or not, you are it. Can I come in?"

I stepped back and let him in. "I'm afraid I don't have my hairdo on," I mumbled, attempting a makeshift French twist with shaky fingers. He walked over to my sofa and plopped down, then leaned over and sunk his head into his long hands.

"Anna Grace, I just got a call from Doc Turner. They did some tests on me last week, and the results just came in. I have prostate cancer. Next week, they'll be taking it out. I guess my life as a macho man is over." He laughed; then cried.

"So, big boy," I said, "Are you here for a last hurrah? Because I can't do that."

He looked at me sadly, "No! NO, Oh hell no! I just thought you might smoke some weed with me and listen to me whine."

I'd never smoked pot in my life. He pulled out a plastic bag and rolled two joints. I thought, "What the heck. This man needs a friend." I took a drag on the lumpy, fat-bellied cigarette.

"Is this, like, a toke?" I was really green.

After a few drags, I felt really good, mellow, whooooo, reeeeaaly mellow. Mama's figurines were dancing again. I started looking at objects in my sitting room, things I saw everyday without really seeing them. Everything I looked at was... intense... way much more what it was than what it had been before. I found myself wondering if having cancer was more intense. That couldn't be good.

Perry started talking in a mumbly voice, "You know before, Anna Grace, that last night here... I think I figured out why that happened..."

I interrupted him, "I know why. We were snookered and I had a lifetime of horny saved up, that, and then there is the fact that you are the only man I can trust not to hurt me." I put my arms around him and laid his head over on my shoulder, while he wept and smoked, smoked and wept, mourning his manhood on death row.

When he finally stopped crying, the pot had done a number on my stubborn moral stance. We made love, sweeter than sweet and sadder than sad, all night long.

2029 Morning Glory Ridge

My eScreen beeps and serves up today's messages. I hit the zoom button and scan the list. Tucked in between dull institutional news items, dreary menus, and depressing death notices, there's a new eNote that tickles my fancy.

SEXUAL SENIORS

Morning Glory Ridge embraces the policy that seniors, health permitting, should be able to enjoy all aspects of life. On Thursday of this week you are invited to the Activity Room for a Sexual Seniors Seminar. Topics covered will include techniques for self-pleasuring, how to request sex enhancing drugs, how to reserve the Privacy Room, sex and your cardiac health, consensuality issues, and a session on "Your Sexy Avatar." In conjunction with the seminar, there will be a Toy Fair, where you can purchase pleasure toys.

2009 Blackshale

My work had been interrupted by a snack attack, and I was sitting crosslegged in the middle of my big square studio table - paying homage to my lifelong craving for crackers, soft cheese, and fancy jellies. The habit dated back to college when food in the dorm was against the rules, and we hungry girls had snuck out to the mom and pop grocery a block behind Highland Hall. The only decent snack "mom and pop" sold were saltines, foil wrapped wedges of soft cheese and tiny jars of exotic jellies... cherry, mint, lingonberry, and pineapple orange marmalade. The forbidden preciousness of those communions by midnight oil had stuck with me through the years.

On my crackers and cheese, everything was red and color-coordinated. There were sun-dried tomatoes, hot pepper jelly, crisp Christmas pickles. In my glass, gogi raspberry juice. RED. Just another weird artist's snack habit.

Munching and crunching and smoothing my tongue across the creamy cheese, I looked around the studio, thinking. The workspace was crammed full of junk waiting to be recycled into art. Every square inch of space, wall, ceiling, and floor, was populated with stuff. I was never closer to heaven than when I was digging through some nasty junk store, but a lot of my treasures were just picked up off the road. Some people might have called me a hoarder, but I was actually a prolific and serious collector of potential art supplies. There were beads and baubles and trinkets and strings, bits of wire, turtle shells, letters and numbers, amputated Barbie hands, mouse bones, and thousands of other doo dads collected over time. Each piece of scrap metal or paper or cardboard that had ever crossed my path was hanging there on my walls imploring "Pick me!"

There was a randomness and play of the accidental in the way some of those elements would come together into a piece of art. Sometimes, it felt like someone else was pulling the strings. Once all the parts were chosen and glued together, I'd set out to batter up the surface with paint and marks and tiny bits of detail that gave the piece the patina of some worn relic. About then, time ceased to exist, and I entered the zone. I could stand there on my swelling feet, painting and drawing and dabbing on dots of glue all night long and never once look up.

At the age of fifty-nine, I quit underwear - went commando. My clothes were washed every day anyway, so what was the point. All that coming and going of cheesy discharges in variations of creamy yellows, pinks and the sudden deluge of monthly crimson were long gone, leaving behind a very well-behaved crotch. I sure didn't miss the death grip of elastic.

The other thing about being post-menopausal was the sleeplessness and mental hyperactivity. Those little wheels in my head started turning like mad. In the land between sleeping and waking, random bits of consciousness would quietly bubble and pop, widely spaced at first, unrelated, weak pings. Then, as the clock ticked on, they'd grow and battle until one or more would rise to the top. With dawn's tender light and bird chatter, the thought, the idea, the must-do, the project, turned into obsession, rolling around in the sheets with me, pushing sleepiness out of the bed. After a tinkle and a blood pressure pill, I'd carry the thought to the computer and give it a home in a do-list or a calendar or in reminder alarms that popped up to annoy me later as I checked my email.

It was in this zombie land, the hours of first light, when my best art was born. After the "pause", I became an unstoppable bundle of artistic energy.

As productive as I was though, I barely made a living. I cared more about making art than conducting business. There was good money to be made painting pastel florals or landscapes, but my work often spoke of things not so pretty. It was the best work of my life, edgy, honest, but it was not what most people wanted to hang in their house.

My work was about the rituals of our lives, we who live in the tribes of Appalachia, birthing, dying, folk wisdom, violence born of ignorance, magical insight, the intensity, narrowing and twisting of religion, the spook in the hollow, the voodoo of the mountains. From these, the fascinations and nightmares of my childhood, my art had been born.

There had been my money from Pap, and I had used that to pay the electric bill and buy groceries all too often. Those coffers were about to dry up. It was becoming clear that I'd have to become an art whore of some sort. My choice was between creating sofa-sized florals in mauves, taupes and teals for interior decorators or freelancing graphic design. The thought of either made me nauseous and consumed with dread. I already had an appointment with an interior design gallery. I knew the time had come when I would have to prostitute myself.

Then came this call. "Anna Grace Tollett, it's Donald McCarvey. I'm an attorney in Knoxville, and I represent a private corporation out of Atlanta. They've been conducting some geological surveys up on your mountain for gas, oil, minerals, that sort of thing. They've been out working up a piece of land that adjoins a property that Frank Tollett owned. You are his daughter, right?"

"Pap owned land on the mountain? I never heard a thing about it." It was news to me. He'd never mentioned current holdings in real estate. I vaguely remembered him dealing land when I was little, but he'd quickly drunk that all away when Mama died.

"Well, I took the liberty of looking it up at the courthouse. It's a right smart parcel, about seventy acres up there, and you are listed as the beneficiary. I don't really understand how you've not been getting a tax bill on it, I guess that slipped through the county cracks. Anyhoo, it had belonged to a man named Yother.

Looks like your dad took it in trade for his funeral services.”

"Oh friggin' terrific!" I thought to myself, "A big pile of back taxes, now that's just all I need!"

"Thing is, every vein they were tracking in the ground up there just worked right back up under your land. It's looking like you might be coming into some worthwhile assets."

"Like, exactly how worthwhile?" I enquired, sucking in a deep breath and hoping for enough to pay the back taxes.

"Well, are you sitting down? The head geologist up there says he wouldn't be surprised to see five million, maybe six, between the mineral, gas and oil rights."

When I came to, a voice in my head was yelling, "Thank you Jesus!

I'm free, I'm free!"

• • • • • • • •

When the Albine Yother property money started becoming a reality in my bank account, the first thing I did was to make sure enough was put back for the highest level of care for Corrine. Then I socked away enough in solid investments to cover my living expenses forever.

There was still money left over. I decided I could use a little more living space, so I called up Mr. Oody at the hardware store and asked him to recommend a good contractor. He sent me a guy who was nutty as a fruitcake, but still a right good carpenter. Horker Holloway showed up at my door with the bill of his cap turned bass ackwards.

I didn't have to ask Horker how he'd gotten his nickname. He was hawking up a splat of Skoal every time he turned around. We went right to work, planning out a larger living room area, a bigger bathroom with a Jacuzzi, and a covered patio where I could work outdoors in the open air.

As he measured and sawed two by fours, Horker got to reminiscing about a remodeling job he'd done for the family who'd bought old man Murphy's house. Horker went on telling his tale, stopping every few minutes to spit.

"Well, ya see, one day I measured off this basement room I was hared to fix up, but then I had to go outside to check the length of a pipe, and walked off the distance to the other end of the basement. Something was aflickin' on and off in my mind, like somethin' wasn't quite right. No sir! The length of that there room was different on the outside of the wall than it was on th' inside! So I go back in and measure it again... And sure'nuf I'm missing fourteen feet! If'n it a been a snake, it a bit me!

I started peckin' around on the wall, and it's hollow soundin'... not like a concrete block solid, so I got my sledge hammer and whacked at that wall hard as I could. Hells bells, would you believe, I get in there and there's stash of bootleg whisky that would' a sent all them Murphy kids to college, had they not opted for careers in crime or got themselves kilt! Course I had to call up the new Sheriff, and I'm honest I stood there 'bout crying when they poured all that fine homebrew out on the ground. But the air shore was smelling great that day!" He lolled from foot to foot, cracking himself up. "Yes mam, smelling real nice!"

I laughed too, "I guess that was Walter Lee Murphy's legacy." Pap had buried Walter Lee in '77, and the last Murphy had finally graced his steel table.

• • • • • • • • • •

The older I got, rules of society mattered less and less. I didn't give a fig what the old dames of Blackshale might whisper about behind my back. So when Perry started coming around again, after he could no longer get it up, and I was no longer fertile, I mean, what the hell. So, he began to spend more and more time with me at the studio house, and one day he brought his fiddle and left it there, so I figured that was a sign he was sliding over my way. Finally, he just up and had a yard sale. He sold off the remnants of his and Bonnie's household and never went back home. He sold his house to a family with teenage boys who once again wore out the river with their canoes, their fishing poles, and the echoes of their shouts.

As for us, we worked out right good. He liked to do my woodwork and framing and was an appreciative tester for the French and Thai and Mexican I had recently learned to make from scratch while watching the Food Channel.

I've spent my life learning about different kinds of love. Now, I'm learning there are different kinds of sensuality, too. Oh, Yes.

For a while after he moved over to my place, Perry kept his distance, aside from cousinly hugs. We were both content, enjoying each other's company. We could have gone on that way too. However... well... we didn't.

One evening after dinner, Perry rose from his easy chair, a gleam in his eye. He wrapped his long bony arms around me, kissed me in a slow, testing, non-cousinly way, and after hearing my breath quicken, he coaxed, "My dear, how would you like to explore the joy of old people's, penisless sex that relies solely on tenderness for its magic?"

Then he laid me down and slowly traced the scar that divides my body into left and right. The tears in his eyes testified how much he cared about me, how he shared that painful event of my childhood. He had been there, after all. Then he buried his snoot in the thinning fur between my legs and worked a certain magic, a pleasure I never expected to be, uh, open to. After I heard noises coming from my body that I could not believe were mine, I lay there smiling, laughing, crying and then feeling guilty for not being able to return the favor.

"Is there anything at all I can do for you?" His doctor had offered the possibility of injections into his penis to facilitate erection. At the time, he had said, "Uh... thanks, but I think I'll pass!" Without that, he was out of business.

"Oh my darling, just being alive and holding you in my arms

is the only thrill I'll ever need, for the rest of my days." Then he picked up his country violin and those long sensual fingers of his made love to the strings as he fiddled the Devil's Dream.

2029 Morning Glory Ridge

My bladder has spasmed itself into retention again, and I'm looking down at the orange and green Mohawk hairdo of a male nurse between my legs, guiding a foley catheter into my most private recesses. If I was a man with something I could aim, I'd let him have it in the face. When he's done, he removes his white latex gloves with a snap and one falls to the floor by my bed. A prompt for a bad memory, but this time it is one of Perry's, not mine. It was another chapter from his mother Nettie's book of nightmares, visited on Perry when he was a young teen.

He had awakened one night, the details of a dream still circulating in his sleepfuzzed mind. Olive, his science lab partner at Blackshale Junior High, had turned to him and reached for his hand, guiding it up under her skirt and between her legs. This triggered some sort of explosion in him and unmistakable new feelings of pleasure. When he pulled back his hand from under her dress, his fingers were curled around the splayed and odorous frog that they were dissecting in class. The frog's eyes bulged crazily from the pressure of Perry's grasp. He floated in a sleepy fog, still savoring the unknown rush of heat and dizzying release, then bolted awake to the horrifying reality that his fingers were in fact curled around his private and not only that, he had wet the bed! It was the stickiest pee he'd ever seen, and he worried that something was bad wrong with his pecker.

The next morning the dream had faded away. Nettie Tollett had been on the lookout though. She'd read a book about growing boys, oh yes, and the things that could happen in their sheets. When Perry got home from school that day, she was even more curt than usual, and after dinner, she called him into the parlor for a talk. On the table were the Bible and a pair of white cotton gloves. In the palm of each glove was a red spot the size of a dime. She read a collection of scriptures about the body being a temple, and then stared Perry down.

"Son, there has been a sign of impure thoughts on your sheets. Satan loves to toy with young men, and he comes to them in the night with temptations. From now on, you are to wear these gloves when you sleep. If you should begin to touch yourself, they will remind you that the hands of Jesus Christ were pierced with cruel nails for your impurity." Perry looked down at the floor, embarrassed. He was so naïve, he wasn't really understanding yet what was what. He took the gloves, and wore them faithfully. The sheets stayed dry for a while.

Then one night, he awoke with Olive on his mind again. Apparently the gloves had worked on a subconscious level and prevented his body from spewing. That was good. But the more he thought about that day in class when Olive had dropped the tweezers and bent to retrieve them, and he'd caught a glimpse of soft jiggling breast, he couldn't go back to sleep. The more he couldn't go back to sleep, the more he thought of jiggling breasts, and then his thoughts dropped lower to the mystery between her legs. The more he tried to crush the thoughts on account of Jesus, the more his organ began to rise and swell. All at once, Jesus, the cruel nails, and Nettie Tollett were forgotten and off came the gloves. Perry had his first purposeful session of bed banging self-satisfaction, so loud and overwhelming that he failed to notice Nettie where she stood in the doorframe. She was staring down at the white glove on the floor, one open, praising hand and her eyes raised to Heaven, the other snapping a studded belt on the floor.

She beat his bare hips bloody, until he passed out. He came to curled up on his side, his wrists handcuffed behind his back. His skin and his bowels were on fire. Nettie spoke out of the darkness. "You have been purified. For your own good, you will sleep in these from now on." She closed the door and in a few hours, Perry cried himself into troubled, jerking slumber.

The next morning, he feigned sleep while she unlocked the handcuffs and inspected his wounds. She opened a bottle of iodine and began to paint the breaks in his skin. When he moved like lightening and shoved her up against the wall above his bed, his elegant hands turned threatening and wrapped around her throat.

"Listen here Maw! I ain't evil. I ain't sleepin' in handcuffs or gloves. I will not be purified by you. If you don't like this, you and me can go up to the school and talk to my guidance counselor about a foster home. I'm gonna look out for my own soul, and you better do the same!"

He lowered her to the bed, and stalked out. She was terrified of being left alone, so from then on she let him be. Instead, she prayed herself silly for hours, asking God to keep her boy Perry from the ways of sin.

I watch the nurse pick up the limp glove and throw it at the receptacle. Thinking back, Perry was remarkable and his mother was a freak. How miraculous that he stood up to her at such a young age and was able to go on to a normal emotional life. What a miracle I, too, was able to overcome my wounded childhood and enjoy love in the last lap. What a wonder that he and I had gotten together at all. Miracles! My tears well up and I'm filled with admiration and gratitude.

· · · · · · · · · ·

Tiffany is having a bad day. It should have been a good one, as it is the only day in three years that her daughter, Felicia, and her granddaughter, Jennifer, have come to visit. Not that Tiffany would notice at all.

However, Tiffany has a bad bladder infection, which requires a catheter to be inserted. Usually, visitors are asked to step out for a minute, but Gourdhead, lacking that much common sense, just asks them to sit at Tiffany's head while he works under the hood.

Six-year-old Jennifer is an inquisitive munchkin, agog over the medical environment and apparatus. When Gourdhead lifts the sheet over Tiffany's knees and approaches with the tube, Jennifer reacts suddenly, yelling in her outdoor voice, "Hey! Mr. Doctor! Are you gonna stick that thing in my meemaw's monkey?"

It's the one time I see Gourdhead soften into kindness. He must have a tender spot for kids lurking inside his exhibitionist heart. He puts down the cath tube and walks Jennifer over to the desk. Drawing a stick figure of a grandma, he shows Jennifer where pee comes out. He explains in a matter of fact way that sometimes a meemaw's pee burns, and he has to help her feel better. It sounds like a reasonable, everyday occurrence and not at all scary. Hmmmm. Another side of Gourdhead. Who knew?

After the procedure is done, Tiffany's company moves around to the side of the bed and keeps trying without success to gain eye contact and recognition. After seeing nobody is home, they don't last long. Felicia is bored, and Jennifer is whining. As they start toward the door, Tiffany looks for a minute like she cares and hollers, "Hey!" They stop and turn back, hopeful for conversation. "Pie!" she spits, and instantly falls asleep with her head lopped over to one side, mouth open and slack.

She wakes right before lunch. Gourdhead changes her and props her up in bed. He pokes spoonful after spoonful into the saggy little mouth. After her pureed asparagus, and pureed squash and pureed turkey, he says, "Time for your treat!" and starts shoveling in sugarfree vanilla pudding.

That naughty Tiffany saves up a mouthful of it in her jowls like a crazy squirrel, and blasts it right back into Gourdhead's face. Once her mouth is empty, she mindlessly chooses her word and spews it out also, "June bug!"

• • • • • • • •

The portfolios are stacked in a corner by my bed. Mrs.

Gundersen has kindly volunteered to go through each one, holding up the work so I can make a sound judgment with my weak eyes and feeble mind. In my investment account is more money than I can ever spend, with no one to inherit it. Coming up with ways to make good use of it has been challenging.

Some funds have gone to Pearlie's church in her honor. Lord knows they needed a new roof. Before she left, I had visited a service with her. The white headed preacher remembered my dunkin' in the river and he praised God for it. Uncomfortable as I was to be singled out, they seated me on the front row in a place of honor and introduced me to the church. When he climbed up into the pulpit to testify the grace of Jesus, every answering echo of the congregation was punctuated by loud splats of rain into buckets on the floor. "You tell 'em, preacher!" Plop. "Good God!" Plop. "Mmmm huh!" Plop! "Talk it, brother!" PLOP! "Amen!"

After arranging an endowment for the art building fund at Mount Highland, we advertised a five-year art scholarship including a year in Europe, a full ride to any art school in the country, and posted the deadline for portfolios. Only students within a fifty-mile radius of Blackshale need apply. The resulting entries are in front of me.

Some are expensive leather zippered affairs and others homemade from duct tape and cardboard, tied up with sisal. There are twenty-seven, all told.

Eighty percent of them are snoozers, stiff copies of cartoons and magazine pictures. The others show promise, students making an effort to observe their world and make fresh statements about it. I am relieved to see these and know they are the ones who will end up making it in a competitive art world, if they work hard.

Then there is *the one*.
Before Gundersen even opens it, I feel a flush of excitement. The outside of the handmade folio is rich with subtle markings.

Inside are works far beyond the maturity of a teen - the essence of Blackshale mountain unfolds, naked and honest, as she peels over sheet after sheet. Malevolent chickens, strange unnamable objects hanging on the outside wall of a barn, emotionally intrusive portraits of wary kin, the sunlit corner of a well house, quilt patterns used as tiny symbols, rusty objects from a toolbox merged into new realities. I have no doubt. I require no second look. This is my scholarship winner.

"OK, Gundersen, this is it! Get me the name and address. Let's make this young artist's day!" She unfolds the envelope, revealing the information.

Name: Josiah Bodine
Address: 454 Climbersville Road
Blackshale, Tennessee 37844
Father: Clyde Bodine (Deceased)
Mother: Moriah Yother Bodine (Deceased)
(Alamandra Yother, custodial grandmother)
Phone: 865-250-6938

I can't believe my eyes. By what strange synchronicity did the hands of fate knit together the source of my wealth and the recipient of my gift? Albine and Piney Yother's great-grandson has won the scholarship. All is well with the world.

· · · · · · · ·

From time-to-time, I have the most intense olfactory memory. The smoke from the small fires along Blackshale Road in the autumn comes wafting back, and I can picture like yesterday my six-year-old self, walking down the crumpled red brick sidewalk to school. It goes so fast- life. I'm so damn introspective today. To use the oldtimey phrase, "I got the blues." I don't want to get up. Where's that grim reaper when you're hot for him?

I lay my head back down on the pillow and stare at the ceiling, finally close to the edge of sleep when I hear it... the teeniest little clicky noise... faint and far away... widgie, widgie, widgie, widgie,

widgie. It gets louder and louder until the WidgieWalker turns in my door. Tiffany yells a welcoming word, "Cornhoe!"

The rider is tiny and bent, barely able to see over the gimmick-laden deck of the WidgieWalker.

"Is there an Anna Grace in here? Anna Grace Tollett?" A diminutive voice squeaks.

It doesn't matter that I can't see more than a blur of the little figure, I could never forget that voice in ten thousand years.

"PinkyToe!" I bellow. "What are you doing here?"

"I live here, fool!" she squawks, "And I just today found out you live here too! Ain't that just the greatest?" She rolls over to my bed and slides in next to me. The mattress barely registers her weight. She can't be more than seventy-five pounds soaking wet. Her pumpkin colored hair, now peppered with grey, puffs out all over her head in a short, thin fuzz ball. Her beady little eyes, devoid of lashes, squint over at me. "I can't believe it! I thought I'd lost you. Now we can be together again."

Pink grins up at me and yanks off her slipper socks. She wiggles her toes, showing off her thickened, gnarled toenails painted in multi-shades of pink. "I guess we're grounded, huh?" she says with an impish grin.

• • • • • • • •

Now that I have Pinky for company, I've stopped taking meals in my room, and we join all the other inmates in the dining room. We enjoy hanging out and making fun of all the pathetic old people in there, but damn, the food sucks! No salt, no sugar, no fat, no nothing with a bit of taste. It's a sick joke on me, being bone thin and able to eat anything I want but having nothing edible in sight. We miss the food of our youth, the greasy treats from the drive-in or anything Pearlie had country fried in lard and sprinkled with salt. I've been having wet dreams about dip dogs.

On this eventful day our overzealous nutritionist drags

her presentation nano-gizmos in at lunchtime to explain that many are living into their twelfth decade now, and it is precisely because we are so much more knowledgeable about nutrition. Because we are supplying our bodies with the antioxidant power in healthy vegetables like kale, and eschewing the unhealthy fats and preservatives of previous generations, blah, blah, blah, blah, we all get to live longer. "So we have time to suffer much more," I badmouth to Pink under my breath.

"Of course," the Nutritionist continues, lying through her teeth, "We are always open to the residents' input on what you would enjoy eating for an occasional treat!" Uh oh, saying that was probably a mistake. We are sitting on each side of her, and I can see Pink deciding, sure, she'll be happy to provide some input!

PinkyToe clamps her bony hands on both sides of the insipid woman's moon round face, and starts shaking her back and forth. "Bite me, vita-breath. You can stuff your food pyramid up your ass!" The food lady pulls her electronics back protectively and starts calling for backup. But Pink is just getting started.

"I am sick to death of all this or-gan-ickky food, and I don't want to live to be a hundred and twenty! I just want a God-Damn-Ba-Con-Cheese-Bur-Ger! If I have to eat one more stalk of super broccoli I'm going to soylent green my pants." With that, Cobert Pitosky yells "Yeah! FOODFIGHT!" and before you can say "super foods" the air is thick with flying raw vegetables and blobs of probiotic yogurt. Even the most sedate seniors are roused up out of their stupors and start throwing handfuls of low fat pudding! Tiffany is stuffed in her wheel chair and observes the fray with glee, as the strap digging under her arms keeps her from keeling over. She has pureed spinach in her hair... but is grinning happily. Her little round mouth begins to open and close like a fish, as if she's trying to come out with her one comment, but the word sputters and fails in the excitement of the day.

2009 Blackshale

Sudy Pelfree Templeton is now in the loving care of her daughter Marlene, who lives with Sudy full-time. In a plastic box with little sections marked M,T,W,T,F,S,S, there are twenty-seven medications and supplements that must be carefully tracked and administered at nine different times during the day. Sudy is diabetic and has to have blood sugars and shots before each meal and at bedtime. The hourly rates of caretakers who could meet Sudy's needs are far beyond Marlene's means. For now, Marlene May has found her calling in life, twenty-four/seven. She is glad that she can be there for Sudy in her waning days. A tiny part of her though, is resentful - mad as a wounded rooster at a cockfight.

Sudy's nursing career makes her a bad patient. She knows all too well what is coming. This knowledge fills Sudy with a churning, sleep-murdering anxiety. Sudy is completely bedridden, on daily laxatives, incontinent in both departments, and her needs are mammoth. Just navigating the maze of dietary restrictions for her diabetes and kidney failure is a fulltime job for Marlene. Marlene is loving, willing, but all the same, overwhelmed.

Tonight Sudy has finally drifted off, talking in her fitful sleep. Whispering sexy baby talk to the cowboy who had ridden off into the sunset back in sixty-two. Conley had been displaying an increasing interest in rough sex. He had a thing for ropes and knots, being a cowboy, and he also had a tiny little horsewhip he liked to apply to Sudy's behind once she was all tied up. At first Sudy was turned on by the dark experiments. After all, her sex life with Faron had been somewhat off the beaten track too, but when it became clear Conley enjoyed hurting her more than the sex, she balked.

"That's enough!" she had protested, coughing and sputtering, demanding to be set free from the noose that was cutting off her wind. She started out whimpering but against her will, ended up in a full-out crying jag.

"What's the matter, you got a cinder in your eye? Hush that up!" Conley took the rope off from around her neck, and spat on the floor. "Aw shitfire, Baby, this is gettin' to be a drag... you ain't no fun any more. If I want a plain old fuck I got a field full of heifers tighter than you."

"Get the hell out!" She bluffed, thinking he would come back. He never did. She heard a few years later he was still living in Nashville, drinking and screwin' his way from one barfly to the next. Apparently Sudy's aging brain has filtered out the bad memories. She smiles and mumbles, "Ride, Cowboy, ride!" before her mouth droops open, slack.

In the waking world, Marlene smells like sex, the musty, fishy woman part minus the sweating, swimming pool scented man part. Go fish. After two glasses of Moscato, a mindless horny haze sets in and her hands move all on their own, seeking pleasure. After all, there is nothing else to look forward to. As they say, too much of nothing. In the next room, Sudy is snoring, giving Marlene a brief respite from duty.

She had wanted so badly to attend Miss Miriam's funeral. Instead she got drunk in her honor - remembering how, at the age of twelve the teacher had given her lingering looks, and there had been some kind of new feeling, a strange magnetic pull that made her look forward to the lessons that had cost Sudy two dollars an hour. Marlene has never had lesbian tendencies, not at all, but in retrospect these moments seemed to be the first glimmers of romantic feeling. Looking back, the teacher must have been one, a lesbian. As they say now, a cookie licker, a carpet muncher. She is quite sure that Miss Miriam never actually munched anybody's carpet, only that there were longing looks for certain ones of her own sex that she never managed to conjure up for her hunchback husband, Harbin. The teacher had never crossed inappropriate lines, just dispensed the lessons with her Mona Lisa smile. Still now, Marlene feels that odd, undefined connection to Miss Miriam, enough to want to stand in the long line at her wake and touch her rubbery face.

Marlene is not gay! No! Never! The thought of being physical with a woman is abhorrent to her. And yet, the one to whom she would spill the contents of her heart, whose eyes she would meet with an inward quiver, her secret crush, her true love... is a woman. The name she calls out when she touches herself is... Anna Grace. Marlene nursed the lifelong crush, and had even told her, "I don't have it in me to be gay, but if I did, you would be the one I love." Anna Grace had laughed, taking it as a joke over too many glasses of draft beer.

She rises and scrubs her hands quietly in the bathroom, trying not to awaken Sudy with her long list of needs. Apparently Marlene has inherited her mother's dislike of self-pleasuring, because she finds the smell of herself on her own hands totally revolting. Her cousin, Siese, has BOB for those kinds of needs. Marlene had seen it in her bathroom, and when she asked what it was, Siese had laughed and said, "Oh, meet BOB, my Battery Operated Boyfriend! Marlene had shot back, condescendingly, "Getting out for a date with a real man might be a good plan too." But now she is no better. Everybody gets horny sometimes.

Sudy wakes, anxious, fretful, and sullen. On her way to Sudy's bedside, Marlene trips over the garbage can the home nurse left out in the walkway. "That nurse could put things back where she found them!"

Sudy squints her eyes and puffs. "I really wish I could please you Marlene!"

"I wasn't talking to you, oh, never mind..." Marlene answers listlessly. She studies her mother's eyes. Lately she notices that they seem to be shrinking and weakening, becoming tiny, red lemur's eyes.

"Can you think of something tasty you'd like to eat? How about some chicken and dumplin's?" Marlene proffers brightly as she busies herself straightening the bedside table, where hundreds of small items, medicine bottles and boxes, nail files, floss, toothpicks, pens and pencils and tablets, unpaid bills attempt to reside, but scatter to the floor every time Sudy flails out her hand.

"No, I'm not hungry. Can't you understand, Marlene, all this medicine makes me sick. Just bring me a can of Ensure."

"Oh come on, you're not doing much for my inner chef!" Marlene quips, straining toward cheer. "By the way, the home health nurse called and says she's not coming today. Her son's got some big important soccer game."

"Well, you know what? Shit on her!" Sudy spits venomously and purses her lips.

Marlene walks back down the hall, chuckling in amazement. Her mother has never used language like that, at least in front of her. Apparently Sudy had a big do-list saved up for the home health nurse.

When Marlene returns, Sudy says, "I'm never using that word again.

It's nasty, and I hate it. I don't know what's wrong with me. This medicine makes me feel like I have little breezes blowing through my head."

Some days, Sudy is a touch off her rocker and embraces childish, annoying behaviors. She picks up the house phone and calls her own new cell over and over, just to hear the ring tone she's picked out. Every time she declares, "I just love that." Every other day she plays all the twenty-eight ringtones, just to be certain she really does like that one best. Several times an hour, she taps the button on her atomic watch to hear the robotic digital voice say the time and date. "This is the best thing I ever bought!" she repeats every time. Marlene knows Sudy has to be bored out of her tree, so she suggests activities.

"Mom, how's about a game of Scrabble?" Marlene asks hopefully.

"Marlene! I told you I'm sick of being managed. You just go do your own thing like you do all the time anyway." Marlene rolls her eyes wearily, trying to remember the last occasion when she had pursued her own interests.

Sudy likes to think of activities for Marlene, too. She recalls a lovely greeting card she got in 1994 from an old friend. It's somewhere in one of forty-something keepsake boxes in the barn. She sighs and says she would so love to see it again. Would Marlene mind to find it? It would mean so much. Marlene spends the day sweating in the hot barn, raffling through boxes. She finds the card at the bottom of the next-to-last one.

Sudy plans impromptu dinner parties, telling Marlene at the last minute that she has invited guests. She just knows the company will love the bread that Marlene fries up carefully one slice at a time, in butter.

Every day, Sudy dictates three or four page lists of her complaints for Marlene May to type up and fax to her doctors. Marlene is quite sure this drives the doctors bonkers, especially since Sudy presents every insignificant, unrelated complaint to a specialist, say, her cardiologist. She pictures what the heart specialist says when he reads the fax that says "my toe hurts a little and I feel like my brain is fluttering." She thinks, as a former nurse, Sudy should know better, but she obeys.

Her mother has always been so strong and smart and perfect. Now, when the medications grind and blend themselves into poison in her belly and filter into her psyche, she is demanding, obsessive, unreasonable, sometimes hateful. For Marlene, every day is a sine wave oscillating to extremes, sweetly attentive to angry to conciliatory. Every morning she starts the day with irenic intentions. Every day Sudy starts in with her list of current criticisms and moves on to cataloging Marlene's long past mistakes. Every afternoon Marlene ends up boiling in anger, stalking off and leaving Sudy in mid-sentence, charging down the hall whispering, "Fuck me!" Sudy maintains her negative stance, harshly argumentative on every point, until she falls back to sleep. Then Marlene stands over her, watching the fragile chest hesitantly rise and fall, overwhelmed to tears by an unspeakable love and tenderness.

She sighs and gazes out the screen door, listening to Sudy's old dog vocalizing his loneliness. Snowball was once a pure white dog, but now he's the color of dirt. When he barks, he yaps once and then tacks on a mournful howl that sounds like a starving cow. Resting in her rocking chair while Sudy naps, Marlene locks into the pattern… yap-moooo, yap-moooo, yap-moooooo… and rocks herself to sleep.

Sudy has run through a long list of home health nurses. Normally, the same nurses cover a case continually, but for some reason Sudy's nurses keep asking to be reassigned. A new one knocks now, rattling the storm door and hitting the doorbell button for good measure.

"Any one of those would be quite sufficient," Marlene thinks to herself and opens the door to a chunky black woman wearing cartoony scrubs and white rubber scuffs. Her nametag says "Tawneesha." She waddles down the narrow hall, sweeping alternating walls with a swishing sound. She bends over the hospital bed exposing a barely visible tramp stamp that reads, "I Love Me Some Jesus." She opens her eyes wide and ducks below bed level, playing peek-a-boo with Sudy, who is in no way amused.

"Well, well, well, Miss Cutie Pie, jes' look. Yo cute as a button. Dey been tellin' me to look out for sweet little Miss Sudy. Yes mam, sweet as pie!"

Sudy fixes her beady eyes on the round black face and pulls herself up in the bed, angry at the attempt to be babied and fussed over.

"Well!" Sudy spits, "YO just might have to change YO mind about DAT!"

Mortified, Marlene wishes to melt silently into the floor. For the briefest instant, shock flits across Tawneesha's face like an invisible slap, but she never misses a beat, flipping sheets, flapping pillows, carrying on like a professional. Sudy is far too medicated to be ashamed of herself.

Marlene sits in Sudy's easy chair like one of the living dead, waiting for the shoe to drop, listening with her heart for the big hurt. She can't imagine life without her mother. She has an uncommonly detailed memory of being a baby and can recall the decal on her crib, Little Bo Peep with her lamb and her crook. She can remember nursing in Sudy's arms. Breastfeeding was out of style then, but she can picture the glass bottle in Sudy's grasp, its rounded rubber nipple dripping warmed milk into her mouth. She recalls being a toddler. She remembers, most of all, her stick.

Marlene knows it could happen in the blink of an eye, that hard, horrible moment when she can no longer ask her mama how long leftovers keep in the fridge, who to call to fix the dishwasher, the name of Uncle Howdy's first cousin once removed, how many minutes to reheat the cornbread muffins.

She isn't sure she can stand it. Marlene is between a rock and a hard place, you see. The only way she will get her life back is to lose the person she loves the most.

Marlene patters on bare feet to the kitchen and climbs up onto the faded red Formica, rising up on her aching knees. She digs far back into the recesses of Sudy's cabinets and finally finds it - the glass baby bottle, rubber nipple hardened and riddled with hairline cracks. She fills it with merlot wine and carries it to her bedroom, where, laying back on a stack of pillows, she curls into fetal position and sucks.

Marlene has had a lukewarm life. When she figured out that Sudy's fag husband was not her father, she tracked down Conley Porter the cowboy, who took her in on a lark but was clearly not father material. She spent her later teenage years with him in Nashville, without guidance or structure, trying to wrangle some love out of him, getting none. She was running wild and married badly, but then again it didn't last all that long.

After a week of being a wife, she woke one night with urine splashing on her face. She sat up sputtering, her drunk and naked husband's yellow stream still cutting the air in a perfect arc. The next week, he went home with a girl from the office and stayed for three days. He seemed to think it was no big deal. Marlene went back home to Conley's bachelor pad looking for sympathy, wanting his help with a quick divorce and a return to the status quo. The cowboy pouted in a black silence for a week. When he finally spoke he railed: "You're the one who was fool enough to marry that polecat. Well, I reckon when you go and get a blister on your butt, you'll just have to sit on it!"

Marlene left him and the peeing husband. She went back home to Sudy who was not at all above saying "I told you so!" for the rest of her life. When Marlene carries in the dinner tray to Sudy's bed, she tries to start up normal conversations, but they always end up with Sudy saying things like "Here you sit in the shit of everything you ever done. I'm not stepping in it, it's your stinky business."

Marlene has a shameful covetousness of her friends, not just the ones who have no parental responsibilities, but also the ones whose charges are part-time or somewhat agreeable. One acquaintance even has a live-in octogenarian mother who drinks wine. They go on outings to the liquor store together and use the walker as a shopping cart. The mother picks out her favorites. "Here's a nice Chardonnay, ... Oh look dear, my favorite - Proseco! We can add a spoonful of raspberry sherbert!" In the evenings, the imbibing mother has a lovely glass and is even more pleasant than she is during the day. The thought of this leaves Marlene wallowing in a pissy green jealousy.

She is not, however, jealous of her friends who have farmed their parents out to Morning Glory Ridge. Another friend of Marlene's, Paisley, took her mama Frances to the Ridge three years back, the minute the old lady smelled of trouble. Mourning her home, Frances declined steadily. Paisley told Marlene that she visits her mother's bedside at Morning Glory Ridge only when they call and report a problem. Checking in, she lets her eyes roll up and down the guest log, averaging the length of visits, getting a feel for what is considered acceptable. She sits for the expected period of time, thinking over and over, "Would you please do me the honor of dying!" Marlene feels superior to Paisley - far superior.

One night, Marlene catches Sudy rubbing herself with a suspiciously regular rhythm. She stands openmouthed, staring in disbelief at the familiar movements under the sheets. Sudy looks up suddenly and sees Marlene watching her. They both look shocked, then simultaneously combust into laughter.

"I guess that little feller down there never stops itching for attention!" Sudy squeaks with a little laugh, her lemur eyes pinching.

Marlene thinks to herself, "Well, well, well, Mama always was oversexed." She quickly turns to leave the room for a private chuckle, but the shamefaced, vulnerable look on Sudy's face fills Marlene with sympathy and love. The child is now the parent.

Marlene says, red-faced and giggling, "Don't be embarrassed, sweetie. We all do it. I sure do it. Once we've tasted the Big O, we never get over our need for that sweet release." She pats her Mom's arm and leaves the room, but instead of a private chuckle, she has a heart wrenching private cry. After that, the sine wave flattens, and mother and daughter journey peacefully through their final days together.

2029 Morning Glory Ridge

We are in the open showers, naked as jaybirds in our little seats made of poly tubing. I am paddling along with my toes, complaining. "For some reason, no one thinks that someone of our age cares any more about privacy ... MY COW! Take a gander at the bush on Taloola!"

PinkyToe looks up, then rolls right over to Taloola, bending over to the level of her crotch to inspect her impressive mons pubis. "What is THAT?"

"It's a merkin dear. All of us theatre people wear them. I have a fabulous collection!"

"A WHUT?" PinkyToe has her "you are a nutcase" look on.

"A merkin... it's an artistic little wig for your privates. I have them in every possible color. Some are sequined and bejeweled. You know I was in the revival of 'Hair' back in twenty-ought-ten!"

"Yeah, and I bet you needed that merkin thingamajiggy like crazy then! Let's see, you would have been sixty somethin'... I bet you were already bald as a billard ball down there." Pinky observes with her usual candor. "Looks to me like a great place for crabs to nest!"

• • • • • • • •

We are polishing off a box of chocolate-covered cherries some do-gooders dropped off in our room. Pinky swirls her tongue around a cherry, savoring, babbling on about how chocolate must be eaten sacredly.

"Anna Grace," Pink says warily, "Do you remember when Jake and Harley got sent to the reformer school for drownin' their baby brother in the ditch?"

"Yes, PinkyToe, I am painfully familiar with the sordid history of the Murphy clan. And it's reform school." Pinky has a slew of expressions that have refused to grow up past her country childhood, and sometimes I let it annoy me.

"Remember, they said a little girl saw them and ratted on them?"

"Yep."

"It was me. I was the little girl peeing behind the tree." Another piece of the puzzle tumbles into place with a click. Apparently our abuse at the hands of the Murphy boys had not been totally random after all.

"Anna Grace."

"Yep."

"While I'm confessin', there's something else. I mean, I don't want nothin' on my conscience when I go. No secrets between you and me."

"Yep."

"The Jake and Harley thing. The thing they made you do."

"Yep." I swallow hard as the memory painfully flashes across my mind's eye.

"Jake was right. I did like it."

"GEEZ! Pink!" I am grossed out, and make a freaky face at her.

"No, NO, not that it was you, but the idea of a girl... well... ok, here goes, I was just plain born gay I reckon. I had crushes on lots of girls, when I was really young. I can remember having a crush on Miss Miriam, and I could swear she liked me back. But never on you. You've got to believe me, you were always my best friend. Just my best friend. All through college and after, my affairs were with women. I've never been with a man."

"Well, son of a bitch, Pink, I'm not sure how to take that. I mean, was I all that friggin' unattractive...?" I'm laughing, trying to make light of the moment.

Then I turn serious. "Well, there are different kinds of love, and I think we are what we are, and love who we love. As for me, I could never see myself kissing a girl let alone wanting to do anything else."

I squinch my eyes against the mental picture. "Eeeeyuk!" I regret my reaction instantly when Pink gets her hangdog look on. "That said, there have been some women I've loved deeply, and I love you. I love you most of all."

Pinky hauls all her little bones up into the bed, and I hold her in my arms, stroking her small fuzzy head.

· · · · · · · · · ·

Anna Grace, avatar, has gotten an eNote from Herbert Miles, avatar. The real Herbert Miles bedridden in 322 C is bald and has a big old hairy potbelly. Herb the avatar is slim and trim with a head full of black hair. He walks upright too.

Herb queries, "Would you like to sit out in the virtual Arbor with me and enjoy the evening breeze?"

My artistic curiosity overwhelms me. I type, "Ok, what time?"

"Seven-thirty." He types back. "Be there or be square."

I look over at Pinky, plopped in my visitor's chair painting her toenails purple, and stick my two fingers down my throat. Herb already makes me feel like yakking.

"Come over here, purpletoe. We are going on a virtual date! I wanna see how this works!"

I use my finger on the screen to walk my obviously hot, desirable avatar to the virtual 3D arbor. I sit her down, cross her legs and have her light a virtual cigarette. What's the harm? There are picture buttons for expression, so I choose the one labeled "cool."

In less than a minute, Herb the avatar saunters up. He has chosen "cool" for his expression as well.

He crashes on the virtual arbor bench and slides his arm around Anna Grace.

"Hey, hotstuff! I've noticed you at the Sports Plaza. You're lookin' good!"

PinkyToe pushes me over and types, "You too, Herb, that's a fine lookin' toupee you have." Apparently this is a double date.

I smack at her, grinning. "Get over on your side, lesbo."

Herb the avatar, a mover and shaker, is wasting no time. One greasy virtual hand is sliding down under my avatar's tube top feeling up my virtual boobs while the other one is headed up my skirt. Herb is multitasking.

I change my expression to "Annoyed" and type "Hey!"

"I'm feeling frisky tonight, baby, how about you?"

PinkyToe says, "Blow 'im!"

Anna Grace, avatar, slaps his virtual face and stalks off. Then Anna Grace, the real woman, pushes PinkyToe off the bed.

Herb types, "Pricktease!"

2010 Blackshale

Perry was a happy man. He had me, after all. He had let go of the past and enjoyed every day for the blessing it was. He loved to walk, covering several miles every day. One day when the waterline was low, he was powerwalking down on the edge of the riverbank.

Chugging right along, getting his heart rate up, he ran slam bang into something hard and tripped head over heels, landing on his back in the sand. For a minute he flailed his limbs like a flipped turtle, but finally pulled up to a crawl and came up eyelevel to a concrete block. A concrete block attached to a chain, a chain embedded in the wet sand with a pile of bones. Little did happy Perry suspect that those bones were what was left of his grandmother Eliza, who had in fact died quite happy herself. He hopped up, with a badly stubbed big toe but the rest of him only a little sore, and headed for the house, where we had a good wine and slow, sweet, one-sided sex.

I felt like a teenager again. Life seemed to vibrate, brilliant and super-saturated. Perry's uncomplicated affection, not to mention the sexual release he gave me once in a while, made life just grand. Without money worries, I had every art supply known to woman, and was throwing out work like crazy - good work. There were more galleries and clients waiting for the next piece than I could supply.

I had relaxed into my art making – made room for the accidental in my work. I waited patiently as elements found their way to me before I married them into a meaningful piece. Sometimes it took days or weeks or months for them to fall together into a perfect whole. I loved clipping oblique, isolated phrases out of newspapers, or collecting bits of ephemera that appeared magically at my feet during a walk. Sometimes I could swear some higher power was providing the elements and making the choices. I never felt so blissful as when I was sitting quietly, picking through boxes of scraps and bits and sticking them to a scumbled surface with dabs of glue – unless, of course, it was when I was poking through a flea market in search of more random elements. Walking up and down the aisles of other men's trash, there was often a voice in my head telling me to take this turn or that. All I had to do was listen – listen to the voice.

Every few months, Perry and I traveled. We'd spend weeks at a time in New York. I hit museums, galleries, and shopped junk stores while Perry lolled in our penthouse hotel room between gourmet meals. With all those restaurants to choose from, we never seemed to pick a bad one – good food, good wine, a good friend to laugh with. What else was there?

He and I spent a summer in Tuscany. I took cooking classes and together we bicycled through the countryside. With the sun warming our achy bones, we sat out on our tile piazza popping cork after cork after cork. I filled sketchbooks with Italia, with my happiness being there. My work became less dark, but was still cutting to the chase of my experiences.

Back at home, I fed the birds, listed every species in a spiral bound book, and watched foxes slither through the woods. We drove the curvy roads back and forth across the mountain. We hiked the local trails, golfed badly, and played the penny machines in the Indian casino - won some, lost some. We Facebooked, iPhoned, texted, and tweeted. I bought a huge HD screen, and we watched movies at night, cuddled in a knot. If I was having myself a whiney-fest one day, Perry was there to wrap me up in his arms and tell me how good things were. There were Yoga classes at the hospital, and my Wii, and running. I thought I was in the best shape of my life. Life was so damn good, everything in a precise balance. I should have been more guarded. I forgot that Karma was waiting around the corner. And remember, bad things often happen in threes.

In the middle of one night, a cell ringtone jangled my nerves. The MS Center was calling about Corrine. Without waking Perry, I jumped in my car and raced to Knoxville. By the time I got there, she was gone. They didn't know yet why, but were thinking there had been a rare side effect from one of her steroids. During my tearful drive home, I thought about the woman who had given me life, who'd left me on the doorstep, but loved me enough to stay close and to come back into my life.

I'd had two loving mothers and lost them both, and Pap. Now I was truly an orphan. I sounded it out, testing the effect on my psyche, little orphan Anna. When I got home, Perry was still snoozing. I went downstairs and rustled through a trunk, digging down through strata of diplomas and yearbooks, letters and grade cards, until I found the Abandonadas mourning amulet. I hung it around my neck and settled in for a few hours of non-stop sobbing.

When Perry woke, I soaked his shoulder with my tears. He petted me for a long while and then helped me make Corry's arrangements. Over and over that month, I thought, "What would I do without him?" A week later, the question became more pressing. He'd had a checkup with his cancer doctor, and the numbers didn't look good. They scheduled a cat scan for the next week.

I went with him for the scan. "No sweat," he kept saying. But the doctor called a few days later with the news that there were several metastases - colon, bones, right lung. Chemo and radiation both were in his future. He took it so well, charging ahead a day at a time, continuing to enjoy life. Staying happy. Even when the radiation burned and the chemo brought on heaves, he was sweetly cranky. My sweet Perry had always been of good cheer through everything.

"At bay," the oncologist reported, "We've got it at bay for a while." We got back in our routine with a new mantra, "enjoy the moment." Perry, the sick one, was able to do that. My moments were turning black.

Again, my art darkened. Tubes and other frightening medical paraphernalia appeared. Doc Turner gave me an antidepressant. Losing Corrine, seeing Perry sick, I had months where I lost interest, laid around low, quit making my bed. A sense of foreboding was heavy on my shoulders. Perry kept trying to cheer me up and that made me ashamed of myself. One morning when he was gone for a checkup, I got up off my ass and got going. I grabbed my iPod, put on my favorite hip hop song at top volume and hit the treadmill hard.

At the top end of my target heart rate, there was a new sensation. At first just a bad feeling, but the bad feeling rapidly became a crushing lack of breath. Note to self: "My God! I'm having a heart attack!" I called 911, took an aspirin, unlocked the door, and sat down. Then I went to a foggy place, where sirens and voices and actions were sliding in and out. I heard someone say, "Bag her." I remember hoping they weren't talking about a body bag. I somehow knew I was still alive and not ready for that quite yet.

When I came to, it was the next day and I was gagging on a ventilator. Perry was next to my bed looking as serious as he ever gets. I knew I wasn't in Blackshale Hospital because there were too many high end gizmos. Perry began to fill me in, trying to avoid tubes and needles as he patted my hand.

"Hay Babe... you've had yourself a bad coronary, but you're gonna be ok. You had a wild helicopter ride in there too... you're in St. Thomas." He said they'd be taking the ventilator out soon, and that I'd be having bypass surgery as soon as I was stable. He started crying and couldn't finish his report. "I just remembered something else I forgot to tell you. I love you."

After they took out the tubes, I was trying to talk with my

scratchy throat. "That's so funny. I was born here. I almost died in the same place I was born."

Perry said, "Oh yeah, I'm rolling on the floor laughing! ROTFL!"

Then I started crying hysterically and couldn't stop.

After that, I woke in the middle of the night, anxious, thinking bad thoughts in the dark, wondering about the unknown place I had almost gone... to the great beyond, the next level, whatever and wherever that is. I'd had my wake-up call. Now Perry and I were partners in some serious shit, but I had gotten a second chance. Even though he was snoring, I reached out for his hand and whispered, mainly to myself, "You and me, baby doll, we're going to make the most of every minute!"

2029 Morning Glory Ridge

I'm waiting on Taloola to get her false eyelashes affixed so we can go to Bingo. She has accidentally glued the top and bottom lashes of her left eye together and is industriously prying them apart. Finally, we widgie down the hall to the elevator. The room next to the elevator is a couple's room. Mr. and Mrs. Chokowsky. Mr. C is deaf as a post. He has the missus cornered behind the TV alcove, yelling extra loud, "Polly! Do you want to fuck?" Polly looks terrified. I don't think she wants to much.

I back my WidgieWalker up and head around the other way. Taloola looks at me.

"Where are you going Tollett?"

"There's entirely too much excitement in this place. Goin' back to bed!"

· · · · · · · · ·

According to the master schedule, Anna Grace Tollett, 326-A, was to be absent from Morning Glory Ridge on Tuesday morning, the fourth of March. She was to be taken by van to Pineville Memorial Hospital for a chest x-ray and echocardiogram and be returned late that afternoon. And all that has happened all right, just much speedier than planned. Also, the van driver opted not to stop for lunch because she is fasting, contrition for a sin with a married man that she's told me about in shocking detail all the way to Pineville. When we get back, I choose the Ultraquiet setting on my WidgieWalker so I won't wake Tiffany when I go rolling back in the room. A sleeping Tiffany is a good Tiffany!

When I get to the door of 326, it's pulled to. I crack it open a tiny bit and peek in. I follow the gaze of her bugged out eyes to the end of her bed, where a hand pumps an enormous glistening cock. When I nudge the door open a tiny bit more, I can barely see that the cock is attached to Gourdhead. His hand picks up speed and his back arches, so I take advantage of his distraction. I pull my phone out of my pocket and aim it blindly.

CLICK! I record the moment for posterity, just as he shoots a stream of his own pudding onto Tiffany's lap. He hears the click and starts for the door, but I back out, hollering at anyone who can hear, "Help! Somebody help me!" I truck my Widgie on high speed down to the director's office. Gourdhead takes off in the opposite direction, bursting through the back doors - never to be seen again at Morning Glory Ridge.

"Great detective work, Anna Grace!" the director says. We've been suspecting him of abuses for a long time, and have been waiting for the funding to install hidden security cams over every bed. But you caught him, uh, red handed with your little phone! I roll back into the room feeling a grand aura of accomplishment. Old people rock! Tiffany looks over the end of her bed and says, "Fucker!" She'd finally made sense.

2010 Blackshale

After my surgery and recovery, I went to rehab and made the habit of exercising every day. I was in the best shape of my life, what with my rebuilt heart and my new motivation for fitness. All that jogging and bouncing and gravity sends your female organs south, but aside from birthing my own uterus once in a while, I'm in pretty good shape. When that happens, I just reach down, stick it back in and move on.

I didn't much like Perry's looks though, his color was bad. We'd had our first fight when he told me he was not going to have any more treatments, he just wanted to stay home with me and live life for as long as he had.

As if I didn't have enough to worry about, Perry's situation and keeping up my own health, I got to thinking about Dory laid out over there in the basement of that place that no longer belonged to family. I kept picturing somebody out there in the future digging down into her bones to remodel that basement. The problem of course, was that Corrine had neglected to mention the basement bone yard to Bobby Oody at the time of the sale. So, I called him up.

"Hey Bobby" I said, "I should' a told you about this before, but, uh, my pap buried a few people in the unfinished basement over there and one of them is Mama. The rest of them were homeless folks or poor folks that couldn't afford a plot."

Bobby Oody laughed his head off. He was a nice guy who always did the right thing. As I listened to him snorting through the phone line, I visualized his face and was reminded that Pap had called him "Sluggo" after the comic strip character, because of his squashed pig nose.

He offered, "Tell you what let's do. You pay to get Dory moved to the cemetery, and then you and I will split the cost of a good thick concrete floor in there."

"Well, actually, there'll be two for me to move." I told him about Hum.

"How 'bout this. You go over one day and mark off the exact places where Dory and Hum are layin'. I'll hire some men to move them. I doubt if you want to be around when it's all going on. Have you got plots for them already?"

"Pap bought ten plots all together up there on cemetery hill. I reckon he expected me to have a houseful of kids. Anyway, there's plenty of room for them, and me too. Corrine's already there."

"You mean you want… Hum… in there with your family?"

"You bet I do, him and Pearlie too, when the time comes, as I reckon she is still alive. They were our family."

· · · · · · · · · ·

When death comes snooping around Sudy Templeton's back porch, she has the healthcare expertise to recognize it for what it is. She has seen it all before, the heaving chest of heart failure, the shaky weakness, kidneys goofing off on the job. She is now subdued, soft voiced, clinging to her only child for comfort. Without the lifelong dialog of blame, Marlene loses her anger and clings back, holding on desperately to this new version of her mother who is now sadly slipping away.

Marlene becomes an obsessive caretaker, super vigilant about small details, the visual and numerical markers of Sudy's condition, drips in the foley, ejection fractions, kidney functions, the swelling of ankles, all to no avail. There is nothing she can do.

Toward the very end, there is a day Marlene will refer to later as "The Big Rigmarole." It begins when the yard boy, a burly sort that Sudy has developed an old lady crush on, comes to pick up his paycheck. It's been one of her bad days, meds reducing her to crossed brain wires, garbled phrases and sleep, so Marlene has spent the day in a chair by Sudy's bed reading magazines. When she hears the yard boy's rumbling pickup, Sudy perks up and asks for her lipstick. This cheers Marlene, who has always known that the day Sudy fails to put on lipstick will be her last.

The yard boy kneels at Sudy's bedside, and she bats her eyelashes and asks him to lean down close. Marlene, still in the room, hears her say, "I am in big trouble here… I need help!" Then she pulls him closer and whispers something in his ear. Marlene can't help but think Sudy's flirtation is cute.

Less than an hour later the doorbell rings, and a policeman is at the door, dripping wet, ducking in from a lightning storm in full swing. He asks if it is the home of Sudy Templeton and Marlene says yes.

Clearing his throat to shore up his authoritative voice, he explains, "Mam, I am here for a welfare check!"

Marlene laughs. "Oh, Mom's not on welfare… she does get a little Social Security check though…" It has occurred to Marlene that he thought Sudy had gotten someone else's welfare check and was there to get it back.

"What I mean, mam, is that there has been an anonymous report by a concerned citizen regarding Sudy Templeton's personal safety in her environment!"

Marlene is clueless. "Well, how nice! Which neighbor called? They have been so good to check on her in storms and power outages and what-have-you, but I've been living here quite a while now, so she's just fine!"

The officer quickly tires of Marlene's bewilderment, and pushes through the doorway, "Look, I have to see her for myself and make sure she's ok!"

Marlene balks, blocking the door with her arm. "Well sir, how do I know you are really who you say. Men use fake uniforms all the time to prey on women alone. I'm not about to let some strange man with a gun on his hip in my house!"

He pushes her aside and walks back to where Sudy lays, glaring up at them.

"Mom, are you ok?" Marlene asks and reaches out to touch her shoulder.

"Don't you dare touch me, girl!" Sudy yelps fearfully, jerking away from Marlene in disgust and terror. Sudy's reaction mystifies and hurts Marlene. It has never happened before.

The officer looks down at Sudy's hands, black and blue from PT testing, then casts suspicion on Marlene. For whatever reasons though, he fails to pursue it further. He stares her down and warns, "You know we keep an eye on our elderly here in Blackshale!" With that, he places his hand on his gun, drawing power from it, and stalks out.

It finally hits Marlene that she, she, the one who has cared for Sudy day in and day out for two years, is the suspect! She reasons that the unknown caller had to be the yard boy. After giving herself a while to calm down, she goes in to Sudy.

"Mom?" She says quietly, "Did you tell Charlie to call the cops on me?"

Sudy is incensed! The picture of righteous indignation. "Of course not! Pffffft! That's ridiculous!"

Marlene steps into the bathroom and mixes a dose of laxative, loads a toothbrush, dumps nine pills in a paper cup. Then the faintest little voice floats up from the bed and through the door.

"Well... yes, I... did."

"You did what?" Marlene asked absentmindedly.

"I did tell Charlie to call the police."

Marlene freezes. "But why Mom? Have I ever hurt you or made you feel afraid?"

"No, no..."

"Well, why in the name of Heaven would you have Charlie call the police?"

The voice shrivels smaller and smaller, "I don't rightly know." She sounds like a little child that has been caught being bad. "The medicine..."

Marlene is overwhelmed with the desire to laugh - at that moment it just seems funny. "You've got to be kidding!" She stands rolling her eyes upward, then she says, "OK, I'm going to choose to believe that you were not in your right mind from the meds when you did that."

"Right."

Sudy's mind seems to clear as she ponders the repercussions of her invented drama.

"Did you get a ticket?"

"They don't give tickets for elder abuse, Mom, they put you in the pokey!"

Marlene dispenses the meds and lays down on the bed across the room, finally falling asleep around midnight. At two a.m., the unearthly voice she's come to expect jolts her out of sleep, "Marlennnnnne, I think I have to poop."

"Ok." Marlene jumps up, grabbing a chuck.

Sudy neglects to tell her things are already underway. Marlene has no gloves on yet, and when she slides the pad under Sudy's butt, her hand plunges into a pile of steaming wetness.

"Ick," she says softly, swallowing bile.

She heads into the bathroom to clean her hand, and she just can't help herself. "It's just a good thing I'm not in jail tonight, or who would do this job?"

Sudy lays there shrinking and silent, her eyes pinched closed. After a while Sudy says, tiny little voice quivering, "I'm sorry I pooped in the bed, but I was asleep when I woke up."

Marlene finds that cute, even though it is, again, the meds talking.

Then of course Marlene feels bad for being a smart ass. After cleaning up six rounds of loose bowel product over the next two hours, she rubs cream on Sudy's butt, tucks her in, hugs and kisses her. She still feels betrayed, slapped across the face with a plank, but she knows she has to ride the wave of forgiveness and understanding.

Sudy's eyes continue to shrink. They are so small now the glints of eyeballs are barely visible when they are open. Sudy focuses the itty-bitty peepers up into her daughter's face with a hard stare. "Will you scratch my back?"

Marlene scritches and scuffs, working her fingernails around the maze of moles on Sudy's back, then she slathers on lotion and massages her shoulders. As she turns to leave for the kitchen, Sudy mumbles up from down in that deep haunted well where her voice now lives, "I love you."

"I know you do Mom. I love you too, so much."

Marlene makes decaf, and sinks into the recliner to wait out the 5:00 meds. When the hour comes, half way through the poking down of eight pills, Sudy projectile vomits them and a quart of water out across the bed, soaking her gown, bed jacket and all the bedding. Immediately she sputters, "I have to poop again! Now!" Marlene should have never let Sudy have those mango smoothies.

Marlene rolls her up on a hip, listening to the diarrheal explosions, wipes and creams and changes pads through three more rounds of cleanup. There are four more that day, the last one of course, at the precise moment Marlene's dinner comes hot off the grill. What can Marlene say? It's been a shitty day.

· · · · · · · · ·

Hard to believe, but there is a sequel to "The Big Rigmarole" which Marlene later refers to as "The Rigmarole Grande." Three weeks before Sudy's death, she rallies, requesting favorite foods. On the morning Marlene walks in and sees Sudy sitting up, pink of cheek, requesting fried eggs and bacon, she decides to do something she has not done in nine months. She decides to go out. After a few phone calls, she engages a qualified sitter and heads to the Mall for a manicure, lunch and a matinee. If she hops right along, all that can be fit in between diabetes shots. She sighs when she turns the key in the ignition of her car, hoping it can remember how to start.

The sitter, Mrs. Tibley, settles her bumper crop of cellulite into the recliner and proceeds to throw unsolicited details of her personal life at Sudy. Sudy clamps her tiny eyes shut to filter out the annoyance.

Mrs. Tibley has forgotten more about her obsolete practical nurse's training than she recalls, but has assured Marlene she can clean up poop messes. She immediately gets her big chance, as Sudy has been wolfing down mango protein smoothies all morning. After three poop changes, a bed bath, and four hours putting up with each other, both Mrs. Tibley and Sudy are tuckered out. The sitter is happy to see Sudy finally settle down for a nap. On the way to raid the pantry and turn on the TV, she puts all the bedclothes in the laundry to soak. Mrs. Tibley has found some popcorn and a cold soda. She puts oil in a saucepan and dumps in the kernels. The stove eye is slow as Christmas, so she plops down in front of the TV to wait for the first pop.

She flicks on her favorite soap opera. Low and behold, Doreena has just come out of her coma! Entranced, Mrs. Tibley, who is hard of hearing, turns the volume way up! Excited about Doreena's miracle and unable to hear the popping, she forgets all about the hot oil on the stove. It's only a small fire, which Mrs. Tibley douses with baking soda once she hears the kitchen fire alarm blare.

Sudy springs awake to the smell of smoke, energized by her protein intake and clean bowels. She spies her cell phone, which has been sitting dormant in the charger for weeks. She flips the case and hits the #9 button.

"911, what is your emergency?"

All at once, Sudy is not exactly sure what the trouble is, so she improvises. Her words have been indistinguishable for weeks. This drugged, stunned quality adds credence to her distress.

She mumbles, "A home invasion. Help! We have a home invasion! And, they are burning down our house!" The operator asks her to repeat it several times, because Sudy is barely comprehensible.

Marlene pulls in the driveway just behind of three Blackshale police cruisers, two hook and ladder units, an ambulance and the Fire Chief - all with sirens blaring. Marlene is sure Sudy has died, but doesn't understand why so many emergency vehicles are required for one small octogenarian. She runs down the hall, tears welling and heart pounding, just in time to hear Sudy telling the emergency crews, on their knees alongside her hospital bed, about the alien who has started the fire in her house and abducted her daughter in his flying craft. Marlene notices that Sudy has thought to put on lipstick.

"You've just got to do something! Marlene hates flying," Sudy says, shaking her head gravely.

In the last week of Sudy's life, Hospice waltzes in toting the big guns of pharmacy. All her obsessions and cares float away, and she begins to slide down the last slithery slope into oblivion. At times she fixes the beads of her eyes on Marlene as if she were perceiving some profound new truth about her, possibly a harsh new criticism she no longer has words to voice.

Most of Sudy's words to Marlene now are fantasies.

Sudy grabs Marlene's shirt with both hands and pulls her down to disclose a shocking truth. "Do you know there is a whale swimming across your t-shirt?" On one occasion Sudy reports that Anna Grace has been killed in a fiery car crash. Marlene, unsure, calls Anna Grace in a panic, relieved to hear her voice.

Near the end, Sudy rarely knows Marlene, or if she does recognize her only child, she doesn't give a rat's behind. Only one minute of clarity gives Marlene the peace she will need to go on alone.

Sudy, the last of the red-hot lovers, has always been undemonstrative with her child. So, when she pops up out of her occlusion and begs her daughter to lie beside her in bed and hold her, Marlene snuggles gratefully against the unfamiliar warmth until they both fall asleep. Short lived, that serving of tenderness, for when the five o'clock med alarm sounds and Marlene touches her Mama's unadorned lips, dry and chapped without a trace of lipstick, they have already gone cold.

· · · · · · · ·

When it's certain that your days are numbered, it becomes your work to fill every minute with good things and quality time. Perry did a great job of that. He almost wore me out living life at warp speed in those last months when he felt decent enough to enjoy life. I wanted every meal to be memorable, so I was cooking up something different and fancy for each one, desperate to get all those culinary experiences stuffed into his mouth before his appetite was gone. I must have been impressive, because one night over our candlelight dinner and wine, he said, "Hey sugar, do you want to get hitched?"

I gave him a hard, distrustful look and ranted, "I knew it, you grabby son of a bitch, you were after my money all along."

He laughed, but continued, "Seriously, if it would make you feel better, I'm willin."

"Nothing will make me feel better," I mourned tearfully, "except being with you as long as I can, and I have that without the benefit of hearing "Here Comes the Bride" played in my honor. The fact that you offered is sweet, but I think we're good like we are. And besides, isn't it illegal for first cousins to marry? Geez, that's all I need Perry-boy, ending up in the slammer at my age."

2029 Morning Glory Ridge

PinkyToe is now in 326-B, and though it's sad that Tiffany has gone on to a better place, Pink and I are giddily happy to be roomies. Truly, the looney wing is a much better place for Tiffany. I'm acting ten years younger now that PinkyToe and her madcap ways are back in my formerly dismal life.

Not everything is perfect though. Flotilla has worked up a special dislike for PinkyToe. I leave Pink napping peacefully, but when I come back from a Widgie with Daphne and the others, she is furious.

"A. T.! She slapped me! Flotilla slapped my face!"

"What did you say to her, Pink? She must have been provoked."

"Flotilla was trying to poke something down my throat and I said, 'Bite me!' I said it nicely, I did, Anna Grace. And also, I may have called her Flotilla instead of her real name." Pink puts on her innocent face, one I had seen many, many times.

"Oh that was so PinkyToe-esque! You kook. Wowsers, here's our big chance to report her!"

"Sure," Pink says with resignation, "My word against hers, and guess who always wins that battle. If I can get a cam, at least she can't do it again."

She's propped up in her bed firing off an eNote to the director, requesting a video camera to be placed over her bed. She is shaky, her face is red, and the BP monitor on her screen is beeping an alarm. I talk her down, as I always have throughout our friendship. She's always been the spitfire, me the damper.

Now that we are roommates, we have time to catch up, tell each other all the things that happened when we had lost contact. I tell her about my happiness with Perry, about losing him and

Corrine, how my work had developed, and how Pearlie had left to marry.

She tells me Tilla had killed herself, when she finally realized her child was not ever coming to find her. I mused on it, "How awful. We all had wicked hard times when we were young, and we could'a all crawled up in a big black hole and died of it, for sure. When you think about it, you and I were the lucky ones. We had our art to save us. Tilla had nothing, nothing but her sadness."

Pinky opens up and tells me about the love of her life. Her name was Belle. She was a well-known and highly published photographer. Pink had met her on a shoot, and they had lived together for most of the years we had been out of touch. It's hard for me to explain how I feel as Pinky talks about loving someone so much. Had it been another best friend, I'd be consumed with jealousy, but Belle was her lover, her love. I am still in the best friend position.

"What happened? How did it end?" I asked quietly.

"Breast cancer. Three recurrences and the third time was a bad charm." Pinky brought out a photo from the drawer in her bedside table. I studied the picture. The woman was tall and willowy, brunette, a face strong with character. I could understand how anyone, male or female, could love her.

"She's lovely," I say, "I'm sorry you lost her."

· · · · · · · ·

A month later the monitor screen over Pinky Thomas' bed is beeping. I cripple out into the hall and add my breaking voice to its cries, frantically calling for a nurse. The nurses' station is empty. Ten minutes later, the monitor impassionately reports a myocardial infarction. "Resident Terminal," the screen says, displaying a flat line graph and the 3D image of Pink's dear heart, motionless and still. By the time Flotilla saunters in from her overextended break, my lifelong pal, my feisty PinkyToe is gone.

"Pink... Pink... Pink", I lay over her body, bawling.

"Es el deseo de mi corazón estar unida contigo."

It is the desire of my heart to be at one with you. At this moment, I am so ready to die myself.

The theory that every cell in your body has some kind of brain function, that it knows, feels, the state of your consciousness, must be true. My body is giving up. It's lost everyone I love, and every little cell is testifying, "It's over, time to go!" I've gone off my feed, taking only the tiniest bird bites. As a result, weakness is setting in, and my days are spent in bed.

One thing, more than any other, assures me it's time to leave this world. I no longer care one whit about art – mine or anyone else's. The artist I have been all my life has already passed away.

It is at this new low time in my life that Mrs. Evangelist of Jesus decides to come back for another whack at me. I hear her heels clicking down the hall, and I can tell from the purposefulness of her stride that she is a woman on a mission. She has heard I've lost my best friend and has decided that she should forgive me for the faked crazy spell and the string of F-words.

"Forgive me? Woman! I've got bigger fish to fry here, I've got a death to die. Now leave me the hell alone!" I flap my hands at her crazily, and she retreats yet again, deleting my name from the book of life in her mind as she clicks back up the hall.

2012 Blackshale

Driving along Blackshale Road in a pelting rain, I passed a huge semi, a stock truck. I could see through the round-cornered rectangles that it was empty, the squealing pigs and moaning heifers already head-hammered into the next world and on the way to someone's gas grill. Even though they no longer occupied that space, I clearly heard their bovine and porcine protests in my mind.

Bobby Oody's office was in a strip mall several miles away, between the Walk-in Prayer Clinic and the "As Seen on TV" junk store. To get there I had to rely on my GPS unit. There was a detour, and the unit kept recalculating over and over and over, directing me around in circles for half an hour. I went ballistic. "Have you lost your fool mind?" I was slinging complaints at the unit on my dash. Finally, after a round and round born of new technology gone awry, I found Bobby's office, picked up the keys, and headed back to my old home.

I walked though the top level of the house. Strange to see it empty, but like the stock truck I'd just passed, it echoed with voices. Dory, Frank, Corrine, Pearlie, and even a "hummmm" here and there. I sat on the floor for a while and let them speak to me, then, I bypassed the second floor. That floor housed other people's sad vibes. Down the next flight, I was back in Frank's workroom. His stainless steel furniture was still there. The discolored tube of the embalming machine dangled without purpose, no more bodies left to suck dry.

The downstairs bathroom hadn't changed much. The stucco walls were a couple of shades dirtier and had more curls of peeling paint, more cracks. But there it was, still, the history of all those Blackshale folks Pap had tended to over the years. It took me a while to read over all the names, their causes of death, pictures the young artist, the mortuary child Anna Grace, had faithfully drawn to tell their final stories. A chewed carbon pencil still lay there. I picked it up, added Frank and Corrine. Next to Frank, Heart Attack. Next to Corrine, Unknown Complication of Multiple Sclerosis.

I stepped into Pearlie and Hum's room. The twin beds were still there, mattresses dripping stuffing dense with mildew. A flowery bedspread edged in faded ball fringe the color of mustard rotted in a corner. Flakes of dust swam in the sunbeams falling from the single window. I ran my hands over artifacts Pearlie had left behind.

On the wall still hung framed pictures of Jesus and the Virgin Mary. The frames were encrusted with miniature shells, now thick with dust. Under Hum's bed, I found a Hadacol fishing lure still in the box, with a birthday card signed, "Love, Anna Grace."

Starting at the top, I opened every drawer of her bureau. All were wiped clean as a pin, until I got to the oversized drawer at the bottom. The drawer was locked. I went into Frank's workroom and grabbed a pointed tool, and picked the lock. The drawer was swollen, unwilling to open, stubbornly guarding its contents.

I finally pulled it free and I lifted the lid of a large box. My heart almost stopped. It was filled with tiny bits of color, sequins, beads, broken glass, doodles, glitters, cobachons, strings and threads, small found objects. I dug in both hands, palms up, and let the colors filter through my fingers. They sparkled in the stream of light from the window. There was another box with glues and paints. My first reaction was, "Wha... What in the name of Heaven was she doing with all this stuff?"

In the other boxes, my question was answered. I pulled out panel after panel of intricate masterpieces: drawings, paintings, ornate multimedia collages and objects crusted with collected and hand drawn tidbits.

Pearlie, precious Pearlie, had been an artist. Not just an artist

- a genius. All that time I'd been with her, I'd never known it, never seen a hint of it. What else could she have done with all the free time she'd spent down in that dreary basement room alone. Pearlie, untrained, without ever visiting galleries or studying art books, had taken all her pain and trouble and everyday experience and found her way to the most breathtaking visual truths. In a language she had invented for herself, with whatever materials she could forage, she had created her own joy and magic. Pearlie had made something out of nothing.

Early on she had discovered the pure happiness of drawing that required no more than scraps of paper and a pencil. Drawing had released her demons and preserved her memories.

As I dug down through the layers in the drawer, I could see her growing - exploring other kinds of art, surface design, and sculptural forms. Downstairs in her basement room, she had worked into the night, bent over and focused, lost in constellations of beads and stitches. During the day, her pockets had bulged with bits of nothingness she collected: pieces of lint and string, scraps of papers, leftover sequins, orphan shirt buttons. The more humble the bit, the more she felt called upon to make it a player in something spectacular, to raise it up to stardom.

I'd heard that Pearlie's husband had died, but I had no idea where she was, or even if she was still alive. How I longed to talk to her about her work. All that time, she had been making art right there, right under my nose. I hadn't known, I hadn't even known. I wept raggedly, a weeping half regret and half joy.

I placed red flag markers around the space where Dory lay, then moved over to Hum's spot to place his flags. On the rectangle surrounding his grave, there were small gifts Pearlie had left, a small homemade headstone, a plastic frog, a faded funny book, some rusty jacks, a moldy picture of all of us we'd taken at the carnival one happy summer.

I gathered Pearlie's work carefully into boxes, and took it home. I hung it all over the walls of my studio, letting it inspire me. She had been unfettered by academics, unafraid, using anything she came across in a bold way. I wanted to be more like her. My work took on her audacity and became more raw, more colorful. It all came together, my training and experience, the arsenal of materials at my disposal, my new influence and fearlessness. I was finally making work that I would rather keep than sell for any price.

I called the gallery in Nashville where I had exhibited several times.

"Belinda, I have something I'd like you to see." We made an appointment for the following week. I kept trying and failing to find Pinky, hoping we could get together while I was there.

After Perry had gotten sick, and I had my heart attack, my long distance friendship with Pinky slowly withered. We weren't mad, we were just busy and lost each other along the way. I was trying to remedy that and get back in touch, but her phone number was no longer right. I tried every search tool known to Internet, but I kept reaching dead ends. PinkyToe had vanished.

• • • • • • • •

"Dear God in Heaven!" Belinda was about to go reeling off her tuffet. She had spread out the stack of Pearlie's pieces across her desk. "Who is this person?" I told her the story, saying that I didn't know what had become of her. I did the math and came to the sad assumption that Pearlie might no longer be living.

"This is phenomenal," she drooled, "There's plenty here for an exciting show, but without knowing about the artist or her heirs, I can't hang it. Too many legalities. Be sure to let me know if you find out anything more that might allow us to show the work!"

I was at least glad to have my opinion confirmed. That Pearlie, in her teeny basement hovel, after the dishwashing and laundering and floor mopping, after the corn shucking and greens looking, after the childcare and selfless companionship to ladies of the house, had created a lifetime of brilliant work.

"Now, what about you! Let's plan a huge retrospective!"

"Nope!" I protested, "I just want to look at it myself for a while. Since I have no kids and have outlived all my loved ones, you can have the whole damn pile of it after I die. Just give my percentage to the Knoxville MS Center."

She was smiling sweetly, fanning her hands, and earnestly protesting the idea of my mortality, all the while heading for her filing cabinet, a contract and a pen.

· · · · · · · ·

Marlene has hit the bottom of a second glass of Merlot, and sinks back into the comforters on her bed, ankles and wrists crossed, spine in an embryonic arc. In her present, pleasant buzz, it's easy to pretend she's floating against spongy uterine flesh. Sudy is out there vibrant and alive, belly bumping against the Formica as she wipes the supper dishes, swaying to the latest hit parade tune. She waddles to the sofa and sinks in, tilting her occupied womb... whoopseedaisy baby... as she props up her swollen ankles on the slipcovered ottoman. She hands the TV Guide to Faron who ponders a minute, then turns the dial to watch Liberace. Daydream turns to dream, but when Marlene May wakes, Sudy remains dead.

In the past weeks, Marlene has gone through probate court, wrestled paperwork, straightened out finances, cleaned out closets and drawers, and disposed of every artifact of Sudy's life that she doesn't want to keep. She has cried and bucked up, cried and bucked up, cried and bucked up, and cried some more. The sadness remains, and she knows it will, probably forever. But floating around in her newly orphaned soul, there is something new. She's bored. She doesn't need money. Sudy left her enough to get by on, but she wants to get out of the house, be with people. She needs to feel useful – and soon. She slaps the Pineville paper on the kitchen table and runs her fingernail down the classifieds. Help Wanted, General. "That's me," she thinks dolefully, "I am about as general as I can get."

Blackshale Hospital needs a phone receptionist on the second shift. She stirs sweetener into her morning coffee and picks up the phone to call about the job. The receptionist who answers knew Sudy well, and when she finally quits going on and on about that, she gives Marlene the number of the person to call.

Putting on her best phone voice, she dials the number and speaks with Mrs. Mahoney. They set up an interview for the next week, but already Marlene is soaked with apprehension. She can tell over the phone, Mrs. Mahoney is one of those strictly business, humorless, naturally judgmental sort of women. She sounds like she has a corncob up her nitpicky ass. Still, Marlene thinks maybe she can charge through the barbed wire of Mrs. Mahoney's personality to a vocation.

Marlene is also lonely. The only men her age in Blackshale are married, gay, crazy, or still shacking up with good old mom. Her friends have been on her case, trying to get her to put up a profile on Match.com. Crap. She is not that lonely.

But she is horny. Since Sudy died, any attempts at relief have failed. She just knows Sudy is there, looking down on her. "What if she is? I'm only human, I have needs!" She tries to convince herself that it's healthy. Even the medical websites say so. But she can't let go and relax.

That afternoon, Marlene sets out to work in the yard, ready to attack the legions of weeds that have taken over during Sudy's illness. She pops her cell in the back pocket of her jeans and sets it to the loudest volume so she can hear it over the weed eater. She digs and pulls and sprays. Good therapy! She comes back in at naptime, sweaty and exhausted, flopping backward on the bed.

Waiting to get sleepy, she thinks random thoughts about weeds and the job interview and how much she misses Sudy and yes, how she is horny. Then, all at once, Hoo-ee! There it is from out of nowhere, the urge she knows is hopeless, the unscratchable itch. But, what the heck, you never know until you try.

Maybe it's the exercise, the long pent-up need, or maybe Sudy has moved on to another plane and given Marlene her personal space. For whatever reasons, Marlene's libido is suddenly a charging bull, unstoppable, and joyfully out of control. She is groaning in obviously sexual pleasure and screaming out loud with total abandon.

Then Marlene hears a voice other than her own.

"Hello? HELLO? Are you all right? Is someone hurting you? Should I call 911?" Mrs. Mahoney is yelling from the back pocket of Marlene's jeans, while she reads Marlene Templeton on her caller ID and raises an eyebrow in shock.

After the pocket dial, Marlene skips the interview. Nupe, nupe, nupe, not gonna happen! She can't face it. She's betting that even a sourpuss like Mrs. Mahoney would know what she'd been up to. But, life is not all bad. At least she's got her mojo back.

· · · · · · · · · ·

Two weeks later Bobby Oody called, "It's done," He said, "you can go up and visit any time you want." Although Perry couldn't be left alone for long, I went that afternoon. I counted out ten stones on each monument. Ten for Dory, ten for Corry, ten for Frank and ten for Hum. My darling dears finally at rest, their loving lives accomplished. I glanced at the empty plots. I knew that before too long, another would be filled, and someday I, too, would lie here on this breezy hill alongside them. That was fine with me.

In a few weeks, Perry was buried in one of Frank's plots. We had been more of a loving family to him than Aunt Nettie had ever been. She was in that same cemetery, but I never visited her grave. As far as I knew, she lay there without ever getting a single posy in her permanent vase, real or plastic. Sad to be gone with no one giving a damn, but I have to say she deserved what she got. Some day I would try my best to muster forgiveness for her, for all my abusers, just not yet. Not yet.

Over the course of Perry's illness, hope flittered in and out of our lives like an elusive dragonfly until finally, it left us. When he began to have unbearable pain and difficulty breathing, Hospice came every day to dole out doses of Morphine. He slept a lot, but when he was awake I stayed close, read to him, held his hands in mine. His last day on earth was grueling, the inability to draw a breath must have been pure terror for him. He was heaving hard, hungry for the air I was unable to feed him.

He was so brave, so beautiful, up to the end. "My love," he predicted with a weak cough and a shudder, "I think I'm going now." Embracing every second, I lay on the bed wrapped around him, trying my best to sink into him. The spaces between his breaths grew longer and longer and longer until his breathing ceased.

2029 Morning Glory Ridge

Mrs. Gundersen worries that I am obsessed with dying and anxious to go. She is trying to convince me that there's still a lot of quality time left in my future. So today, she is taking me on a field trip. We start down the hall. She is huffing and puffing to keep up with my WidgieWalker.

"OK, where are we going, Trudy?" I ask her with a lackluster sigh.

"We're going to see the hundred and fifteen year old woman."

An ancient figure is sitting up straight and queenly in a day room exercise chair.

The irises of her eyes are white as snow and her skin is papery.

"What's her name?" I ask Trudy.

Trudy says she doesn't know, but I can ask her myself because she's still somewhat lucid. "Do speak up though!"

I say loudly, "HELLO, Ms. G here thought I would be inspired to meet someone older than me. She thinks I need encouragement to keep on going. What's your name, honey?"

There is a purposefulness to every movement, every word out of her mouth. But when the dried-up-prune-textured mouth opens, slowly, slowly, it says, "Well... child... glad to have myself a visit! They call me Pearl... Pearl Washington!"

After I get over the shock of being called a child, the name takes a minute to register. The man with the ring that she'd called a rock, the man driving the old beat-up Pontiac, his name was buried deeply in my memory. All at once it bubbles to the surface, "Samuel," she had announced back then, "Samuel Washington." My mind swells with joy, and I feel my heart doing the pony and the mashed potato from too much excitement.

"PEARLIE!" I cry, "It's me, Anna Grace!"

We squall like babies, wringing all the surprise and love out of our soggy old souls.

I run my fingertips over her twisted hands, touching the "rock" still in place on her gnarled ring finger. "Tell me what all happened to you after you left Tolletts!"

"Well," she says, "Me and Mister Samuel Washington, we done loved him to death! Naw, he pass from the sugar." She chuckles. "Mr. Sam, he had a little money from his concrete bidness up there in Pineville, so I lived on by myself in his house a few years, until I fell and broke me a hip, then I come here to the medicaid."

"Pearlie, I need to ask you about your work that you left in the drawer of your bureau at Tollett's. Why did you leave it there? It's incredible. You should have let someone exhibit it!"

She clouds for a minute, and I'm afraid she can't remember. Then Pearlie's artistic past comes back to her with a smile.

"Why, Miz Anna, I left them pictures there for you. You was the onlyest one with de eyeballs for it!" She rolls her head back, closes those white eyes, and lets go of a big old Pearlie horse laugh, up out of her gut. "You do with it what you want, unnnh huh!"

"I found it long after we sold the building. I was so shocked to see that you'd been making art. It was amazing work, Pearlie. Can you tell me why you started making it? What moved you to create all those wonderful things?"

"Why Miz Anna, it was you, baby. I seen you, a bitty girl no bigger than a piss ant, sittin' in de floor studyin' on everthin' in front yo face. Turn'in round makin' a picture of it so's everybody else could see jus' how you was seein' it. I say, 'Pearlie Bean, you kin do that your own self!' "

• • • • • • • •

Mrs. Gundersen has been acting antsy ever since our first visit to Pearlie three weeks ago. She's taken me back every afternoon or so. If Pearlie is having a fairly good day, I am there taking advantage of it. After all, how much social life can we have left?

Today, Mrs. G plants herself in the green visitor chair next to my bed and says, "Oh boy, oh boy! I could get fired for this." I think she means that she would get fired for sitting down, and I shoot her a sympathetic look.

"For crying out loud Gundersen, surely you can take a load off your feet once in a while!"

She reaches over me to my screen and types in a code. "A few weeks after she came here, Pearlie told her story to the eScreen. This is so against the privacy laws. Supposed to be locked as long as they are livin', but I know how much this will mean to you." She clicks her way to the Pearlie Bean Washington button in the Biography Library, and Pearlie's deliberate, raspy voice floats out over my bedspread.

"This here Febwary. History Month. Lady from church, she come up here and tole me if I have a mind to, I kin talk the story of my long, long time livin' into this tv. I gone to, too. Best I can. I still talks old time. Most folks now talks good. Dey been goin' to white college long time now. Me, Pearlie Bean, I never got no schoolin'. My talk never change, I jes keep on de same.

"When I come here to the Mornin' Glory, they check the box say 'non-caucasian.' I done know that aready 'cause I been tole. I be call black, Afr-i-can A-Mer-i-Can, colorert, of color, coon, spook, negro, picaninny, nigra, jigaboo, jungle bunny and on back, nigger, nigger, nigger. Fact is, I never kere much what they call me, I's jes Pearlie Bean, child a God.

"All colors marry up with all colors now. Fade out da wash, so all people the same color. Or all of 'em some shade so different it don't matter no more. They jes folks, like it always been and the good Lord Jesus lovin' ever one the same.

"I was 'leven when my mama die gruntin' my baby brother in the world. He die too. 'Fore too long, my daddy they call Mean Nigger Bean comin' home drunk and thrown me down. 'Fore long, gruntin' out my own baby boy. Joseph Jerimiah Bean. I was old enough to know my daddy wrong, wrong, wrong to mess wid me. But I loves dat baby. Loves 'im. Four years on, only thing outta that boy's mouth is "hummmm." I know. I know he ain't right.

"One night, my daddy come home drunker'n a polecat. It cold. Down 'round zero. Me and Hum up in de bed. Pile on them patch quilts my mama make, outta floursackin' one stitch at a time. I be prayin' to the black Jesus up on the wall we don't freeze. My daddy take up a stick and jerk off all them quilts, whoopin' my blue black legs bloody red. Callin' me lazy for not fixin up a heater. I don't know how and that's the truth. Don't know nuthin' 'bout heater. Hum, he hangin' on me, cryin' for his mama and get a few licks on his own self. Him jes'a sweet, freezin' baby boy. Hmmmmp!

"My daddy out in the dirtyard tryin' fill up dat heater, but he so drunk coal oil sloshin' all over 'im. He testin' it out, but it ain't workin and he kickin' it and cussin' Goddam sombitch stove. More coal oil. He strick dat match. WHOOSH! He hollerin' like he in hellfire. I never reach for no water bucket, you think I did? Never done it. I jes watch him burn. Don't feel nothing but froze.

"Might maybe be some sinnin' trouble here. I be needin'a baptizin'.

"The reverend, he say Lord Jesus know our trouble. He know I let my daddy burn up, but he know Pearlie Bean is jes froze.

"Reverend like to drown me under dat water, but I come up praisin' and singin'. Reverend say, Pearlie Bean you a child a God. He forgive on accounta Jesus. He do. I sing it. I sing it everday.

"Can't get no job doin' for'a white lady. Can't leave Hum. My friend Sallie, (she high yellow and she think she bettern me mosta time) she get me piecework from the mill where she work. She do for Miss Peavine but dat lady get too hateful, Sallie quit her. I'm good with my hands and sell some 'broideries. Sallie hep me. She know a lady take it to souvn'ir shop in the smoke mountain.

"I set out a garden. Got poke salat and two chickens in the dirtyard. We get by, bellies full, watch the river run, we happy as doodlebugs in our little wood house.

"Hum, he grow up tall but still all he say is "hummmm." Hum has got hisself a soft heart, never hurt nothin'. If he step on a roachbug or a toadfrog, he cry. But he big, tall as our house, and he dark. He walk funny, and look differnt and I reckon he skeer somebody. All I know, sheriff say some boogyman musta want us outta here, cause when our little wood house burn up, they nothing left but coal oil cans and a black cross of Jesus out in da dirtyard.

"Sheriff take us down to de station. He callin' and callin'. Then Mr. Frank Tollett, he come load us up in some old bang up hearse. I think Lord, Lord, dey gone kill us and take us straight to the ground. Maybe we better off.

"That first day at the Tollett, I reckon Miz Dory kinda shock. But after one day a me cookin' and helpin', she soften right up. First day, she say me and Hum kin take some of the cookin' down to our room for supper, mighty kind.

"Next mornin', she say, "Well, shoot! Why don't y'all just sit yourselves down here with us. No point in you being down there just the two a y'all in the dark! And she pass the plate of hoe cakes to Hum, even 'fore she pass to Mr. Frank." After breakfast, me and Miz Dory standin' at the sink, I wash, she dry. Back then, Pearlie Bean too dumb to know dis here stranger than a two headed milk cow.

"Nowadays I know it, that wern't how other folks was. Before Tollett I never work before, 'sides do for my daddy, get whipped, get throwed back on the tickin'. I not heard Sallie tellin' bout folks treated bad, some like dogs. Some was treated po-lite, but looked down on like they dirty or never think real human thoughts. In mosta house on Blackshale road, maid serve up dinner in the dinin' room, go in the kitchen 'n eat a ham cathead biscuit alone. Before Dr. King get kilt at dat motel and Mr. Evers get shot up on dat crack in his own driveway, and start up the slow, slow, slow changing of how things is. Still slow. But still, gettin' better.

"Now, I 'low, Dory probly want me upstair to see to baby boy and baby girl, hop up and pour the tea, so's she and Mr. Frank can sit and eat in peace. But time pass, me and Dory bury our boys, work side by side, raise our sweet orphan girl, we more like sisters in a house, jes livin' and workin' side by side. I be paid help, I know dat, I ain't dumb after livin' almost a hunnert years. But I know this here, sure as the day is long, back at the Tollett, we all love each other like famly.

"Now you look here. Miz Corry, that lady a whole new can a fishin' worm. Later on, after Miz Dory get kilt by that crazy white man, I bout go crazy my own self. Then, here come Miz Corry, say she da mama. If anybody gone be mama now, Pearlie Bean gone be! The one been rockin' dat baby since she come up out that drawer on the front porch! Changin' her nappie, stirrin' her puddin'. Lovin'. Lovin' like my own baby girl I never have.

"Fore too long, Miz Corry hangin' around, greasyweaselin' herself in here, suckin' her way in on Anna Grace and Mr. Frank like a leech in the crick. Mr. Frank, well that man deaf, dum and blind wid da grievin'. He don't care 'bout nothin'. Back then, all he thinkin' 'bout Corry is a hep for Anna Grace, so he kin take his bottle of Jack and crawl in a big black hole. Took a while, on after they marry, for that Corry to weasel in wid me. But, she done it, she did. Yes she did. You hear me right. She love that girl too, and a girl like Anna Grace can't have too many lookin' out. Way I see it, Anna Grace Tollett had her three fine mamas, Dory, Corry and big, tall non-caucasian me.

"Anna Grace, now there's a name I can chaw on all day long. That baby full of sunshine, she come up outta that bureau drawer smilin' and she never stop. She love Pearlie Bean, even when I say "No no, baby girl, no no" she jes come over and give me a love pat, lay that shiny little black head down on my lap. You think she make my life easy? No, Lord have mercy! Soon as she walkin', crayon markin' come up all over them walls. Miz Dory break her from walls, she in the floor, scribble, scribble colors all day long on papers, hittin' the papers some of the time, floor most of the time. So here I comes with the ragmop. When she not colorin' she up cuttin' up shirt cardboards and toothpickers, pipe cleaners and cotton balls, glue'in it all into some kind of sumpin', who knows what. That girl a maker. She make and make and make. She get older, she start lookin'. Sumpin' tickle her eyeballs, and there she go… layin' it down in one them sketchin' books. That girl jus one big suckin' up eyeball. And if she not seein' it, she makin' it plumb up outta her head!

"Hmmmph! Got my girl a baptizin'. Yes I did.

"Mr. Frank downstair with his dead folks in the sad place. I cleans the parlor days in between, but I kin hear them white folks moanin' and a groanin' in my head. I smell them sick, sweet flowers and feel them deaduns hangin' around waitin' to go in the ground. I pulls out my asphiddy and squeeze it tight in one hand, dustrag in the other. Lord, Lord, yes I'm skeered a haints, yes I am.

"Upstair, in our sunny place, we never thinks about them folks, them ones dead, or them livin' ones left behind feeling like dyin' they own selves and right then jes as soon. We jes havin' happy times. You hear me, I'm tellin' it, Mr. TV. Miz Dory, Mr. Frank, Anna Grace, Hum, and me. We jes walkin' and talkin' and workin' and playin', weavin' in and out, in and out of them sunbeams, dancin' in the light.

"Seem like nothin' good never last. Lord, Lord, hep me Jesus to tell it.

"Mr. Frank, he knock easylike on my door like he skeered to.

He never come to my room. Not to say nuthin. Not to set a spell. Mr. Frank here now, and he shakin' like a minner in a minner bucket. Oh Lord, sumpin' bad here.

"He look at me and get out "Hum" and commence to cry. Man like that, cryin', I know right off, my boy *gone*. Mr. Frank sit wid me long time, ain't nothin' he can say. Miz Dory tell me to stay down, take a good rest, long as I want to, even after Hum in the ground down in the basement. I know I got to get my body up and goin', else I gone lay there and die my own self. So I go on up the stair, fill up them pans, push the broom, give all the smile I can to my sweet girl. She know I sad, she know. She know somethin' bad 'bout Hum, but she know not to ask. My hands go on and do for Miz Dory, but my head be dark and cold and buzzin' with sad a long, long time.

"One day, Hum been gone a while, me and Anna Grace out in the yard. Me in the shade breakin' stringbeans, she skippin' rope in the sunshine. She done took off her haltertop, sittin' there in her shorty shorts. Back then mamas didn't think nothin' about little girl titties. She drawin' birds. She look up to me and say, "Pearlie, you got a picture of you and Hum?" My breath all swoosh out.

"No'me missy, we never got our picture took." My sad come back bad.

"Anna Grace wiggle them little knees 'round and stand up. Brush the dirt off her little bottom and tie on her halter. She come over to me and never say a word, but she set that sketchin' book and a pencil in my lap, stare me in a eye real hard, and jes sashay off.

"That night in my room, I take up that pencil. I do. I close my eyes thinkin' hard… what do my Hum head look like. Then his eyes and his nose and mouth. I draw them things on over and over, page after page, and then I draw Hum big as life, again and again. My sweet Lord Jesus! It look like Hum! Then I go look in the mirror and draw what I see there. I look old and sad, but I draw me next to Hum on the page. We together again. Pearlie made it.

"Then on, when I pick up a pencil, I feel happy. Like all my sad slide out my hand down through dat pencil right onto the paper. I draw every single something I see in my room. Coffin sellin' man leave a big stack of pads downstairs for the takin' and grocery boy give me free pencils. I draw the chamber pot. I draw Black Jesus and Mary. I take the back off the larmclock and draw all them things windin' around in there. Dead bird on the window ledge, feet up in the air. Houseshoes Anna Grace give me for Christmas. Mouse bones in the corner. Hum's fishin' ties, china Tennessee cowboy Miz Dory bring me from Nashville.

"Then I start drawing things I see's in my head. Hum flyin' up to Heaven. Anna Grace, a different bird on ever finger, When I make a picture, it's mine. Make it whatever I damnwell please. Sometime pretty and sparkle to cheer me up, sometime scary and dark and sad like I feel right then and I can tell it. I start sewing on pictures. If I got a string, a button, a bead or sparkle sequin or paper scrap, I glue it in. I cut and paste and draw and paint on top. I paint with colors I make my own self out of flour and pokeberries but they gets moldy. I walk to Blackshale to the five and dime and buy a watercolor paint set. I make and I make and I make 'til up in the night. I make my own happy, but I have 'bout wore myself out.

"No'me, I never stop makin. I'm getting' on, 'bout too old to stand on my feet all day, helping Anna take care of Corry who got the MS, but I keep on makin. One day I run out of storebought paint. I ax Anna Grace can she run me to the new Walmarks. She head for the produce aisle cause she love a fresh mushmelon, she do. I'm trying to pick between the plastic paints and the watercolor paints, when I see this… gentleman. Same brown as me. He look me over foxy.

"He laughin' at me wid his eyes. I can tell. He thinkin'… what do this old woman want paint for? I grab up my paints and go to pay, go hide in the car and wait on the girl.

"That night, the phone ring twice. That same man he say in a deep smooth talk, 'Please may I speak to the artist of the house?' He say, he done walk all over that Walmarks axing everybody he see, 'Who is that fine lady?' until he find out where to call me at, me, Pearlie Bean.

"I call him a fool.

"He say, "I am in love at first sight when I see you buying that paint in the Walmarks, and I be please to take you to dinner in Pineville, if you don't mind."

"He talk in a kind voice I like. I do.

"A month later he down on his knees with a big rock. You heard me right. Me eighty-five, and all them up at the church lookin' for me to march down that aisle like a kid. Now you look here! You lookin' to see me moppin' up the floor with some swishy long white something or other, you lookin' for me wrong! I get me a nice suit instead, but I do go walkin' down the aisle with a rhinestone crown up on top of my wighat. He standing up at the front wid the preacher. He commence yellin' out, 'Unh, unh, unh! Preacher! Preacher! Kin I jes run down that aisle and get her right now cause I can't wait?"

"I ride away from Tolletts a bride in Mr. Samuel Washington's great big gold colored Pontiac. By then, my girl Anna Grace done grown, so I reckon she gone be ok.

"Me and Mr. Samuel Washington rockin' that bed. Folks think old people don't get 'em some love, but we could tell them a thing or two. Unh huh! Dat man, he struttin' around like he the King of Tonga.

"Now Mr. TV, you maybe think Pearlie so busy lovin', she forget all about makin'. I leave all my makin's and pencils and paints at the Tolletts. You listen here! Once somebody knows 'bout makin, how that feel happy and free, like sittin' up in the driver seat in the front of the bus, they has to keep on doin' it with whatever they got. So after me and Mr. Samuel Washington get up at the house, I go and fall in love all over again. With concrete. You heard me! Mr. Sam got all the cement I could ever want! So we out on the yard at Pineville Concrete and Block Supply, pourin' cement and sand and everthing in the world Pearlie can think of into molds, ever shape in this world. Mr. Sam love concrete. Now he makin' too.

"Mr. Samuel Washington, he finly pass from the sugar. We had us some happy years though, we sure did. We had us some fine sweet love."

· · · · · · · ·

More and more, I feel my heart fluttering out of rhythm. And with this gizmo on the screen, if I chose to, I could see it too. There's a real time three dimensional, Ultra HiDef scanner image. It's so accurate, you can see your colon in spasms or the tiniest quivers of your mitral valve. If I had that kind of clinical interest in the final failings of my own body, I could have a ringside seat! I could watch my own ticker have a heart attack! Now wouldn't that be a trip?

I'm not that interested in the morbid mechanics of it, but I do think about it - death. I'm not at all afraid - just curious about what the crossing over is like. I've never been to church much, but my idea of God has always been my invisible friend. My loving friend is here now, sitting on the edge of my bed, watching, waiting.

On my playlist, "I'll Fly Away" is number one on the hit parade – it's even beat out all my "The Grateful Dead" songs for selections most played. What a happy, happy dyin' song! It makes me downright cheerful about my departure, I will be grateful.

I believe a higher creative power had to have designed the complex beauty of this masterpiece Earth. I believe the power abides with us, guiding us through life, urging us home. I'm certain there's a Paradise of the spirit when we take our leave. I believe we must forgive, and I have. Yes, I have. All of them. It may well be that my soul is too blackened and heavy to float, yet, somehow, I have a sure faith that it will. I'm ready.

2029 Nashville

The Director uncrossed her ankles and rose from her seat. She took a ladylike sip from her water glass before clinking it with her gold pen to silence the well-dressed people gathered in the room.

"Good evening! Thank you for joining us on this special occasion. The Music City Gallery is proud to present the work of Pearlie Belle Bean Washington. Pearlie was the live-in housekeeper for the Frank Tollett family of Blackshale, Tennessee from 1948 until 2010, when she left to marry at the age of eighty-five. Several years after she moved away, the Tollett property was sold. The daughter of the family, Anna Grace, found this amazing body of work locked in a drawer in Pearlie's small basement bedroom. Pearlie had never mentioned making art, nor did she ask for or discuss buying art supplies. She simply went to her room in the evenings and quietly created these remarkable pieces using what she had at hand. Although she was not able to join us for the opening this evening, she is still living at the age of one hundred and fifteen. Please direct your applause and comments to the video camera, so she can enjoy your presence and your praise. Again, thank you for coming and please visit the wine and cheese buffet as you view the exhibition!"

2029 Morning Glory Ridge

Ok. OK. This is it! Here I go. Oh God, I'm coming - crossing the dark glass. Up, up through the clouds, a siren swimming the sky, my mermaid form cleaving the ether into thick heady folds. The force of my soul pushes up through smoke, shifting rapidly from thin to thick to thin to thick - up toward the loving light. Who knew. The birdsong is exquisite, bejeweled with joy, more varied than the most prolific mockingbird left back on earth, laboring at his pale inadequate tune. Soft staccato puffs of light bounce off my face in icy sensations. Oh, the perfect peace! I have no weight, no pain, no anxious dread. I am free. I know everything but care of nothing. I'm part of all. What I used to be – the transient shell that housed my spark of life - has already gone up in smoke, leaving behind only those things I created. By them, I will be remembered.

I focus joyously ahead. Then I see them - all the others, the ones before, the ones I loved, the ones who will come after. We are one.

At least, this is what I think it will be like!

SMOKE FROM SMALL FIRES
Supplementary Materials

The artworks of Anna Grace Tollett, Pearlie Bean, and other characters, Book Club discussion questions, and other supplementary materials for "Smoke From Small Fires" may be found online.

Look for "Smoke From Small Fires" on Facebook and Pinterest. Visit Annepowers.com, and Amazon Author Pages for information about the author, Anne Powers.